And the Bull Saved Me

Alex Rose

PublishAmerica
Baltimore

© 2007 by Alex Rose.
All rights reserved. No part of this book may be reproduced, stored in a retrieval system or transmitted in any form or by any means without the prior written permission of the publishers, except by a reviewer who may quote brief passages in a review to be printed in a newspaper, magazine or journal.

First printing

All characters in this book are fictitious, and any resemblance to real persons, living or dead, is coincidental.

ISBN: 1-4241-0852-7
PUBLISHED BY PUBLISHAMERICA, LLLP
www.publishamerica.com
Baltimore

Printed in the United States of America

CHAPTER ONE

In a world teeming with almost five billion people, you wouldn't think one single life would matter, not when you considered the numbers, the huge mass of humanity inhabiting the earth. A world in which every few seconds, a soul is either entering or leaving it. One life in such a vast ocean of people should be insignificant, inconsequential, lost in the multitude. But in spite of the immeasurable numbers, one life *did* matter very much. It mattered so much that the two souls caring for that one life managed to somehow transcend the bounds of nature and spiritualism to continue protecting that life. Those two people were Adam and Kathleen Kerr and the life they were watching over was their only child, their son, Marcus.

Their love for Marcus was interminable, a force so strong that it could overcome the hurdle of life itself, extending to a place past earthly limits and corporal existence. The only thing stronger than their love for Marcus was his love for them. They were his light and he was theirs. It was a faith and devotion that the three of them thought could never be broken. But that faith was put to the test when Marcus was seventeen years old and his parents were both killed in an automobile accident.

Everyone around him seemed to think he was coping well with the loss. Only he knew why he was able to go on without falling into despair. It was because of his faith in his parents' love. His grief was cushioned by that love, surrounding him, comforting him. It was a faith that became his strength, his rock and that he refused to give up on. And after a time that faith spawned a new belief.

That his parents were still with him.

It was a belief that he wouldn't let die and allowed to blossom into full bloom. As the idea took shape in his heart and mind, he clung to it, just as he had clung to their love. Very soon he became convinced of it. Otherwise how could he explain the strange things happening to him? It had to be the only explanation.

He was being haunted.

It wasn't a haunting like those he'd read about in books, with clattering chains in cold, damp castles or old houses full of cobwebs. This haunting was taking place in everything and everyone around him, causing him to experience a series of episodes that completely ignored the law of averages. It was a manifestation that propelled him from one calamity to another. The catastrophes were never huge or mountain moving. They were personal disasters, centered directly around him, as if some unseen and invisible force was guiding him down a path towards what?

He didn't know.

But what he DID know was who was pushing him towards those adventures—

His parents.

He knew beyond any doubt that it was them, in their unique and witty way, showing that they were still with him. He was not alone. He didn't have to face the rest of his life without them. And because of that belief, he never minded the strange things that occurred. Why should he? It was simply their way of communicating, letting him know that they were watching over him. Their love had reached out past time and space and found him.

And for that one reason, he accepted what was happening to him.

So for the next ten years following his parents' deaths, he endured his "haunting," a condition that everyone else considered to be a curse, not a blessing. His affliction became known to not only his closest friends and co-workers but to a great number of people in northern Ohio. The citizens of Kirklin, where he lived, regarded him as some kind of oddity, a freak, to be stared at and whispered over. But he ignored the whispers and stares.

How could they possibly understand?

How could they know that it wasn't a curse at all?

It was a gift. From them. His parents.

Thus he went about his life, dealing with his *gift* the best way he knew how, with quiet tolerance and acceptance. He decided that his life was no different than anyone else's. He merely suffered from a slight case of being accident-prone. Many people experienced the same thing. It was no big deal. The fact that the incidents happened ten times more frequently than other people didn't matter. It simply put him on the heavier end of the law of averages scales.

At least that's what he told himself.

And things would have been fine, just the way they were going. He was happy. He held a job he loved, had friends he could always depend on and he was smart enough to know that any man with that kind of luck was most fortunate. The only thing he lacked was another person to share his life with. Someone who could love him and that he could love back. But alas, that one thing eluded him. After a time, when it didn't happen, he didn't become bitter about it. He accepted it, just as he'd accepted the other things that happened to him. And just when he'd decided he would end up a confirmed bachelor to the end of his days, it happened.

He fell in love. And he was never the same again.

He first caught sight of her walking across the main intersection next to the courthouse in downtown Kirklin, Ohio, the place where he grew up, lived and earned his living. He'd been driving home from his job as manager of Crystal Lanes, the bowling alley located at the edge of town off Highway 77. It was the same route he took every night after work. His lived on Hancock Street, two blocks south of Main and his apartment was on the second floor of a fabric store. Shoppers in the store were never noisy so he enjoyed peace and quiet most of the time. He could have been unlucky enough to have the upper apartment five doors down, above the music store. It was also available when he was shopping for apartments and even though the rent was cheaper, he knew that the place would be inundated with soaring decibels from the music students testing out amps or the latest Fender Straitocaster.

The reason he knew this was because the store's music instructor and manager, Ben Hollinger, happened to be his best friend. He'd spent many an afternoon at the store observing Ben teaching the area's teenagers and citizens the finer points of music appreciation, a job he was born to do. Ben was one of those rare breeds of teachers who were not only inspired by their choice of vocation but also shared that inspiration and enthusiasm with every student he came in contact with. Now Marcus was experiencing that same inspirational spark.

When he first saw her.

As he drove by, she was walking along, swinging her purse at her side. She was alone but her lips were moving as if she was talking to someone. He then realized she was singing. He'd seen people singing to themselves before but they were usually joggers or walkers wearing headphones that were connected to a CD player or radio. She wasn't wearing headphones, at least not that he could tell. She looked to be in her middle twenties, had an average build, although a bit on the slim side and had light brown hair. Her hair was one of the first things he noticed. It was curly, hung down just past her shoulders and bounced as she walked along. She was wearing a pair of gray dress slacks and a wine colored blouse that had a ruffle near the neck.

She'd just passed The Farthest Point, one of three bars in the downtown area and one of his favorite places. Many of his friends were regular patrons at the bar and he and Ben played on the bar's dart league on Monday nights. The Farthest Point bar had been a fixture in town since he was a boy. He (or anyone else, for that matter) had never figured out exactly what it was the farthest point from. Although for a few of the regulars who got tipsy and left their cars in the parking lot, they were lucky the bar wasn't the farthest point from home. On a few occasions, he was the one opting to leave his car in the lot and walking home, especially if his dart team was celebrating a victory, which lately, seemed to be every other week.

After seeing her that first time, his thoughts kept drifting back to her. He wanted to know her name and what song she'd been singing. She looked like she was a couple years younger than he was. He began wondering if she'd gone to Kirklin High. If so, her picture might be in his yearbook among the other underclassmen. It was only after he dug the old book out of storage and started leafing through it that he knew something strange was happening to him.

It was as though he was an over-stimulated teenager, looking for a pin-up girl. He knew that loneliness was motivating him into looking up her picture but rationalizing the behavior didn't stop him from doing it. He was by no means a teenager and had enjoyed his fair share of intimate encounters with other women. If nothing else, his *gift* hadn't robbed him of that pleasure, just the opposite. Some women were intrigued with a man who made strange things happen. After witnessing one or several of his "incidents" some of them became quite enamored with him.

He accepted the fact that those same women only went to bed with him to see if his affliction caused any zealous bedroom escapades, which at times, it did. For a long time he looked forward to seeing his *gift* periodically make an appearance during those times, causing his partners to leave the trysts in different degrees of emotions, ranging from laughing hysterically to screaming in terror. Whether it was running naked with his partner through a soybean field after a freak hailstorm destroyed their tent or waking up next to a redhead and a bunch of lizards, the calamities were always interesting. He enjoyed not only the episodes themselves but also the appreciation of his partners who many times felt compelled to reward him for such an adventure. It was an exchange of sorts between willing adults, satisfying both his libido and his partners need for fun.

But lately, the experiences had left him feeling hollow, empty, unfulfilled. And after seeing yet another adventuress leaving one morning, he realized the sad truth. Once his partners had their curiosity or passion satisfied, the result was always the same—

He was left alone again.

As his thoughts drifted back to the singing girl, he faced another hard truth. To consider that she might be different from the others was foolhardy. Women were basically the same and no female in her right mind would want to spend her life with someone who was thrust into a catastrophe every few days. Even normal people had trouble finding love and happiness. Thinking he could do it with everything that was stacked against him seemed nearly impossible. Just the same, he found himself driving home that next afternoon at precisely the same time, looking for her. He drove slowly down Hancock Street but after passing the first intersection without spotting her, the disappointed kicked in. He didn't know exactly why he was so disappointed. It wasn't like he knew her. He didn't even know her name. If he were smart he'd forget about her and go home.

But something began to nag at him, telling him not to give up.

He gave into the feeling and turned left at the next intersection, driving around the block and heading back up to Main Street. There was a car backing out of diagonal parking space near the corner of Hancock and Main and he pulled his Pontiac Sunbird into it. He shut off the engine and turned the key to "accessory," allowing him to still listen to the radio. The song "I Knew I Loved You" was just finishing as he glanced down at his watch. 5:15. He did some quick calculating. He had to be back at work at 7:00 for a meeting to set up fall leagues. Time enough to pursue the chase for a little while more.

He ran his hand over his face. There was a slight indication of five o'clock shadow but not enough to show too much. Because of his black hair and fair complexion he'd made the habit of shaving close and often. Letting the whiskers go, even for a day, made him to look like one of the hard-core drunks who made The Point their home. He glanced out of the passenger side window and down the street. Groups of people were exiting the buildings but the singing girl's face wasn't among them.

He glanced at himself in the rearview mirror again. He hated mirrors. They had a habit of making you view yourself honestly, forcing you to see yourself as others saw you, a task not easy for some. It was hard to believe that some people could treat others like shit and still manage to face themselves in the mirror every morning without feeling remorse. Anyone with a halfway decent conscience couldn't do it without performing some degree of self-evaluation, walking away a little more enlightened because of it.

Self-reflection was exactly that for some, including him.

Beads of perspiration began to form on his forehead and he pushed the buttons on the door console, rolling down the two front windows. A warm, gentle breeze blew in through the windows. It was the last part of July and although it had rained earlier in the day, it hadn't cooled things down much. He'd worn jeans and a cotton shirt to work that morning but ended up putting on a sweater later in the day. The sweater was a permanent fixture in his office because of the air conditioner. The vent was located directly above his desk and constantly blew down on him, chilling him even on the hottest days. He'd tried to shut it off more than once but doing so completely cut off the air, turning the office into a sauna. Wearing the sweater was easier than sitting around every day, sweating off five or ten pounds.

He looked out the front windshield to the clothing store on the corner. The two female mannequins standing in the display window were dressed in summer clothes and their heads were turned away, which made him happy. The mannequins at the mall stores that faced front always made him uneasy. Seeing those lifeless eyes staring out at nothing or no one gave him an eerie shudder, not to mention that some of the mannequins looked too real for comfort. More than once he would bump into one and ended up muttering, "Excuse me," thinking it was a real person. He always felt stupid making such a mistake. Afterwards, he'd look around to see if anyone had seen him do it. But he knew, even before checking that there would be someone watching. There was always someone watching, especially whenever one of his *moments* occurred. It never failed.

He stared at the mannequins again. The one on the right reminded him of a woman he'd dated the previous year. Marilyn. She'd been the one and only relationship that had lasted more than a couple of nights. Three weeks to the day, a personal record and one he had yet to surpass. It had also been the happiest period in his life since his parents died. It was the first time he'd ever enjoyed both a sexual and emotional bond with a woman. What's more, she knew about his problem and for a time, seemed to be okay with it.

He met her in the music store while she was purchasing some sheet music for her violin. She had long, lovely legs and a smile that instantly lit up his heart. He asked her out and the first date went fine, at least in comparison to some of his other first dates. They were driving back from a club in the nearby town of Summit when her car broke down. They'd been drinking so she elected to take the back roads home, away from the state troopers on the main routes. But after zigzagging around the rural curving thoroughfares for over an hour, they both experienced a need to relieve themselves. They made a rest stop in a secluded cornfield and adjourned to their respective sides of the roads.

However, upon coming back to the car, she discovered she'd locked herself out. With no other cars in sight, they made the decision to hoof it down to the next house. After they'd gone about a mile it started to rain. They spotted an abandoned barn and sought shelter inside. Their clothes were drenched and after finding a few bales of straw and some half-full feed sacks they could use as pillows, they decided to strip down and curl up together. It wasn't exactly the Hilton but their enthusiasm pursuing each other's passion overshadowed the inconvenience and made it a fulfilling and satisfying interlude. The next morning she even commented that it was the first time she'd made love to someone in a place other than a bed. Her attitude seemed quite pleasant and he was relieved she wasn't upset about the escapade. But a few minutes later she did become upset—

When the pigs showed up.

The two of them were still nestled in each other's arms when four large and angry looking swines came rumbling into their part of the barn, which turned out wasn't as abandoned as they'd first thought. He figured out later that the animals must have been after the feed in the sacks, but at the time it seemed as though the pigs were charging at them. And these particular pigs weren't the "Babe" type that Hollywood portrayed. They were full-grown farm hogs, and pissed hogs at that. They looked like small tanks with enough weight on them to do serious damage to anything or anyone who happened to be in their way. He and Marilyn quickly decided not to argue with the angry porkers and made a hasty retreat out the door, not even stopping to pick up their clothes.

Once they fled the barn they constructed some makeshift clothes from cornstalks and made their way to a farmhouse a mile or so away. After first seeing the cornstalk clad visitors on her front porch, the woman living there threatened to call the police. But they finally calmed her down enough to explain the situation and soon found a sympathetic ear. After they called a tow truck, the woman offered them some old clothes from her attic. They gratefully accepted. They arrived back at her apartment a little while later (along with her car) and laughed at how funny they looked wearing clothes made to fit a hefty farmer. She dismissed the whole thing as a once in a lifetime adventure and seemed amused by the whole incident.

So she didn't give up on him. At least not yet.

Even after receiving a gash on her head during their second date when he sneezed and accidentally turned his denture into a flying projectile, she took it all in stride. She didn't even mind that he was without his plate for three days while it was getting fixed or that he looked like the toothless abominable snowman from the *Rudolf the Red Nosed Reindeer* cartoon. But he saw the handwriting on the wall once the episodes started escalating.

After getting his denture back they decided to celebrate in the privacy of her apartment. She was still wearing the bandage on her forehead and didn't want to be seen in public anymore than she had to so they stayed in. He rented a couple of videos and she made a big bowl of popcorn. He chose two horror films, knowing full well she'd get frightened and snuggle up with him on the couch. She eagerly went along with the ruse, even adding a blanket to the mix. Before the credits rolled on the first film, they were enjoying their own little romance film on her couch, which they found much more comfortable than a pile of hay.

They fell asleep in each other's arms and it was a few hours later when she woke him abruptly, claiming to hear someone moving around outside her front door. The TV screen was filled with snow and gave out the only light in the room so he had to navigate over to the door aided only by it and one of the couch pillows, which she gave him to cover himself up. In his other hand was an empty beer bottle, leftovers from earlier, which he wielded tightly in his fist, ready to strike the intruder.

Beyond her front door was a hall that was accessed by the five other apartments on that floor. The lights in the hall were always on and as he glanced down through the crack in the bottom of the door, he could see a shadow moving around suspiciously. He reached down to turn the doorknob when something suddenly hit the door hard, causing him to jump back and scaring Marilyn so bad that she let out a gasp of fright. He approached the door again and carefully listened. It sounded like the person was scratching at something near the doorknob and he assumed they had been picking the lock. He threw the pillow aside and reached down, quietly as he could and unlatched the lock. He knew that the movement would probably scare the intruder away and he wasted no time, he was determined to catch the culprit red-handed.

He threw open the door, let out a yell and stood poised, ready to strike with the beer bottle. But as the door swung inwards and the light trickled in from the hall, he saw that it wasn't a burglar at all. It was a large black cat, hanging on to the three-foot high angel decoration hooked on the door. The decoration was a homemade craft made of burlap material and the cat's claws were dug into the angel's face, hanging on with fury as the cat chewed the cloth button eyes. He reached out to grab the animal off the decoration when Marilyn screamed. A second later a yellow blur flew past his face, missing it by centimeters and something breakable crashed against the door, hitting the cat's tail. The cat let out a howl and jumped at him, claws out. He managed to dodge the worst of the attack, flinging the animal back out the door where it landed hard, hissed and sped off down the carpeted hallway.

    He stood still, not sure he should try venturing forth in his bare feet with all the glass on the floor. Marilyn began apologizing profusely for throwing the popcorn bowl. As she carefully walked towards him, she explained that because of the dim light, she thought the object on the door was a bat instead of a cat. It was an explanation that made sense to him. The first movie they'd watched was about vampire bats and no doubt her fear had enhanced her imagination. Not to mention that you didn't usually see a cat sprawled out across your front door, trying to gnaw the eyes off your angel decoration.

    He started to bend over to retrieve the pillow to cover himself up when she let out a yelp and ran back over to the couch. He turned to ask her what was wrong when he was suddenly surrounded by a bunch of people flooding into the apartment. He reacted instinctively and covered himself with his hands.

    There were six or seven of them and they all began talking at once, demanding to know what all the commotion was. Marilyn was now wrapped up in the blanket and hurried over to rescue him. She opened the covering just enough to let him in and then tried to explain to her disgruntled neighbors what happened. Most of them shook their heads in understanding and began to file out of the apartment, a few of them cursing softly as they inadvertently stepped on the shards of glass littering the floor. But one of the neighbors, a short, bald man with a bushy mustache, didn't leave. Instead, he stood and lectured them at length about cruelty to animals being against God and how pets were a blessing. It was then that Marcus realized that he must have been the angel-devouring cat's owner. The man finally finished speaking his piece and left, tiptoeing carefully around the broken glass pieces as he went out the door.

    That's when her questions started.

    She began commenting about the lousy luck they seemed to be having on their dates. He offered no explanation, only "hemmed" and "hawed" while shaking his head and agreeing with her at the unfortunate succession of mishaps. She was obviously wondering what the odds were that all three dates would end up in calamity and he desperately hoped she didn't wonder about it too long. After some coaxing and more than a little bit of lying, he convinced her that it was one of those odd circumstances people would sometimes talk about. She finally agreed with him and he inwardly breathed a sigh of relief.

But he was only avoiding the inevitable and the "inevitable" showed up a few days later, putting all her doubts about him to rest.

The gash on her forehead had healed enough to allow the removal of the bandage, so they decided to celebrate by going to dinner at a nicer restaurant in town. The dinner went fine but the drive up to Carswell Point, the local lover's lane, didn't. After the barn episode, he decided to use his own car, not only because it was reliable but because it had a roomy back seat. He was hoping for a little tryst under the stars. On the way to their rendezvous, they picked up a couple of soft drinks at a fast food place. He'd parked at the top of the hill, giving them a spectacular view of the stars and town lights as they snuggled together, sipping their drinks.

After finishing the sodas, he got out of the car and threw the empty cups into a nearby trash can. As he walked back to the car, his right shoe sunk down into the mud. It had rained quite a bit the few days previous and the ground had become saturated. He picked up the shoe and hopped the last few feet to the car. He'd just sat back down on the driver's side and was wiping the mud off his shoe with one of the leftover napkins when the car suddenly lurched forward. He looked out the front windshield and figured one of the front tires had sunk down into the mud. He slipped on his shoe and started the car, to back it up. But as he put it into reverse, the car lurched forward again. This time the movement was more pronounced and the car was now listing forward toward the hill's edge.

"Oh, my God," she said, her voice full of concern. "What's happening?"

His mind went into overdrive, trying to think of a way to say it without scaring the shit out of her. He strongly suspected that the rain soaked ground had given way underneath the vehicle's weight and that the car was on the verge of tumbling over the hill. He started to tell her not to move when the car suddenly lurched forward, sending it toward the dark abyss. She screamed and he grabbed on to her as the car slowly rolled over the edge. She clutched at him and kept screaming so loud that he couldn't hear anything else. He waited to feel the momentary weightlessness as the car hit the open air, falling the hundred or so feet to the woods below.

The sensation never came.

He opened his eyes a few seconds later and looked out the back windshield. The top of the hill was about five or six feet above them and the car was sitting at a forty-five degree angle, stuck between a bunch of large tree roots sticking out from the side of the hill. The branches were dense and thick. A few of the smaller ones were sticking in the front passenger side window.

They were both pushed against the dashboard and the radio knob was sticking into his ribs so he quickly adjusted his body to compensate. She was stilling clinging tight to him and trembling so he asked her if she was okay.

"Yes..." she said, not quite sounding sure. "Where are we?"

He explained to her about the tree stopping their descent and added that the roots seemed to be supporting the weight of the car nicely, hoping the news would relieve some of her anxiety.

A few seconds later someone called to them from above, at the top of the hill, letting them know that help was on the way. "Are you guys okay?" the voice asked.

Marcus called back to them, replying that they were. "See?" he told Marilyn. "It's going to be just fine."

She slowly pulled away from him but retreated back into his arms a second later when she saw the branches sticking in the window. "It's all right," he whispered to her, trying to comfort her. He knew it wouldn't do any good to tell her the truth, that in all the years of enduring his *gift* he'd never been seriously hurt. And he also couldn't share with her how amusing it was to see the episodes manifest themselves in such a wonderful variety of ways and methods, each new one more amazing than the last. It was like riding a roller coaster and never quite knowing exactly how scary the next hill would be. And he had ridden this particular ride for over ten years and was getting used the track. But telling her wouldn't ease her fear. There was a big difference between standing on the safe ground, watching someone else ride a roller coaster and having your butt stuck in one of the seats beside them.

Half an hour later a tow truck and wench arrived and within minutes both they and the car were back up on top of the hill. The car exterior was muddy and the paint was scratched but to him it was no big deal. Since buying the car three years earlier he'd been forced to get it repainted several times due to similar situations, just like the other four cars he'd owned over the past ten years. And because of his history of frequent mishaps he had to resort to paying very expensive high-risk insurance. If no one else in the world appreciated his *gift*, at least his insurance company did.

It was the young couple parked next to them that had phoned the police on their cell phone after watching their neighbors suddenly disappear over the ledge. Once back up on the hill, he noticed that the police had made all the other vehicles back up at least twenty feet to prevent any other cars from trying to fly. The following day the town counsel passed an ordinance to build a fence along the top of the hill, assuring that no other lovers would end up at the bottom of the ravine. It was a public service that directly resulted from one of his *moments*. There was yet another result, but this one much more personal.

Since exiting the car, he noticed that Marilyn's expression of horror had diminished but not nearly as much as he'd hoped. She walked around silently among the people as the officers took down the statements, acting as though she was in a daze. He knew she was still feeling confused and frightened by the incident and it didn't help matters any when one of the officers made a comment under his breath that she was just asking for it going out with the *Kirklin Klutz*. The comment was loud enough to draw snickers and laughter from the people standing around, lovers who'd decided to temporarily adjourn their festivities to watch the show.

He took her home a little while later, knowing she must be wondering about the comment. She'd only recently moved to town and hadn't yet had the privilege of hearing the rumors about the strange man who ran the bowling alley. However, chances were good that by the next morning, she'd be asking more than a few people about it.

When she called him the next evening and cancelled their date, he figured she'd gotten all the answers she needed and decided not to tempt fate any more. But a week later, when she called him back and made another date, he knew she'd opted to buck the odds and give it another try. It was a decision that moved him deeply and demonstrated her determination to be with him, something no other woman had done. Thus, because of her brave attempt, he made a vow to himself, to do everything he could to make sure nothing else went wrong.

The next evening he showed up at her door, anxious for a second try. He was determined not to have her experience any more misadventures and made the date as low risk as possible. They weren't even going to use a car. Just a simple picnic in the park a couple blocks down from her apartment. He even prepared the dinner himself, making sure the food was not at risk from contamination by a freak accident at the packing plant or possible spoilage. He kept it simple, peanut butter and jelly sandwiches, potato chips and cartons of apple juice.

AND THE BULL SAVED ME

The date began smoothly. They took a blanket with them to the park and sat next to each other, enjoying the warm, early evening breeze and sounds of children laughing, playing on the nearby swings and merry go round. They talked and laughed, telling each other about their lives. He neglected to tell her anything about his condition or the episodes, hoping to avoid the issue entirely. But he happily listened as she told him her dreams, hopes and experiences. It wasn't long before she was snuggled up close to him and he was starting to think that the relationship might go the distance after all. She was even gracious enough not to say anything when her eyebrows shot up in surprise over his dinner selections, which they both munched down in short order.

Afterwards, they walked around the park, hand in hand, viewing the duck pond, bridge and pavilion, which was now empty of people. As the stars appeared and the children's voices faded away from being called home, they found themselves alone to enjoy the park in privacy. She told him that she wanted to ride on the swings. After a brief few seconds of trepidation while he tried furiously to think of what catastrophes could occur while using the playground equipment, he agreed. He hadn't been on a swing in more than a few years and matched her enthusiasm as they both kicked their feet and pumped away, laughing and swinging together in the dark. A little while later, as they walked home arm in arm, with him carrying the blanket and her carrying the empty picnic basket, his heart began to float away with happiness. He couldn't have asked for a more perfect date. She asked him up to her place and he happily accepted. He was on a high from experiencing a calamity free evening and was looking forward to capping it off together with her, in the comfort of her arms and passion.

But he should have known better.

His condition was, if nothing else, persistent.

Because the night had turned cooler, she elected to leave the air conditioner off and open the windows, which he helped her do. As he finished raising the window in the living room, the aroma from the rosebushes below filled his nostrils. He had observed the flowers the first time he came to her place and how neatly manicured the landscaped border around the building was. The plants consisted of a rosebush and hosta fern every few feet with a freshly painted scalloped, two-foot high wooden fence bordering the perimeter. The rosebushes had even been cut to almost the same height, giving the effect of a perfectly symmetrical garden. After commenting about it, she told him that the gardener was her landlord and that he lived in the apartment directly across from hers on the second floor. He had also been one of the neighbors who witnessed the episode with the cat hanging on the door.

He called her over to the window, knowing she would enjoy the aroma floating up from below. As she breathed in deeply, she gave him a smile that made his pulse race. He felt a sudden desire to kiss her. He still had the blanket over his shoulder and she pushed it off as he pulled her close, enjoying the mixture of sensations, the aroma of the roses and sweet warmth of her lips. She moaned and leaned against him, pushing him back towards the window. He became aware of the fact that there was nothing behind him to support his weight and reached back with his right hand to grab the window frame for support. But his hand hit dead air and he quickly groped around for something to grab. The weight of her body against him caused him to lose his balance and he started shuffling his feet in an attempt to regain his footing. His hand suddenly came in contact with something but a second later he realized it was the window screen and knew it would afford him no kind of support.

He stopped kissing her long enough to grab her shoulders, trying to steady himself. A second later his body tipped far enough backward to lose his footing and he fell against the screen. When she saw him falling, she let go, trying to keep her own balance. At the last second she reached out, trying to help but it was too late. The force of his body hit the screen and it ripped open. She screamed as he groped around desperately for something to hang on to. He felt the edge of the blanket and clutched at it just as his body went tumbling backwards out the window. He was hoping the blanket would cushion him when he hit the ground and waited for it to go slack, signaling that it had made the journey out the window with him.

His vision adjusted to the disorientation of the street and car lights flashing past his eyes as he completed the somersault. But he didn't fall to the ground. The blanket suddenly went taut and he gripped it firmly in his hands. His body bumped hard against the building as the momentum of the fall impacted itself. He tried to shake the momentary queasiness and lifted his head. Marilyn was leaning out the window, holding on to the other end of the blanket. He heard some of the adjoining windows being thrown open and knew that her screams had alerted the other residents to his plight. Voices now filled the air, among them a very angry man yelling at everyone to call the police. Marcus felt great respect for the man at the concern for his safety but changed his mind an instant later when the same voice yelled at him not to fall on top of his prize rosebushes and ferns.

He glanced down and saw that indeed, he was now hanging approximately ten feet above one of the rosebushes. The angry man's voice went away so Marcus concentrated on to holding tight to the blanket. But there was no way he was going to be able to hold on long enough for help to arrive in the form of a fire department jump canvas. He was going to have to let go and fall on the man's rosebush, an idea that made all the hairs on his legs suddenly stand on end, imagining the thorns piercing the material of his trousers and embedding into his skin.

The fatigue announced itself in his arms as the muscles seized up with pain. He glanced back up at Marilyn still holding on to the other end of the blanket and told her to let go so he could use the blanket as a shield against the thorns. He braced himself for the fall as she loosened her grip on the covering. A second later the night was filled with a man's screams which startled Marcus so bad that he almost let go. It was the angry man's voice, yelling at the top of his lungs, informing him that in no way, shape or form was he to fall on his prize rosebush. Marcus gripped the blanket tighter and grunted to the angry man that he couldn't hang on any longer.

The man began cursing loudly, the sound of his voice moving to the left and then coming back a few seconds later. "Okay!" the man yelled. "Go ahead and drop now."

A scream came from above and Marilyn yelled at the man to take it away.

Marcus glanced down and saw what she was referring to. The man had placed a plastic patio chair on top of the rosebush to shield it from the intruder about to fall upon it from above. He wanted to laugh at the ridiculousness of the man's attempt to save his rose but his arms were aching so bad that he couldn't make a sound. The man grunted in anger and started to lift the chair off the flower to set it aside. A second later, the blanket suddenly went slack and Marcus sucked in a breath as he finished falling down to the flowerbed below—and directly on top of the man trying to protect his rose.

His feet connected with the man's back and as the rest of his body weight followed, the man let out a considerable yell and shoved him hard, inadvertently diverting him into the grass next to the flowerbeds. He landed with a thud, bending his knees to protect his legs from enduring the whole impact. With the help of the blanket, he'd managed a somewhat soft landing and quickly stood up and surveyed himself.

Nothing broken. All okay. He brushed the grass from his clothes and glanced over at the landlord who was still standing in the flowerbed, the patio chair lying in the grass next to him. The man appeared to be unharmed and was bent over, doing something. Marcus went up to him, wanting to thank him for helping to break his fall but also knowing he was about to be read the riot act for invading the man's garden. But the man didn't look up. He was cussing and picking at his legs and arms.

That's when Marcus realized.

As he fell upon him, he'd forced the angry little man down onto his own rosebush. It was now the landlord covered with thorns, not him. He watched in amusement while the little man cussed a blue streak and plucked the thorn from his skin. Marcus tried to keep a straight face and walked back towards the entrance of the apartment. Marilyn had come down from upstairs and met him at the door. He handed her the blanket and she asked him if he was all right.

"I'm fine," he told her with a smile. "But your landlord is still picking the thorns out."

"Serves him right!" she grunted angrily. "Acting like a damn plant is more important than a person. He would have let you break your back on that chair! All to save that stupid flower! That's why I let go when I did."

He stopped smiling and asked her what she meant.

She glanced over at the flowerbed. "When he took the chair away," she whispered, "I realized that as big as he was, he'd make a good cushion. I knew you wouldn't drop down on him, so I made the decision for you. And I was right. It worked."

He threw his head back and laughed.

The landlord stepped out of the flowerbed, picked up the patio chair and stomped off towards the back of the apartment house, grumbling all the way. Marcus turned back to Marilyn, expecting to see her enjoying the joke too. But he quickly stopped laughing when he saw the all-too-familiar sad smile on her face.

He recognized the look. He'd seen it many times before.

She opened her mouth to say something, but nothing came out.

It was just like all the other times when the women he'd dated were searching for the words to give him the brush off. It was never done with rudeness or anger, exactly the opposite. They were always cordial and polite. It was usually something like "I think you're a very nice man, but…" or "Perhaps we should only be friends…" Getting rejected on a regular basis made him an expert at what to expect and he waited to hear it.

"Marcus…" she whispered.

He could see the pain in her face and decided to give her a break. He put on a brave smile, trying to mask his disappointment. "Uh, I've been thinking," he told her. "I'm not really ready for a serious relationship yet. I think it might be a good idea if we slowed down a bit. You know, give it some time before we start heading towards anything serious."

"I agree," she replied, her face full of compassion. "I'm also not ready for any kind of complications in my life..." She stopped and glanced down, her face flushed with embarrassment. A few seconds later she seemed to gather her composure and looked back up at him. "We could still remain friends. I'd really like that. And who knows? We might even end up back together in the future. Maybe you could give me a call sometime."

    He knew she was only trying to be kind and he loved her for it. She was opening the door for him to begin the relationship again but it was clear her heart wasn't in it. He leaned forward and kissed her on the cheek. "I tell you what," he whispered. "If you decide you'd like to get back together sometime, give me a call. If nothing else, we can meet for coffee, as friends. How about that?"

    She nodded yes, the sad smile still showing on her face.

    They exchanged good wishes and promised to call one another sometime. But as he walked away, he knew it would never happen. She'd decided that hanging around with a bull in a china shop wasn't for her. He couldn't blame her. Living with or even being involved with a man whose whole life revolved around catastrophe was not for the squeamish or faint of heart.

    He gripped the steering wheel of the car and stared at the mannequin in the shop window, a sudden, deep sadness filling his heart. Was it so wrong to hope for another Marilyn? Was it even fair to put someone else through such an ordeal in his quest to find a life mate? He looked at his reflection in the rearview mirror and frowned. He couldn't give up trying. He shouldn't give up.

    They never would have given up.

    He stared at the steering wheel, seeing his parents' faces in his mind. So many times over the last ten years he wished they'd been there to talk to. Not only to share his troubles or problems, but to share his life, his success. He still had his best friends, Ben and Jack, to tell his woes to but it would have been nice to talk to his parents, even if it was only one more time.

    He closed his eyes and pushed the thought out of his head. He'd always been against the sport of self-pity. All it did was shove unattainable dreams in your face, reminding you of what you didn't or couldn't have. Who the hell needed that? Life wasn't about guarantees. It was about surviving and making do with what you had. Besides, he was lucky. He wasn't alone. They were still with him, watching over him. So he had to keep trying to find someone to share his life with. They found each other and they'd want him to find someone too.

    He glanced out the passenger window again and suddenly saw her, walking down the street near the courthouse. He immediately recognized her. She was wearing a short sleeve, white blouse and dark blue skirt that showed off her well tanned legs. She stopped at the corner and crossed the street on the walk light with the other people, swinging her purse at her side and moving her lips, singing. He watched her, mesmerized. It was as if she was oblivious to the people around her, lost inside her own happy, little musical world. She crossed the intersection, passed in front of his car and headed off down Hancock Street.

He shut off the key and exited the car to follow her. He had to hurry to catch up and managed to get within a few steps of her as she approached The Farthest Point. He observed her as she walked along. She looked about four inches shorter than he was, making her about five feet six inches tall. She had light brown hair, which bounced up and down on her shoulders as she sang, almost in time to the tune. It was only because her stride was matching the rhythm of the song but the affect was hypnotizing. He tried to look inconspicuous and fell into step behind her, trying to make out the song she was singing. A familiar word would reach him now and then and a few seconds later he recognized it. It was the song he'd just heard on the radio, "I Knew I Loved You." He smiled and followed along behind her.

She walked past the small market and bookstore down from the bar and as she approached the corner of the first block she slowed down. He hadn't realized how close he'd been following until a moment later when she swung her purse backwards, causing him to dodge to the side to avoid being hit and detected. She stopped at the corner and pushed the button to activate the walk light. He stood behind her, watching and listening. As she waited for the light to turn, she started singing louder. It was as if she was putting on a performance for no one but herself. He became entranced and continued watching the show.

A couple of seconds later she grabbed hold of the light pole and started swinging herself around it. Before he knew what was happening, she circled the pole and was coming directly at him. It had taken him completely by surprise and he jumped back, barely missing crashing into her.

She stood up straight and let out a gasp. "Oh I'm so sorry. I didn't know anyone was behind me."

He was at a loss for words and felt his mouth fall open in surprise. He was still trying to think of something to say when she spoke again.

"I guess I got wrapped up in the music. I heard that song right before I left the office and couldn't get it out of my head. I didn't mean to frighten you."

He started to say something, but it came out froggy sounding so he quickly cleared his throat. "Oh, you didn't frighten me."

She smiled up at him and he felt a pang of desire as her eyes seemed to shine at him. "You should have seen the look on your face," she said, giggling softly. "I was afraid you were going to have a heart attack or something."

He felt his face redden with embarrassment. He could only imagine how startled he'd looked when he thought she'd caught him following her. "No. I'm fine, really," he told her, avoiding her gaze.

"Good," she replied, with an air of relief. "Well, looks like we missed that light."

He glanced up and saw that the walk light had blinked off. She pushed the button again to activate it. He quickly realized that once it came back she was going to walk out his life, maybe forever. He tried to strike up a conversation. "Uh...I really like that song you were singing."

Her face brightened, showing the dimples in her cheeks. "It's Savage Garden. I love their music. I've got the CD and play it all the time."

"I've been meaning to buy that CD, myself," he said, telling a white lie.

"You'll love it," she told him. Then she looked across the street to the parking lot next to the fire station. "Are you parked over there, too?"

"No," he told her, pointing back towards The Farthest Point. "I just came out of there and was walking home. I live down the street."

"Oh," she said, still smiling at him.

The traffic slowed down and the walk light flashed to life above them. She started off across the street and he desperately tried to think of a way to get her to come back.

She turned and called back to him, "Nice to meet you and sorry I scared you!"

He waved to her, feeling the disappointment settle over him like dark cloud.

There was no way he could follow her now without looking obvious or making her suspicious. He stuffed his hands into his pockets and strode down the street toward the next block. He'd already admitted to walking home. It was best to keep up the pretense in case she saw him while she drove away. He went as far as the music store then cut behind it to the alley that led back up to Main. As he drove home a few minutes later, he started running scenarios through his head, thinking of ways to accidentally run into her again. Following her after work every day wouldn't work. She'd assume he was a wacko or something even worse than a man who was an accident magnet.

A pleasant thought suddenly occurred to him. Maybe he could follow her around for a while as she sang to herself and went through her day. Perhaps she would go walking at night down by Currant Creek in Majestic Park, one of his favorite places. She could stroll out across the green lawns next to the tennis courts as the stars and moon shined down upon her, with him following quietly behind. And as long as she never turned around, nothing bad would happen, nothing would go wrong.

He would be safe and still with her.

He pulled into his regular parking space behind the fabric shop, got out and locked the car. He started thinking about the possibilities and hope crept back into his heart. Maybe she would be different than the others. Maybe this time it wouldn't end up a disaster. He smiled and headed up the outside stairs to his apartment, the sound of her voice singing softly in his mind.

CHAPTER TWO

It was few days later, on Saturday. Marcus sat in one of the corner booths of The Farthest Point with Ben, talking and enjoying a couple of beers. Smoke hung in the air as the patrons watched the baseball game on the TV, sitting on a high shelf behind the bar. The place was pretty busy for a Saturday afternoon. All the barstools were taken, as were most of the booths and the two pool tables located at the back. To the regular patrons and most of the townsfolk, the bar was referred to simply as The Point. Back when he and Ben had attended school at Kirklin High, it had always been a status symbol to brag about spending evenings at The Point, even though the boasts were nothing but lies. The owner/barkeeper didn't allow underage patrons on the premises after 9 PM unless accompanied by their parents, something no teenage boy was about to admit to his friends.

As Marcus finished taking another swig of his beer, the place erupted in cheers. He glanced up at the TV. One of the Cleveland Indians had scored a double with a line drive. The bar owner was an Indians and Browns fan and the TV was always tuned into their respective televised games. The Point was a friendly neighborhood bar, a throwback to the days before the advent of sports and theme bars decorated with their respective memorabilia. The Point boasted its own eclectic collection, including several impressive display shelves housing trophies from the bar's dart, pool and baseball leagues, which the proprietor proudly sponsored. The owner was a second-generation bartender, inheriting the tavern from his father. And like his father, he exercised the same deep pride running the establishment, making him respected among the townsfolk and patrons. The bar was also a miniature museum of Kirklin with a large assortment of pictures from the horse and buggy days adorning the walls.

The man was also a bit of a historian and loved telling stories that had been passed down through generations in his family. The patrons got to enjoy both the photographs and library of knowledge from the man behind the bar pouring the drinks. A trip to The Point resembled something akin to a history lesson and more than one inebriated customer would head home happy and full of not only their favorite brew, but several stories of Kirklin's past to go along with it. It was a place where most people could feel comfortable socializing and had become a favorite haunt for him and Ben. It was also a place where he, Ben and Jack could talk privately about his *moments*, a ritual they'd developed over the last few years.

Somehow, talking about the episodes afterward made him feel better. Jack and Ben would react to each telling with guffaws and snickers but the mirth wasn't because they were making fun of him, just the opposite. Once the laughter died down both of them would offer advice on how to handle the aftermaths of the calamities. Whether it was merely lending a sympathetic ear or giving advice on things like how to remove skunk stench from car upholstery and how to repair electrical fixtures, something he was becoming an expert at. After every *moment* discussion, he walked away feeling better about his condition and thankful he had friends he could talk to.

He'd known Ben since kindergarten, when Ben had inadvertently given him his nickname, Magic. After hearing the teacher announce his name, Mark Kerr, Ben asked her if he was a Magic Marker like the ones in his art kit. The other kids laughed and from that day forward he was known as Magic, a moniker his parents found quite endearing and also adopted for him. The name seemed to fit him and once the episodes began occurring when he was eighteen, the townspeople thought the name fitting as well.

Jack, his other closest friend, was a man in his early sixties who worked as his assistant at the bowling alley. Jack smoked a pipe and had a laid-back manner approximating Atticus Finch from *To Kill a Mockingbird*. He was quick-witted and saw humor in almost everything, the proof of which showed in the deep laugh lines around his mouth and eyes. He was also a bit of a philosopher, deeply religious and didn't mind sharing his views on either subject with his friends.

The patrons at the bar suddenly let out howls of protest. Marcus glanced up at the screen and asked Ben what was going on.

"Chicago's pitcher is trying to get even for that last call so he hit the batter. Uh-oh, it's about to get interesting."

Marcus joined him watching the game. They were both die-hard Indians fans and had been so since they were kids. Seeing someone take a cheap shot at one of their favorite players was enough to keep their eyes glued on the action.

They'd started out an hour earlier, playing darts at one of the three machines along the back wall of the bar. After losing four straight games to Ben (and taking a good deal of ribbing about his aim being off) Marcus asked Ben to take a break over a couple of beers. Before the action had heated up on the ballgame Ben had been discussing a problem he was having with his live-in girlfriend, Sue. Marcus listened patiently; acting like he knew nothing of what Ben was talking about. What Ben didn't know was that he'd already discussed the problem at length, with Sue, the night before.

"Well, they sure missed that opportunity," one of the men at the bar said, acting disappointed.

The inning ended without either side erupting into a fight, much to the chagrin of a few of the bar patrons who responded with grunts and angry waves at the set.

"So like I was telling you," Ben said, turning back around to Marcus. "One of Sue's friends brought her new baby over the other night to show us. You've seen what big fuss women make over babies and Sue was no different. She held it for over an hour and didn't want to give it up. She didn't even notice I was in the room. All she saw was that baby." He paused and started turning his glass around in his fingers.

Marcus stifled a smile. It was a gesture Ben would always repeat when he was approaching a delicate subject, or probably in this case, about to talk about something that made him uncomfortable.

"What happened next?" he asked Ben.

"After her friend left, Sue got in this really weird mood."

"What kind of mood?"

Ben paused and ran his hand across the top of his head like he was thinking about it. His hair was blonde and cropped short on the sides and top, a style he'd had since high school. He was five feet six inches tall, a few inches shorter than Marcus. But what he lacked in height he made up with in muscle. He was a star wrestler in high school and still worked out a couple times a week with a set of barbells he kept in his basement.

"She kept avoiding me like she was pissed off about something," Ben told him.

"What could she be pissed about?"

"Beats the shit out of me. So I thought, what the hell, and asked her why she was upset."

"And..."

"And nothing," Ben said, his tone exhibiting irritation. "She wouldn't answer me. She got this hurt look on her face and ran off to the bathroom. I thought maybe she was sick so I followed her, calling to her through the door and asking her if I could do anything for her. She wouldn't answer me. She locked herself in and wouldn't come out for over an hour. I ended up having to go out back and take a piss in the rosebushes."

Marcus snickered. "That must have made the roses happy."

"Hey, I was doing them a favor. We haven't had any rain in a week. They looked like they needed it."

Marcus asked him what happened next.

"She finally comes out a little while later and gets into bed with me. But her eyes are red and puffy, like she's been crying. So I got mad and demanded she tell me why she was acting so loony."

"And I'll bet that made her cry even harder, right?"

"Yeah," Ben said, acting surprised. "How the hell did you know that?"

Marcus tried to keep from grinning. "Mr. Tact, you're not, Ben. It's obvious that Sue's thinking about having kids."

"I may not be a master of diplomacy but I did, at least, figure that much out. Especially after she cried herself to sleep in my arms."

Marcus picked up his beer and tipped it at him in toast gesture. "Good. Then you've got it all worked out."

"Not exactly."

"What do you mean? Didn't you talk to her about it after she stopped crying?"

Ben started turning the glass around in his fingers again. "Well, uh, no. She never said anything else so neither did I. Besides, talking about having kids is a taboo subject with us."

"Jesus, Ben. You two have been living together for almost eight years. You mean you never talk about it?"

"We discussed it a few times the first year we moved in together and I guess she figured we'd eventually get married and start a family like everyone else. Of course, we never did. But I wasn't sorry. I always figured we were smarter than those other couples. We weren't committed legally to each other so we both chose to stay in the relationship and work at it. We stay together because we want to. But having kids is different."

"How?"

"You know, the whole parenting thing. Car pools, PTA meetings and dirty diapers."

Marcus got thoughtful for a moment. "Gee, that kinda sounds like fun."

Ben smirked. "Dirty diapers? Fun? I think there's more than your aim off. We'd better check you to make sure one of those darts didn't penetrate that noggin of yours."

Marcus chuckled and ignored the sarcasm. "I wasn't talking about the dirty diaper part. I meant the other things."

"What other things?"

"Oh, I dunno," Marcus said, picking up his beer and smiling thoughtfully. "I was thinking about how much fun it would be to do all the kid stuff again. Things like kickball, little league and going fishing down at Summit Creek. But this would be even better because we'd be doing it with them, your son or daughter. Showing them all the terrific things we discovered when we were little, reliving those same great memories."

"Or maybe even making a few new ones."

Marcus stared at his best friend and smiled. It wasn't easy leading a horse to water. Getting him to drink, however, was something entirely different. He decided to find out if the trip was for nothing. "So?" he asked Ben. "You maybe changing your mind about it?"

"You mean about being a father?"

"Yeah."

Ben tilted his head slightly and shrugged. "I guess it wouldn't be so bad at that."

Marcus grinned and drank his beer, an image of Ben dressed as a horse and taking a big drink from a pond in the back of his mind. He set down the beer and charged forth with the mission. "So?" he asked Ben. "Why not talk to Sue about it?"

"I can't," Ben said flatly.

"Why not?"

"Because. If I bring it up, she'll think I'm pressing her to make a commitment to be a mother and then she'll expect me to make a commitment and marry her."

"So what's wrong with marriage?"

"You know what's wrong. Look at all the kids we graduated with. Some of them have been married and divorced a couple of times already. I don't want that to happen to me and Sue."

"It won't. Trust me."

"What makes you so sure?" Ben said, eyeing him carefully.

"Because I know you. I know Sue. You'd be great parents! And what's more I think you know that. But talking to me about it isn't going to help, man. You've got to sit down and discuss it with her. Otherwise it's going to drive you crazy."

Ben sighed and stared down at his beer. "Yeah, I guess you're right. Sue and I are going to have to break the communication barrier and clear things up."

"Good," Marcus said, "and don't think you're alone in the communication gap between the sexes. Look at Jack and Mavis. They've been married for over forty years and Jack says they never talk to each other. When she talks, he just nods his head like he's listening and she does the same thing when he talks. Jack says that it's a system that's worked for years so it should work for you and Sue, too."

"We're not that bad," Ben grumbled.

"Maybe not yet," Marcus said, enjoying needling him, "but give it time. In a couple years you won't have to talk to each other at all. You can use visual communication like the apes do." He stuck his arm out at Ben, grunting like an ape. "Like this. One grunt to tell her you want a beer. Two grunts for some bananas…uh, I mean your dinner." He could see Ben getting irritated and decided to drive the point home. "On the other hand, there might be another good reason for you two to have a kid. There'd be someone for both of you to talk to, that is, since you won't be talking to each other. Then if Sue wants you to do something, she can tell the kid to tell you and vice versa. Of course, you'll have to wait a few years until the kid can understand the words, especially the four letter ones."

Ben took a half-hearted swat at him. "Okay, Magic. I get the message. I'll talk to her about it today."

"Glad to hear it. Besides, if you and Sue have a kid, that'll make me an almost uncle."

"What do you mean 'almost'?"

"You know what I mean," he told Ben, picking up his beer again. "Because we're not brothers."

Ben expression turned angry. "I've known you since we were six. We grew up together. Shit, I practically lived at your house. And your dad and mom…you know what they meant to me. If it hadn't been for your dad…" He stopped and folded his arms in front of him, taking a second to compose himself. "So don't sit there and tell me you're not my brother. You know damned well you are."

AND THE BULL SAVED ME

Marcus felt a pang of guilt for hurting his feelings. Ben very seldom showed so much emotion. He was always the epitome of self-control and patience, a job hazard that came from teaching restless teenagers music.

"Ben. I didn't mean anything by it. I only meant…"

"Oh, forget it," Ben said, waving him off. "Don't mind me. I've been a little nuts lately. I've been putting all kinds of hours in at the store, getting it ready in case the loan goes through."

Marcus suddenly figured out what was bothering him. "You were thinking about dad, weren't you?"

Ben nodded yes. "Today would have been his fiftieth birthday. I was thinking about all the fun we used to have with your mom, planning his surprise parties. But we could never fool him. Remember the big act he'd always put on? Like he knew nothing about it?"

"Yeah. He was always a big ham. Mom and I loved him for it."

"What I loved was the way he'd always keep encouraging me, always telling me to never stop chasing my dreams. Even if the loan to buy the store doesn't go through, it would have been nice to share it with him."

Marcus decided it was time to share a long kept secret. "I saw you at his grave this morning."

"You were there?"

"Sure. Just like you. Didn't you see the flowers by the headstone? I put them there."

Ben leaned forward, lowering his voice. "I never told you but I go there every year on his birthday."

"I know."

"What? But how?"

Marcus explained it to him. "Dad's first birthday, after he was killed, I followed you to the cemetery. You didn't see me. I stayed a couple of rows over. I know you visit Mom's grave sometimes, too. I see the flowers you put there every Mother's Day."

"You never said anything."

"I know. Ironic, isn't it? Looks like we're both experts at not talking about things. And here I am, trying to give you advice on how to talk to Sue. I think we could both use a lesson in communication."

Ben smiled again. "I'll check with a couple of my students and see if there's any classes being offered up at the high school we could sign up for."

Marcus replied that he'd take a pass. "The teachers would all go on strike if I showed up there again."

"Oh, things weren't *that* bad, Magic."

Marcus smiled at his friend's attempt to downplay it. Truth be known, his last year in high school was the worst year of his life. But thankfully, that was a long time ago and now only a fragmented memory that periodically haunted his dreams.

"Here we go again!" one of the guys up at the bar called out. "Their pitcher just hit another batter. Gonna be a fistfight for sure."

Ben directed his attention to the TV and Marcus took advantage of the minor distraction and excused himself to go to the john.

"Don't fall in," Ben smirked, his eyes still glued to the set.

Marcus got up and headed towards the john at the back of the bar. Just before ducking into the men's room he glanced back over his shoulder to make sure Ben wasn't watching. He then turned and hurried over to the pay phone at the other end of the hall, next to the women's room. He picked up the receiver, pulled two quarters out of his pocket and put them in the slot. He dialed the number and waited for her to pick up.

"Hello?"

He cupped his hand over the receiver. "Hey, Sue. It's me."

"Magic?"

"Yeah."

"How did it go?"

"Great. It's all set. He's going to bring it up tonight so prepare yourself and act surprised."

"Are you sure it's okay?" she asked, her voice sounding a bit shaky. "I mean, do you think he's really in favor of the idea?"

"Not only is he okay with it, he's already talking about little league for the kid."

He heard her suck in a breath and could almost see her breaking into a huge smile.

"I'm so glad," she said. "I hated keeping it from him."

He asked her when she was going to tell Ben the news.

"I'm not sure. I want to get him used to the idea first before I spring it on him. I was thinking I'd tell him on your birthday."

Nice birthday present for me, Marcus thought, suddenly picturing Ben's face after he found out he was going to be a father.

"I wanted to wait for his birthday in September," Sue added. "But I'm afraid I'll be showing before then."

Marcus agreed with her that his birthday was the perfect time. "And in the meantime I'll keep working on him. By the time you tell him he's gonna be so happy about it that he'll be running out buying a guitar and amp for the kid."

She giggled into the phone. "The next thing you know he'll be turning the garage into a sound studio." She paused and got quiet for a moment. He asked her if she was okay.

"Yes I am. Now. Oh, Magic. What would I do without you?"

He felt his face flush at the compliment. He didn't have to answer the question. He and Sue had been friends long enough that they could read each other like a book. "I'd better get back," he told her, "before he catches me talking to you."

"Okay. I'll call you tomorrow at The Crystal."

"Good. Talk to you then."

He hung up the phone and headed for the men's room. He knew he should feel guilty for deceiving Ben. But telling a couple of white lies seemed like a fair trade off for bringing happiness to two people he loved. He ducked into the men's room door, thinking how much his dad would have loved being in on deception. It almost seemed fitting that it was done on his birthday. He would have loved it. Marcus got back to the booth a few minutes later and asked Ben what had happened in the game.

"Oh, man, you missed it! The pitcher hit one of our guys in the shoulder and both dugouts went nuts. It looked like a prison movie there for a second. Chicago's manager and the pitcher were both thrown out." He paused. "By the way, where were you? I told you not to fall in."

Marcus downed the last of his beer and remembered what he wanted to talk to Ben about. "Uh, Ben," he said, putting down his empty glass. "I was wondering if you could give me some advice."

"Sure thing," Ben said. "Besides, I'm gonna need the practice. Especially if I'm thinking about being a dad."

"You *better* be thinking about it. With my history dating women, becoming an uncle might be the closest I ever get to being a parent. I'm counting on you. Otherwise, the only parenting memory I'm gonna have is that weekend I babysat Jack's grandson's lizards."

Ben broke into a smile and slapped the table with his hand. "Oh, my God! That's right! The lizards! And that redhead you took home that night. What was her name?"

"Wanda."

"Yeah! That's it. Wanda! I never saw her in here again after that night."

"Nope. She stopped drinking and joined AA. I ran into her one day at work.

She was there bowling with her kids. Says she never felt better. I was happy for her."

"That's great, Magic," Ben replied, grinning down at his beer. He was on the verge of laughing and Marcus knew why. The episode with Wanda was one of Ben's favorite *moment* stories.

"So," Ben remarked, acting like he was only passing the time of day. "Why were you watching those lizards, anyway?"

Marcus sighed. It was Ben's not-so-subtle way of prompting him to tell the story again.

"You know what happened," he told Ben. "Jack and his son's family were going away for the weekend and his grandson had a bunch of lizards that had to be fed. It was his science project. So I volunteered to keep them at my place for the weekend." He thought about it, recalling the incident. "Actually, they were kind of fascinating to watch in that glass aquarium thing. There were eight of them and I sat there a couple of times and stared at them slithering around in between the branches and leaves. Watching them eat reminded me of us on spaghetti night when we were kids."

Ben snickered. "Spaghetti night. I almost forgot about that."

"I guess that's the closest I ever came to having a pet."

"That's right. They weren't allowed in your apartment house. Your dad always felt bad about that."

"Yeah, but he shouldn't have. Besides," Marcus said, grinning at Ben. "I had you."

"Very funny."

"Well, I almost had a pet," Marcus said. "That goldfish we won at the carnival when we were twelve. But you know what happened to it. Ken Simmons ate it."

Ben frowned. "Uh, I forgot to tell you. It seems that Ken is not only coming to the reunion this year, he's also talked his way onto the decorating committee."

"What?" Marcus said, images of Ken Simmons throwing rolls of toilet paper all over the high school gym playing in his head. "Whose stupid idea was that? All he ever does is get drunk and pick a fight with everyone."

"Not everyone. Just you. He's had it in for you ever since that time he took us snipe hunting."

Marcus knew it was the truth. Ken Simmons had been the proverbial class bully, fighting his way through four years of high school. The guy also seemed to have a personal vendetta against him. "You know, I was at the diner a few months ago and he was in the booth behind me," he told Ben. "He was telling whoever he was with that I purposely make the things that happen to me occur, to draw attention to myself. He said he asked a psychologist about it."

"That's bullshit and you know it," Ben grumbled. "Shrinks wouldn't talk to Simmons. He's too warped for anyone to try and analyze."

Marcus knew he was only being a good friend for saying it. From the time they were kids, Ben had always been like the older brother he'd never had. Ben was always there for him, sticking up for him and defending him to others. And the role didn't stop with childhood. Once the *moments* began happening, Ben continued in the role of brother protector, defending him to the townsfolk who would go around complaining that he was a "freak" and making him the topic of conversation at the local coffee shops and restaurants.

He didn't mind that the townsfolk talked about him behind his back but Ben did and would jump on anyone doing it. And what's more, people listened to Ben because he had pull with the area residents. He'd built himself quite a reputation over the last ten years. He'd influenced a good share of the teenagers in town and word had spread about what an excellent teacher and businessman he was. Ben was fast becoming one of Kirklin's leading citizens and having someone with that kind of prestige on your side was always a plus.

"You know, I did talk to a shrink about it one time," he told Ben, deciding to share another secret. "Back when I was in business school."

"Really?"

"I never told anyone. I guess it was my stupid pride getting in the way. But the shrink did agree with Ken Simmons on one point. He said I was causing the things to happen because of my subconscious anger over Mom and Dad's deaths."

"That's bullshit, too," Ben grunted. "If that were true, your *moments* would be happening to me, too. What do shrinks know, anyway? They read a few books, take some classes and think they have all the answers. They don't. Their lives are as screwed up as everyone else's. The only difference is that they put a name on their screw-ups. But naming it doesn't mean solving it. And I'll bet that shrink couldn't find a name for your situation, could he? Not to mention your own theory about it. What did he say about that?"

"I didn't tell him," Marcus said, suddenly feeling ashamed at the admission. "I figured he might think I really *was* delusional and pack me off the nuthouse. So I kept my mouth shut and let him think he'd cured me. Which of course, he didn't." Marcus paused and stared hard at Ben. "Besides, my best friend doesn't even believe it. How could I expect a complete stranger to take it seriously?"

Ben fidgeted, like he was uncomfortable. "It's not that I don't believe you, Magic. It's only that I don't believe in any of that mystical stuff. You know me. If I can't see, hear or touch it, it doesn't exist. But what the hell? I could be wrong."

Marcus smiled and shook his head, amused. They'd been through this particular discussion many times before.

"What I *do* know," Ben said, "is that something unique is going on around you and since it started happening, I've been lucky enough to have a front row seat. I only wish I could have been there for ALL your *Magic moments*. Especially the one involving a certain redhead and some lizards." He paused and raised his eyebrows inquiringly. "So. When you took Wanda up to your place, didn't she see the lizards in the cage?"

Marcus rolled his eyes in exasperation. It was no use trying to fight it. Ben was gonna keep it up until he told the tale again.

"No, she didn't see the lizards," he told Ben. "She was pretty drunk and having trouble focusing in on me. I never did figure out how they got out of the aquarium. There was a piece of plywood covering the top and I put a book on it to hold it down. The next morning the plywood and book were lying on the floor. Beats me how they knocked off the top."

"They might have been intelligent lizards," Ben said, trying to keep a straight face. "Maybe they were trying to read the book."

"Yeah, that was it," Marcus replied, sarcastically. He then paused and thought of something. "You know, it *was* kind of chilly that night and I had the window open. After they got out of the cage, they must have been looking for someplace warm and decided to crawl into bed with me and Wanda. It would have been better if a few of them hadn't decided to make a little nest in her hair."

Ben almost spit up his beer chuckling.

"It's kind of strange," Marcus said, "but when I woke up that next morning and saw one of those little guys lying in the hair on my chest, I wasn't upset about it. It was kinda cool. It was just sitting there, real peaceful with its eyes closed. It woke up a few minutes later and crawled off me. It was no big deal. I was like it's human sleeping bag. I didn't mind and neither did it."

"But Wanda *did* mind," Ben reminded him.

"That's for sure. I turned over in bed and saw about five of them in her hair, snug as a bunch of bugs in a rug, and her sleeping away, completely unaware. I knew she'd be upset if she saw them so I reached up and tried to scoot them along, before she woke up. They didn't mean any harm. They were only looking for a soft, warm place to take a nap. Can't say I blamed them. Wanda did have beautiful hair. That's where I'd be if I was a little lizard looking for a soft spot. Shoot, I thought for sure I could get them all out of her hair before she woke up. But then one of them got a little skittish, ran smack dab, across her face and almost ended up in her mouth."

Ben's shoulders began shaking from trying to keep from laughing.

"She sure woke up after that," Marcus said, picking up his beer.

"I'll bet she did," Ben said, giving into the laughter. "It's not every day you wake up with lizards all over you."

"The bad part came when she ran butt naked out of the apartment, screaming at the top of her lungs. There were a couple of women coming out of the fabric shop and Wanda almost ran over them, trying to get away. I don't know who was more scared, Wanda or those poor ladies. The shop owner threatened to call the cops but I talked her out of it."

Ben stopped laughing. "You never told me that part. How did you manage that?"

Marcus grinned sheepishly. "I told her Wanda was having DTs. She believed that."

"No shit! What with Wanda screaming about little green things in her hair? It's no wonder."

"The lady was real nice," Marcus said. "She ended up giving Wanda a number for the local chapter of AA. I think that's how she got started going to the meetings."

"See? Some good *did* come out of it."

"Yeah," Marcus replied, seeing his point. "I guess it did turn out all right at that."

"You said you ran into her and she seems happy. Why don't you ask her out again?"

Marcus thought about it. The idea had crossed his mind but he knew it would never happen. "She'd never get within a mile of my place again. Not after that. I couldn't even get her to go back inside to put her clothes on. She made me bring them out to her and she got dressed, right there in the back seat of my car. And she inspected them thoroughly first. She was almost blue from the cold but she wasn't putting one stitch on until she knew they were lizard free. I don't know why she was so scared. It was only lizards." Then he paused and thought of something. "It's kinda funny, but when I saw those little green lizards mixed in with Wanda's hair, it reminded me of some of those women you see with beads and things woven into their curls. Like that one girlfriend of Sue's, remember? I heard her telling Sue it took her hairdresser six hours to do her hair and how she paid top dollar for it."

Ben stopped grinning and put down his beer. "What are you saying, Magic? That they should start a new trend? Weave lizards into women's hair?"

"It's only a thought," Marcus said with a shrug. "It would probably be a lot easier than all those little beads. Take less time, too."

"I'd love to see that," Ben chortled. "Some gay hairdresser sticking live lizards in a woman's hair and both him and her screaming like hell. You're right. That could sell. Not only would the customer get an attractive 'do,' everyone in the salon would get a floor show. Quick! Where do I sign up to buy stock?"

"Screw you, Ben," Marcus replied, giving him a healthy kick under the table. But the kick only made Ben laugh louder. Finally, Marcus could no longer resist and joined him. They'd shared more than a few ideas with each other over the years and Ben was a good enough friend to give him his honest opinion on them. The laughter died down and he suddenly remembered what he wanted to tell Ben. "Uh, speaking of my love life, there's something I want to discuss with you."

Ben told him to go ahead.

Marcus began talking fast, trying to tell him all that happened. "Okay, I saw this girl the other day. She was walking down the street, singing to herself but she didn't have on headphones or anything. You don't usually see people singing to themselves like that and I thought it was kind of interesting. So the next day, after she got out of work, I followed her—"

"Magic! You aren't stalking this woman, are you?"

Marcus sighed. "No, Ben. I'm not stalking her. I only followed her because I was curious. Anyway, I was walking behind her and she almost clobbered me with her purse."

"Oh. So she caught you stalking her."

Marcus gritted his teeth, trying not to get angry. "For the last time. I was not stalking her. I was only following her."

"Okay. Right," Ben said, giving him a wink. "That's what I'll tell the cops when they ask me."

Marcus started to protest but Ben cut him off. "Relax, Magic. I'm only kidding you. Go on with the story."

Marcus glared at him, perturbed. "You're having the best time, aren't you?"

"What do you expect? Lizard weaves and purse toting stalker victims? Come on, Magic."

"She didn't mean to hit me with her purse. She was swinging it while she was singing and I got in the way. Anyway, she apologized for doing it but that's beside the point. I ran into her…I mean, I saw her again the other day out at the DMV when I was picking up my plates."

Ben stopped him again, "Hey that's right, your birthday's coming up. We've got to plan for that."

"Already got some ideas. So like I said, I'm out there and see her standing in line, just a couple people up from me. I finally get close enough to hear the clerk ask her when her birthday is and it turns out its August twelfth, two days after mine."

"What's her name?"

"I don't know. I never really introduced myself."

"Too bad."

Marcus continued. "She got her plates and left, so I figured I missed my opportunity. But when I came out of the building, a few minutes later, there she was, in the parking lot. One of her tires had gone flat and she was trying to change it. She remembered me from bumping into me that day on the street. So I offered to change the tire."

"And you got her name and number," Ben said. "Nice move."

"Well, not exactly."

"What? Why not?"

"I got all tongue-tied," he told Ben, trying not to make it sound stupid. "She kept talking to me while I changed the tire, telling me about her car and how much trouble she's been having with it lately and I kept shaking my head up and down, listening. I felt like one of those Cleveland Indians bobble-head dolls they sell at the stadium. So after I get the tire changed, she tries to pay me and I told her 'no thank you, it was my pleasure.' And those are the only words I said to her. She kept thanking me and I just grinned like an idiot, nodded my head and waved to her as she got back in the car and drove away. She must have thought I was retarded or something. And why not? I sure as hell was acting like it."

"I'm sure she doesn't think you're retarded. And don't forget. It could always be worse. She could have thought you were a stalker."

"Maybe I *should* start stalking," Marcus said; suddenly feeling depressed. "Especially considering my track record. If I get to know a woman for more than thirty seconds, my little problem makes an appearance and they all head for the hills."

"What's this? Self-pity? That's not like you, Magic."

Marcus grumbled, under his breath. "Nothing wrong with a little self-pity once in a while."

"Well, get rid of it. You don't need it. Hey. If I can hope to be a daddy someday, then you can meet the woman of your dreams. So don't sit there and cry in your beer. Besides, you're empty."

The men at the bar all started cheering and Marcus glanced up at the television. One of the Indians was sprinting around the bases, legging out a home run. As the ballplayer crossed home plate, the bar was momentarily bathed in sunlight, indicating someone had come through the front door. The light faded and Marcus let his eyes adjust to the smoky atmosphere again as he saw the outline of the person take shape. He experienced a sudden sense of familiarity and tried to focus better on the person. A few seconds later he recognized who it was and sat bolt upright in his seat. Ben noticed his sudden change and asked him what was wrong.

"Shit! It's her!" Marcus said, running his hands through his hair and straightening his collar.

"The singing lady?"

"Yeah, and she's coming right toward us! What should I do?"

"Well, first of all, don't faint or anything, okay?"

Marcus shot him an annoyed glare. "Come on, Ben. I'm serious! What's she doing here?"

"Let's find out. And don't be so nervous. Let me do the talking."

As she walked up to their booth, Marcus felt something inside of himself sigh. She looked lovely. She wasn't wearing anything dressy, just jeans and a sleeveless white tee shirt. Her hair was pulled back from her face with a tie and she had a shoulder purse and a small, paper bag in her hands. Ben stood up, introduced himself and she shook his hand.

"Hi there, Ben," she said. "I'm Vickie Garrett."

Ben offered her a seat. She thanked him and sat down, scooting over enough to give Ben room. She placed the paper bag on the table in front of her and when she looked up a moment later her eyes settled directly on Marcus. His throat suddenly went dry and he reached for his glass to take a swig of beer. But as he tipped the glass up, he remembered it was empty. He quickly put it back down again, feeling stupid for trying to drink air.

"I think it's empty," she said, smiling sweetly.

He nodded yes, unable to speak. He racked his brain, trying to think of something to say but it was no use. He was absolutely blank. Ben kicked him under the table and he jumped, his knees bumping the bottom of the table.

"Are you all right?" she asked.

He nodded yes and reached under the table to rub his sore ankle, wishing he could kick Ben back without her noticing it. She was still staring at him. He suddenly felt self-conscious and clumsy and the temperature in the room felt like it had gone up ten degrees in the space of a few seconds. Beads of sweat were now forming on his forehead and he reached up and wiped them away. He then rubbed the sweaty palm on his pants leg and grabbed his beer with his other hand. But as soon as he felt how light the glass was, he remembered the stupid mistake from a moment earlier and let go of it.

What the hell's wrong with me? he thought. *I'm acting like a complete idiot.*

Ben chuckled and pointed to Marcus's empty glass. "It's a new kind of beer," he told Vickie. "They just started selling it. It's Lite Beer. No calories, no hangover. You can drink all you want and never get drunk." Then Ben poured half of what was left of his own beer into Marcus's glass. "Here. Try some of mine," he told Marcus, giving him a quick wink. "It's not quite as 'lite' but it's definitely got a better taste."

She giggled and Marcus felt the relief wash over him. Ben was saving his ass again.

"Magic told me he helped you with a flat the other day at the DMV," Ben said, pausing to take a swig of his own beer.

Marcus watched her eyes move from Ben to him. "Magic? But they told me your name was Marcus Kerr."

He sat there, temporarily stunned. He couldn't believe she knew his name. "How did you know my name?" he asked her in what sounded to him like a shaky voice. "I never gave it to you."

She took the purse from her shoulder and put it on top of the table, next to the paper sack. "When you wouldn't let me pay you for changing my tire, I phoned the clerk and asked her for your name and address. She wasn't going to give it to me at first. But once I told her what a nice thing you did for me, she changed her mind. I was coming into town today anyway, so I drove over to your apartment to thank you. When I didn't find you there, I remembered you mentioning this place and thought someone here might know what your phone number was." She paused and glanced around the bar. "To tell the truth, I've always been curious about this place. I walk past it every day but I've never seen the inside. Gee, it's kind of quaint, isn't it?"

Marcus sat there, unable to reply. Ben nudged him in the knee under the table, prompting him to speak up but he couldn't. He was afraid that if he opened his mouth again it might come out froggy sounding or squeaky, which it did sometimes when he was nervous.

And one thing was sure, he was nervous.

"Yes, it is quaint," Ben said. "They have karaoke on Thursday nights. You should come up and try it sometime."

"I'll do that," she said, turning back around in the seat. "Some friends and I have tried the karaoke at *Kreigs,* it's a bar over in Barbertown, down by the town park."

As she spoke, Marcus saw those same smiling eyes that had mesmerized him that day on the street. They seemed to shine out with a sweet innocence and vulnerability that made him feel strangely protective of her.

"I know the place," Ben said. "My girlfriend's brother is a bartender there. He says they get a nice crowd on karaoke nights."

"Yes they do," she said. "It's a lot of fun."

Marcus watched as a piece of her hair came loose and fell gently across her face. Even tied back, her hair was lovely and the piece against her cheek looked soft and inviting. She brushed it back and rearranged the elastic tie. As she smoothed her hair down, she glanced up, giving him a smile that made his heart jump. She giggled, showing that she'd caught him staring at her again. He felt his face flush red with shame and quickly averted his eyes, trying not to look so obvious. He cleared his throat and took a big gulp of beer hoping to wash away the awkward feeling.

But he'd taken the drink too fast and some of the liquid entered his windpipe. His body reacted almost instantaneously and he started coughing violently, his insides convulsing and trying to expel the beer from his airway. The coughing quickly turned to retching and as much as he wanted to stop, he knew it would only end when the last of the beer was gone. He tried to hold his breath to make it stop but the retching had drained his lungs of air and he began gasping for breath in between the coughs. He kept his head down, avoiding her gaze but could see her from the corner of his eye, staring at him.

"Are you okay?" she asked, her voice full of concern.

He nodded his head yes, even though he didn't believe it.

"He'll be fine!" Ben said, reaching across the table and smacking him hard on the back.

Marcus coughed up the last of the beer and finally started to catch his breath. His throat felt like raw meat and he took another sip of his beer, this time drinking it very slowly, making sure it went down his throat and not his windpipe. He finally mustered up enough courage to look at her.

"Are you sure you're all right?" she whispered.

"Uh, yeah," he said, clearing his throat again. "Guess it went down the wrong pipe."

Ben picked up Marcus's beer glass and examined it closely. "That happens to me sometimes, too. I think it's from all the foam they put in the stuff. I've seen a lot of guys have coughing fits because of it. Someone should complain to the management about the damn, cheap draft beer."

Marcus experienced a wave of shame at his best friend's noble attempt to make him sound better instead of the truth, that he was idiot who couldn't even control his own body functions. Ben struck up the conversation again and asked her if she worked in town. He was trying hard to downplay the coughing fit and Marcus mentally thanked him for it.

"I work at the water department," she said. "I do the data entry, help keep the records and wait on customers."

Marcus cleared his throat and tried to act normal again. "Do you like the job?"

She told him that working on the computer got boring. "But talking to the customers makes up for it."

He asked her what she meant.

"Meeting all the people. Some of them are a lot of fun to talk to. If it wasn't for them, I'd hate the job." She leaned in closer on the table, like she was about to reveal a secret. "Like this one man," she said. "He's in his early seventies and came in to complain about his water bill. It went from thirty dollars to three hundred in one month."

"You're kidding," Marcus commented, clearing his throat again and trying not to sound froggy.

"No," she said, her eyes opening wider as she explained it. "Turns out some fool who was replacing the water meters put a commercial meter on his house by mistake. The commercial meters are like the ones used on large buildings that only register water in the thousands of gallons."

"Jeez," Ben chuckled. "It's no wonder he was charged so much."

"I know," she said. "And after this man complained, they found out that several other customers were charged commercial rates by mistake, too. They corrected the problem and the people got their money back, thank goodness. Then the elderly gentleman who first complained, his name is John, came back in a few days later and thanked me. He was so sweet. He brought me a great big bouquet of roses from his garden. They were gorgeous. I set them right on the front counter so everyone who came in could enjoy them. Now every month when he comes in to pay his bill, he always stops and chats with me. The other people in the office started teasing me, calling him my boyfriend because he always asks for me."

"He was probably very grateful that you helped him," Ben remarked.

She put her hand to her cheek and blushed. "Well, I think he does have a little crush on me. He always goes out of his way to make sure I wait on him. If there's a line of customers, he waits around, sometimes over an hour, until the office clears out, so we can have time to talk. And I love talking to him. He used to work at the newspaper and knows everyone in town. He's always telling me the funniest stories."

Marcus stared dreamily at her. He was suddenly jealous of the elderly man John, who had somehow captured her attention, time and heart. Before he could think about what he was saying, he asked her, "Is your boyfriend jealous of the old gentleman?" As soon as he asked it, Ben kicked him under the table, as if to say, *nice move*. He kicked back, but harder, to let Ben know he got the message.

"Oh, I'm not going with anyone right now," she said. "I just got out of a relationship with someone not long ago, although he probably wouldn't have cared one way or other. He was more interested in his car than me."

Foolish man, Marcus thought to himself.

"Where the heck are our manners?" Ben said, getting up from the booth. "Can we get you something to drink?"

"Yes, thank you," she said. "I'll have a Coke."

Marcus started to get up but Ben pushed him back down, giving him a quick wink where Vickie couldn't see. "That's okay, Magic. I'll get the drinks. Looks like you and I need a refill too. Be right back."

As Ben took off towards the bar Marcus realized what he was doing, giving him a chance to redeem himself, a chance to do what he wanted to do, ask her out.

He was now alone with his singing vision. He tried hard to think of something to say and in his head he was yelling at himself, *Come on, stupid! She's sitting right there! Ask her already!* But on the outside he was simply sitting in silence, smiling at her.

He *was* a bobble-head doll.

He suddenly felt like a teenager at his first dance, complete with shortness of breath and sweaty palms. So far, he hadn't made much of an impression. He'd exhibited signs of being a retarded, deaf mute and bobble-head doll who couldn't even manage to drink a beer without almost choking to death.

He felt like an idiot and assumed she must have come to the same conclusion.

But fighting adversity was a regular routine for him. His *gift* had not only taught him perseverance but tenacity. He felt his determination return and began thinking of ways to ask her out.

He was hoping to bring up the subject without making it too obvious. The direct approach probably wouldn't work so he began to run a few lines through his head. *Uh, I think you're beautiful and I love the way your hair bounces when you walk. If you're not doing anything for the next fifty years and don't mind living with someone who makes strange things happen...by the way...do you have good accident insurance?*

Nope. Too direct and humor at this point would probably reinforce her belief that he really *was* crazy. He quickly thought of another one. *Excuse me, miss, but I love the way you sing. Would you mind accompanying me back to my apartment? I don't happen to be babysitting any lizards at the present time so I can assure you that when you wake up in the morning, the only thing crawling all over you will be...me.* And as he thought of the line, a smile crept across his face.

"What's so funny?"

As soon as she asked it, his face flushed red with guilt. "Uh...nothing," he said, averting her gaze. He grabbed at his beer and took a swig, reminding himself to drink "slowly" and hoping she didn't ask anything else. He began running lines in his head again but nothing seemed quite appropriate. The silence became thunderous and he glanced up at the bar, hoping Ben would hurry up.

"Oh, I almost forgot," she said, picking up the paper bag and handing it to him. "You wouldn't take any money for helping me with my tire the other day so I bought you a little present."

He opened the bag and took out a CD of the group Savage Garden.

"I know you said you wanted to get that CD, the first day I saw you," she said. "Outside on the street, remember?"

He nodded his head yes, impressed that she'd even remembered. After all, they'd only spoken for a few minutes. He ran his hand across the CD. It suddenly became very important to him because she'd gone out of her way to get it. "Thank you. That was very kind of you," he told her and meant it. He started to think of a way to ask her out, without simply blurting it out. He began running another line through his head when she leaned across the table and put her hand on top of his holding the CD.

"I wanted to ask you, before your friend Ben comes back to the table," she whispered. "The CD is only part of my thank-you. I'd like to take you to dinner, if you're available some night soon."

His mind began reeling. He was still reacting to her touch, so warm and pleasant against his skin. She'd taken him completely by surprise. "Sure," he said, trying not to sound too anxious. "I'd love to. Just let me know when." He tried to act normal but in his head he was dancing around and shouting, like a little kid at Christmas.

"I forgot to ask you where you work," she said. "You don't work nights, do you?"

"I manage a bowling alley. I do work a lot of nights, especially with all the fall leagues getting ready but I could get someone to cover for me."

"He sure as hell could!" Ben said, walking back up to the booth and handing Marcus his beer. Ben then handed Vickie her Coke and she thanked him.

"My pleasure," Ben said, taking his seat. "Magic needs a night out. He works too hard. He runs *Crystal Lanes*. Do you know the place?"

She replied that she did. "My niece bowls there all the time. She's always telling me how much fun she and her friends have there."

"All the kids in town love The Crystal," Ben told her. "Almost as much as they love taking music lessons from me. Right, Magic?"

Marcus smiled at Ben's feeble attempt to sound modest. "What they love is the triple digit decibels coming from those electric guitar amps and pins being knocked down," he told Ben. "It's the noise they love and the louder the better. You're the one always saying it's another way of them rebelling against authority, letting their frustrations and destructive tendencies surface. And what better way to do it than with a Fender Staitocastor or fifteen pound Brunswick?"

"That's an interesting theory," Vickie commented. "How long have you worked at the bowling alley?"

"Magic and I both got jobs there in high school," Ben said, answering for him. "We did everything, short order cook, oiling the lanes, cleaning the bathrooms. Then, while Magic was going to business school, he worked there during the summers. But the place got run-down and was losing money. The owner had moved to Florida and didn't have much interest in it anymore. Magic was offered the job of running the place and everyone figured it was a hopeless cause. That is, everyone but Magic."

"And you," Marcus reminded him. "When we worked there," he told Vickie, "I was always bending Ben's ear about how I would do things different if I was running the place. I had all these crazy ideas about how to make the place a success. When I got the managing job, Ben told me I should put those ideas to use. So I did and it worked. Now the place is making money and the owner couldn't be happier."

"It sounds like you're very successful at it," she said.

"Damn right he is," Ben remarked. "Thanks to Magic's crazy ideas, the place is making money hand over foot!"

Marcus kicked Ben under the table, letting him know he was overdoing it. He never liked people who bragged about themselves and taking compliments had always made him uneasy.

Vickie asked Ben what the crazy ideas were.

"For one thing," Ben said, "he started a mother's league and set up a little room next to the lanes where the moms could leave their kiddies while they bowled. Like a daycare center. The mothers get a break for a few hours and the alley is busy during the day, when most places are usually dead."

"It couldn't have worked out better," Marcus added. "My friend Jack, he works at The Crystal with me, his wife and daughter run the daycare center for me. Jack's daughter Betsy loves kids and doesn't have any of her own so she really gets involved in the job. She's so good with the kids. She plays games with them and sings songs. The kids have so much fun that when their moms come and pick them up, a lot of them don't want to go."

"That's marvelous," Vickie said. "What a great idea. My sister was pretty stressed out when her kids were little. She could have used a break like that. You know, my niece is always talking about The Crystal and she's up there a couple times a week. She told me about a dance game you have. It sounds like fun, but I didn't really understand it. How does it work?"

"That's my favorite program too," Ben piped up enthusiastically, a little too enthusiastically, Marcus thought. "All the teenagers in town love it. My girlfriend and I go up some nights and watch the kids play it. Tell her how it works, Magic."

Marcus pushed his beer aside, eager to explain. "We divide the girls and guys into teams of four in adjacent lanes. They bowl three games and the team with the overall highest number of pins wins. The winners dance with the losers on the dance floor next to the jukebox. Jack and I put in the floor last year. Actually, it was more like Jack told me what to do and I did it. I'm not much of a carpenter but he is."

"Along with a lot of other things," Ben added.

Marcus saw a puzzled look on her face and explained. "Jack's one of those guys whose done almost everything. He's been a carpenter, farmer, worked in construction and plumbing, did some time as a Carney..."

She asked what a Carney was.

"It's one of those guys who travels around with the carnivals," Marcus told her. "Jack said he used to run a ride something like the Tilt O' Whirl. He'd run and maintain the ride, having to break it down and set it up every couple of days in a new town. He said he saw a lot of the country that way. He once told me he's done over fifty different jobs in his life. If there was a buck to be made doing it, he'd do it."

"He sounds like an interesting person," she said.

"He is," Marcus said. "He started working for me after he retired from one of the factories in Columbus. He and Mavis, that's his wife, moved up here to be close to their son and his family. I love to hear him tell stories about his past. He should write a book." He paused, realizing he had gotten off the subject. "Anyway," he said, "about the dance game—the guys bowl against the girls and once one team wins, the other team has to dance with them. But there's a catch. The winning team gets to pick the kind of music they dance to. If it's fast music, they can dance without touching each other. But if the winners pick the slower songs, they have to dance cheek to cheek. As a rule, the girls usually pick the fast music to dance to. But almost all the guys pick the slow songs."

"It's great," Ben remarked. "And it's just as much fun to watch. The girls all protest if the guys win and make them slow dance but they don't seem to protest very long."

Vickie flashed Marcus a dubious smile. "Does anyone complain if they get stuck with someone ugly?"

"They aren't allowed," he told her. "The rules state that you have to dance with the girl whose name is in the same order bowler as you are. The girl number ones dance with the boy number ones, et cetera. However, we don't tell them they can't decide who bowls in what order so the boys are always scrambling for pecking order once they see the girls' names up on the monitor. Some of the kids who are already dating make sure they get put with their steadies and others who are kind of shy sometimes end up with someone they wouldn't normally have the courage to ask to dance. That way, they use the game as an excuse to get together. The kids really seem to enjoy it."

"Enjoy it? Hell, they love it!" Ben said. "The place is packed every night they have it and the lanes are reserved a week ahead of time. I told Magic he ought to start a program for us older folks, too."

Marcus leaned back and laughed. "Yep. Then I'd really be in trouble. The kids are well behaved and act like responsible people when they show up. Some of the adults, however, wouldn't. A lot of the married couples would make sure they didn't get stuck with their spouses and before you know it, there'd be fights over who is dancing with whom. I'd have the cops there every night, the place would be branded a den of inequity and closed up by all the church leaders in town. No thanks. I'll stick with the kids in the dance game. Besides, we have games for the adults, too. We have raffles, trivia contests and Magic Pins."

She asked him what Magic Pins was.

"Jack and I rigged a strobe light on the back wall by the end of the lanes," he told her. "Then we took a few of the pins and painted them gold with black letters spelling out the word 'Magic' on them. At different times during the league games we start the light flashing, signaling the bowlers that it's 'Magic Pins' time. Jack mixes the marked pins in with the others and the first bowler to knock one of the magic pins down gets a prize. The prizes are usually things like stuffed animals, free passes for games or free food at the lunch counter. But we also give away free bowling balls and bags once a month and run specials during football or baseball season and give away free tickets to the Browns and Indian games. The customers seem to enjoy it and Jack says it gives him something else to do while he's back there babysitting the pinsetters."

"Isn't that strenuous work for a man his age?"

"That's what I thought," Marcus told her. "But he loves it."

"Tell Vickie how you came to hire Jack," Ben said. "That's a great story."

"It was not long after I started managing the place," Marcus told her; happy to share the tale. "Jack used to come up and bowl with his grandkids. Back then the pinsetters were constantly breaking down and I was always running to the back, trying to repair them. So one night Jack's lane breaks down and as I'm heading back to fix it I notice he's following me. I figured he was some Budinski but I was too damned tired to argue with him, so I let him come along. He ended up fixing it for me. Turns out he knew all about pinsetters.

He used to set pins by hand when he was a kid, before they had automatic pinsetting machines. Then the place where he worked bought the automatics and Jack knew he was going to be out of a job. But instead of quitting, he learned how to repair the automatics and made himself indispensable to the owners. Now I'd be the one lost without him. He keeps the setters running perfect and knows all their little quirks. Before Jack came along and when I couldn't fix them myself, I'd have to hire an out of state repair firm and sometimes even they couldn't fix them right. Since hiring Jack, I never have a problem. And he loves the job, says he was bored after retirement and felt kind of useless. He works full time for me now. I told him he could cut his hours if he wanted but he doesn't want to." Marcus paused and noticed her grinning strangely at him. He asked her if something was wrong.

"No. Not at all," she said. "It's only that when I first sat down here, you seemed…well…kind of uncomfortable and nervous."

"I was nervous," he admitted. "But I didn't realize it was that obvious."

"Oh, it wasn't *that* noticeable," she replied. "But when you started talking about the bowling alley, your whole attitude changed. You seemed more relaxed and open."

"Yep. That's Magic," Ben said. "The Crystal is like his baby. And why not? He's put his heart and soul into it. He should be proud of his hard work."

"Yes, he should be," Vickie added.

Marcus glanced down at the table; feeling uncomfortable again and wishing someone would change the subject.

"I'd really like to see the place," she said. "Maybe I'll drop by sometime."

"Uh, that would be nice," he told her, beaming inside. "I'd love to show you around. I'm there every day. About the only time I'm gone is when I break for dinner around five o'clock."

"It just so happens that Magic was on his way back to The Crystal before you came in," Ben added. "He could probably give you a tour right now."

Marcus kicked him under the table again, signaling him to lay off. Ben had just taken a swig of his beer and almost spit it up, chuckling. Some of the foam spilled across the table and Ben uttered a quick "sorry" and cleaned it up with one of the paper napkins from the holder in the middle of the table.

"I'd like that very much," she said. "But I've got some errands to run, including picking up my sister." Then she glanced at her watch. "As a matter of fact, I'm late now. I'd better get going."

Ben got up from the booth and let her out. "It was nice meeting you, Ben," she said. "And thanks again for the Coke."

"My pleasure."

Marcus jumped up from his seat and volunteered to walk her to the door. She'd only given him a vague promise to meet for dinner sometime and he was hoping to get something more definite. She smiled and took his arm as he led her away. He noticed a couple of the regulars at the bar give him leering smiles and knew he'd be hearing a few choice comments later. He held open the front for her. "I'm available on Wednesday night for that dinner you mentioned," he whispered. "That is, if you're free and the offer is still there."

She pulled her keys from her purse and looked up at him. The sun was shining in from the outside and lit up her face, making it seem as if there was an aura around it. He experienced a momentary urge to reach out and touch her to see if she was real.

"I am and it is," she said, bringing him back from his thoughts. "I know an Italian place over in Barbertown that has great linguini. Richetti's, do you know it?"

"Sure. It's the place next to the library."

"I live right around the corner from there so you wouldn't have to pick me up. I could walk down and meet you. I'll reserve us a table. Is 7:30 okay?"

"Sounds great," he replied.

She took off down the street and he stood in the door and continued watching her walk away.

"Hey, Magic!" someone called from over at the bar. "Shut the door. We can't see the TV!"

He closed the door and as he headed back across the bar a few of the guys began kidding him about the "the babe on his arm" and asked if she was his new girlfriend. He ignored the comments and sat down across from Ben, the smile still on his face.

"So?" Ben said. "Is there a date on the horizon any time soon?"

He stopped smiling and told Ben about meeting her at the restaurant. "But it's a wonder she's even going out with me. Especially after I had my spazz attack and tried to cough up a lung."

Ben snickered. "I thought you were trying to break your own personal record for having one of your *Magic moments*. I clocked it. Exactly three minutes after she sat down. Come to think of it, that is a record."

Marcus suddenly remembered what he wanted to tell him. "Uh, Ben?"

"What?" Ben said, finishing the last of his beer and setting the glass down.

"Thanks for making me sound so good."

"No problem. Besides, it looked like you could use a little help. You must really like this girl. I've never known you to be that nervous around women before."

"I know. It's weird," Marcus said, thinking about it. "I've been that way since that first day when I followed her down the street. I sounded like an idiot. I couldn't even make a coherent sentence. I haven't been that tongue-tied since I saw my first boob."

"Yeah! Mary Beth Daniels. I remember her. That was the day you promised to show yours if she showed hers. What were we, ten?"

"Eleven," Marcus replied. "I couldn't believe she actually let me touch them. My tongue must have been hanging out a mile." He paused to smile. "And they were sure nice. She always did have big boobs, even at that age."

"She was just plain big. She was taller than all the boys in the class. Ken Simmons used to call her an Amazon and she'd beat hell out him every time she caught him saying it. I also remember how all the guys used to drool over her but no one had the courage to ask her out."

"That's because they were afraid of her."

Ben flashed him a sly grin. "Telling everyone about feeling her up sure made you famous for a while. You're just damn lucky she never found out. Otherwise she would have cleaned your clock."

"Shit! I thought she was going to clean my clock that day! Especially when I started squeezing too hard. I knew it was a once-in-a-lifetime thing so I went for broke. Unfortunately, she didn't share my enthusiasm. She slapped me so hard that my teeth rattled. After that there was no way I was dropping my pants. I was afraid she'd get mad and knee me or something even worse. My balls shriveled up in fear just thinking about it. Thank God you showed up when you did."

"I couldn't figure out what the hell was going on at first," Ben said, shaking his head like he still couldn't believe it. "All I saw was her standing there with her hands on her hips, screaming at you and demanding you drop your shorts. I thought, 'What the hell?' Then you started stammering and making all those stupid excuses, telling her you had the clap and that she could catch it by getting near your dick. And then, when you told her that your scrotum was sensitive to light, I thought I'd crack up laughing."

"It's a good thing you didn't. Otherwise she'd have known it was a lie and knocked me out for real. But damn it, I was desperate! I had to think of something, and quick. Lucky for me, she bought all those lies."

Ben reminded him of the aftermath of those lies when she went around school the next day, asking all the guys what a scrotum was.

Marcus laughed. "Yeah, and then Ken Simmons unzipped and tried to show her and got busted for exposing himself in school. Old Lady Weaver screamed bloody hell and marched him off to the office before he could whip it out. Poor Mary Beth. She never did get to see one."

"She must have seen at least one," Ben smirked. "She's got four kids now. I also heard she's coming to the reunion. Maybe you, her and Ken could get together and she can show her boobs and Ken can whip out his scrotum. We could make it part of the festivities. I'll mention it to the reunion committee."

AND THE BULL SAVED ME

Marcus rolled his eyes in disgust. "I'm sure they'll love the idea. The way Simmons gets drunk every time and starts fights, they'll probably welcome the change."

"It's not the fights they all remember from the last reunion. It's the fire."

Marcus frowned down at his beer. "That's the last time I'm ever going to rent a white suit. The rental guy kept telling me it was a great idea. You should have seen his face when I brought it back to him. He'll never rent me another one."

"You can't blame him. It started out white and ended up green. But I don't know what he's complaining about. He could always rent it out for St. Patrick's Day."

"Not with all that liquor on it. Hell. All I was doing was getting a damn glass of punch. How was I to know Simmons spiked it?"

"Spiked it!" Ben grunted. "More like booby-trapped it! There must have been two full fifths in that bowl. When the DJ's drunken helper crashed into the table and dumped the stuff on you, you smelled like a brewery."

Marcus replied that he felt like one, too. "That was enough for me. After that, all I wanted to do was get the hell out of there. That green punch made me look like a leprechaun. And that suit sure soaked it up."

"I'll say. You were leaving a trail of green ooze all the way across the gymnasium floor. It was like a stick of dynamite, with you as the stick and the ooze as the fuse. But when that guy dropped his cigarette and ignited it, that's when the real fun began. It was just like the pyrotechnics the rock bands use."

"But in this case, there was no team of special effects experts standing by with fire extinguishers," Marcus reminded him. "And the way everybody was screaming, I thought I was in a remake of that movie *Carrie*."

Ben laughed. "You might have ended up like Joan of Arc if that brunette hadn't been knocked down and dropped her blonde wig on the slime trail. Cut that fuse right off."

"Only because the damned wig flamed up and exploded first. And the smell lingered in the air the rest of the night, making everyone sick to their stomachs."

Ben waved his hand in front of him, like it was no big deal. "Hey. No one was hurt and they eventually got the burn marks off the floor so nothing was really damaged."

"Maybe not," Marcus fretted. "But one thing's for sure. It was a reunion the class of 1992 will never forget."

Ben smirked. "Yep. Especially since the whole thing was caught on videotape. Now it will be recorded for posterity and all our future generations. What more could you ask for?"

"Very funny," Marcus replied. "How was I supposed to know one of the wives was filming right then? I guess I should be grateful it never turned up on one of those TV video shows."

Ben commented that it could still end up on one. "I have a copy or two left."

Marcus glared at him, not amused. "Having millions of people see one of my *moments* is not something I'd look forward to."

"Don't worry about it, Magic. You're already famous, at least here in Kirklin."

"You mean infamous, don't you? More like public enemy number one. I'm surprised they haven't plastered my picture on the post office wall with the other notables."

Ben told him to stop feeling sorry for himself. "Besides, you just made a date with your dream girl…I mean singing girl. Things are looking up."

Marcus thought about it. Ben was right. He shouldn't dwell on things he couldn't control. He should keep his eye on the future and right now that future was Vickie.

Ben got up from the booth and Marcus grabbed the CD and followed him to the exit. He waited until they were outside and voiced his concerns once more to Ben. "I just don't want this date to end up like all the others."

"Don't worry," Ben said, patting him reassuringly on the back. "It won't. As far as I know, Richetti's doesn't serve lizards, either on the plates or coming in through the front door so you won't have to worry about that. Besides, green wouldn't go very well with her brown hair."

Marcus chuckled and followed him down the street. By the time Ben left him at the store a few minutes later he was feeling better about the whole thing. Ben could always brighten his spirits no matter how low he was feeling. And as he turned and headed back down the street towards home, he realized that Ben was right.

They *were* brothers.

Only a brother would save you from yourself and come to your rescue without even being asked. Only a brother would suffer through all the disappointments with you and laugh along with you at the crazy situations. And only a brother would love you enough to stick out the worst of times with you, putting his own soul through the same torture.

You didn't have to be blood to be related.

You just had to be lucky enough to know someone who gave a damn about you.

He picked up the pace and his spirits suddenly lifted. One of his favorite

AND THE BULL SAVED ME

Harry Chapin songs began playing in his head and the image of Vickie Garret singing and walking down the street filled his thoughts. What was wrong with singing to yourself, anyway? If you felt good, why not let it out?

He smiled and began to sing the song out loud. He wasn't much of a singer but just hearing the notes and words float out in front of him gave him an incredible sensation of freedom and elation. As he approached the fabric shop and the end of the song, he sang louder, his mood rising proportionately with the volume. It was a wonderfully liberating feeling and one he'd never experienced before, at least not sober.

Maybe she was on to something.

Maybe she *would* be different than the others. Stranger things had happened. He should know. According to some of the townsfolk, he was the King of Strange.

He started up the outside steps of the apartment, a song in his heart and a renewed sense of hope in his soul. Nothing wrong with hope or being happy.

He finished going up the steps and said a silent prayer that it would last.

Even if just for a little while.

CHAPTER THREE

The next few days seem to drag and Marcus found himself looking forward to the date with Vickie, even though he knew better than to expect too much. He'd also been having daydreams about her, something he'd never done with any of his other dates. As a rule, he wasn't what people would call "hopelessly romantic" or "dreamy-eyed" but since meeting her, he'd been experiencing strange new feelings and emotions. He wondered if it was simply his desperation to find a life mate or possibly loneliness affecting his inner psyche. Whatever it was, it was new territory and left him puzzled.

The daydream was always the same. He's at The Crystal, dancing close with her as the song "I Knew I Loved You" plays on the jukebox. Her arms are wrapped tight around him and his head is bent down, on top of hers, the soft locks of her hair surrounding his very soul. He experiences a sense of happiness and well being as they slowly sway to the music. He can almost feel himself float away, surrounded by her warmth and the gentle notes of the music. It's a satisfying and enjoyable vision that fills his heart and puts a smile on his face.

But putting his hopes on such a dream was dangerous, especially if she ended up leaving him, like all the others. Since the relationship with Marilyn, he'd been trying to figure out what went wrong or if he could have approached the subject of his *gift* differently. He'd tried mentioning it up front with a few dates before but they'd either laugh, assuming he was joking or run away, convinced he was crazy. The ones who laughed would only stick around long enough to discover that he wasn't kidding and then they too, would head for the hills.

So telling Vickie about his problem wasn't an option.

At least with Marilyn, by keeping his problem secret, she was able to get to know him before she left. She found out that he was a man, not a monster or someone to be afraid of.

So that was what he had to do with Vickie.

That way she could see "him" and not just his *gift*. She could decide for herself if she wanted to be with someone with his unique problems. Then if she elected to leave, he'd still have a few nice memories to reflect back on. When you were a people repeller, sometimes that was the best you could hope for. But even that course of action had its problems. His *gift* was unpredictable and had a habit of showing up at the most inopportune times. To expect his *moments* to temporarily abate or take a vacation was foolish. The best way to deal with the situation was to ignore it—that and lie a lot. If anything happened, he could make up excuses and try to convince her it was a fluke, one of those odd coincidences people experienced every day. As long as the occurrences didn't happen *too* often, he could manage some decent damage control.

It could work.

He would make it work.

Since acquiring his *gift* he'd become an expert at dealing with it and observing others' reactions to it. For most people, watching small catastrophes take place wasn't an everyday happening so most people witnessing one would laugh or gaze on with awe. However, when you were inundated with such occurrences, it wasn't that big a deal when one of them happened. He was often amused at how people would stare at him afterwards, acting as though he was as fascinating as the events themselves. He knew that part of their surprise was because the incidents didn't upset him. He couldn't make them understand that the events were part of his life, more or less routine. If history had proven anything, it had shown exactly how adaptable mankind was, and he was no exception. It was amazing what you could get used to, especially when you had to.

Therefore, by the time Wednesday, the day of the date with Vickie, rolled around, he'd resigned himself to the fact that no matter what happened, he'd have to deal with it. He'd gotten used to approaching dates the same way, hoping for the best but always expecting the worst. It was a pessimistic way of looking at things but it was a system that worked considering his past history. His reasoning was simple. If the date didn't turn out bad, in other words, if by the end of the night the police, fire department or other local officials hadn't been involved, it was good. That way, even a mediocre date was rewarding. If the date ended with the hint of another date being tentatively planned or with his date spending the night without waking up with lizards on her, it was even better. Most people would consider the reasoning bizarre. But other people didn't have to adapt to circumstances that required such logic. In other words, they didn't have to deal with his *gift*.

He sat at his desk, sorting through a stack of bills and trying to keep his mind on work. He had a bookkeeper to whom he supplied weekly reports and that helped him with the bulk of the financial management but that left him with the everyday expenditures to deal with. It was the one part of the job that he found not only time-consuming, but boring. Unfortunately, it was a necessary process and after first landing the managing job, he was surprised at how much time he was spending, trying to save every nickel and dime in an effort to make the place efficient and profitable. The results were effective but it was a long, drawn out process that he hadn't enjoyed.

The owner and former manager had let everything fall to disrepair and from the start, it had been an uphill battle to keep the place going. But it had been a labor of love and after seeing a marked profit by the end of the first six months, he knew he was on the right track. It also gave him a sense of accomplishment that up until that time, he'd never experienced.

The result was that The Crystal had been exactly that—his own crystal ball where his hard work and dreams came true. With the success of each new program and venture, The Crystal thrived. So did his love for the job. It was the one place he felt free to let his imagination and creativity run wild. Whether it was painting Glow in the Dark stars and magic symbols on the walls next to the lanes, giving a mystic feel when the lights were turned off during the Glow Bowl sessions. Or dressing up like Merlin the Magician and handing out prizes, and ball game passes to the customers.

It was HIS place, HIS ideas that the customers enjoyed and responded to. It was his personal playground where everyone was invited and no one was turned away. It was part of him. It was also something else, something quite extraordinary.

It was the one and only place where his *gift* never showed itself.

In over five years of managing The Crystal, nothing on the level of his *moments* had ever occurred there. It was another aspect of his condition that reaffirmed his belief that his parents' spirits were behind it. It was just like them to give him a place to retreat to, a safe haven, where he could take a break from his *gift*. Things would happen to other people, but never him. It was a bowling alley, so there was the usual amount of incidents involving dropping balls on toes or uncoordinated bowlers accidentally throwing their Brunswicks into the adjoining lanes. There was even an incident a year earlier when a small fire broke out after an inebriated leaguer unknowingly dropped his cigarette on the carpet by the rest rooms. But Marcus wasn't even present in the building at the time and the fire had been put out before it did any real damage.

The fact that nothing ever happened at The Crystal hadn't gone unnoticed by his friends or the townsfolk either, who at first flocked to the lanes to see his *moments* happening live. But the *moments* never materialized and soon the customers stopped watching him like a hawk, waiting for something to happen. Once it became clear that his *gift* wasn't going to show itself, he expected the flurry of business to decline. Much to his surprise, it didn't. The people seemed to think that the lack of his incidents was just as interesting, proving that he was a source of entertainment either way. Some people had even speculated that the building itself was responsible for his condition—a paranormal center for cosmic energy and mystery.

Whatever the reasons, the people kept coming back and he was smart enough to recognize a door of opportunity. If their curiosity got them in the door, he would make it his task to keep them there. So with each new program and promotional success, he saw something akin to magic happening. But it involved no mystic or cosmic intervention; at least he didn't think it did.

That's when he realized.

He wasn't *completely* sure it *wasn't* magic. And that fact alone made it mysterious and fun, giving him the chance to enjoy the same magic as his customers.

But getting to that level of success hadn't been an easy journey. For years he'd been labeled a Jinx or Jonah, and those were some of the nicer euphemisms. Less discreet comments had branded him "peculiar," "weirdo" or "freak," none of which did much for his ego, especially while he attended business school. In all the time since his parents' deaths, the only time he truly regretted having his *gift* was during the two years he attended business college in Columbus. From the start it had been difficult.

At least when he was living in town, he could talk to Ben about the incidents afterwards, also because Ben was present for a lot of the mishaps. But at college, it was different. Once the incidents began happening, exactly two days after settling into his dorm, he was branded an aberration and ostracized. Even the faculty had resorted to watching him closely, like a bug under a microscope, especially after the initial incident when one of his instructors had the unfortunate circumstance to personally witness one of the *moments*.

It had happened during a computer class. The classes contained thirty or more students and the lab rooms were quite large. The computers sat on long tables, each table housing five computers on each side, allowing the students to sit facing each other. The tables were positioned in a square-like formation, allowing the teacher to stand in the middle and instruct the students. Two large printers sat on a table off the main area. They were the type with continuous, perforated paper and the copies had to be folded and ripped off along the perforation. The instructor would guide the class through an exercise and after completing it on their screens, the students would print off the results and hand them in to be graded.

It was during one such exercise when the incident occurred. He'd completed a document on the word processing program and walked over to get the hard copy. The printers were old and sometimes the perforation on the paper didn't roll all the way out to where it could be folded and torn off. Thus, the student had to reach down and carefully pull the page out, making sure not to pull too far, causing the next document to be out of alignment.

But his report didn't seem to be suffering from this problem so he reached down, folded the paper and began to pull it, allowing it to break off at the perforations. But nothing happened—the paper resisted. He leaned in for a closer look, but nothing seemed to be holding the paper back.

He found out later that the person using the printer before him had printed off an extra blank page and set it underneath the printer by mistake. The page was then sucked up with the continuous roll and ended up under the perforated page, doubling the thickness.

However, he wasn't privy to this fact so he continued to struggle with the page, hoping he could free it. One of the female students came up behind him and started making huffing noises, waiting impatiently for him to finish. He pulled at the page again but with no luck. He tried once more, this time pulling as hard as he could. The force caused the printer to slide forward toward the edge of the table, its front two legs dropping off and tilting the machine at a precarious angle. He let go of the paper and grabbed the printer just as it started to fall over the edge.

He cradled it in his arms, thinking that he'd averted a disaster but a second later found out that instead, he'd started one. It was only after catching the printer that he realized that the weight of both heavy machines had caused an equal balance on the table. By removing one, the table became unbalanced, causing it to tip and sending the other printer flying off the end and directly into the legs supporting one of the student tables. The result was a domino affect as the table legs buckled under the weight of the printer and the table listed at a forty-five degree angle, sending every computer sliding towards the end of least resistance.

An ensuing pandemonium broke out as the ten students sitting at the table scrambled to get out of the way of the electronic automatons, which had suddenly come to life and slid down the smooth tabletop toward the floor. A few seconds and quite a few gasps and screams later, the fallen table end was covered with monitors, consoles, mice and cords of every type and shape. The machines on the beginning end of the avalanche suffered the most, resulting in crunched consoles, broken glass from the monitors and a few sparks flying from ripped out electrical cords. The machinery resembled used up battle gear, casualties from a skirmish. After the last of the excitement died down, the instructor and students looked around the room, trying to figure out what had caused the catastrophe.

They didn't have to look far.

He felt every eye in the room turn to him and knew there was no denial to be had. He was still holding the one remaining printer and the student standing behind him was now pointing an accusing finger at him. He lowered the machine down onto the floor and tried to ignore the stares burning holes in his back. Usually, it didn't bother him when people glared at him whenever one of his *moments* would happen. But now it did.

Because for the two days previous to the mishap, no one had known about him.

He'd been completely anonymous, simply one of the other hundreds of students there to get an education. For the first time since incurring his condition, he enjoyed the contentment of being normal, unknown, exactly like everyone else. It was a feeling he quickly got used to and loved. He mingled with the other students, talking and socializing without having someone point at him and whisper disparaging remarks about him. But as he placed the other printer back down onto the floor, he knew his fleeting pleasure at being anonymous was gone forever.

Thus, for the next two years he endured the glares and grunts of both the faculty and students as they were propelled with him through one disturbance after the other. It got to a point where the faculty even suggested he talk to a psychiatrist. He consented, but only because he thought that by agreeing, the people in charge would stop treating him like an oddity.

The psychiatrist meant well and had several theories about his malady, including one that involved his subconscious mind rebelling against the loss of his parents. He listened quietly as the man lectured him extensively about his deep-rooted anger and even though he didn't feel angry with anyone about his condition, he let the man drone on. He walked away from the last session feeling as if the psychiatrist had gotten more satisfaction from the talks than he had. He decided not to tell the doctor about his own theory about his condition, knowing it would probably result in the doctor and faculty sending him packing to the local mental ward. And when for three days after the last session, nothing happened, he thought that perhaps the doctor had been right. But the next day his *gift* returned full force, causing a minor commotion in the cafeteria when one of the machines he was getting a sandwich out of mysteriously went berserk and began dispensing every item in the racks.

A crowd of students quickly gathered as hands shoved and pushed, trying to grab the "free" samples offered by the machine. After one of the faculty members stepped in to break up the small riot, the man noticed him and started giving him dirty looks. The rest of the free sample holders did the same and before long he was enjoying exiled status again.

The student body and faculty walked around him as if he was a living land mine. Some of the students had even dubbed him a "warlock" and "wacko" and hung a sheet with a satanic symbol from his dorm window. He endured the branding with tolerance and for solace, turned his energy towards what he was there for, getting his degree. It wasn't long before he was on the dean's list and earned a summa cum laude honor.

He did not, however, collect his diploma in person at the graduation ceremony. After subjecting the student body to two years of his *moments*, he decided to give them a break and receive his degree through the mail, a decision that he knew the faculty was more than grateful for. He left the school, wanting to put all the memories of it and the humiliation behind him.

Every year the alumni committee would send him an invitation to a reunion but the invitations always ended up in the same place, the wastebasket. Reliving his days at the school was not something he cared to do. Having to periodically attend his high school reunions was bad enough. His *moments* had already made appearances at both his one and five year reunions. To repeat such performances at his college reunions was only asking for trouble. Having the people from his hometown stare and laugh at him was normal, at least to him. Having to endure it from people from all over the state was a notoriety he didn't care to endure. Thus the invitations stayed in the trash.

AND THE BULL SAVED ME

He glanced up at the clock, 2 PM. He did some quick calculating. If he left work at five it would give him enough time to go home and clean up before heading over to Barbertown to meet her at 7:30. He tried to remember if he had anything clean at home to wear. Tuesdays were usually his days to do laundry but he'd neglected it the day before because of a broken pinsetter he and Jack ended up working on most of the day.

If he couldn't find anything clean he could always use something from the emergency clothes bundle in the trunk of his car. His condition had taught him to always be prepared, like the Boy Scouts. His trunk housed among other things, an emergency kit consisting of two changes of clothes, including jockey shorts and undershirts, bath towels and washcloths, a blanket, first aid kit, canteen full of water, matches and tennis shoes.

He kept a second, smaller kit beside the first containing things like a sewing supplies, safety pins, candles, aspirin, shampoo, deodorant and various sundry items. He also kept a standard emergency car kit in the front of the trunk with such items as flares and emergency messages for the back window in case of a breakdown. All three kits had been used and replaced extensively due to the frequency of his personal "emergencies" over the years.

He got back to the task in front of him and had just written down another entry in the ledger when there was a knock at his office door. He uttered a quick "come in" and the aroma of cherry blend smoke quickly filled the air as Jack Kinderbrook entered and took a seat in one of the two leather chairs at front of the desk. He was smoking his pipe and wearing his usual boots, jeans, cotton shirt and fleece, denim vest. The vest was like his armor. He used it as a substitute for a coat and wore it year round, summer and winter both. His boots always had a high shine and his face was always clean-shaven. He never gave the appearance of being sloppy or disheveled, demonstrating not only pride in his appearance but in everything he did.

"That sick pinsetter, number twelve, broke down again last night," Jack told him. "But I've rigged it up good enough that it should be okay for a few days."

"When did you do that?" Marcus quizzed him. "This morning before the mother's league started?"

"No. Last night. I stayed over and worked on it after the late league was done. I finished about two AM."

Marcus shook his head in disbelief. He'd always been impressed with Jack's seemingly inexhaustible energy but at sixty-three, the man neither looked like nor acted his age. He was approximately six feet tall, large in the chest and shoulders but carried his weight well. He didn't have a belly that hung over his belt like some of the other men his age. However, he was large enough to make an imposing impression on anyone who didn't know him. But he didn't use his size to intimidate. On the contrary, he reacted positively to people. Jack once told him that people were the most interesting things on the planet and anyone missing that revelation was also missing the best part of life. The statement fit Jack's personality. For as much as he, *The Kirklin Klutz*, was the novelty attraction that drew people to The Crystal, Jack was what kept them coming back.

Jack practically lived at the alley and made it a point to try and talk to each and every customer, asking them how they were and even remembering the names of their children and family members. He had a keen mind and an ability to recall every fact, a talent that had served him well over the years. He emitted a positive attitude and humor that people picked up on and responded to. The large creases in his face as he smiled were like a highway sign, announcing to everyone who saw them that this person was friendly and prone to laughing. His optimism about everything was contagious. Even the fact that his hair had thinned so much that the light would reflect off his mostly bald head didn't bother him. He took aging in stride, just as he took everything else, with quiet acceptance and a bit of indifference.

It was one of the most endearing qualities he enjoyed about Jack, his ability to bend with the wind and not let things bother him. Jack's reasoning was that life was going to deal you one set of cards and to get worked up because you thought you got a lousy hand was useless. The best strategy was to play the cards you had and make the best of it. Jack sometimes made it a habit of affiliating his philosophical views with poker. He was a die-hard poker player and had been since he was a kid. He'd even admitted to supporting himself through his teens by playing poker and shooting craps.

He ran away from home when he was thirteen and had been on his own since, learning to support himself by any means possible. It was during the late forties and the advent of child welfare agencies or support groups that aided the so-called "homeless." Children living in the street had to learn quickly to adapt. The alternative was death or sometimes a fate worse. It was survival for real, not some television program put on for the amusement of the masses. Jack had never revealed why he had run away, but from the way he avoided the subject or any memories about his childhood, it was clear it had been traumatic. So traumatic that Jack never claimed to have any relatives, either living or dead, anywhere, a fact that his wife Mavis verified. Jack's early years were just as much a mystery to her.

AND THE BULL SAVED ME

"Uh, Magic," Jack said, puffing away on his pipe. "I called the parts place this morning and they mailed the gears yesterday. We should get them in the mail tomorrow morning. I'm taking Mavis to breakfast before I pick up the parts at the post office and I thought you'd like to go with us."

"Normally I would," Marcus replied, putting down his pen. "But I better wait and call you in the morning, in case I don't get in until late. I've got a date tonight…"

"No kidding!" Jack said, sitting forward and acting quite interested. "That's great, Magic. Anyone I know?"

"I don't think so. I only met her last week. We're going to dinner over in Barbertown and I don't know if she'll want to go out to a club later or not. She works at the water department uptown and probably has to get up early." He hesitated and then added, "And I'm also waiting to see if any complications turn up."

Jack removed the pipe from his mouth and eyed him carefully. "Then I take it she doesn't know about…"

"No. I don't think so. And I'm not volunteering the fact, either."

"Do you think that's wise?"

Marcus smiled at him. It was Jack's subtle way of telling him he was taking the wrong approach. Jack would never come right out and tell him he was wrong. He'd merely suggest an alternative course of action, much like a kibitzer would tell a poker player he was about to throw away an ace.

"I know what you're thinking," he told Jack. "I should be honest and tell her first thing. But I've done that before and it didn't work. They either look at me like I'm nuts or hang around just long enough to find out I'm telling the truth and then they *really* look at me like I'm nuts and run away so fast they leave a smoke trail behind them. I kid you not. If you see smoke coming from anywhere in a five mile radius, it's probably not a fire. It's more likely one of my dates breaking the fifty yard dash record trying to get away from me."

Jack chuckled and puffed on his pipe, giving him a fatherly *I know what you're talking about* nod.

Marcus continued, telling Jack about his idea of averting the *gift* issue at least until Vickie got to know him better. "I decided to approach this whole dating business like a scientific experiment. I'm taking it slow and making sure not to rush her, letting her set the pace. She can get to know me and find out I'm not a jinx or oddball. Then maybe she'll think twice before zooming away in a cloud of dust."

Jack leaned forward and tapped some of the pipe ashes into the tray located at the edge of the desk. "And you're assuming that your *gift* will cooperate with these plans?"

There was no sarcasm in the question so he knew Jack was simply making a relevant point.

"You mean, what do I do if one of my *moments* happens?"

"Uh-huh," Jack said. "Unless you're telling me they've suddenly stopped happening…"

"'Fraid not. And lately they seem to be occurring with even more frequency. Did Betsy tell you about what happened yesterday? When we drove down to Deckerville to pick up those new cribs for the daycare center?"

"No. She didn't mention it."

Marcus sat back in his chair and sighed. "Let's just say they won't be filling any more orders for me anytime soon. After I left, they probably posted my picture all over the factory with a warning under it to not let me in the building again."

Jack asked him what happened.

"The drive down in your truck was fine, although Bets does have a lead foot. I figure she got that from you. When you taught her how to drive."

"I didn't teach her. Mavis did and that's who she gets the heavy foot from."

Marcus grinned at him. "Traveling with her was a lot of fun. I think she took some of those bends on two wheels. But it wasn't quite as exciting as what happened at the furniture factory. The guy who sold me the four cribs said he was shorthanded and didn't have anyone to help us load them onto the truck. Betsy and I told him we could handle it ourselves, so the guy gave us the receipt, showed us where the cribs were and left us to it. We drove the truck around to the back dock and used one of those long metal dollies. You know, the ones that look like metal tables with rollers.

So after we got the cribs loaded, I pushed the dolly back over with the others. When I rolled it past the back entrance, a whole bunch of little kids, there must have been about forty of them, came flying out the door. Turns out the place was shorthanded because they were giving tours of the factory to a bunch of area fourth grade classes. Seeing all the kids at once like that startled me so I turned my head to watch them and didn't notice that I was pushing the damn dolly too close to the dock ramp." He paused, gesturing with his hand, turning it at a right angle. "It was one of those sloping concrete ramps that runs from the dock platform down to the driveway below."

"Uh-oh," Jack said, taking another puff on his pipe.

"Yep," Marcus said. "The dolly started tilting towards the ramp and I lost my grip on it. So I tried to grab at it, kind of lunging out to get a better grip when I lost my footing and fell forward, landing belly first on top of it. The next thing I know, I'm rolling down the ramp at top speed, heading straight out into the parking lot. There were some people coming out of the factory from the side entrance, walking towards their cars and I had to yell at them to get out of the way."

Jack took the pipe from his mouth as his face went red from chuckling. "Couldn't you stop yourself?"

"Finally," Marcus replied. "I put my feet out to the side and I ended up laying half the rubber from my soles on the concrete, trying to slow down. I was also helped by one of the people in the lot, a very angry elderly man."

"What'd you do? Knock the old boy down?"

"No. He almost knocked me out, with his cane! He saw I was about to crash into his Lincoln so he grabbed hold of the back of the dolly with his cane and stopped me dead in my tracks. Shit! He didn't look that strong. But I guess he was determined. The dolly stopped a couple feet short of his car but he was still mad as hell. He started hitting me with the cane, yelling that I was nothing but a young hellion with no regard for people's property."

"What'd you do?"

"I just took it for a few seconds. I mean, I couldn't hit him. He was an old man. I dodged the blows the best I could and started dragging the dolly back to the dock, trying to get away from him. And that's when I heard Betsy yelling at me to watch out."

"Watch out? For what?"

"For all the other dollies from the dock rolling down the ramp right at me. Apparently, the kids saw me do it so they assumed it was okay if they did it, too."

Jack snickered. "Didn't their teachers stop them?"

"They couldn't. One of them told me later that the kids went out the back door so fast that they didn't even know what was happening until it was too late. You should have seen it, Jack. It reminded me of all those times Ben and I went sledding down at Kelly's Hill. Except in this case, the kids couldn't stop. There were dollies rollin' all over the parking lot, crashing into cars, rolling into fences. People were running every which way, screaming and trying to get out of the way. It was crazy!"

"I've no doubt," Jack said, his eyes widening.

"You should have seen the kids," Marcus told him. "They were laughing and hollering like they were having the time of their lives. Then the guys from the furniture factory came running out into the lot and started apologizing to all the people. Everybody was mad as hell and they were all staring right at me."

"How did they know you were responsible?"

"The old man. Right after he stopped hitting me with his cane one of the kids crashed a dolly into the side of his car, making a sizable dent."

Jack asked him if the kid was okay.

"He was fine. But I was worried the old man would go after the kid so I went over to protect him. Turns out I was the one who needed protecting. The old man started hitting me with the cane, not the kid."

"Oh no."

"That's right. He blamed me! He kept hitting me and yelling that it was all my fault for showing the kids how to ride the dollies. So here I am, pushing this kid and two dollies back through the parking lot and this old man is walking behind me, beating hell out of my back with his cane. And let me tell you, those damn things sting! Especially that rubber thing covering the bottom. I've got some nice bruises from it."

"Where was Betsy while all this was happening?"

"She was helping the teachers and factory workers gather up all the kids and dollies, which wasn't easy. They were everywhere, on the dock, between the cars. One even managed to roll all the way over to the lot exit and almost ended up in traffic. Luckily Betsy caught him first. Everyone finally managed to herd the kids up and get them back on the bus."

"Then no one was hurt?" Jack said, acting concerned.

"No. There was a lady who got knocked down by one of the dollies but she was okay, only got a little dirt on her pants. A couple other cars got dings in them but they belonged to the employees and the factory manager said he'd take care of settling up with them. Other than that, no other damage was done. The kids seemed to think it was some great adventure. They were laughing and asking to ride on the dollies again. Of course, the factory manager didn't let them. Actually, he was pretty nice about the whole thing. I was surprised he didn't demand I pay for the damages to the cars."

"How could he?" Jack said, tapping the last of the burned out tobacco from his pipe into the ashtray. "They were the ones who had the dollies out there in the first place. It was a safety hazard. The manager knew that." He paused and gave Marcus a curious stare. "Your *Magic moments* as Ben calls them, they never seem to cause any real damage, do they?"

Marcus asked him what he meant.

"No one ever tries to sue you or gets seriously hurt, not even you. Judging just by the *moments* I've witnessed, that's quite remarkable."

Marcus thought about it for a minute. Even with some of the more bizarre or destructive *moments*, ones where someone's property was damaged, no one had ever threatened to sue him or demanded that he make reparations. "I never really thought about it," he told Jack. "But you're right. I guess it is kind of amazing."

"Not so amazing. At least not when you consider what's already been happening to you."

Marcus smiled down at the paperwork in front of him. He knew Jack was about to give him his views, whether he wanted them or not.

"You know, Magic. I've been around for a lot of years and seen some pretty peculiar and astonishing things. But what's going on around you is nothing less than incredible. There's a greater power involved in all this and even though you can't see the whole purpose behind it, doesn't mean it's not something good."

"I've already told you what I think is happening."

"I know, I know," Jack replied, waving him off. "But maybe there's something else going on here. You know, God has a purpose for all of us. We can't always see what it is, but it's still there."

Marcus paused, trying to think of how to word it so he didn't hurt his friend's feelings. "We've had this discussion before, Jack. I know you think it's something miraculous, but it isn't. Look at me. I'm not a religious man and I haven't gone to church in years."

Jack held up his index finger, like he was making a point. "But you *do* believe in God."

"Yes I do. But I don't believe in religion and you know why. I've never bought into that idea of having so many different churches and beliefs. It's okay to have the freedom to worship whichever way you choose but it's wrong to use religious conviction as an excuse to commit every sin those religions are preaching. I mean, come on. Where's the logic in killing each other because of one's beliefs? Like nature isn't doing that fast enough already with cancer, HIV and whatever new virus is lurking out there and that we haven't unleashed yet. It doesn't make any sense."

Jack agreed that it didn't. "And unfortunately, the zealots doing the killings are always the ones getting all the press." He paused and regarded Marcus carefully. "But what you don't see or hear about are all the other things, the wondrous things going on behind the scenes. Things like what's happening to you."

Marcus stared at him, moved by his friend's conviction. He almost wished he could believe like Jack and maybe there was something behind what he was saying. After all, if his parents' souls were behind it, someone or something had to be helping them. "I understand what you're saying," he told Jack. "But I don't believe it's anything holy or has to with miracles. I'm simply an ordinary guy, like a billion other guys, trying to get through the day, pay the bills and make sense out of it all. Simply because I experience more than my share of 'accidents' doesn't mean God is behind it or that it's some kind of divine intervention. Besides, it's not that uncommon of a phenomenon anyway. Shoot, look at *Ripley's*. There's a lot more amazing things out there than a Calamity James character."

Jack snickered. "Calamity James?"

"That's the name Bets gave me. She calls me her personal Catastrophe Cowboy. She also thinks it's wonderful every time one of my *moments* happens."

"That's because nothing ever happens here at The Crystal," Jack reminded him. "The only time she gets to see anything is when she goes somewhere else with you."

Marcus knew it was true. "You know," he told Jack. "It's funny but my *moments* seem to happen more around Betsy, too. Almost like she's a catalyst and sets them off. Lucky for me she enjoys them so much. She always laughs her head off, no matter how bizarre the *moment* is. She's the first woman I've ever known who makes me feel good about myself and my *Magic moments*."

Jack flashed him a mischievous grin. "Mavis and I always expected that you and Betsy would get together someday. We were always plotting, thinking up ways to get you two together, inviting you to family outings, pushing ourselves into your life. We were hoping nature would eventually take its course. I guess it wasn't meant to be."

Marcus stared at him, not sure how to respond. He knew Jack was being honest and decided to reciprocate. "I don't think of Betsy that way. At least not any more."

Jack asked him what he meant.

"Betsy was the first woman I've ever been friends with. She knew all about my condition but it didn't bother her. She was like you, she thought it was great and loved it every time something would happen. She didn't treat me like I was strange or a curiosity. That was something new for me. I found myself falling for her and she knew it."

"So what happened?"

"She's the one who put the stops on. She said she valued our friendship too much to get involved with me. She was afraid that if it went bad down the road we might not be friends anymore." He paused and smiled. "She was also afraid it might put my friendship with you in jeopardy. She didn't want to take that chance. I finally saw her point and deferred to her judgment. I know now that she was right, although at the time I didn't. I thought I was in love and love doesn't have any logic or listen to reason. But I got over it. Now I think of her as the sister I never had."

"Well, she sure thinks highly of you," Jack said, giving him a wink. "She also agrees with me about what's going on with your *gift*."

Marcus scoffed. "Don't tell me you've got Betsy believing your theory."

"She's no fool, Magic. She can see what I can, that something quite extraordinary is going on."

"I'm not putting down your theory," Marcus told him, trying not to smile. "But I don't see anything happening here on the scale of Moses parting the waves or a burning bush. Although I did literally set the dance floor on fire at my last high school reunion."

"I know. Ben told me all about it."

"I just don't think it's anything holy or miraculous."

Jack gave him a hard stare, as if he was studying him. "But you *do* think it's your parents' souls behind it."

Marcus fidgeted in his chair, suddenly feeling defensive. It wasn't the first time he and Jack had talked about it and Jack never put down his belief. But discussing it with anyone always made him uncomfortable. "I know it sounds a little crazy but you had to know them to understand why I believe it. They were always playing practical jokes, on their friends, on me. It was their trademark. They were like two big kids who never grew up. If they weren't planning a practical joke, they were helping their friends with one. And they always included me. My dad would take me with him on dry runs, going over the plans in minute detail to make sure it all went smoothly. My mom was the same. If it sounded fun, they did it—same with our vacations. If Dad heard about some new place opening up that he thought we'd enjoy, he'd spend every penny he had to get us there. Both of them instilled in me a sense of fun and thrill seeking."

"Did any of the jokes get dangerous?"

"Heck, no. They'd never do anything to put anyone in danger. It was good, clean fun. They lived for it and all their friends loved them for it. So did I. I was their only child and my mom had several miscarriages before she had me. Both of them had given up on having kids. They tried for seven years without any luck. When I came along, they were shocked. Dad used to call me his little 'miracle,' but that's the only time I've ever been referred to in that reference. They doted on me. I never doubted their love for me." Marcus paused, trying to find the words to make him understand. "They were both very special people. I was lucky to have them as long as I did. Mom and Dad used to tell me that love could conquer anything and I believed them. So when the things started happening right after I got out of the hospital, I knew it was their way of showing me that love *could* conquer anything, even death. It was their unique way of showing me they were still with me. It was their trademark showing itself all over again." Marcus paused and smiled. "When I was little, I once asked them what they thought Heaven was like. They told me it was a wonderful place where you could play practical jokes all the time. So I figure that's what they're doing, playing practical jokes again, but this time on me."

Jack got a thoughtful look on his face. "Maybe they're not only watching over you, maybe they're steering you towards something."

"Like what? You mean awareness? Faith? God?"

"Perhaps," Jack replied, sitting back like he was thinking about it. "But even with you believing that they're behind it, you have to admit something, someone is behind them."

"You mean God."

"Yes. So doesn't that show you that it's His work going on here?"

Marcus laughed. "Not unless God thinks it's a good idea to have me wake up with lizards or end up naked at the top of a papier-mâché volcano in the high school gymnasium."

"I never heard that story," Jack said. "What happened?"

"It was at the senior play. I was wearing a loincloth and knelt down inside the top of an eight-foot fake volcano. At the appropriate time, I was to stand up and be seen coming out of the volcano. But there was a nail sticking out from the chicken wire holding the papier-mâché in place. It caught on my costume just as I was standing up and pulled down the loincloth. It was supposed to represent mankind emerging from the Forest Primeval. Instead, I looked like Adam emerging from the Garden of Eden in his birthday suit. It was the hit of the play, I can tell you that."

Jack laughed. "I'll bet."

"That's why it can't be anything miraculous," Marcus said, making his point. "God would have to have a pretty strange sense of humor to be behind it."

"Perhaps He does."

Marcus studied his face and realized he was serious.

"I remember reading one time," Jack said, "that God was a comedian playing to an audience that was too afraid to laugh. Makes you wonder, doesn't it? Love makes you feel good inside and God is love. Laughter also makes you feel good inside, so why shouldn't God be behind the laughter, too? It's not such a big step. Personally, I think God is behind every good thing in the world. And laughter and humor have to be included on that list."

"Okay," Marcus replied, giving into his reasoning. "But if He is behind it, I hope He's too busy to send me on one of my *moments* tonight. I'd like this girl to get to know me first before she wakes up with lizards or ends up in a volcano."

Jack got up from his seat and gave him a wink. "Go ahead and put your trust in Him, Magic. He knows what He's doing."

"I'll keep that in mind."

Jack wished him luck on the date and headed back out the door.

Marcus glanced at the paperwork in front of him and smiled. Jack's unshaken belief in God's power was moving. But believing God was behind the *moments* was absurd; especially considering the first time Jack witnessed his affliction in action. The circumstances were neither biblical nor holy. It happened in a bar. The last place in the world you'd expect to see anything miraculous. He thought back to that afternoon, five years earlier...

It happened several months after Jack started working at The Crystal. Because he liked to mingle, Jack began hearing *Magic Marker* stories from the customers. At first he thought his leg was being pulled because he was the new kid on the block. But when the stories kept surfacing, Jack decided to confront Marcus for the truth.

Because nothing ever occurred at The Crystal, Marcus knew Jack probably wouldn't believe him. So he called upon someone else to do the convincing, namely Ben, who was more than happy to talk about his best friend's *gift*. It was done one afternoon at The Point, where he and Ben also introduced Jack to the finer points of darts. Jack immediately took to the game and eventually joined the dart team with them. After playing several games, they broke for a beer and Ben proceeded to give Jack the lowdown on his boss, a.k.a. *The Kirklin Klutz*.

Marcus sat in silence, repairing one of his darts as Ben started from the beginning and told Jack about a few of the events that occurred during their last few months at Kirklin High, following his parents' deaths. Ben then gave Jack a *Reader's Digest* condensed version of his *moments* over the past five years, including a few embarrassing ones that he'd wished Ben had left out. Jack had only recently moved to town so he hadn't been privy to the back fence gossip that had been floating around about one of the two town curiosities, the other being a creature called "Yellow Eyes," a local legend resembling Big Foot whom the townsfolk periodically spotted in the wooded area adjoining the reservoir.

Jack's reaction turned from skepticism to near shock as Ben regaled one episode after the other. It had been Ben's aim to illustrate the bizarre nature and sheer volume of the events in an effort to prove that he wasn't making it all up. However, the clincher came a few minutes later when Jack got to witness one of the moments in person.

Marcus had just finished replacing a flight on one of his darts. The flight was the detachable, plastic piece at the bottom of the dart that helped guide it as it was flying through the air. He threw the broken flight across the table to the ashtray sitting in front of Jack. But the flight missed the tray and skidded off the end of the table. Marcus ducked under the table and saw it lying next to the single circular support located in the middle. He gripped the table and bent down to pick it up when he heard Ben yell, "Whoa!" Marcus glanced up and saw all three beers, the ashtray and napkin holder sliding across the table directly towards his face. He then realized that he'd accidentally tipped the table to almost a forty-five degree angle.

He immediately let go but the centrifugal force and single support caused the table to swing back dramatically the opposite way. Jack and Ben jumped up from their seats as the table catapulted the beers, ashtray and metal napkin holder into the air. Marcus lunged forward, trying to grab the glasses but only managed to touch the bottom of the napkin holder before belly-flopping down on top of the table, landing with a resounding thud. He looked up in time to see the three beer bombs, glass ashtray and napkin holder hurtle towards a booth full of unsuspecting men sitting next to them.

His weight caused the table to tilt forward and as he slid down onto the floor he heard the sound of shouts and broken glass. He pulled his knees forward and sat up, still gripping the edge of the table for support as his butt landed on the floor. The four men who'd been assaulted were standing next to their booth, cussing loudly and wiping beer off of their clothes.

Marcus heard a scraping sound and turned his head back to the still tilted table. The dart he'd been working on earlier was sliding, point forward, down the tabletop and directly toward his hand. He let go of the table just as the dart reached the edge but quickly realized his error as the table swung wildly in the opposite direction like a top, catapulting the dart high into the air. He scrambled to his feet and ran around the table, never taking his eyes off the dart's trajectory. It arched toward the ceiling, almost touching it and hanging momentarily in midair before beginning its trek back down.

As he sped forward, he saw the barmaid standing with her head tilted up, watching the dart, which was now descending directly at her. A look of fright filled her face and a split second later she threw up her hands, one of which was holding a tray full of drinks. The drinks were slung backwards into a group of patrons sitting at the bar and another round of broken glass and shouts ensued. He rushed her, seeing only the white, exposed skin of her neck and upper breast from the low cut blouse she was wearing. Just before slamming into her, she glanced down at him and let out a scream he was sure had burst his eardrums. He didn't have time to explain to her that all he wanted to do was push her out of the dart's path. She stopped screaming and let out a grunt as he crashed into her, sending her flying backwards into the people at the bar who were still busy cleaning the drinks off their clothes.

As the momentum of his body weight pushed her back, he noticed a large, hairy man in a greasy baseball cap wiping the remnants of a Bloody Mary from his Cleveland Indians tee shirt. Marcus closed his eyes as he and the barmaid collided with the man, throwing him off balance and sending the three of them sprawling to the barroom floor. He opened his eyes a second later and found himself face first in the waitress's ample bosom. She let out a groan and began shoving him off of her. He got to his feet and helped her up, relieved to see that she wasn't hurt.

The man with the baseball cap was having some trouble getting up so Marcus bent down to give him a hand. He started to apologize for crashing into him, when the man starting grinning like crazy.

"I'm not a bit sorry," the man grunted, his breath heavy with beer. "I always thought she was a looker. Anytime you want to shove a pretty girl at me, you're more than welcome!" The man then snickered licentiously and went over and got back up on his bar stool.

Marcus headed back over to where Jack and Ben were still standing next to the table. Ben was slapping Jack on the back and laughing.

"What'd I tell you? See what I mean? It's uncanny." Ben then directed his attention to Marcus. "Nice touch, Magic! Talk about a demonstration!"

Marcus gave Ben a grunt of disapproval. "I didn't exactly plan it, Ben. You know I can't control the damn things! If I could, I'd stop them altogether." He then turned his attention to Jack. His mouth was hanging open and an *Oh, my*

God expression filled his face. Marcus knew it must have been a shock for him. It wasn't every day you found out your boss was a walking disaster area. Jack came out of his temporary daze and began looking across the barroom floor.

"Where did your dart go?" Jack asked.

Marcus snapped his fingers, suddenly remembering. "Be right back," he told them and went back over to the bar. The bartender had come out from behind the bar and was helping the barmaid clean up the dumped drinks. Some of the customers were still grumbling, wiping the liquid from their clothes and all of them appeared to be in a surly mood. All except one, the man in the baseball cap. His shirt was still covered in red and he was grinning lecherously at the barmaid, who was exposing a fair amount of skin as she bent down in her mini skirt to pick up the drinks.

"Sorry about the inconvenience, folks," the bartender said, helping the barmaid clean up the last of the alcohol from the floor. "Next round of drinks is on the house!"

The bar erupted into applause and Marcus went over to the bartender to apologize.

"Sorry about that, Terry."

"Don't worry about it, Magic," the man said, patting Marcus on the back. "I already owe you big time. Half the customers show up, just hopin' to catch one of your *Magic moments*." He paused and grinned. "And you never disappoint them…or me." He chuckled and walked off behind the bar to fill the drink orders.

"I want Delores to bring me my drink," the man with the baseball cap told Terry.

"Then maybe Magic can shove her into my lap again."

Delores glared daggers at the man, showing that she didn't appreciate his remarks. It was then that Marcus remembered what he was there for and tapped her on the shoulder. "Excuse me," he said as she turned to face him. He thrust his fingers into her cleavage and carefully pulled out the dart. She gasped and her mouth fell open in shock.

"Thanks, I was looking for that," he told her, quickly turning and walking away. He knew she'd soon be recovering from the shock and if he hung around too long, he'd get his face slapped. He walked towards Jack and Ben and held up the dart. "I saw it when I landed on top of her. She never even got a scratch!"

They both began laughing. But a second later both of them abruptly stopped.

"Duck!" Ben yelled.

Marcus quickly crouched down and a split second later a large serving tray whooshed past his face like a silver Frisbee. Jack and Ben ducked down and the tray careened over their heads and crashed into the far wall, next to the restrooms. Marcus turned and glanced back to the bar. The barmaid let out a "hmph" and stomped off with a satisfied look on her face, showing that she didn't appreciate being accosted all for the sake of a dart. The bar erupted in laughter and Marcus went over and rejoined his friends.

Marcus let his mind drift back from the memory and smiled. It wasn't exactly the way he would have liked Jack to find out about his condition, but it proved the old adage.

Sometimes actions *did* speak louder than words.

The results of the demonstration were threefold. Jack finally found out that the *Magic moment* stories were true and that his boss wasn't a nut after all. The second result was that after that night, Jack was always included in the *post moment* meetings with Ben. The last and most important result was one that Marcus had never counted on but had always been grateful for, Jack became a close friend. And even Jack would agree that good friends were also a *gift*.

Marcus glanced up at the clock again. 2:30. He was going to have to get a move on if he wanted to leave by five.

He picked up his pen and got back to work.

CHAPTER FOUR

Marcus entered the front foyer of Richetti's and paused to let his eyes adjust to the dimmer light. The entrance walls were draped with red and white velvet and the aroma of burning candles permeated the air. A hostess was standing behind a small podium, a few feet away, arguing with a group of seven or eight people about a lost reservation.

He glanced around the podium to the main area of the restaurant. There were about twenty tables and booths scattered throughout the room, all with red-checkered tablecloths and lazy Susan condiment containers holding wine bottle candles. The walls were decorated in a nautical theme, with anchors and pictures of boats of all kinds, from small sailboats to a large picture of the Queen Anne hanging above the back wall. The place was pretty busy and only a few tables weren't occupied. He spotted a booth in the far, left corner and saw Vickie waving at him, trying to get his attention. He straightened his tie and headed across the room. As he circumvented the tables, he observed the other patrons and was relieved to discover he hadn't over dressed. Most of the men were in dress pants, shirts and ties like him and only a few were wearing jackets.

As he approached the booth, his senses were bombarded with the wonderful aroma of Italian cuisine and spices wafting throughout the room. The candles on the tables were all burning and the flickering light added to the ambiance of the setting. The booth where she was sitting was shaped in a semicircle and he slid in next to her, making sure not to sit too close and crowd her. She looked even lovelier than the last time he saw her. She was wearing a white, cotton skirt and a light blue, silk blouse. A small silver heart necklace adorned her neck and glistened when she moved. Her hair was down and outlined her face, accenting her soft features. He also noticed a small birthmark near her right earlobe that hadn't been visible that day at The Point. Her hair had been pulled back and must have been concealing it.

"I made a reservation but I got here early so we could get a good spot," she told him. "I know how busy they usually get."

"Smart move," he said, glancing around the crowded room. "I can't believe they're this busy during the week. The food must be good."

"It is," she said, handing him one of the menus lying on the table in front of her. "Just wait until you taste it."

He opened up the menu. It was the usual Italian fare, although a few of the entrée names he didn't recognize but assumed they were fancy titles for different types of pasta. A waiter appeared and placed two water glasses in front of them. The man was tall, thin, twentyish and had several small moles on his right cheek, almost as if a grandmother had pinched his cheek when he was little and the mark stayed. His teeth were perfectly straight and white as he smiled cordially at them. His dress was the same as the other servers, red trousers, white, ruffled shirt and red-checkered bow ties. He asked them if they were ready to order and Vickie told him she wanted to order some wine.

"You don't mind if I pick the wine, do you?" she asked Marcus. "Their house wine is my favorite. I think you'll really enjoy it."

"I don't mind at all," he replied, glad she was the one picking. He wasn't much of a connoisseur when it came to spirits. His expertise ended at choosing between Bud Lite and Heineken.

The waiter took the wine order and started rattling off the daily specials. "And we're famous for our calamari," he added.

"Sounds great," Marcus said, handing him the menu. "I'll have that and a salad with French dressing."

The waiter wrote down the selection and asked Vickie if she wanted the same thing.

"I don't care for calamari," she said. "I'll just have the linguini in clam sauce and a salad with sweet and sour dressing."

The waiter wrote down the order and as soon as he left, Marcus noticed Vickie smiling strangely at him. He asked her if something was wrong.

"No. But I am impressed. You're obviously one of those people who enjoys a lot of different foods."

He shrugged, not sure what she was referring to. "Sure. I love Italian food. Any food that ends in an 'I,' I'm crazy about. Spaghetti, ravioli, you name it. I couldn't get enough of it when I was a kid. My mom used to call me the Spaghetti Kid."

She tilted her head and smiled, as if she was observing him. He usually didn't like people staring, but with her it was different. It sent warm waves of pride and pleasure through him, causing his pulse to quicken.

"Some of my friends really like different foods like calamari," she told him. "They've also accused me of being old-fashioned and not trying new things. But I'm not *that* old-fashioned. I simply believe in being careful."

Careful? he thought. *Uh-oh. That doesn't sound too good.* His life wasn't exactly a model of stability.

"But honestly, how can you make an intelligent decision about anything, until you hear all the pros and cons?" she said. "I'm practical, that's how I was raised. We're all what our parents make of us, you know what I mean?"

He nodded, realizing that he would have agreed to anything she said. It was a pleasure just listening to the sound of her voice. And that, mixed with the sweet smell of her perfume was having a hypnotic effect on him.

The waiter brought the wine and glasses and poured a sampling for them. Marcus downed the wine and filled his glass again, this time to the top. He noticed Vickie had also finished her sampling and offered to pour her some more. She nodded yes and he obliged, only filling her glass half full. He didn't want her to think he was only interested in getting her drunk, although the idea had crossed his mind. If she was inebriated, she might not notice if one of his *moments* happened.

He started on his wine again, downing half the glass in two big gulps. He hadn't realized how thirsty he was and the wine was both smooth and tasty, tingling his throat and taste buds. He decided that her selection was a good one.

"So," she asked him, "are your parents that way, too? You know, practical?"

He looked away for moment, suddenly seeing his parents' faces in his mind. The tingling sensation of the wine faded. "My parents were killed in a car accident when I was seventeen."

She gave him a sad look and told him how sorry she was for his loss.

"Thank you," he said, feeling awkward. He sat there in silence, trying to figure out how to start the conversation again. Death wasn't exactly what you might call an icebreaker.

She reached out and touched him on the arm. "I'm sorry if I made you think about them."

"Oh, it's not that," he said, once again trying to think of something to talk about.

She asked him what they were like.

"I guess you'd call them free spirits. Ben used to say that my parents were two kids that never grew up. They liked to have fun, all the time. They loved going out, dancing, going to amusement parks, movies."

"They sound charming," she said. "Tell me more about them."

He stared at her, not sure why she was asking. None of his other dates had ever inquired about his life. They always talked about themselves. He sat up in the booth, quite eager to discuss it. He'd wanted her to get to know him better. Now was his chance.

"Dad used to say that his favorite sound in the whole world was the one you'd hear at amusement parks—people laughing and screaming at the same time, having fun on the rides. Dad called it a contagious piece of joy. You couldn't help smiling or laughing when you heard it."

"It sounds like your dad was a lot of fun."

"He was. And Mom was just like him. She used to make up silly songs and her and Dad would sing them to me and Ben. We'd play games and work on projects or practical jokes. Ben loved it. He never wanted to go home. But Mom and Dad weren't what you would call practical. At least not when it came to money. They never managed to save a penny."

She asked him what his father did for a living.

"He was a mechanic in a machine shop. He made pretty good money and we lived all right but if they had a chance to spend their money on a vacation, outings to the theater or any other thing we could all enjoy, they did it."

She put her hand on top of his. "It must have been hard for you financially after their deaths."

"Oh, they didn't leave me penniless or anything," he told her, suddenly feeling a bit defensive about it. "They had good insurance policies that paid my way through business school and left me a little nest egg besides. But they weren't afraid of having fun. They didn't get depressed or bogged down with worrying about every little thing. They made every minute of their lives count for something."

"It sounds like a very nice way to grow up," she said, squeezing his hand.

"It was," he replied, enjoying the warmth of her hand against his own. "And when I think about it, it was kind of prophetic. It's almost as if they knew they were going to die young and were taking advantage of every moment, never letting an opportunity pass by where they could enjoy themselves. I used to think all parents were that way. It was only after they died that I saw how unique and wonderful they really were."

"It reminds me of a line from a song," she said. "Something about 'you don't know what you've got 'til it's gone.' I guess that's true, isn't it?" Her eyes seemed to shimmer as she said it, conveying not only sympathy but also curiosity. It was as though her eyes were trying to communicate with him somehow. Say the words she couldn't. Ask him what she couldn't. He could almost hear her whisper the question.

"Who are you really? And be honest with me."

But of course, she didn't say it. She only stared at him with that same questioning look while she held on to his hand. His heart began to ache with regret. If only he *could* tell her. If only he *could* trust that she wouldn't run away after he did tell her. If only.

"Marcus?" she said, letting go of his hand and acting concerned. "Are you all right?"

"What?" he said, jarred from his thoughts. "Yes. I'm fine. Uh, what was I saying?"

"You were talking about how wonderful your parents were. It's too bad everyone's parents can't be that way."

"Of course I didn't always think they were so wonderful," he said. He then told her about when he was fifteen and had quite a different opinion of them. "I was at that age where I was full of myself and couldn't see things straight. I thought they were weird and didn't understand me. So one night the three of us had a big fight and I came out and told them how I felt. I accused them of being immature and told them to grow up and act like adults. That I was tired of being the most mature person in the family." He paused and sighed, recalling the memory. "I thought they'd react like they always did, laugh and brush it off. But they didn't. They acted like I'd stabbed them in the heart. I hurt them, I mean really hurt them, and I knew it, too. It was written all over their faces. Once I saw that, I ran upstairs to my room and ended up crying myself to sleep…"

He broke off as soon as he heard the words said aloud. A wave of shame washed over him and he avoided her gaze and grabbed on to his wine glass. How could he have told her something so personal? It was a memory that he hadn't even shared with Ben and Jack. And here he was. Telling it to a date, and a first date to boot. He suddenly felt vulnerable and exposed. How could he be so stupid? What the hell was wrong with him? Maybe he was on the verge of a breakdown or something worse. Was it possible that he was subconsciously trying to drive women away? Perhaps his inner self was pushing him towards behavior that his conscious self wouldn't permit. He started wondering if he should check the yellow pages for a local shrink when he felt her hand on his again. He glanced up, afraid to see the expression on her face. But it wasn't the look of disgust he expected.

She was smiling at him.

"Not many men would admit to crying," she whispered. "I think that's quite exceptional." And she gave him a look that was more intoxicating and sweet than the wine. He experienced a warm feeling of elation. Not only because she'd responded to his honesty but because she'd touched him again. And just as before, it had a dizzying effect, making his heart race and face flush.

"Uh...thank you," he said, reaching for his wine glass. He gulped down the rest of it, letting the wine's effects add to his feeling of euphoria. He grabbed for the bottle and as he refilled his glass, she asked him where he went after his parents died.

"I went to live with Ben and his parents. But it wasn't easy for them, having to deal with two depressed seventeen-year-olds."

"What do you mean two?"

He pushed his hair back around his ear, feeling warm. The room was air-conditioned and he knew it was probably the effects of the wine. "I mean Ben," he told her, loosening his tie. "I never had any siblings, so Ben was...is...like my brother. I think he loved my folks more than I did. He spent more time at my house than his own. He thought my parents were Peter Pan and Santa Claus all rolled into one. And Mom and Dad thought the world of him, too. When Ben decided to become a musician instead of joining his dad's lumber business, Dad supported his decision..."

"You mean Hollinger Lumber? That's Ben's family?"

"Yeah. And Ben's father was mad as hell when he found out my dad helped Ben not only apply for college, but get financial assistance. Ben's father didn't talk to any of us for a solid month, he was so angry. He expected Ben to help him run the business but Ben's heart wasn't in it and my dad knew it. Ben wanted to study and teach music and Dad told him if he didn't pursue that dream, he'd regret it for the rest of his life. But it all worked out in the end. Ben's younger brother now runs the business with his dad and Ben teaches music and is a member of a small orchestra that does benefit concerts. Right now he's trying to get a loan to buy the music store where he works. The owner's retiring and wants out."

"You mean Cromwell Music?"

Marcus nodded yes. "Frank Cromwell wants to move out to California where all his kids are. Ben's been working for him for three years and knows the business pretty well. It's a good investment and he's doing something he loves. Dad was right. Ben would have been miserable in the lumber business."

She asked if Ben's father ever accepted Ben's decision to study music.

"Eventually. After my parents were killed, it happened a few months before Ben and I graduated, he changed his mind about it and agreed to pay Ben's tuition. Ben also talked his parents into taking me in to live with them. They could have forgotten about me but Ben wouldn't let them. I had no other relatives and was still underage so the state stepped in and said they were going to send me to a foster home. Ben threatened to run away and go with me so his parents finally decided that one more mouth to feed was easier than chasing after Ben all the time. They're decent people, really. They were very kind to me. We're still friends today. And Ben and his dad get along great now. But they'll never be as close as Ben was to my dad. A couple of friends from school told me that Ben cried like crazy at Mom and Dad's funeral, he was so broken up."

"But weren't you there?" she asked, acting confused.

"No. I was in the hospital, recovering from a head injury I got during the accident. I was in the car with them when it happened. A tractor-trailer went out of control, crossed the median and hit us head-on. All I remember is Mom reaching back to me in the back seat, trying to shield me. They found me in a field, about fifty yards from the car. I must have been thrown out the window. Either that, or Mom pushed me out. They both died from the impact. I was in a coma for two weeks before I finally came out of it. I must have smashed my mouth on part of the car as I went flying out, because when I woke up all five of my front teeth were missing. My mouth was pretty torn up, too. I healed up okay, but now I have an upper plate." He paused, suddenly remembering all the mishaps he'd had with his plate over the last ten years. He wanted to make a joke and tell her about some of them but to do that would mean revealing his *gift*, something he wasn't ready to do.

"That must have been terrible for you," she said. "I can't even imagine losing one of my parents, let alone both of them." Her expression turned sad and her eyes seemed to shimmer, conveying an emotion that couldn't be expressed with words. It made his heart jump and his body responded with warm waves of desire. His throat went dry and he reached for his wine, trying to fight off the feeling but at the same time, wanting to revel in it.

The waiter brought the salads and rolls and Vickie immediately started in eating. But Marcus didn't. He just sat there, drinking his wine, happy at how well things were going. The sweet fragrance of her perfume added a wonderful footnote to the mixture of aromas and flickering light surrounding him. That, along with the wine's effect gave him a feeling of warmth and love, the likes of which he hadn't known for a good long time. He started daydreaming about the possibilities and suddenly saw an image of himself, sitting there with her, not on their first date but celebrating something else. Maybe an anniversary. Their one month anniversary. He'd never lasted that long with anyone else but it *could* happen. He let his imagination take him even farther. It wasn't their first month anniversary, it was their first year anniversary, a wedding anniversary. He could see them sitting together, laughing and snuggling there at the same table, their table. They'd made it their regular table because it was where they'd had their first date. Perhaps they would even order a small cake to celebrate the anniversary. No. Better yet, they still had the top layer of their wedding cake, frozen in the freezer of their new house. He could almost see it. The top layer of a wedding cake with the little plastic figure of a bride and groom.

He was no longer alone. He had someone to share his life with…

"Aren't you hungry?"

Her words jolted him back to reality and he sat up, trying to collect himself. He grabbed his fork and looked down at the salad. The impression of his fantasy was still lingering in his mind and he happily let it drift back as he pushed the salad greens around with his fork. He glanced over at her, trying not to stare as she picked up her wineglass and drank from it. He could almost see her, raising her glass in a toast to their anniversary.

"You look happy," she said, grinning over the top of her glass. "What are you thinking about?"

"Oh nothing," he said, knowing he must have been grinning like an idiot. "I was thinking how nice it is in here." He started to eat some of the salad but a moment later the waiter brought their selections and placed them on the table. He pushed his salad aside and decided to give the entrée a try. He sampled the first few morsels and was pleasantly surprised at how good it tasted. He quickly filled his fork again, realizing how long it had been since he'd eaten. He'd only had toast and coffee for breakfast and had been so busy at work that he'd skipped lunch.

He dug in with zeal and finished over half the plate within a few minutes. He was drawn out of his feeding frenzy a few minutes later when he heard Vickie giggling.

"It must be good," she said.

He grabbed his napkin and wiped his mouth, hoping to hell he didn't look like a hog, rooting away in his slop trough. He nodded and grabbed for his wineglass to wash it down.

"I've always wondered," she whispered, leaning closer. "What's it taste like?"

"It's kind of like shrimpy onion rings with breading. It's delicious. Would you like to try some?"

She laughed. "No. That's okay. You go ahead and enjoy it. I'll just stick to my noodles."

He did as she suggested and dove back into his plate. The food was a treat to the palate and he finished the rest in short order. He came back up for air a few minutes later and downed some more of his wine, enjoying the sated and satisfied feeling. She'd also finished her entrée so he wanted to get back to the conversation again. He remembered her elderly friend John and asked her if she'd seen him lately.

"As a matter of fact, he came in today," she said, pushing her mostly empty plate aside. The noodles looked tasty and he wanted to ask her if he could finish them but decided not to. Then she really would think he was a pig in a troth.

"I told him I had a date and he wanted to know who I was going out with," she said.

He decided to tease her. "He didn't get jealous, did he?"

"No," she said, blushing slightly, "but he wanted to know all about you. I told him who you were and that you ran The Crystal."

He stopped smiling and put down his wine glass, worried. She'd been asking about him. That could only spell trouble. He decided to approach the next question very carefully. "Uh, did he say anything about me…I mean, has he heard of me?" He was almost afraid to hear the answer. She hesitated for a second, like she was thinking about it. His heart dropped. He began clutching at straws in his mind. Maybe the guy hadn't told her anything. Maybe he didn't know anything. And even if he did know something, maybe he hadn't told her the truth, only rumors. Rumors could be dispelled and dismissed as mere innuendo. That is…if he was lucky and she hadn't heard too many of them.

He leaned in closer, trying to read the answer in her eyes. He waited for her to respond, praying that whatever the man told her wasn't anything too terrifying.

"No," she said. "John's never heard of you. He said he's been in The Crystal plenty of times and he knew the owner, the man you said moved out of state. John used to be in the Rotary with him."

AND THE BULL SAVED ME

He let out an inward sigh of relief. She hadn't yet found about *The Kirklin Klutz* and he hoped it stayed that way. He tried to get off the subject and asked her more about John. She told him a few more stories about the elderly Kirklin resident and he sat back and listened, enjoying the sound of her voice. He finished off the rest of his wine and pushed the empty glass aside, letting both the wine and calamari settle. She was into her third story about John when she was interrupted for a few seconds while the waiter seated a middle-aged couple at the table next to them. The waiter went into his spiel about the specials but the woman held up her hand and stopped him.

"No thanks," she said. "I don't do tentacles!" Then she laughed and her husband joined her.

Marcus chuckled and leaned in closer to Vickie. "Did you hear what she said about tentacles?" he whispered. "That was funny."

"Well, I can't blame her," Vickie said, nudging him in the elbow. "Not everyone is as adventurous as you and likes to eat squid. I know it's considered a delicacy and even though you told me how delicious it was, I still don't think I could eat it."

"Squid?" he said, not sure he heard her right.

She waved her hand at him. "Oh, I know. You squid lovers like for it to be called by its Italian name. Sorry. I meant to say calamari." She then resumed her story about John.

He smiled and continued to try and listen but it wasn't easy. The word was still repeating itself inside his head.

Squid!

He'd eaten squid. How was that possible? He racked his brain, trying to remember the menu. He'd only read part of it because he'd gone on the recommendation from the waiter. He glanced down at the empty plate in front of him. His stomach rolled over, picturing the calamari that had been heaped there a few minutes earlier and that was now filling his belly. He suddenly felt betrayed. It was Italian for Christsakes! Italian like spaghetti noodles and ravioli! Where the hell did squid fit into that equation? It didn't taste like squid or at least how he imagined squid would taste. It resembled shrimp mixed with onions, not something slimy.

His tongue felt thicker all of a sudden and he reached over for his untouched water glass and took a sip. It didn't help. The chlorine only enhanced his realization that he had just eaten a plate of squid—no, a great big plate of TENTACLES.

Pictures began forming inside his head. It was a scene from *Twenty*

Thousand Leagues Under the Sea. A giant squid was wrapping itself around the submarine *Nautilus*. As the tentacles encircled the sub, his stomach tightened up. It was as though the same tentacles were wrapping around it, too. Vickie was still telling a story about John and as much as he tried to focus on what she was saying, he couldn't. Images of giant squids and suckered tentacles kept popping into his head. Another image took shape. It was the movie *It Came from Beneath the Sea* that he'd watched once with Ben. Three, huge suckered tentacles rose up out of the water and crashed down on top of a concrete bridge, buckling the pavement. His stomach did another flipflop and sweat beads began to form on his forehead as the temperature in the room seemed to jump up twenty degrees. He loosened his tie as once again the vision of the suckers protruding from the tentacles flashed in his head. He closed his eyes and swallowed hard, trying to wipe the image from his thoughts.

"Are you all right?" she asked him.

He opened his eyes and managed a weak smile. "Yeah. I'm fine," he lied, hoping she didn't see through it. "Please, go on with your story."

She started talking again and he tried to maintain the smile, in spite of the nausea that was now announcing itself with a gurgling noise from his midsection. He loosened his tie a little more, praying the queasiness would pass. His stomach gurgled again and he cleared his throat, trying to cover up the sound. His intestinal tract was reacting to both his imagination and the fact that he'd mixed the squid with several large glasses of the wine. Another image appeared, this time it was a giant squid puking up red liquid. He pushed the wine bottle away from him, wishing he could push the nausea and images along with it.

Jesus Christ! he thought, the anger burning inside his chest, adding to the rest of his body's intestinal upheaval. How was he supposed to know that calamari was squid for crying out loud? What kind of word was calamari anyway? Obviously it was Italian for tentacles or squid! If they were going to sell something so repulsive they should at least add a disclaimer to the menu. Something like: *This dish is Italian for squid tentacles. Ingestion may cause nausea or vomiting.* As he saw the word *vomiting* in his head, his stomach lurched, causing a burp to come up. The taste had a strong hint of acid and only added to his nausea.

He started thinking about all the other Italian foods and if their names were also masking what they actually were. Perhaps ravioli was Italian for eel. And what did that make spaghetti, his favorite food in the whole world? It was probably Italian for worms or larvae. He would sometimes eat cold spaghetti, he loved it so much. Now he wondered about all those times. It probably wasn't really larvae but the thought made his stomach roll over like crazy. He heard Vickie's voice again.

"So then John's wife developed Alzheimer's and John retired so he could stay home with her. Have you ever heard of anything so moving?"

He braved a smile and nodded. He wanted to answer but his throat was dry as the desert and he was having trouble swallowing without the nausea coming back up. She started to tell another story about John. He tried to listen but his mind was on his stomach, gurgling and rolling like a crazed swamp alligator. After a few more minutes, his face began to flush and he experienced fuzziness in his gut. But this wasn't the warm, cozy feeling someone would get snuggling up in bed. This was the all too familiar feeling that would come after drinking too much and having to puke.

He tried thinking of other things, mountaintops, trees, race cars. But as he imagined the cars speeding around the track, his head began to spin, adding to the discomfort. When he'd watched the movies as a kid, it was cool to watch the squids attack people. But now it wasn't cool. Now the squid was attacking him and seemed determined to come back up the same way it went down.

His stomach lurched again and he quelled a desire to run from the table. She was in the middle of a story and he didn't want her to think he was rude by interrupting her or better yet, that he was an idiot and didn't know what the hell calamari was. Another wave of nausea hit and he said a silent prayer that he didn't throw up on the table. He smiled, anxiously waiting for her to finish the story so he could excuse himself and retreat to the restroom. His stomach started making rumbling noises and he put his arms up on the table trying to hide the sound. A couple minutes later she wrapped up the story and he got up from the table.

"Uh, will you please excuse me a minute?" he told her. "I've got to go to the john." He was afraid of talking at all, fearing that something else would come out of his mouth besides the words.

"Sure," she said, smiling up at him.

He started walking towards the back of the restaurant, not sure where he was going but wanting to get as far away from her as possible. Then if he did have to let go before finding the restroom maybe she wouldn't see it. He quickly scanned the room and spotted the sign for the men's room in the far right corner. He headed towards it, wanting to run but afraid to, knowing that any more jostling would make him heave for sure. As he hurried past the tables he tried not to look at the other customers' food. Seeing someone else eating calamari would push him over the edge and it wouldn't do the place much good if he threw up all over someone else's dinner. A waiter came out of the kitchen with a tray of food and he ducked out of the man's way and hurried over and through the men's room door.

There were two stalls, one occupied, so he headed for the unoccupied one. He passed a fiftyish looking man standing in front of the urinal who was smoking a cigarette with the longest ash he'd ever seen. It must have been three inches long. He wanted to get a closer look but there were more pressing matters to attend to. He ducked into the stall just as his stomach made another huge lurch and he hadn't even had time to shut the door before he began heaving into the bowl, freeing the chewed up tentacles from his tender and unforgiving gut.

The toilet flushed next door. Obviously the occupant had been hurried along by all the retching noises. Marcus hung his head over the bowl and for the next few minutes expelled the entire contents of his stomach. He was aided by the images of the giant squids attacking idiots who stupidly didn't know how to choose an appropriate entrée, namely him. He made double sure he was done before finally flushing and reemerging from the stall. He went over to the sink, splashed some water on his face and rinsed his mouth, trying to get rid of any residual taste.

The room was now deserted except for the ash man who came over and gave him a sympathetic nod. The man staggered when he walked, showing that he'd been enjoying more than a little of the house wines.

"Bad linguini, huh?" the man said, patting him on the back. His words were slow and slurred. "Yep! Thass happent to me, too. That clam sauce can curdle in your stomach fastern greased owl shit!"

Marcus began picturing Vickie's linguini in his head, covered with owl shit. His stomach rolled over again and he leaned down, splashing more water on his face, trying to wash away the image. Why didn't the asshole shut up? He finished cooling his face with the water and glanced up at the mirror. His face wasn't green but it felt that way. He could see the man's reflection in the mirror. The long ash was now gone from the cigarette, as was the flame. But the man was still puffing as though it was still lit.

"Nesht time you order," the man said, swaying unsteadily, "do yourshef a flavor…don't get the linguini, get the calamari, that won't go sour on ya." And as he slurred the word "calamari" Marcus could detect the stale smell of wine on the man's breath.

That was all it took.

His body began dry heaving and he fled back to the stall, vacating what he thought was an empty stomach. After another five minutes his stomach finally began to calm down and he went back to the sink. After splashing some more water on his face, he glanced around the room and was thankful to see that the ash man had left. He got back to cleaning up and after rinsing out his mouth about a hundred times and checking to make sure he didn't smell like puke or calamari, he exited the restroom and headed back to the table.

"Sorry I was so long," he said, retaking his seat. "There was a line."

"I'm not surprised, as busy as it is," she said.

The waiter had removed the plates and water glasses from the table and Marcus was thankful that any evidence of tentacles was no longer in view. In spite of still feeling green in the face, she didn't seem to notice anything different. She began talking about her job and he was happy to sit and listen as his stomach returned to normal. He only spoke a few words, interjecting an "Oh really" or "That's interesting" every once in a while to let her know he was listening. She had a soft voice and it was having a soothing affect on him.

A few minutes later he noticed himself getting warm again. But the warmth didn't seem to be internal, it was external, as if someone had shut off the air conditioner. He looked around the room but didn't see any of the other diners looking red in the face from the heat or exhibiting signs of being uncomfortable. He dismissed it as being an after effect of puking and got back to listening to Vickie. The waiter came up and asked them if they would like dessert. He was glad when Vickie declined. Staring or smelling at any more food would only bring back the unease his intestinal tract was still rebounding from. The waiter finished writing the check and as he laid it down on the table Marcus felt something like a bee sting near his right ankle. He grunted in pain and the waiter asked him if he was all right.

"I'm fine," he replied, reaching down and groping around his ankle. He touched the cuff of his pants and a burning sensation shot through his hand. He yelped and jumped up, out of the booth.

"What's wrong?" the waiter yelled, his voice close to a scream.

Marcus backed away from the table and looked down at his right pant leg. It was smoking.

"Oh, my God!" Vickie screamed, scrambling out of the booth. "You're on fire!"

The burning sensation increased dramatically and Marcus began shaking his leg vigorously, hoping it would extinguish the smoldering material. His hand was still burning from where he'd touched the cuff and he didn't relish sticking it in harm's way again. He started to grab for the wine bottle but quickly realized that the alcohol might make the smolder turn deadly. So he grabbed one of the cloth napkins instead and began beating it against the smoking cuff. He'd just finished making a couple of swipes when the napkin burst into flames. Vickie and the waiter both screamed and Marcus dropped the napkin to the floor and stomped on it.

He managed to extinguish the napkin but now the smoldering in his cuff was threatening to flame up and a few seconds later it did. The waiter let out a piercing scream and Vickie ran towards the couple in the next booth. Marcus started dancing around in a circle, trying to keep the burning material away from his skin. He looked around frantically for something—anything, to put out the fire. He finally decided that alcohol or not, any liquid would help and began jumping towards the table to get it. He reached out for it but was cut off as Vickie charged at him, carrying something in her hand. It was a pitcher. A second later there was a whoosh of air as a cool splash of water washed over his lower leg, dousing the fire. He breathed a sigh of relief and leaned down to survey the damage. There was a burn hole the size of an orange in his cuff and some of the pant leg was singed off. He inspected his skin beneath it. Some of the hair was missing but other than that, it looked unscathed.

He began to stand up to thank her when a streak of red came hurtling towards his face. He jerked backwards and a second later the smell of marinara sauce filled his nostrils as something thick and wet slapped against his legs. The waiter was standing a few feet away, his face frozen in horror, holding an empty platter with the remnants of someone's dinner. The waiter let out a gasp and took off with the platter towards the kitchen.

"Where's he going?" Vickie said, turning to grab the other napkin from the table. She bent down and helped Marcus wipe off the noodles and sauce off his trousers. Some of the sauce had splattered on her white skirt, turning it into a giant napkin with crimson splotches.

"Your skirt's ruined," he told her, hoping she wouldn't be too upset.

"I think the waiter was only trying to help," she whispered, standing back up. "Did you see how scared he was when you caught on fire?" She paused and giggled. "Did you ever hear a man scream like that? He sounded like a woman."

He searched her face. He expected her to be upset, but she wasn't. She was smiling. He'd never seen one of his dates act so laid-back after one of his episodes. He wasn't sure how to react. "Are you okay?" he asked, thinking that perhaps she was in shock.

"I'm fine. But you're a mess. You really are the Spaghetti Kid now." She gazed into his eyes, a glow of happiness showing in her face. He couldn't believe it. She was acting as though she was having the time of her life. He was left speechless.

The waiter came running up with two other servers and all three had handfuls of paper towels. They went to the task of wiping up the floor as the waiter apologized for throwing the food. The man was visibly upset, almost to the point of babbling and Marcus tried to keep a straight face as the man droned on. The waiter then observed Vickie's skirt and started babbling apologies to her.

"It's no big deal," she told him. "I'm gonna duck over to the ladies room and clean some of this up."

Marcus watched her walk away, wondering if she was taking the opportunity to get away from him. He was relieved when he saw her turn towards the restrooms instead of the rear entrance. So far, so good. She hadn't been scared away, at least not yet.

"I can't understand how you caught fire!" the waiter exclaimed. "Did you bump against one of the candles?"

Marcus told him about the man in the restroom and how the ash must have dropped off into his cuff.

"Oh, that explains it," the waiter said; his anxiety quickly replaced with indignation. "We've told the customers time and again that they're not supposed to smoke in there. I'd better call the manager." The man left in a huff, as if he was on a mission.

Marcus headed back to the rest room to clean up. He'd been hoping for an uneventful evening but should have known better. As he passed the women's room door, he wondered if Vickie was crawling out the back window, trying to escape. Other women had left him for less. It wouldn't be the first time. And who could blame her? Calamari and flames? Even Chef Boyardee would have run for the hills. Maybe he should consider himself lucky. It could have been worse. At least this time the fire department or police hadn't been called.

He pushed open the men's room door, a depression descending upon him like a black cloud. He was hoping that *this* time he could make it work. It had seemed like destiny; from the first time he'd seen her, as if fate had stepped in, pushing him towards something, towards her. He went over to the sink and cleaned himself up. A few noodles were still clinging to his knees and within a few minutes the worst of it was cleaned off, leaving wet stains over his lower half. He washed his hands and looked at himself in the mirror. He suddenly envisioned his father's face, looking back at him, smiling. It was his conscience, reminding him to not wallow in self-pity. He could almost hear his father's voice, consoling him, telling him not to give up. He then pictured Jack, sitting at a poker table, holding a set of cards and frowning. But the frown turned to a smile a few seconds later as Jack laid down a royal flush.

Marcus sighed, straightened his tie and smoothed back his hair, feeling his determination return. He wasn't going to stand there and feel sorry himself anymore. If she'd left, he could accept it and move on. His life would continue, same as before. He would simply keep looking for someone to share his crazy life. There was *someone, somewhere* out there. There had to be.

But as he headed for the bathroom exit, a ray of hope brightened inside of him, hoping she hadn't run away. She was different than the others. When he looked in her eyes, he saw wonderful possibilities and dreams, dreams he hoped would have a chance to come true. He held his breath and opened the door, ready to deal with whatever hand of cards Destiny was going to deal him.

And that's when he saw it.

A royal flush.

She was standing in the hall, a few feet away, smiling and waiting for him. He walked up to her, a lump forming in his throat.

"I did the best I could," she said, "but I still smell like spaghetti."

He moved close to her, no longer able to hold back his happiness. "Like I told you," he whispered, "spaghetti is my favorite food. I love the way you smell." And he flashed her a smile, showing her he meant it. She gazed up at him, giving him a look that made his heart jump.

She hadn't been repulsed or run away.

She'd stayed.

He was overcome by the moment. He reached out and gently stroked her cheek with the back of his hand. She tilted her head and closed her eyes, enjoying his touch. She parted her lips, signaling him to kiss her. His heart leapt and he leaned down, anxiously anticipating the warmth of her lips against his own.

But he never quite got there.

Someone was poking him hard on the shoulder and he turned to face the waiter.

"I called the manager," the waiter said, his tone businesslike and placating. "I told him about that other man smoking in the men's room and how you caught on fire. I also told him about me throwing the spaghetti. He wanted me to extend his deepest apologies for the accident and asked that you call him.

Here's his name and number." The waiter handed him a slip of paper with the information written on it. "He's picking up your check and wants you to send him a bill for you and your wife's clothes that were ruined."

Marcus heard Vickie giggle at the *wife* remark and offered no correction.

"Thank you," Marcus told the man. "My wife and I would like to thank your manager for his kind consideration for our safety and welfare. I also appreciate your heroic efforts to save my life and I'll be calling your manager tomorrow to tell him personally how grateful I am for your quick thinking." The waiter's face flushed with pride. Marcus thanked him again and led Vickie toward the exit. As soon as they went out the front door, Vickie started laughing.

"He didn't save your life! All he did was throw spaghetti at us!"

"I know," he said, grabbing her arm and leading her into the parking lot, "but his heart was in the right place and that should account for something. Besides, if you hadn't saved me first, that spaghetti might have."

"Oh," she replied, nodding as if she understood his reasoning. "Wait a minute," she said, pulling away from him. "Where are you taking me?"

"I'm driving you home."

"But I only live down the block."

He took her arm again and led her to his car. "Now what kind of husband would I be if I let my wife walk all over town with spaghetti sauce on her?" She giggled and got into the car. He shut the door and headed over to the driver's side, his mind spinning, trying to come up with a way for her to go out with him again. He began running ideas through his mind.

He already had her in the car. Maybe he could just take her home with him right now. She hadn't seemed to mind the waiter thinking she was his wife. Perhaps she wouldn't mind accompanying him and living out the real thing.

But he wouldn't.

His plan had been to take things slow and not rush her. Not to mention that his *gift* seemed to be working overtime. He suddenly had an image of Vickie waking up in bed with a giant squid. There were hundreds of lizards scrambling around the room, crawling everywhere, trying to get away from the squid attacking them with its tentacles. Vickie was frantically defending herself with the only weapons available, the bed pillows.

He got behind the wheel and shut the door on both the car and the image.

Taking her home could be disastrous. He dropped the idea like a lead weight.

"We could go somewhere else," she said as he started the car.

"Well, we could try that bar you and Ben talked about, the one with the karaoke."

"Yeah, but I couldn't go like this..." she said, glancing down at herself, "but if you run me back to my place, I could change my clothes."

He quickly agreed and put the car in gear. He followed her directions and drove down the block, turning into the first drive past the red light. Her apartment house was a two-story corner building that looked like it had been recently remodeled. The aluminum siding looked new and the windows still had the manufacturer stickers. He pulled up near the back entrance and put the car in park. She started to get out when he reached across the seat and grabbed her, pulling her back against him. He leaned down and kissed her, not giving her a chance to object. He knew it was a bit forward, but his *gift* left him no choice. He was determined to get at least one kiss before anything else happened.

It was everything he'd imagined it would be, and better. Her lips were warm and inviting and he wrapped his arms around her, wanting to surround himself with her soft caress and touch. He'd just begun to enjoy himself when he heard someone clearing their throat.

"Uh...excuse me. Am I interrupting something?"

He let go of Vickie and looked out the passenger window to a young girl's face. She was about sixteen and had Vickie's same facial features and hair color. Vickie pulled away from him and asked the girl what she was doing there.

"Mom and Dad dropped me off a half-hour ago and I forgot my key. They thought you were home. They didn't say you were on a date."

Vickie got out of the car and as soon as the girl saw Vickie's skirt she started laughing. "What the heck happened to you?"

"I had a little accident with some spaghetti. And you don't have to tell Mom and Dad about it or that I was out on a date."

The girl agreed to keep her secret and Vickie led her back over to the car. "Marcus, this is my little sister Marty. Marty, this is Marcus Kerr."

Marcus shook the girl's hand and a look of awe filled her face. "Are you Magic? Magic Marker?"

As soon as she said it, Vickie took the girl aside and whispered to her. After a quick discussion both of them came back to the window.

"Marty was talking about the kids at school calling you Magic Marker," Vickie told him.

"Yeah. That's what I meant," Marty said. "A lot of the kids bowl at The Crystal and have mentioned that you run the place."

The girl's words sounded sincere but Marcus could see something else in her eyes and wondered what she knew, if anything. Vickie walked with Marty over to the driver's side of the car. "I wish I could go to that club," Vickie told Marcus, leaning down by the window. "Maybe some other time," and she gave him a sad smile.

He knew that her sister's arrival had put the stops on the rest of their date but was hoping she would agree to see him again. "I could get away from work Saturday," he told her, trying not to sound too anxious. "We could go to a movie or dinner."

Vickie started to agree when Marty cut her off. "You can't! We've got plans! Remember?"

"Oh. I forgot," Vickie said. Then she told Marcus that she and Marty were going to a costume shop in Columbus. "Marty joined drama club this summer and they're putting on a medieval festival in a couple months. We're going to the costume shop to pick out an outfit for her or maybe get some ideas on how to make one ourselves."

He asked her which costume shop it was.

"Grogan's on Hayden Road. I've only been to Columbus a couple of times so I'm not sure exactly where it is."

Hayden Road, he thought. The same area as the furniture factory where the dolly fiasco occurred. "I know where it's at," he said. "I'd be honored to take you both there. It would be my way of making up for what happened with the spaghetti. There's a little place near there that has great barbeque if you like ribs. It would be my treat."

A smile crept across Vickie's face and Marty grabbed her arm, coaxing her to accept the offer. "I love ribs," Marty said. "And he knows the way so we won't get lost. Can't we go?"

Marcus wanted to thank the girl for the added support. He still suspected she might know about him but if she did, she wasn't letting on.

"It's a date," Vickie said. "And I'll make sure to wear something red in case we have a problem with any exuberant waiters carrying trays of ribs."

"Good idea," he said. "What time should I pick you up?"

Vickie told him they'd be ready about noon. As soon as she heard Vickie say it, Marty began clapping with glee.

"Hurray! That means we won't get back until late and I won't have to go to that dopey family reunion Sunday with Mom and Dad."

Vickie shook her finger angrily at Marty. "Oh yes you do. You already promised you'd go with them." She turned to Marcus. "I usually go to my parents on Sunday for dinner but this week they're going to Toledo for a family reunion." She then leaned down and whispered to him, "So it looks like I'm free on Sunday. We could do something together, just the two of us…"

He couldn't help but smile. She'd committed to not only one date, but two. He quickly agreed and started thinking of places they could go where the risk level for his *gift* would be less likely to occur. He began to suggest a nice quiet trip to the lake for a picnic when Vickie asked him if he'd ever been to the zoo in nearby Mayer.

"The zoo?" The words almost got stuck in his mouth. Zoo. Animals, lots of animals. He didn't have a good track record with animals.

"Yeah! The zoo!" Marty exclaimed, putting her hands to her mouth, trying to cover up the grin. "That would be a great place for a date!"

Marcus studied the girl's face, trying to figure out what she meant. But Vickie squeezed his arm and broke his concentration. "They have a new dolphin exhibit," Vickie said. "I've been reading about it in the paper and I'd love to see it."

He knew he was being backed into a corner and couldn't give her a good excuse for not going without revealing his secret. "Uh, yeah. That's fine," he said, swallowing hard and trying not to look worried. "It might be a lot of fun."

Vickie leaned in and gave him a peck on the cheek. He turned his head, hoping to get a kiss on the lips but she backed out too quick and he missed his chance. His heart began beating like thunder and his face flushed with desire. In the space of a few seconds his body had gone into full alert, pumping adrenaline and sending waves of yearning through every pore. She was like a strange and exotic perfume that he wanted to immerse himself in.

"See you Saturday," Vickie said, grabbing on to Marty's arm and leading her towards the back door of the apartment house.

It was only after they'd disappeared through the door that he came back to his senses. He put the car into gear and drove towards the exit, suddenly remembering what he'd just committed to. The Columbus trip seemed safe enough, except for the usual deadly potential every other driver experienced on the turnpike in traffic. It was two hours in the car down and back with only a couple of stops to the costume shop and dinner. Costumes, inanimate objects, clothes. Nothing deadly there. And the rib place should be safe as well. Even if they spilled barbeque sauce, seeing people wearing hot sauce in a rib joint was a regular occurrence. The zoo was the worry. The potential for a problem increased proportionately with the addition of living, breathing creatures capable of spontaneous behavior.

He shrugged it off and decided that he was being paranoid. His *gift* didn't always make an appearance on dates. Sometimes it would stay dormant for as long as a week. Maybe it wouldn't even show. Besides, the zoo animals were in controlled surroundings, cages, aquariums and gated pens. They were all monitored and secured.

It should be okay.

He saw an opening in traffic and pulled out onto the street, stopping almost immediately behind a couple others cars lined up for the light. As he waited with the others, he glanced out the passenger window to Vickie's apartment house. A few seconds later Marty emerged from the back entrance, taking off in a run across the lot. He raised his hand, waving to her and as soon as she saw him, she stopped dead in her tracks. He wondered if maybe he'd scared her and started to wave again. But he stopped when he saw her double over, as if she was in pain. He began to worry that something was wrong when the sound of her laughter drifted in through the window.

The light changed and the car behind him began honking their horn, audibly complaining and telling him to get a move on. He stepped on the gas and glanced up at the rearview mirror. He could still see Marty, standing in the parking lot, laughing herself silly.

Wonder what she's laughing at? he thought as he headed towards the route home. A voice inside his head answered, *Hope to hell it's not me.*

Ben leaned out of the booth and glanced at the back door. "Not yet," he told Jack, sitting across from him. "But he should be here any minute."

True to form, a few seconds later the back door opened and Magic filed in with a couple of the regulars. The regulars headed for the bar and Ben waved Magic down, motioning to the full beer sitting in front of the empty seat beside him.

"You don't waste any time, do you?" Jack asked, taking a drag on his pipe.

"Go ahead and poke fun," Ben whispered. "But you're just as anxious as I am."

Jack chuckled. "True. But at least I'd give him a minute to go to the bar and order a beer."

Ben ignored the sarcasm. "Hey, after hearing about the spaghetti and fire, this must *really* be good. Get ready...here he comes." Ben shoved over in the booth, leaving plenty of room. But as Magic sat down, he noticed something different about him. His face was bloated and his eyes looked splotchy, as if he'd been on an all-night bender. Ben pointed to the beer and prompted him to drink it. "You look like you could use it." He waited while Magic took a couple healthy swigs and then told him. "Let's hear it. First of all, what the hell happened to your face? Were you in a fight?"

Jack sat forward, the pipe smoke wafting in the already smoky filled air. "It must be good to get us to meet at midnight. Mavis is going to think I've got a girlfriend, going out so late."

Marcus put down his beer and smiled. "Does that mean you're in hot water with her?"

"Not after she and I heard what was broadcast on the police scanner. We knew it had to be one of your *Magic moments* making a curtain call."

Ben took a half-hearted swipe at Jack. "You never told me your heard it on the scanner! And I've been sitting here with you for fifteen minutes waiting for Magic to show." Then he gave them both a warning glare. "So? Are the two of you gonna tell me what happened or do I have to read about it in the paper?"

Marcus's face went white with fear. "The paper? Shit! I never thought about that! You don't think they'll print it, do you?"

Ben felt himself getting pissed. "I know you're about to panic," he told Magic. "But I'm the odd man out here and don't know what happened. What did you do, Magic? Set fire to the courthouse or something?"

Jack put his pipe in the ashtray and cleared his throat. "Not exactly. But one of Kirklin's oldest monuments *did* show up tonight. Or I should say, one of the oldest legends."

"What's that?" Ben asked him. "Some kind of cryptic message? Well, I forgot to bring my decoder ring. What local legend are you talking about?"

"Yellow Eyes," Marcus replied.

Ben frowned at him, not sure he heard right. "That werewolf creature legend? The one people have supposedly spotted in the woods outside of town?"

"That's the one," Jack said, confirming it. "I'm not from around here but I've heard the customers talk about it. It's reported to be some kind of creature that walks like a man but looks like a werewolf, right?"

"That's the myth," Ben said, not seeing where the town legend was fitting into the picture. "He's usually spotted by the hunters during deer season. Although some people think it's just a bunch of drunk hunters making up tall tales. But what has that got to do with Magic's face?" And he directed the question to his best friend sitting next to him.

"I wasn't expecting anything to happen," Marcus said. "We were only going to Columbus to try on some costumes. It seemed safe."

Ben and Jack told him to go on.

Marcus wrapped his arms around his glass and sighed. He told them about Marty needing a costume for the medieval festival and how he'd volunteered to take her and Vickie to the shop in Columbus. "It started out fine. We got to the place and Marty found a costume that she liked right away. I figured we'd be a while, you know how picky women are with clothes. But since we had some time to kill, all three of us decided to try on some of the other costumes. So we spent a couple hours dressing up. It was fun. I only tried on a few of them, an ape costume, Dracula, that sort of thing. But the third costume I ended up buying."

Ben started to see the plot unfold and smiled down at his beer. "Uh, Magic. The one you bought, it wasn't by any chance a werewolf costume, was it?"

"It was on sale," Marcus said, acting defensive about it. "You know how Jack and I always dress up for Halloween at The Crystal. I usually use my Merlin costume but thought I'd do something different this year. And the guy told me I could save ten bucks if I bought it now. He also said that if I waited until October, the best costumes would be gone."

"Sounds like a hell of a salesman," Jack commented and Ben bit his lip, trying to keep from laughing.

Marcus continued. "After the costume shop, I took Marty and Vickie to dinner at that rib place on Hayden Road. Dinner went fine. The food was delicious and the three of us had a great time talking and laughing. Marty seemed kind of cold towards me at first and I still wasn't sure if she knew about me or not."

Ben nudged him in the elbow. "She never mentioned about laughing at you, when you dropped Vickie off after Richetti's?"

"No. And if she *did* suspect something, she never said anything about it to Vickie. Otherwise Vickie would have cancelled the date or asked me a thousand questions about being *The Kirklin Klutz* and she didn't. So anyway, I stared telling Marty some of Jack's jokes over dinner and she seemed to change her mind about me."

Jack relit his pipe again. "A good joke is better than liquor," he said, pausing to puff on his pipe. "It's what I used to make Mavis fall for me."

"Well, it also worked for me," Marcus said. "I had both of them in stitches with all the dumb jokes. We were having such a good time that I decided to keep the laughs going and put part of the costume on for the drive home. It came with a pair of those large, hairy arms so I put those on along with the mask. The mask had eye holes plenty large enough to see out of so I could drive with no problem. You should have seen the other drivers staring at me on the interstate."

"No doubt," Ben said. "It's not every day you see a werewolf driving a Pontiac Sunbird."

Jack asked him what happened next.

"The trouble came when I got to the next to last exit on the interstate. I started getting this burning sensation and my skin started itching like crazy."

"Uh-oh," Ben said, seeing what was coming.

"I know," Marcus said, shaking his head yes. "The damn mask must have been made with latex. I didn't notice because of all the hair on it."

"Magic's allergic to latex," Ben told Jack. "He found out about it when he was eighteen. It wasn't long after his *moments* began happening. He had a reaction to the latex and ended up at the hospital."

"From gloves?" Jack asked them.

"No," Marcus volunteered. "Condom."

Jack almost spit up taking the pipe from his mouth. "Holy hell! I'll bet that was uncomfortable!"

Ben snickered "For the girl, too."

"It's true," Marcus said, lowering his voice to a whisper. "She freaked out when she saw my dick swell up *after* we had sex. She started screaming at me, accusing me of giving her the clap or herpes. I had to fight her off with one hand while I drove to the hospital with the other hand. She was ready to kill me. It took two of the doctors to explain to her that I was having an allergic reaction. I never went into anaphylactic shock or anything but my dick and balls swelled up like a balloon and itched like a son of a bitch until they gave me a shot."

"So that's what happened to you tonight?" Jack asked him. "The mask made your face swell up?"

"Yep. And I didn't want to alarm Marty or Vickie so I thought I could make it back to town before it got too bad. I took a shortcut and came in by the Old Town Road, figuring it would be faster. The hospital's on the other side of the woods. But just as I got to the end of Old Town Road, my car got a flat. I was starting to have trouble focusing and neglected to see a dead branch in the road. I ran over it and blew out my right front tire. I could have changed the tire but I didn't have time, I had to get to the hospital for the shot. My face had already begun swelling and when I tried to take the damn mask off, the zipper got caught in my hair. Vickie tried to cut it with some scissors I had in my trunk, but she was afraid she'd get my scalp by mistake. It was dark by then and we only had the dome light to work with."

Ben felt Jack poke him in the leg under the table and he bit down on his lip to keep from laughing.

Marcus continued. "So after that, I decided to make a run for it through the woods and to the hospital. We didn't see any other cars on the road. It's not traveled much so we couldn't flag someone down. I told Vickie and Marty to stay with the car and I'd send back help."

"And did they?" Ben asked him.

"Marty did. But Vickie didn't. And thank God she didn't."

"Why?" Ben asked him.

"Because of what happened next. A few minutes after I ran off into the woods, I came upon some teenagers camping out. They had a fire going and must have been passing around a couple of joints; the air was thick with the smell. My eyes were swelling shut so I followed the light of their campfire, thinking it was the hospital lights on the other side of the woods. The kids took one look at me and jumped to the wrong conclusion, that I was 'Yellow Eyes,' in the flesh. I tried to tell them what had happened but they went scattering in all directions, screaming and yelling. I'm sure the weed didn't help. The shit will make you paranoid in the sunlight, let alone a dark forest. So it turns out that one of the kids has a stun gun in her backpack and she grabs it and comes after me."

"Holy shit!" Ben said, holding back the smile.

"Couldn't you explain to her what happened?" Jack asked.

"I tried," Marcus said. "But she wasn't listening. All she saw was this hairy thing coming to attack her and she was going to fight back. She lunged at me and all I could hear was that electrical current sparking out of that damn gun as she tried to hit me with it. She was all over the place, attacking trees, the tents. She even got one of the other kids by mistake. The kid went down like a sack of potatoes! She finally got me backed up against a tree and was about to zap me when Vickie came running up and stopped her. She told the girl what happened and got her to let me go. Then Vickie led me the rest of the way to the hospital and we sent one of the ambulance drivers to pick up Marty."

Jack asked him if Marty got scared.

"No. She was fine. Vickie says she's used to being near woods. Her parents have a couple acres of it behind their house and her and Marty used to play there when they were kids." He paused and took another couple swigs of beer. "I probably shouldn't be drinking this, what with the shot the docs gave me. But what the hell?"

Ben asked him what happened next.

"After the docs gave me the shot they went to work on the mask. They had to cut it in half to get it off. Shame, too. It really *did* look authentic."

Ben couldn't help smiling. "Authentic enough for a few kids in the woods, anyway."

Jack's eyebrows shot up. "Not only the kids," he said, "but a few of the neighbors around the woods, too. I was just getting home from The Crystal when Mavis told me she heard on the police scanner that 'Yellow Eyes' had attacked someone. From the sounds of it, the cops sent out half the force to check it out."

"That's rich!" Ben said, giving in to the chuckles. "I can only imagine what kind of story the cops got from the kids smoking the weed. They could have said they saw flying saucers and no one would have believed them."

"Thank God for that," Marcus replied with a grunt. "I sure as hell don't need any publicity. Vickie must be wondering about the last two dates already. I've got to get a handle on this thing before she starts asking too many questions." And he stared down at his beer, a worried look on his face.

Ben stopped smiling and watched his best friend. In spite of the telltale swelling, it was clear Magic was upset with the turn of events. Jack had also noticed the sudden change in demeanor and asked Marcus if he was all right.

"I'll be okay. I guess I was hoping for too much, that's all."

"You mean with your *gift*," Jack said, taking the pipe from his mouth and pointing it at him. "You thought you'd be safe from it for a day, didn't you?"

Marcus nodded, confirming it. "I was worried more about going to the zoo tomorrow..." And his voiced trailed off as though he was thinking about something. He spoke again a second later, in a whisper. "Maybe I should call her and break the date. If something else happens, she's gonna be suspicious as hell."

Ben glanced over at Jack and saw his own worry reflected in his face. Magic was running scared and was considering getting out before he got in too deep.

Jack took the pipe from his mouth and slowly tapped the ashes into the tray in front of him. "Is that what you want, Magic? To stop seeing her?"

"Well, no...not really."

Ben could see the hesitation in Magic's expression and knew exactly what Jack was up to. Jack never openly offered advice. His approach was much more subtle.

"It seems to me," Jack said, sitting back and narrowing his eyes like he was giving it some thought, "that if you really liked the girl, you wouldn't give up on her."

"But I'm not giving up on her!" Marcus protested. "I'm only trying to save her from getting hurt!"

Ben decided it was time to add his two cents. "Maybe she's not as frail as you think she is. Maybe she likes having a boyfriend who has adventures."

Marcus shot him an annoyed glare. "Adventures? You mean like catching myself on fire and throwing spaghetti on her? No one in their right mind would *enjoy* something like that."

"So maybe she's not in her right mind," Ben said, trying to stifle the snicker. He felt a kick under the table as Magic let him have it in the shin.

"The point is this..." Jack said, giving them both a fatherly nod. "You shouldn't be making that decision for her. If she's willing to stick it out a little while longer, then you should respect her judgment and stay with it, too. Don't give up so soon."

Ben watched Magic think about it.

"What if something else happens?" Marcus asked.

"You mean *when* something else happens, don't you?" Ben reminded him.

"Yeah. So what do I do when the next thing happens? Lie to her and tell her it's only a coincidence? At this rate that excuse isn't going to last long."

Jack leaned forward, resting his elbows on the table. "A little white lie now and then can't hurt, especially when it comes to matters of the heart. Trust your own good sense and instincts. If it's not meant to be, you'll know soon enough. This way you can give it the 'old college try' before walking away. Don't you think she's worth at least that?"

Ben watched as Magic deliberated on it. If nothing else, Jack's logic was always impeccable, and hard to argue with. He was a master at the soft sell and right now the recipient of the sale was considering it.

"Okay," Marcus said with an uncertain look in his eyes. "I'll give it another try. I do owe her that much."

Ben patted him on the back. "Great! Now all you have to do is stay away from any squids and lizards at the zoo and you should be fine."

"I'll take along some anti-lizard repellant," Marcus said, his smile returning. "Either that or I'll get myself one of those stun guns. That thing looked like it could take down an elephant."

The three of them got back to their conversation and changed the subject Jack suggested they get in a little dart practice before the next game so they grabbed a couple of extra sets Terry kept behind the bar and headed to one of the machines against the back wall. They played two games and by the time they adjourned an hour and a half later, Magic seemed like his old self again.

A little while later, as Ben drove home, he couldn't help thinking that Magic was in for a hard ride. His *moments* were infamous and unleashing such a phenomenon at a place inhabited by wild animals, even ones behind bars, was tempting fate. He hoped it didn't end up in a situation where a stun gun or even lizard repellant would be necessary.

But with Magic's *moments*, anything was possible.

Yellow Eyes, no less!

What next? The Abominable Snowman?

CHAPTER FIVE

A gentle breeze was blowing through the open windows as Marcus drove his car into the parking lot of Vickie's apartment house. The day was warm and the sky was clear without any hint of cloud cover. The forecast had been for temperatures in the 70s and low humidity, so it looked like it was going to be a fine day.

Talking to Ben and Jack about it had helped, the same as it always did. What's more, he knew they were right. He was wrong to give up too soon. So far she hadn't badgered him with a lot of questions about what had happened on the first two dates. It was reasonable to assume she'd merely chalked it up as simple bad luck.

There was another good reason for not giving up.

The kiss. The one and only kiss he'd gotten from her.

It was more than sensual; it was like a prelude to a beautiful concerto, the first sweet notes of an allegro and the musical promise of things to come. He couldn't give up before he heard the entire concerto. He'd have to keep trying. Besides, it might be his last chance for happiness. With something that important riding on the outcome it demanded his best effort. He was going to stick it out, at least as long as she did and no matter what happened.

He knew what he was letting himself in for. It was the same as challenging his condition to a duel, daring it to show itself so he could defend against it and possibly defend it as well. After all, it was part of him. Whoever chose to share his life would have to accept that fact. They'd also have to deal with living through more than an occasional disaster or catastrophe. It was better to know now if she didn't have the courage or stamina to put up with such frequent calamities. Either way, he could accept it and walk away with a clear conscious, knowing he'd done everything possible in his quest for a life mate. And with any luck, he could walk away before experiencing the loss that came with falling in love with someone inaccessible, a blow that would leave definite psychological scars.

He saw Vickie standing near the back entrance with someone. As he drove nearer he could see the man clearer. He was short and appeared to be in his mid-forties and was wearing a faded, blue coverall. The two of them were talking like old friends but as soon as Marcus drove up the man stopped smiling, gave him a cold, angry glare and went back inside. Vickie waved to Marcus and went over to the passenger side to get in. She was wearing jeans, a white, short sleeve tee shirt and had a light blue sweater dangling from her shoulders. Her hair was down and there was a blue bow tying part of it up in the back. He waited until she was inside the car and asked her who the man was.

"He's a friend of mine," she said, leaning across the seat and giving him a kiss on the cheek. The unexpected affection caused him to flush red and he was glad he had on a pair of sunglasses so she couldn't see it.

"His name is Sanun," she said, moving back over to her side of the seat. "He also happens to be the building manager."

As she pulled away, he could detect a new perfume. The fragrance was barely detectable and gave a seductive hint at things to come. He smiled and headed the car back out onto the street. The interstate was only a few blocks away and as he pulled out onto the ramp, he tried to get a conversation going. It was a twenty mile ride to the zoo in Mayer and it would give him a chance to feel her out about the previous night's mishap. She was leaning against the door, looking out the window and humming. Her hair was blowing in the wind and he found himself envisioning the same fantasy about dancing with her, his face buried in her hair. But this time the image was enhanced by her presence, only two feet away. He recognized the song she was humming and smiled. It was one from the CD she gave him.

"I know that song," he told her.

She smiled back at him. "Then you've been listening to the CD I gave you?"

Her voice was filled with enthusiasm and he felt himself drawn to it. "I'll bet I've played it ten times already," he told her. "I'm thinking about putting a CD player in my car so I can hear it on the way to work. Uh, speaking of my car, I wanted to apologize again for the predicament last night with the mask. I had no idea it was made of latex."

"No need to apologize," she said. "That could have happened to anyone."

"That was nice of your sister to come pick you and Marty up at the hospital," he said, trying to make sure he worded it carefully. "I hope it didn't scare Marty too bad."

"Oh, no. She was fine. As a matter of fact, she thinks you're wonderful. She was telling my sister all about you on the way home."

Uh-oh, he thought. He cleared his throat and tried not to show any fear in his voice. "Really? What was she telling her?"

She moved across the seat and wrapped her arm around his. "Marty told her what a sweet person you were and how funny you were. Marty was quite taken with you. She's very shy and never had a man pay so much attention to her before. To tell the truth, I was getting a little jealous there for a while."

He leaned his head against hers and brushed his face against her hair. "No need to be. I only wanted her to feel more comfortable around me. I don't think I made much of a first impression."

"Well, she's impressed now. She thinks you're terrific. She also told my sister how the kids at the high school think you're 'awesome' as Marty puts it. That's hard to believe."

"I don't know," he said, teasing her. "Maybe I am awesome."

"I didn't mean that," she said, squeezing his arm. "I'm just surprised the kids think so highly of you. They're teenagers. They're supposed to hate all adults. You must have a real connection with them."

He wanted to tell her truth, that the kids knew his reputation and anyone causing regular mayhem was bound to enjoy elevated stature among the local youth. Being infamous sometimes had its advantages, too.

"I wish I could get Marty to open up more with other kids her age, the way she did with you," she said. "My niece is always talking about all the fun she has at your bowling alley and I know Marty wants to go."

"Why doesn't she go with your niece, then?"

"Stephanie, that's my niece, is eighteen, two years older than Marty. She's asked Marty to go with her lots of times but Marty doesn't feel comfortable around Stephanie's friends. I guess it's the age difference and Marty's always been so shy. But I know she's dying to go. There's a boy she likes that bowls there a lot."

"What's his name?" he asked her. "Maybe I know him."

"Tim. I think his last name is Prescott or Prentiss…"

"Tim Prentiss?"

"Yeah. That sounds like it. Why? Do you know him?"

"Sure. Tim's a regular on one of our senior leagues. He's good, too. Went to state tournament last year and had a respectable showing. He and his friends are always up at The Crystal." Marcus paused as an idea formed in his mind. With a little careful planning, it could work to his advantage. It would be a way to get Vickie to visit him at The Crystal and do a favor for Marty, whom he'd developed a kinship towards in the last few days. Being an outcast was never easy for anyone, whether it was because you were painfully shy or the town klutz. "You said Marty wouldn't bowl with your niece. Do you think she'd bowl if you went with her?"

"I'm sure she would. Why? What did you have in mind?"

He gave her the basics of his idea. "But I'm going to need your help with it. Marty can't know it's a set up. Otherwise she'll bolt faster than a streak of lightning. Do you think you can keep it a secret and still talk her into going?"

"Are you kidding? She'd do it in a heartbeat. Especially when I tell her that you've invited her personally." She then squeezed his arm and smiled up at him. "Now, let's get down to business. Tell me everything."

They spent the rest of the ride discussing the details and by the time he pulled into the zoo parking lot a little while later, they'd worked out a pretty good plan. As he pulled the car into an empty spot next the perimeter fence, he thought about how good it felt to have someone in his life again. Someone not only to talk to but be with and do things together with. Living alone wasn't easy. Dining alone, going to movies by yourself and never having anyone to share things had its consequences. It sometimes forced you into becoming an island onto yourself, trying to shut out the rest of the world while walking through it. Loneliness was a hard road and a rocky one, too. But he still had hope. Hope that someday soon he'd be leaving that road. Heading for a more populated road. One with music, dancing and love. Maybe even an occasional concerto now and then.

"What are you smiling at?"

He took the keys from the ignition and turned to her. "Oh, nothing. I was just thinking how long it's been since I've been here. I wonder if they have the same animals they had when I was a kid."

"Only one way to find out," she said. "Come on!"

They exited the car and as they walked across the lot towards the entrance, she took hold of his hand. He suddenly felt like a teenager again and couldn't help but smile. There was a family of six, two adults and four children, coming back through the main gate. The parents looked whipped but the kids were all carrying cartoon balloons and had dirty but happy faces. As the kids passed, the two oldest, boys around nine and ten, began pointing at Marcus and Vickie and snickering. The boys then began making kissing noises, causing the two youngest children to laugh.

"I think they're making fun of us," Vickie whispered, squeezing Marcus's hand tighter.

"I think you're right," he said, happy about the whole thing.

He ushered her to the entrance, paid for the tickets and followed her into the park. The smell of sawdust and mixture of flower scents immediately propelled him back to his childhood. So many times as a child he'd accompanied his parents there, taking in the same sights and sounds. It was like stepping into a time machine and going back twenty years. The rest of the world had moved on but here, time had stood still.

"Is it just as you remembered it?" she asked him.

"It's incredible," he whispered, still in a kind of daze. "It's like stepping into a time machine. Even the trees and shrubs look the same!"

She laughed and he was jarred back to reality.

"What?" he said, not sure what she was laughing at. "Did that sound childish or something?"

"Yes," she said, grabbing his arm and pressing her body against him. "And I love you for it."

He smiled with pride and led her down the path to the first exhibits. Yep. It was going to be a good date, all right. He could almost feel it.

They talked and walked along, stopping to view every exhibit. They saw a variety of animals, including llamas, giraffes and gazelles and with each new site she responded with a childlike excitement. It was as though she was seeing the zoo for the first time and he ended up sharing her enthusiasm. For the next hour he took it all in, enjoying both the exhibits and conversation. He also learned quite a bit about her.

Her family was originally from Columbus but her father relocated the family to Kirklin two years earlier. He thought a small town would be a better influence on his youngest daughter, Marty, and because it was closer to his oldest daughter in nearby Barbertown. Vickie had attended OSU for two years but dropped out after she and Greg, her ex-boyfriend, decided to get married. But the relationship ended before the union took place.

She had another older brother who lived in Cleveland but said the family didn't have much contact with him. She didn't elaborate so he assumed it was a sore subject. Her older sister Karen lived in Barbertown with her sixteen-year-old daughter Stephanie. Karen had gotten pregnant when she was fifteen and the father had skipped town to avoid any responsibility for the child. Because of that, Vickie's parents, especially her father, had become very protective of his two youngest daughters, almost to the point of obsession. The man kept close tabs on both girls and didn't let them make any kind of decisions about their lives without his approval first.

As Marcus heard this particular revelation, he couldn't help wondering how her father would react to hearing one of his daughters was going out with *The Kirklin Klutz*. Anyone that protective wouldn't want one of his offspring hanging out with an "accident" magnet.

He decided to come right out and ask her. "Does your father know you've been going out with me?"

"No. I've kind of been keeping that a secret. I made Marty promise not to tell either. You don't mind, do you?"

"No, no. Of course not," he said, relieved. Then another question came to mind. Why *didn't* she tell her father about him? They'd just reached the monkey house and he stopped with her on the front steps. "Um, is there a particular reason you didn't tell him about me? I mean, do you think he might not approve of you going out with someone like me? You know…someone who runs a bowling alley?" He was careful how he worded it, hoping to make it sound like an innocent inquiry.

"Don't worry," she replied, grabbing on to his arm and giving it a squeeze. "My father's not that provincial. But he did drool a bit when he found out what Greg did for a living."

"And what's that?"

"He's a junior executive for a corporation based in Columbus."

She turned and went into the building and he followed behind her, wanting to hear more. From the sounds of it, no one in her family knew who he was and he hoped to keep it that way.

At least for a while.

The exhibit was nothing more than one large room containing cages on both sides. There was a waist-high metal observation bar that extended out from the cages and ran down along both sides of the exhibit. In the middle of the room was a round, bricked off area containing various jungle, type plants and a tree whose branches reached almost to the ceiling. Several wooden benches sat up against the bricked-in foliage area but at present all were empty. There were only six or seven people in the exhibit, including a man and woman standing near the orangutan cages with their two boys, the oldest one about twelve and the younger one approximately five.

Marcus and Vickie walked past the family and headed down to the look at the spider monkeys, which she said were her favorites. There were four or five of the animals hanging and swinging from the tree limbs inside the cage and Vickie quickly became engrossed with their antics. He watched with her, waiting for an opportune time to bring up the subject of her ex-boyfriend again.

"So, I take it your father liked your boyfriend."

"Greg?" she asked. "Oh, sure. Dad *loved* him. Greg's the type of person who'll go far in the corporate world. He knows how to impress people and my father was no exception. However, my mother saw right through him."

"What do you mean?"

She sighed and leaned against the observation bar. "Greg never loved me. My mom and I both saw it. He thought of me as one of his possessions—like his car or his collection of medieval swords. But he was what my dad thought I needed. Someone with a good job and conservative, like he is."

"Conservative?" he asked, not liking the sound of it.

"Yeah. Dad's made a very comfortable and structured life for him and Mom. He's a successful investment analyst and believes in neatness. You know, the marriage, big house, nice car and job dream. He thought Greg was all those things and wanted me to be secure. The only time I saw my dad say anything disapproving about Greg was when he found out Greg and I were sleeping together. I thought Dad would go through the roof. He doesn't believe in pre-marital sex and even though Greg and I were engaged at the time, he still didn't approve. He never got over the shock of my older sister getting pregnant and he's determined something like that doesn't happen to me or Marty."

Uh-oh, Marcus thought. *There goes my chance of spending the night.* "But how did your father find out about it?"

"Well, it's partly my own fault," she said, rolling her eyes in exasperation. "He drove by Greg's place one morning very early and saw my car parked in the drive. He never said anything to Greg about it but that night he gave me and Marty a four-hour lecture on promiscuity. Poor Marty. You should have seen her face. She's only kissed a boy once and that was in the fourth grade and on a dare. Hearing my father talk graphically about sex almost killed her."

"Didn't your parents ever have the sex talk with either of you?" he asked, at the same time thinking how lucky he was to have a parking lot behind his apartment building, not in plain sight from the street.

"My mom did when I was about twelve. And I know she's talked to Marty, too. But the talks weren't very helpful. Mom didn't really tell me anything, just kept bringing up the love thing, only having sex with someone you love. The whole discussion lasted a total of five minutes and it made her so uncomfortable that we never talked about it again. I had to go to my older sister to learn anything really useful. My mom comes from a generation that didn't like to talk about things like that." She paused and grinned. "But that day with my dad, he was so determined to make his point that he completely transcended the generation gap. He went into great detail about men's and women's anatomies and how men were only out for one thing. He didn't pull any punches about it, either. He would have made a great sex ed. teacher. He graphically described every aspect of having sex and left absolutely nothing out. I thought Marty was going to faint at one point. I wanted to laugh but was so shocked that I was left speechless. He's never done anything like that before."

More trouble brewing, Marcus thought to himself. Any man who would overcome his puritanical beliefs to protect his daughters wouldn't approve of someone who was known as a "The Town Menace."

"I suppose he was only trying to protect you," he told her, not sure how to respond to her candor.

She leaned closer, brushing up against his chest suggestively. "Why?" she whispered. "Do I need protection from you or are your intentions 'honorable' as my father would say?" She then smiled up at him provocatively. "According to my father, all men have only one thing on their minds. Is that true?"

He could feel his face turn red and suddenly felt like a kid who'd been caught with his hand in the cookie jar. "Uh…" he said, scrambling to think of a response. "My intentions?"

"I was only kidding," she said, laughing and pulling at his sleeve. "Come on. Let's go look at the rest of the monkeys."

He walked with her over to the other side of the room, thankful for the break while he caught his breath and gathered his wits. He would have to think carefully before asking any more questions of that kind.

She stopped in front of the gorilla cage and turned to him. "I know I sound a little silly, talking that way about sex."

"Oh, I don't think talking sex is silly," he said, immediately feeling stupid at the way he worded it. "I mean, it's nice that you can be open about it with your father."

"But that's just it," she said, a look of regret showing in her expression. "My father is open about it, but only as far as it pertains to us avoiding pregnancy. He doesn't understand that other things can complicate matters. Things like love. He's forgotten what it's like to be young and in love. He thinks that by holding on to Marty and me he can control our feelings, too. But he's gotta let us both go. To live our own lives and make our own mistakes. He has to learn that there are some things you can't control, no matter how much you try."

No shit, he thought to himself. Some things were next to impossible to control, as the last ten years had shown him.

"I didn't mean to shock you with all that talk about my father," she said.

He told her he wasn't shocked, only a bit surprised at her honesty. "Most of the women I've gone out with don't reveal things that personal."

"Why not?" she said, giving him a sexy smile. "Don't you get personal with them?" And once again she rubbed up against him provocatively.

"Uh…well…" he said, unbuttoning the top button of his shirt and suddenly feeling warm. "It's not that I don't like getting personal…It's just that…"

She giggled and reached up and gave him an innocent kiss on the cheek. "Don't worry," she whispered. "I was only playing with you. I like trying out my seduction routine every once in a while to make sure it still works."

It works all right, he thought, collecting himself. And how!

"I do it to all the guys I go out with," she said and then she rolled her eyes like she was exasperated. "That is…for the meager few dates I've been on since breaking up with Greg."

"So…" he said, trying to think of a nice way to put it. "You purposely…uh…"

"Try turning my dates on?" she said. "Yep. It's what I call my own personal 'character test.' When I first did it a few minutes ago, I expected you to proposition me or at least try and kiss me. That's what most guys I go out with end up doing. But you acted like such a gentleman that I wasn't sure you were for real. So I decided to try it again, to find out."

Oh, he thought, realizing that he'd been playing into her hands.

"It may sound childish," she said, acting apologetic. "But after hearing my father grill me for years, telling me how every man out there is only trying to get into my pants, it got me wondering."

"I've no doubt," he said, trying not to smile.

"So now I conduct my own little survey with guys I go out with. It's a quick way to find out where I stand with them."

"But you didn't do it the first two times we went out."

"No," she said, staring at him, like she was thinking hard about something. "But you were different. You didn't come on to me right away like most of the other guys do. All you did was kiss me. So I began to wonder if you were even interested in me at all."

"Oh…I was interested…" he said.

She put her finger on his lips and gave him a smile. "I know that now," she whispered. "That's why I gave you my little test."

"And did I pass?" he asked her, quite interested in the answer.

She took his hand and prompted him to walk with her. "Yes you did," she said, leading him down along the observation bar. "You proved that you were a perfect gentleman and that your intentions were quite 'honorable.' In other words, my father would definitely approve of you." She stopped and directed her attention back to the monkeys, which was only fitting.

Because he now felt like one.

In one fell swoop he'd ruined any chances of taking her home and possibly put an end to any future plans as well. There was no way now that he could suggest she accompany him back to his apartment. It would be out of character for him. He'd passed her test.

He was a gentleman.

He sighed inwardly and tried to console himself. Maybe it was for the best. It didn't sound like her father would be the type to approve of a boyfriend with his history, anyhow.

"Marcus?" she said, turning to him. "You looked worried about something. I didn't scare you off, by any chance, did I?"

"No," he told her, knowing that if she knew the truth, it would be *her* that was scared off. He decided to keep the tone light and not make her suspicious. "I didn't mind your little test at all. But now I wish I'd flunked it. Then at least I would have gotten a kiss."

"Then let me make it up to you," she said, grabbing on to the front of his shirt and pulling him down to her.

His heart danced with happiness and he closed his eyes, waiting for the soft touch of her lips. But once again he was interrupted, as something pulled hard on his pant leg.

"S'cuse me, mister."

Marcus glanced down to a dirty, but angelic face staring up at him. It was the little boy he'd seen earlier standing with his parents. He was hanging on to the observation bar with one arm, his feet dangling underneath him.

"Are you gonna kiss her, mister?" the angel face asked him.

Marcus grinned at him. "As a matter of fact, I was."

Vickie bent down to the boy and asked him his name.

The boy got down from the bar and stood up straight with pride. "My name is George Alexander Martin."

"Hi there, George Alexander Martin. My name is Vickie. Do you like the monkeys?"

The boy's face lit up with excitement. "Yeah, they're funny. They was throwing stuff at my big brother, Rob. Rob's mean to me sometimes." George grabbed on to the railing with one arm; swinging back and forth and making Marcus wonder if he wasn't part monkey, too.

"I'm glad they throwed stuff at Rob," George said. "Rob throws stuff at me sometimes and I don't like it!" Then George smiled at Vickie. "You're pretty. Are you gonna kiss that man?" And the boy pointed accusingly up at Marcus.

"Yes I am," she said.

"Why?" George asked.

"Because he's cute. But I think you're cute, too."

"No kiddin'?" George said, giggling like crazy. "Would you kiss me?"

Before Vickie could answer, the older boy, Rob, came walking up and grabbed George boy by the arm.

"Come on, George!" he grumbled. "You know you're not supposed to talk to strangers!" And he emphasized "strangers," making it sound like a dirty word.

Marcus observed the older boy's expression. It was hard and cruel and reminded him of some of the meaner kids he used to see in grade school. The boy started pulling hard at George's arm, jerking him away from the bar and yelling at him to mind.

"I don't wanna go," George whined, trying to pull away from his brother's grasp.

"Damn it, George! Come on!" the older boy said, pulling harder on George's arm. "If you don't get movin', I'm gonna get Dad to spank you good!"

As soon as George heard the word "spank" he stopped struggling and obeyed his older brother. As he was being led away, George turned and waved to Vickie.

"Byeaa," he said, giving her a sad smile. "I gotta go now." And then his brother jerked his arm again, making him turn back around and follow.

"Oh, Marcus," Vickie whispered. "Look at his little face. I just want to scoop him up and take him home with me."

Marcus watched as the older boy steered George back to his father, a large man standing next to a thin, tired looking woman wearing a wrinkled print dress. Both parents looked about forty and the man was five feet ten or eleven inches and resembled some of the construction workers that would frequent The Point, right down to the black jeans and leather work boots. There was a leather belt adorned with a large buckle around his waist that was partially hidden by the man's stomach, hanging over it. As the older brother approached with George, the father leaned down and opened up his hand menacingly, threatening to hit his younger son. George cowered down in fear and whimpered as he put his hands over his head.

"I'll be good," the boy whispered to his father. "I pwomise!"

As Marcus saw the display, he fought off the urge to go over and deck the man, making him cower down as George had. Watching parents correct their children wasn't a new sight to him. He'd sometimes witness the same thing at The Crystal and as a rule he didn't meddle unless necessary. Most parents didn't take kindly to advice on how to discipline their kids. The only time he'd interfered was when a man slugged his teenage son in the jaw for not listening to him during a tournament. The father then tried to hit his son again and it was only after engaging the man physically that Marcus was able to stop him. In the end the police got involved and the father was taken away and charged with assault. Marcus expected the wife and son to be relieved but they weren't. They were mad as hell, at him.

The wife called him a son of a bitch for interfering and threatened to sue him once she got her husband out of jail. The son wasn't vindictive but his humiliation seemed to magnify after his father was hauled away by the police. The whole experience made Marcus wary of interfering with domestic altercations. It was a combustible mix that was based on something completely unpredictable, extreme human emotions.

"Poor little George!" Vickie said. "How could his father be so cruel to him? All he was doing was talking to us."

Marcus tried to calm her down. "He's all right. His father didn't hit him. He only threatened—"

But she didn't stick around long enough to hear him finish the sentence. She stormed off across the floor towards George's family. Marcus chased after her, trying to stop her but it was no use. She'd gotten too much of a head start. By the time he reached her a few seconds later she was already giving George's father a piece of her mind.

"For your information," she yelled, shaking her finger at the man, "your son was only talking to us. He wasn't hurting anything. You didn't have to make him cry!"

"Who the hell are you?" the man grunted. At first his expression was angry but it quickly changed after he gave Vickie the once-over, eyeing her up and down and grinning lecherously.

"See something interesting, friend?" Marcus sneered sarcastically, glaring at the man angrily.

The smile disappeared from the guy's face and he directed his attention back to the monkeys. "I see monkeys," the man said, keeping one eye on Marcus. "That's all. Now leave us alone and mind your own business."

"This is our business," Vickie told the man. "You've got no right to treat your son like that."

George started crying softly and his mother bent down and shook him by his shoulders, telling him that he was bad to upset his father.

Marcus decided that he liked the mother about as much as her husband.

"You people have no right to interfere!" the woman said, standing back up and yelling at Marcus and Vickie. "How we raise our kids is our affair, not yours!"

The woman's voice must have struck a note with a few of the chimps, for a few seconds later both she and her husband were pelted with tiny objects resembling stones or food pellets. George pulled away from his mother and grabbed hold of the observation bar, grinning up at the site. The bombing finally stopped and the husband added his own two cents.

"That's right!" he said, acting indignant. "Mind your own damn business! You've got no right telling us how to discipline our kids!"

Vickie's response was immediate and angry. "Discipline is one thing! And hitting is another! I should report you to the authorities!"

Marcus expected the man to respond with anger at the threat. But he didn't. Instead he smiled licentiously at Vickie and gave her the once-over again.

That was all it took.

Marcus walked up to the man and stood toe to toe with him, getting directly into his face. "Mister," he said, narrowing his eyes and speaking through clenched teeth. "You ogle my girl like that again and you're gonna end up in the cage with those monkeys."

The man had forty pounds on him and was an inch taller, but Marcus knew that if it came to blows, he could take him. He continued to stare the man down, waiting for him to respond. He'd drawn the lines and only given the man two options. Either back down or fight. One or the other.

A flash of fear showed in the man's eyes and he took a step back and relaxed his posture a bit.

He was capitulating.

"Look," the guy said, acting apologetic. "I didn't mean to stare at your girl. I was only…"

But he never got to finish the thought. Just then something black came flying around at him, hitting him square in the jaw.

"Ow!" the guy yelled, throwing his hands up to his face.

Marcus jumped back and threw up his fists, thinking the man was trying to throw a cheap shot. But then the black object came around and hit the man in the face again and Marcus realized the guy wasn't trying to attack him after all. Instead, *he* was the one being attacked.

"Shit! That hurts!" the man cried as the black object hit him in the forehead. It retreated a second later, finally revealing what it was—

His wife's handbag.

"You we're ogling her?" the woman yelled, hitting her husband again. "Goddamn it, Hank! I told you next time I caught you doing that you'd pay for it!"

The blows came faster as the little woman released her disapproval across her husband's face. He threw his arms around his head, trying to ward off the worst of the blows. The woman began yelling again and the monkeys in the nearby cages started squawking in protest at the commotion. A few seconds later another volley of projectiles came hurtling towards the man, his wife and the older brother standing beside them.

Marcus grabbed Vickie by the arm to pull her away from the barrage. She leaned down and grabbed George's hand and the three of them stepped aside, out of the line of fire. George never took his eyes off the spectacle.

"What's the monkeys throwin'?" George asked them.

Marcus couldn't resist the temptation and bent down to him. "They're throwin' what they always throw at people they don't like."

"What's that?" George asked.

"Their turds."

George started laughing, let go of Vickie's hand and ran back over to the bar in front of his family. He grabbed it and began swinging like a little monkey himself as he watched the chimps wreak revenge on his family.

"Look at him," Vickie said, giggling. "He's having the time of his life."

"Why not?" Marcus agreed. "It's not every day you get to see your parents as targets in a shit storm."

They headed for the exit, the sound of shouts, pinging and George's laughter filling the room behind them. As they emerged out into the sunlight Vickie started laughing.

"Well, that was fun. Let's get going to the next exhibit and see what other trouble we can cause." And with that she hooked her arm through his and began leading him towards the next building down the way.

Hmm, he thought, sneaking a glance over at her smiling face. *She doesn't seem to mind a little adventure. Could be a good sign.*

She suddenly stopped walking and pulled at his arm.

"What is it?" he asked her.

"I just thought of something," she said. "What if that man would have started a fight with you?"

"Don't worry," he said, lacing his arm through hers and leading her down the path again. "I've taken on bigger guys than him. It pays to have a best friend who's a wrestler."

"You mean Ben?"

"Yeah. He placed second in the state tournament when he was a senior. My parents and I went to all of his matches."

"But you didn't wrestle," she said, making it more of a statement than a question.

"No. But I might as well have. Ben wasn't happy simply practicing with his teammates. He'd come home every night and practice on me, too. I had to learn to wrestle or get creamed." Not to mention that having a condition that sometimes pissed people off had also taught me how to defend myself, he thought. "My dad would act as referee," he told her. "He loved doing it."

"So why didn't you wrestle like Ben?"

He shrugged, thinking about it. "It wasn't my thing. I never cared for all the contact sport stuff, wrestling or football. I just like to watch it. In the four years Ben was in wrestling, Mom, Dad and I never missed one of his matches. We were his own personal rooting section."

"Didn't his parents go the matches?"

"No. His dad was always too busy and his mother said she couldn't take seeing someone beat up on Ben."

"No wonder Ben was close to your folks. They did more than his own parents would. At least my parents showed up to all my soccer and volleyball games."

Volleyball, he thought as he followed her towards the next building. Hmm. *There's volleyball net over at Kirklin park.* Maybe he could talk her into going one afternoon after work and giving him a few pointers. Nothing had happened to him that night he went to park with Marilyn. Maybe it would prove to be safe again.

They followed the main path, stopping now and then to enter the buildings and view the animals inside. The sunlight was bright and the day had turned out warm and comfortable. He didn't talk much, just nodded in agreement and listened to the sound of her voice as she commented on the various exhibits and made conversation. He was happy simply walking next to her and feeling her close. It was only after passing several animal enclosures a little while later that he realized he hadn't even noticed the inhabitants, or even seen them.

He'd only been looking at her.

As they approached the lion compound she began talking about her friend John again and his wife's battle with Alzheimer's.

"She was a teacher," she said. "And she used to keep in touch with some of her students. Even after she got sick, they still wrote to her. John said he would read her the letters over and over."

"But how could his wife understand the letters if she had Alzheimer's?"

Vickie stopped and turned to him. "I asked him that. He told me that even though it seemed like she wasn't there, he knew there was some part of her that understood what he was reading to her. Isn't that beautiful? Even her disease wouldn't stop him from trying to reach her. It must be wonderful to love someone so much that nothing can separate you, death, or even life, for that matter."

He didn't answer her. He just stared at her, moved by her compassion. She was different. She had the ability to see things most people couldn't or wouldn't. She had a passion inside of her that gave her an insight into people's feelings. She wouldn't merely scoff at a bold new belief or idea. She'd study it and try to understand it. And maybe…he thought…just maybe she would understand his own ideas. About his condition and who he thought was behind it.

"Marcus?" she asked. "Is something wrong?"

He searched her face, trying to figure out if she would believe him or not.

She smiled at him. "What is it? Do you want to tell me something?"

Yes, he thought to himself. More than anything in the world he wanted to tell her his theory about his parents. But something stopped him. It was too risky. There was still the chance that she might not believe him or worse yet, run away.

He couldn't do it. Not yet.

"Oh, nothing," he said, trying to think of another subject of conversation. "All this talk about teachers reminded me of my days at Kirklin High, that's all."

They got back to watching the lions. The cages were the two-sided kind with bars housed in a large building, allowing visitors viewing access both from the outside and inside. There were four Bengal tigers, all in separate cages and all four were busy ravaging some raw meat.

"Must be feeding time," Marcus observed, watching with fascination.

"Yech. That's disgusting," Vickie said. "Don't you think it's gross?"

"Not really. To tell the truth, I think it's kind of cool. It brings back fond memories."

"Of what?" she said, acting disgusted.

"The high school cafeteria for one thing. Especially when the football players and wrestlers were eating."

"Oh," she said. "You mean it's a guy thing."

"Not necessarily," he told her. "Our wrestling team had a girl on it and she could eat just like that."

She nudged in him in the arm and accused him of teasing her.

"No. I'm serious. We did have a girl wrestler. And she was pretty good, too." He leaned against the outer bar and thought of something else. "It also reminds me of spaghetti night at my house. There was this one time when Ben and I were about twelve. We made such a mess eating spaghetti that Mom made us take our plates and finish eating out in the back yard behind our apartment. Ben and I wanted to get back at her for exiling us outside so we proceeded to not only 'eat' the spaghetti, but also 'wear' it. We covered ourselves from head to toe with it."

"Did she get mad at you?"

"Nope. She got even. She took out the garden hose and sprayed us down. And once Dad saw her doing it, he helped her. He kept telling us afterward what a good idea it was and how all restaurants should offer the same service. That way you could get a meal and a bath at the same time. Mom went right along with Dad and told us she was going to send in the idea to one of those restaurant magazines."

Vickie laughed. "And did she?"

"She said she did but I think she was only saying that for my and Ben's benefit. She and Dad were always doing things like that."

"You were right about your parents," she said, tilting her head thoughtfully. "They were different, weren't they?"

"Oh, they weren't like that all the time, just sometimes. Didn't your family ever get a little crazy and do funny things like that?"

She sighed and leaned against the observation bar. "I wish. Dinners at our house were like some of those old prison movies. You know, where the inmates couldn't eat until the guards blew the whistle first."

"Oh, you're exaggerating," he said, not quite believing her.

"Oh yeah? Well if you don't believe me, just ask Marty. She used to call them forced food drills. Us kids would sit at the dining room table every night with our napkins in our laps and elbows off the table, acting like proper little ladies and gentlemen. And we weren't allowed to talk or make casual conversation while we were eating, either. It was almost puritanical. The closest thing to conversation was when my dad would tell us about his day at work." She paused and rolled her eyes sarcastically. "Let's just say that my dad's business isn't exactly exciting. More than once I almost fell asleep and ended up face down in my mashed potatoes."

He chuckled. "What about your mother? Didn't she talk at the dinner table?"

"Sure. But it was mostly to tell someone to pass the peas to somebody or stuff like that. She would also comment on Dad's stories, acting interested in them but I don't think she really was. She hardly ever talked about her own projects at the table."

"Oh. Does your mom work outside the home, too?"

"Kind of. She's a professional crafter. She makes crafts and sells them at shows. She's built it into a pretty good hobby, actually. Even my father was shocked to see Mom make a profit."

"That's great," he told her, observing the look of pride in her face as she talked about her mother's accomplishments.

"Marty helps Mom with the crafts, too," she said. "And she's really good at it. She loves to paint and draw and her art teacher at school is always telling her how good her stuff is. You should see some of the little paintings she does on the glass jar crafts she makes with Mom. They're beautiful." And as she said the word "beautiful" he heard the same word repeat in his head, about her.

They continued walking to the next attraction and up ahead the path forked off into two directions. They took the turn to the right, leading to the bears. It was an outer compound encircled by a large fence and moat to keep the animals and humans at a safe distance from one another. The habitat consisted of man-made caves and small pools of water, one of which was presently occupied by a large, white polar bear.

"He looks cool," Vickie said, nodding at the polar bear. "Marty would enjoy this. She says her biology teacher looked like a polar bear."

An image formed in Marcus's head. "Mr. Kloppenhurst?"

"Yeah. I think that's the name she used."

"I thought he retired years ago. I had him when I was in school, too."

"Marty's always talking about how he falls asleep during class. She said sometimes he even starts snoring and the kids all crack up laughing."

Marcus nodded, remembering the scenario. "It was the same with my class. And sometimes when he'd fall asleep, the kids would let all the animals out of their cages. We spent half the year chasing after gerbils and mice. The girls were always screaming."

"I'll bet that woke him up," Vickie said, seeming to enjoy the joke. "Marty also said that it was because of Mr. Kloppenhurst that all the locks were taken off the closet doors in school. There was some student a few years back that accidentally got locked up in the biology room closet after Kloppenhurst fell asleep. The poor kid had to spend all night in the dark with a bunch of biology specimens and a human skeleton." She shivered, like she trying to shake it off. "It's a wonder the poor kid didn't end up warped after something like that."

Marcus stopped smiling as he realized the kid she was talking about was him. His mind flashed back to the memory, ten years earlier. The biology closet episode had left an indelible mark on his heart. Not because he'd spent the night trapped in the dark. But because it was the same night he became convinced that his parents' spirits were behind his *moments*.

Being stuck in the closet was no picnic. But after some initial investigation and a great deal of inspection, he discovered that the skeleton was nothing more than molded plastic. The only other "specimens" locked up with him were a few dead butterflies encased in plastic and mounted on a small glass display box. The closet was dark, but roomy, and left him free to move around. After finding nothing more menacing than charts and boxes of microscope slides, he sat back and got comfortable. He created a makeshift bed from some anatomy charts and sang songs to keep himself occupied. He'd hoped that Mr. Kloppenhurst or someone walking by the classroom would hear him but as the night wore on, he knew that it was no use.

He continued singing but his thoughts finally drifted back to his parents and the despair returned. It had only been a month since their deaths and he was still feeling the loss. He started singing louder, trying to fight off the despondency. After a while, he started to hear someone singing with him. He knew he wasn't dreaming it. He was wide awake and could feel the cold closet floor beneath him. The voices became louder and gradually more distinguishable until he suddenly recognized them. It was them. His parents' voices, singing to him, just as they had when he was a little boy, cowering under his bed covers, frightened by the sounds of a raging storm. It really was them. Coming back, showing him that he wasn't alone. His heart burst with happiness and he sang along with them as the fear and desolation left him, floating away with the soft notes of his favorite songs. He fell asleep with the sounds of their voices, surrounding him, comforting him. They were still with him. He wouldn't have to face the rest of his life without them. He reemerged the next morning from the closet with a renewed determination and purpose, able to face his life again.

"Hey, there's the new dolphin section I read about in the paper," Vickie said, bringing him back from his thoughts. "Come on. Let's go see it." She took his hand and he walked with her down the path towards a large rectangular, concrete building twice as big as the monkey house. It had a small dome on the top and the sides were dotted with alcoves every few feet cut into the stone. The shadows darting out from the alcoves gave a surreal feeling to the structure and exhibit. There were two large holding pools on either side of the domed structure and in the front was a set of steps leading down into a lower level.

They decided to look at the lower part first and quickly headed down the steps. The temperature fell at least ten degrees as they entered a large room full of windowed enclosures housing various sea creatures. The water-filled enclosures all had topside access to the outside, allowing the sunlight to stream in through the water and cast shimmering reflections across the dark blue carpeted floor. It gave the impression of being inside a huge aquarium.

The room was dotted with fifteen to twenty people and others could be seen peering down into the water from the topside holding pools containing the sharks and porpoises, the sharks on one side of the building and the dolphins on the other side.

For the next half-hour he enjoyed not only the view and cool retreat of the exhibit but her company. They strolled around the room, examining the sea life and she read aloud from the signs above the exhibits, explaining details of each specimen. The only time he experienced any trepidation was when they approached the squid exhibit. His insides were still trying to recuperate from the calamari incident and the thought of seeing one of the creatures alive and up close made him queasy.

He managed to steer her past the glass window without much trouble and guided her over to the shark tanks a few yards away. But a few more people had come into the aquarium and were crowded around the viewing tank so they headed over to the other side of the room to see the dolphin display, which at present was empty of any sightseers.

As they approached the bar separating the viewing area from the tank, she let out an "oooh" of delight at the dolphins swimming effortlessly in the tank. "Isn't that lovely, Magic? Look at them swimming together."

He stared at her, a bit surprised. "That's the first time you called me Magic."

"I know," she said, acting unsure of herself, "but everyone else calls you that so I thought maybe I should, too."

He pulled her close, wrapping his arms around her waist. "I always hated my name when I was younger. But I really like it when you say it."

She hugged him back and leaned against his chest as she watched the exhibit. The silence and shimmering light from the tank lulled him into a state of tranquility. He could feel the slow and regular rhythm of her breathing and that sensation mixed with the view of the dolphins swimming in silent unison made him feel at peace.

"I wonder what they're thinking?" she whispered, her voice full of wonder.

"I dunno," he replied, smiling and laying his head down upon hers. She was so different from the other women he'd known. From the first minute they'd entered the zoo, she'd exhibited an exuberance and almost childlike enthusiasm that was contagious. He found himself experiencing it along with her, marveling at all the sights and sounds. She was like a fountain of youth that showered life and vitality upon anyone she was with. People were drawn to it. People like an elderly man named John.

Better yet, people like him.

"Look at that," she whispered. "They've got a baby."

He turned his attention back to the exhibit. Two full-grown dolphins were swimming together in a circle around the edge of the tank. The smaller of the two dolphins had a miniature version of herself swimming directly beside and in time with her. The little dolphin's tail was moving swiftly to keep up with his mother's pace. The larger dolphin, obviously the male, was gliding ahead of the mother and baby, its head moving back and forth periodically, surveying the water like a sentinel protecting his family. All three moved together, their body movements and strides mirroring each other in unison, as if moving as one. It was like watching a melody being played out but the motion was more dramatic because the absence of any sound.

"That's amazing," he said, thinking out loud. "Look how they swim in unison. It's like watching music."

She looked up at him, her eyes shining sadly and a look of sweet compassion on her face. "That's the most beautiful thing I've ever heard." She reached up and gently stroked his cheek. "Oh Marcus," she whispered. "You're such an incredibly romantic soul."

He couldn't stand it any more.

He leaned down and kissed her, the warmth of her lips sending him into sweet surrender. It was as though he was back in the closet again. Surrounded not by his parents' voices, singing softly to him but by her love. Wrapping him up like a warm blanket and whisking him away.

He no longer cared about the rest of the world. It didn't matter that she knew nothing of his "condition." He didn't care if it seemed hopeless. That was the future. This was now. And right now all he wanted was to lose himself, in her caress and kiss.

She moaned softly and he kissed her more passionately, wanting with all his heart to whisk her away with him. To a place somewhere far away. Where only their love for one another mattered. Where nothing and no one could touch them.

He wrapped his arms around her tighter and seemed to lose track of time and space, drawn away to a place he'd never been before but that seem strangely familiar. From somewhere far away he could hear someone singing. It was her, singing that same song from the CD she gave him. The soft notes of her voice surrounded him, lifting him up and floating him away. Other voices slowly drifted toward him. It was the sound of children laughing. The laughter suddenly got louder and a second later the warmth of her lips was taken away. He opened his eyes and saw her smiling at him.

"We're being observed," she said, darting her eyes to the right.

He looked over to where she was indicating. A group of about twenty people were laughing and staring, not at the dolphins, but at him. His face immediately flushed red and the people began clapping at his reaction. Vickie grabbed him by the hand and led him through the gathering. A couple of women "oohed" and "awed" as he passed them and a few of the men gave him hearty congratulations and pats on the back. A few remarks like "this must be a new exhibit they didn't tell us about" and "it's even better than the dolphins" followed them as they made their way to the exit. A few of the children scampered after them, making mock kissing noises as he and Vickie headed back up the stairs.

They exited the aquarium and continued down the main path towards the tourist center. He waited for her to comment on what had happened and was relieved when she started talking about something else. He was still enjoying the fading sensation of the kiss and hoped to repeat the experience again later, this time without an audience. They stopped for lunch at a small cafeteria between the information center and the reptile house and he was relieved to find nothing even closely resembling calamari on the menu.

They enjoyed "gorilla" burgers, "lionized" potatoes, fries with cheese, and drank from cups with pictures of zoo animals on them. After lunch they browsed the gift shop and he offered to buy her something. She picked out a hair ornament with a tiny picture of a zebra on it. She asked him to clip it in her hair and he gladly obliged, enjoying the soft sensation of the curls against his fingers.

They started touring the facility again and spent the next hour viewing the reptile house and aviary. By three o'clock they'd seen everything but the largest animal exhibits, namely the giraffes and elephants, and set out for them. They had to double back on the same path, past the monkey house to where the main path branched off towards the back of the zoo, right near the new addition. There was a popcorn cart near the dolphin and shark house so they stopped to buy a large box and two sodas from the vendor, a man who had a long, thin moustache and looked like Luigi from Super Mario Brothers. The cart was one of the old time type, painted with red and white stripes resembling a barber pole. It was on wheels and about the size of a Volkswagen. All four sides had large glass windows, displaying the vendor's wares and the air was filled with the smell of fresh popped corn.

From there the path turned to blacktop and veered left, up a hill and past a small train crossing. The train circumvented the park and gave rides to the patrons. They boarded the train at the crossing and rode it around the park, getting off at the stop near the building housing the elephants. They'd finished most of the popcorn and she commented on how good it tasted.

"It does," he told her, grabbing another handful from the box as they walked along. "Maybe it's the memories that go along with it that make it so good, recollections of being at the zoo or in the park. I always loved smelling the popcorn cooking. I even bought a miniature version of one of those carts for The Crystal. The customers sure seem to like it."

"I can't wait to see the place Friday night, when I bring Marty," she said, handing him the popcorn box.

The late afternoon air had warmed up and she took off her sweater and draped it over her back, tying the arms together around her neck. He could once again detect the scent of her perfume and smiled, enjoying both it and the popcorn.

They walked over to the large building housing the elephants. It was almost as large as the new aquarium and had massive cages cut into the sides. Steel bars extended from the concrete foundation to almost the top of the building and from the thickness of the metal, it looked like it could even contain King Kong.

The massive pachyderms lumbered around behind the bars, sometimes in what looked like slow motion from the sluggish movements of their bodies. At the back of the building was a circular enclosure roped off from the public. Thirty or so people were standing at the ropes, watching the zoo personnel work with the elephants. Two men were in the process of leading one of the mammoth creatures back into the building and two others were hosing down a second elephant that was about 2/3 the size of the first elephant. A man dressed in a zoo personnel uniform was standing on a podium near the building, making an announcement.

"Mike and Ted, two of our trainers are leading Timbor back to his cage now that's he's nice and clean," the man said into the mike. "And as you can all see, our head elephant trainer Stan, and his new assistant are in the process of giving Benji a nice wash down. Benji is a new addition to our zoo and even though he's only a little fellow, we're sure he's going to fit right in with the other elephants."

"If you can call an eight-foot elephant a little fellow," Marcus remarked.

"As you can see," the announcer said, continuing, "Stan is showing his helper the proper do's and don'ts to giving an elephant a bath. Don't forget to wash behind his ears, guys!"

The comment brought a flurry of laughter from the crowd as the two men bathed the so-called "little" elephant. The head trainer, Stan, ran water from a hose across the elephant's back while his assistant scrubbed the elephant with a wooden brush attached to a long stick which he would periodically dip into a big tub of water next to his feet. The elephant was held in place by a large metal chain wrapped around his front, right foot. The other end of the chain was hooked around a round metal object resembling an anchor chain hold from a ship.

Marcus helped Vickie finish the last of the popcorn and drinks as they watched the elephant show with the other patrons. After the men finished the job, the announcer spoke again.

"And now that he's done with his bath, our friend Benji is ready for his afternoon nap. Stan and his crew are going to be giving some of Benji's friends a scrub down later this afternoon about five, so be sure to come back and catch the next show. Thanks, everyone!" The announcer then replaced the microphone on the podium and walked over to the back door of the building.

The crowd began dispensing and Vickie asked Marcus for his empty drink cup and popcorn box.

"It's all gone," he told her, showing her the empty box. "Too bad. I was going to offer some to Benji."

AND THE BULL SAVED ME

"You'd need a lot more than one box," she said. She took the empty containers over to a trash bin a few yards away.

He directed his attention back to the men attending the elephant. The older man, Stan, was walking over to a spigot in the middle of the enclosure to shut off the water. The assistant was bent over with his back to the elephant, unwrapping the chain from the animal's foot. He finished getting it undone and pulled the heavy chain across the concrete, out of the way of the animal's foot.

Marcus suddenly experienced an all-too-familiar tingle at the back of his neck. It was the same sensation he would get sometimes, right before one of his "accidents" happened. He continued to stare at the scene as the young man dragged the chain away from the elephant's foot. The animal took advantage of the situation and began to slowly back away from the young trainer.

Marcus just stood there, fascinated that such a large animal could move so silently or at least quiet enough so that the assistant didn't notice that he was losing control over his charge.

Vickie came walking back from the trash can and Marcus grabbed her hand, still not taking his eyes off the elephant. "Uh-oh," he muttered.

"What's wrong?" she asked him.

He wanted to explain, but there wasn't time. For at that very second, both trainers had suddenly noticed the elephant backing away. The younger assistant yelled at the animal to stop and Marcus wanted to laugh at the absurdity of yelling at an eight-foot elephant. But before he could even crack a smile, Benji reared back, trumpeted and broke into a run towards the rope enclosure. Marcus froze for a second, not wanting to believe it was happening again. But it was.

The elephant was charging...directly in his and Vickie's direction.

"Holy shit!" he said, squeezing Vickie's hand and pulling her away from the ropes. He managed to get out only one more word. "Run!"

She glanced back into the enclosure and let out a yelp. "Oh, my God!" She wasted no time, picked up her feet and joined him running. A second later there was a crash and shouts filling the air and Marcus knew that Benji had knocked down the posts holding the ropes, an idea that seemed absurd anyway. How could mere ropes hold back an animal that size to begin with? He and Vickie sped down the side of the building and onto the main path leading back to the monkey house, a couple hundred yards away. The sounds of Benji trumpeting and men's shouts filled the air behind them, although how far behind he wasn't sure and he wasn't about to stop to figure it out. He knew they could probably duck into the monkey house for safety and headed for it, never letting go of

Vickie's hand. But as they approached the building, a group of people came crowding out onto the front steps. The only way he and Vickie could enter would be to run down a couple of adults with their kids first. He pulled at Vickie's hand and steered her away from the building, yelling a warning over his shoulder to the people as they hurried past.

"Elephant!"

A flurry of shouts and screams ensued as the parents shoved their kids back into the safety of the monkey house. Marcus took a second to glance behind him. Benji was still in hot pursuit with the trainers chasing after him. To make matters worse, it appeared that the animal was picking up speed and gaining on them. He was surprised at how fast the animal could move. Vickie let out a gasp, signaling that she too, had noticed the elephant's progress. She began running faster and he knew it was probably the result of an adrenaline rush.

Having elephants chase you would do that, he thought with a smirk.

They fled down the path past the outside exhibits. A few of the animals had stopped grazing and were directing their attention towards the drama playing out on the midway. *And why not?* Marcus thought. Zoo animals were always being stared at to perform. Why not watch a couple of the observers for a change? Especially when they were being chased by one of their fellow inmates? They ran past the llama enclosure and one of the llamas bellowed at them. He wondered if the animal was trying to tell them something, like maybe "run faster." He glanced around, looking for a place they could duck out of the way but animals inhabited the entire area. Venturing into unknown habitats could be dangerous, especially if it was populated with lions, tigers or bears.

Oh my, he thought with a footnote.

His lungs were now starting to burn from exertion and his muscles ached with strain. Benji trumpeted again and Marcus could tell from the sound that the animal was getting closer with each step. The men's voices had multiplied, indicating that the trainers must have picked up help along the way.

"He's gaining!" Vickie shouted, glancing behind them. She then put some steam into her step and he opened his stride to keep up with her, hoping like hell they didn't trip or run into a dead end. They rushed past the lion cages and headed towards the bear compound, as the shouts of the men got louder. He wondered how close the elephant was and wanted to glance back but knew that even a second's delay could result in them both getting run over.

He got his answer a few seconds later when the elephant let out a roar that sounded WAY too close. Vickie suddenly started sprinting harder, probably motivated by the sound, and she moved a step or so in front of him, pulling hard at his hand to follow her. He picked up the pace again and they approached the large aquarium building at top speed. He tried to mirror her steps and she suddenly veered to the left as though she knew where she was going. The men's shouts followed them through the turn and he knew that Benji must have taken the same path.

As they approached the first alcove along the aquarium building, she half-jumped, half-leapt towards the opening, pulling him in with her. She threw herself against the wall, turning at the last second as he went crashing in after her, his body weight shoving her hard against the stone wall. She was facing him and he felt the sweater on her back partially cushion the impact. A few seconds later something gray lumbered past them, followed by what looked like six or seven men.

It appeared they had successfully diverted becoming elephant toe jam.

He pushed himself off her and asked her if she was all right. She was still out of breath and nodded her head yes. He peeked out of the alcove to where the men were still carrying on the chase. The elephant had slowed down and stopped next to the popcorn cart.

Vickie leaned out and joined him watching. "What's he doing?" she said, catching her breath.

He watched as Benji pushed his trunk against the front window of the cart. "If I didn't know better, I'd say he's trying to get some popcorn."

"Look at the trainers," Vickie said. "They look silly."

Marcus saw what she was talking about. The men were gathered around the elephant, trying to help one of the trainers get the chain around the animal's foot. But every time they got near it, the elephant would sidestep a bit and just miss being corralled.

Vickie giggled. "Looks like Benji is trying to teach the trainer a new dance."

The elephant began pushing his trunk against the side of popcorn cart, tipping the two front wheels a few feet up off the ground. A couple seconds later the popcorn vendor came flying out the side door of the cart and fell down onto the pavement. *No wonder*, Marcus thought. It wasn't every day that you had an elephant for a customer.

The vendor scrambled to his feet and slowly and carefully began to back up from his large customer. Benji paid no attention to the man. He just kept shoving the front of the cart, tipping it backward a little bit further with each push of his trunk. The cart teetered on the brink of no return and the men began shouting to each other to look out.

"There she blows!" Marcus whispered and a second later the cart tipped over backwards, crashing onto the blacktop. The sound of glass breaking filled the air as popcorn and boxes went spilling out all over the pavement, looking like a miniature snowstorm against the black path. Benji started pawing curiously at the cart contents with his trunk and the popcorn vendor shook his fist and cursed profusely at him.

"Good Lord," Vickie whispered. "Does he really think cussing at the poor animal is going to do any good?"

Marcus chuckled, enjoying the joke. "Not unless Benji's been hanging around a few bars and knows what those words mean. Now that's what I call one popcorn loving pachyderm!"

"Now that's something you don't see every day," Vickie said. "An elephant causing a circus instead of the other way around."

He stopped watching the elephant show and observed her, instead. She should have been upset or at the very least, scared. But she was neither. She was smiling.

Incredible.

A whistle sounded and they both peeked out of the alcove. It was the zoo train, making its trek around the park. The whistle blew again and Benji trumpeted, as if in reply. The men had managed to get part of the chain around his foot. But a moment later the elephant reared back and stepped out of it, trumpeting again to the train whistle. He then broke free and ran down the hill towards the train crossing.

"Uh-oh," Vickie said. "Maybe he thinks the train is talking to him."

The men rushed down the hill after their charge and the two men hefting the chain followed them, their faces red with exertion from dragging the heavy load. The train had entered the crossing and blocked the path just as Benji approached the tracks. He let out a couple more trumpets and the people aboard the open cars started clapping and waving with enthusiasm.

"Oh, my God!" Vickie said, laughing. "They think its part of a show! Now that's funny!"

"And that's just from one of the little fellows," Marcus added. "Just imagine what kind of show the full grown ones put on!"

The men had caught up to the elephant and because the train blocked Benji, it looked like the men would get their chance to corral the beast. But once again Benji swung around at the last minute and eluded capture.

"Reminds me of the Keystone Cops," Marcus remarked.

"Hey!" Vickie said. "Isn't that George's family?"

Marcus followed her gaze and saw George's father, mother and older brother walking toward the downed popcorn cart.

AND THE BULL SAVED ME

"Where's George?" Vickie whispered and Marcus scanned the area, but didn't see the boy anywhere in sight.

The older boy Rob bent over and picked up some of the popcorn from the ground. He began to put it in his mouth when his father abruptly slapped it out of the boy's hand and yelled at him not to eat it. The boy grimaced in pain and rubbed his hand against his pant leg.

"Oh, no!" Vickie exclaimed. "Here comes Benji!"

The elephant came running up the path from the train crossing and headed back over to the popcorn cart again. George's father was the first to notice the approaching visitor and let out a yell, turned to flee and almost ran over his wife and son, trying to get away. The wife glanced down at herself, straightened her dress and started bellowing at her husband to watch his big clumsy feet. The boy looked up and saw the elephant, gasped with fright and then turned and broke into a run behind his father. The mother still had her back to the elephant so she didn't yet know what was going on. She yelled at her husband and son, demanding to know where they were going. A second later Benji trumpeted and she spun around to the pachyderm approaching her at full steam.

Vickie gasped and Marcus felt a jolt of panic for the woman's plight. He started out of the alcove, to help her when a high-pitched shriek startled him. It was the woman, screaming in three digit decibels. He watched in amazement as the woman stood still, put her hands over her ears and screamed like a banshee. Benji stopped a few feet in front of her, raised his trunk, trumpeting at her in what sounded like a protest to the noise. It didn't seem to deter the woman, she kept screaming in a continuous drone. Benji suddenly decided that the popcorn wasn't worth having to put up with a screaming woman and slowly lumbered around her. He then trotted off down the same path that the husband and son had taken. The woman was still screaming and didn't seem to notice that the reason for her fright had departed.

"How do you like that?" Vickie grunted disapprovingly. "Her husband just ran off and left her there, to face the elephant alone!"

"She seems to be doing quite nicely," Marcus said, meaning it as a compliment to the woman's diligence.

"Holy cow!" Vickie said. "I think she's louder than the elephant!"

Marcus smiled. "Shit! She probably scared him more than he scared her."

Just then a whole crowd of men ran past the mother who had finally paused to take a breath from screaming. It looked like half the staff was now in on trying to catch the elephant and all of them looked beat. "I don't know," Marcus remarked. "After this, Benji's not the only one who's gonna need a nap."

"Look!" Vickie said, pointing to the popcorn cart. George was standing behind the downed cart. He had a box of popcorn in his hand and his face was red from laughing.

"Good for him!" Vickie said, her voice full of glee.

"Can't blame him for laughing," Marcus said. "Now, that's what I call 'elephants on parade!' It's better than going to a Disney film. Now all we need is a musical score in the background." Vickie started laughing and he looked down at her. Her face was flushed from smiling and eyes shined up at him.

"Benji didn't want to hurt anyone," she whispered. "He only wanted some popcorn, that's all." She gave him a look that made his heart ache. The sun was shining in and lit up her face and hair, giving them a soft aura and making her resemble one of the angels he'd seen in the story books his mother used to read him. He reached out and touched her cheek, wanting to make sure she was real. He suddenly remembered the kiss in the aquarium and longed for that feeling of sweet abandon again. He leaned in to kiss her and she closed her eyes in anticipation. As his lips met hers he experienced that same wonderful feeling of being surrounded by her love. She moaned softly and wrapped her arms around his neck, hugging him tight. He began to drift away into sensual oblivion when he heard a child's voice and felt something pull at his pants leg.

"Are you still kissin' that man?"

Marcus opened his eyes and glanced down. It was George. His face was a little dirtier than when they saw him that morning and he was still holding his box of popcorn.

Vickie bent down to him. "Hi, George. Are you having fun?"

The boy smiled so large that it took up most of his face. "Yup! I got to see effalunts and they was runnin' all over the place! One even chased Rob and my dad! It was funner even 'an those monkeys throwin' turds!"

"Come on," Vickie said, taking the boy's hand. "Let's get you back to your mom."

Marcus followed after them, mentally noting the kid's incredible timing. So far he was two for three in cutting him off from kissing Vickie.

"Mama!" George yelled, letting go of Vickie's hand and running up to his mother.

But his mother didn't seem to notice the boy. She was sitting cross-legged on the pavement, her face scrunched up in frustration as she rummaged through her purse. What looked like the rest of the contents of the purse were scattered on the ground around her.

"What's she looking for?" Vickie whispered to Marcus.

"I don't know. But I hope to hell it ain't a gun." He hurried in front of Vickie and bent down to where George was sitting next to his mother. "Pardon me, ma'am," he asked apprehensively. "Can I help you find what you're looking for?"

She stopped rummaging through her purse and looked up at him, bewildered. She blinked, acting like she was coming out of a trance. "What?" she murmured. "What did you say?"

He repeated the question.

"No, no thank you," she replied, starting to regain some of her composure. Her face was still red, and her voice was a little raspy, no doubt worn out from all the screaming. She got up and brushed herself off. "I was looking for my cell phone," she said, picking George up in her arms. "I can't seem to find it. I need to call my sister to come and get me out of this mad house!"

Vickie asked her where she lived and the woman replied that she lived in Barbertown.

"We're going that way," Vickie said, smiling sadly at Marcus. "We can give you a lift if you like."

"Sure," he said, trying to mask the disappointment as he realized they weren't going home alone.

"Oh, thank you!" the woman replied, acting relieved. "I just need to find my other son first..." She turned towards the path her husband and son had run down a few minutes earlier.

Marcus started to volunteer to go look for the boy when the woman let out a sigh of relief.

"Thank God!" she said, looking towards the path. "They finally caught the damn thing!"

Marcus glanced down the path with her and saw Benji. He had a large chain around his right foot and was being escorted by what looked like ten men. All the humans looked pooped and Benji seemed to have lost some of his former spunk. As the group went past, Marcus noticed George's dad and brother bringing up the end of the procession. The boy ran up to his mother and started talking excitedly, telling her how the elephant had chased him and his father. From the way the boy told the story, it was clear that he had the time of his life, running for his life. No doubt he was going to be the envy of his neighborhood. That is, if anyone even believed the story in the first place.

The mother hushed the boy and then directed her attention to his father, who looked more than a little tired himself. "I'm getting a ride home with these nice people," she told the man, her voice full of anger. "Me and the kids are going home. If you want to stay around here and play with the animals, well, that's your business!"

The man began to protest but she stuck her hand in front of his face, cutting him off. "I've had enough for one day!" she yelled. "And I don't need to look at your ugly face or spend one more minute with you!"

The man tried to reach out to her but she adjusted George in her arms and swung her purse at her husband with her free hand. He jumped back, barely avoiding getting hit.

"Stay away from me!" she grumbled at the man. "I'm going home. As for you…you can go straight to hell!" Then she turned heel and stomped off down the path, glancing back only to bark at her older son to follow her. As the boy ran after her, Vickie bent down and picked up the few items from the purse still scattered on the ground. Marcus bent down and helped her.

"I'll show them where your car is," she told him, juggling the items in her arms.

"I'll be right behind you," he said, standing up and pulling the keys from his pocket. "I'm gonna stay a minute and have a word with George's father." He handed her the keys and she took off after George's mother.

Well, that's that, Marcus thought to himself.

It seemed that the trip to the zoo was now over.

He went over to where George's father was still standing by the downed popcorn cart.

"I guess I really screwed up," the man said, acting sorry and kicking at the black top with the toe of his right shoe. "What am I gonna do? She's really mad at me!"

Marcus studied the man's face. There was nothing left of the angry expression he'd exhibited in the monkey house. Now all that remained was a hopeless, melancholy "hang dog" look. He almost felt sorry for the man.

"I wanna apologize for ogling your girl earlier," the guy said. "You had every right to be mad. I'd be pissed too, if someone was doing that to my wife." Then he paused and began kicking at the pavement with his shoe again. "Looks like I'm about to get my just desserts, though. Last time she got that mad I was in the doghouse for a month! Shit! This time I'll be lucky if she ever lets me out."

Marcus felt his sense of fair play kick in and decided to give the guy a break. "Don't worry about it," he said, patting the man on the back. "She'll get over it. It's nothing a dozen red roses and nice romantic evening away from the kids couldn't cure."

"Do you really think so?" the guy said, his face showing a flicker of hope.
"Sure. Works every time. Best thing for runaway elephants."
"Thanks, man," the father said, vigorously shaking Marcus's hand. "And thanks for giving my family a ride home, too."
Marcus told him that it was no problem.
"I'd better get cracking on lining up those roses and dinner," the man said, pulling something from his pocket.
Marcus smiled when he saw what it was. A cell phone. Probably the same one his wife had been searching so frantically for.
"I wonder which restaurant she'd like," the guy said.
"Try Richetti's," Marcus told him. "I hear they have great calamari." And as he heard himself say the word out loud, his stomach churned, remembering the entrée. The man thanked him again and Marcus took off for down the path towards the exit. With any luck he could get George's family home and still have time to take Vickie somewhere else, maybe for a drive up near the lake. He quickened his pace and began planning.

It was a little while later. Marcus sat behind the wheel of his car, taking another sip of a strawberry shake as he drove down the interstate. George was next to him; giggling as Vickie wiped chocolate ice cream from his mouth. In the back seat were George's mother and older brother, the brother eating an ice cream sundae and his mother enjoying a root beer float.

After they'd all left the zoo, George's mother had broken into tears and even George's hugs and angel face couldn't console her. Marcus felt sorry for the woman. She'd only wanted an outing for her kids. It wasn't her fault that she had the misfortune to pick a day when one of his *moments* would wreak havoc. He was forced to live with his affliction. Seeing others suffer through it was sometimes a difficult task.

He'd spotted a Tasti-Freeze not far from the zoo and pulled in, wanting to make amends for what the woman had suffered through. After a little coaxing and an offer to make it his treat, she finally agreed. The ice cream wouldn't take away the harrowing memories but what it did do was dry her tears and put her in a better mood.

Now the only problem left to deal with was George.

Because they wanted to give the mother a break, Marcus and Vickie had George sit in the front with them. But from the time the little tyke took his seat, it was clear that his mind was on only one thing besides his ice cream—

Vickie.

George immediately commanded all of her time and attention, asking her questions and giggling at everything she said. He then asked Vickie to hug him harder and inquired if she would like to be his girlfriend, Marcus knew it was silly to be jealous of a six-year-old. (George had volunteered his age after asking Vickie hers.) But in spite of the young age, George was smart enough to know a pretty girl when he saw one. To make matters worse, Vickie seemed completely taken in by the cherub face and adoring demeanor. But when George continually asked Vickie to kiss him on the cheek and she happily obliged, Marcus had to fight the urge to give kid a quick jab in the head with his elbow. He knew the move would not be taken well by either Vickie or George's mother, but the simple truth was that the pint-sized, future hormonally overzealous youngster was trying to beat his time.

He was thankful when Vickie finally took a break from doting on George and struck up a conversation with his mother. (She told them her name was Maggie.) He listened in as they discussed the pros and cons of living in Barbertown.

"We don't even have a movie theater," Maggie said. "We have to take the kids over to Kirklin when we want to see a movie."

Just then George offered Vickie a bite of his cone and Marcus had to smile at the kid's persistence. Vickie declined the offering and turned back around to face George's mother. She asked Maggie if she and the kids ever went bowling.

"I used to go when I was young. But I've never taken the kids."

"The reason I asked," Vickie said, leaning back across the seat, "is because Marcus runs Crystal Lanes in Kirklin. I've never been there myself, my sister and I are going Friday night, but everyone says it's a lot of fun. Maybe you should try it sometime."

The older boy, Rob, stopped eating his sundae and began prodding his mother to go.

"Me too, Momma," George said. "I wanna bowl too."

"But I don't own a ball," Maggie replied.

Marcus explained to her that she didn't need one. "We have racks of balls for every member of the family. We even have ones that George can use, it's our bumper bowling league." He told them about how the bumpers in the gutters allowed the little kids to bowl right alongside the older kids.

George giggled and turned to Vickie. "Could you show me how to do it?" he asked her.

"No. But Marcus can. He runs the bowling alley."

AND THE BULL SAVED ME

The little boy glanced up at Marcus, giving him a soulful look. "Is it hard?" the angel face asked him.

Marcus couldn't help but smile. The kid was irresistible. "No," he told George. "It's easy, and a lot of fun. We've got a lady there who loves to show kids how to bowl. Her name is Betsy."

"Is she pretty as her?" George asked, pointing to Vickie.

"She sure is. And she's a lot of fun, too. She'll teach you how to play games and sing songs…"

"They sing songs while they bowl?" Maggie said, acting surprised.

Marcus explained to her about the daycare center for the mother's league and how the league was always looking for new members. "It's in the mornings and the mothers not only bowl, they help organize fundraisers and parties for the kids. We're having a flea market in a couple weeks to raise funds to send the junior and senior league to tournaments. The mother's league only takes a couple hours out of your day and Betsy and her mom are great with the kids."

He watched her face in the rearview mirror as she considered it. "It sure sounds like fun," she said. "And I used to be a pretty good bowler in high school."

"We've also got junior leagues for Rob," Marcus added. "Those are held on Saturday mornings and the league is going to start in a couple weeks."

Rob started jabbering excitedly and his mother finally agreed to look into it.

George handed Vickie his cone, stood up on the seat and faced his mother. "Please, Mama. Can we go?"

Marcus glanced in the rearview mirror and saw Maggie smile tenderly at George. It was clear that she too, was used to being influenced by her youngest son's angelic face.

"Okay," she said. "I'll call first thing in the morning."

Both boys let out whoops of happiness and George sat down again on the seat. Vickie handed him his cone and he smiled up at her.

"Will you be there, too?"

Marcus marveled at the kid's tenacity. He was also thankful that the kid was only six. The tyke had moves most young men would envy.

"I wish I could see you bowl," Vickie told the boy, "but I have to work."

"But I wanted you to see me bowl!" George whined. Then he flashed that same cherub smile at her.

Vickie gave in to it, just as George's mother had. "Well, maybe I could stop by at lunch sometime," she told George. Then she asked Marcus what time the bumper bowling was held.

"During the mother's league we always keep a couple lanes open for the kids who want to bumper bowl," he told her. "That's from nine to twelve during the weekdays. You could come over and watch George bowl and then I could take you to lunch." He took a second and marveled at his own tenacity. He was using George's persuasive methods to get Vickie to agree to another date. George started pulling at Vickie's sweater sleeve, pleading with her to agree.

"I'd love to," she said, giving them both a smile.

"Oh, boy!" George added. "And maybe I could go to lunsh with you, too."

Not if I have anything to do with it, Marcus thought. The kid may be determined, but so was he. He wasn't going to share Vickie if he didn't have to, especially with a pint-sized Romeo. "We'll see," Marcus told the boy, making sure not to promise anything. "Besides, there's a lady there named Betsy who'll probably be busy feeding you some of her mom's famous chocolate chip cookies."

I'll make sure she does, he thought. "Everybody loves those cookies," he told George. "You sure wouldn't wanna miss out on that."

He watched George give it some serious thought. It was hard to be six and have to decide between chocolate chip cookies or the attention of a pretty girl.

"How big is them cookies?" George asked him.

Marcus smiled down at him. "They're huge. They're as big as a bowling ball!"

That was all it took. George's eyes lit up with glee and Marcus knew that he'd have no problem luring the little Casanova into staying with Betsy while he and Vickie snuck off to lunch.

Vickie was kept busy the rest of the trip, cleaning up George as he finished his cone. By the time they drove into Barberton a few minutes later, most of the cherub face was visible again.

"It's the next street over," Maggie told Marcus. He headed the car to the next intersection and turned where she indicated. The homes were older but well-kept, with lush, green lawns and landscaped borders and flowerbeds. She pointed to a two-story white house in the middle of the block with two elm trees in the front yard. There was a porch attached to the front with a hanging wooden swing. As they neared the house, he noticed George's dad standing in the yard, holding something in his arms. Marcus pulled into the driveway and smiled as George's father walked towards them.

He was carrying a big bouquet of roses.

Pretty damned impressive, Marcus thought. The man had not only obtained the flowers quickly but on a Sunday, to boot.

AND THE BULL SAVED ME

Maggie stepped out of the back seat and her husband walked up to her and began apologizing in spades. The speech seemed somewhat rehearsed but the man managed to sound sincere. He handed his wife the roses and she reluctantly took them as the man lowered his voice and pleaded with her to forgive him. She was silent for a few minutes and Marcus began to wonder if she'd heard anything the man had said to her.

"What's wrong with Momma?" George said, standing up in the seat and looking out at his mother.

Marcus took off his sunglasses and observed the woman closer.

"Look at her eyes," Vickie whispered to him.

That's when he saw it. There was a sad smile on her face and tears were running down her cheeks.

"Oh, Hank," she said, throwing her arms around her husband's neck.

He put his arm around her waist and led her back across the yard. He paused and called back over his shoulder, "Robbie, get George, will you?"

Vickie helped George out of the front seat and both boys went running across the yard and up the front steps of the porch. George's father whispered something to his wife, kissed her on the cheek and hurried back to the car, going over to the driver's side window.

"I wanted to thank you again for bringing my family home," the man said, leaning down to Marcus and extending his hand to shake. "And thanks for the tip about the roses and Richetti's. I made reservations for tonight! It's going to be great! Thanks again!" And with that the man rushed back over to his wife and put his arm around her shoulders, leading her up the steps of the porch.

"You told him to get her roses and take her out to dinner?" Vickie asked Marcus.

"Yep. And as long as they don't run into any customers smoking in the restrooms, they should be fine."

She moved over in the seat next to him. "That was so sweet," she whispered, putting her arm through his. "You just made two women very happy—Maggie and me." And she pulled him down to her and gave him a kiss on the cheek.

"Glad to be of service," he said. He then turned to her and saw a look of such longing in her eyes that it made his pulse quicken. He was immediately propelled back to the aquarium. And the kiss. He leaned down to kiss her, wanting to relive that moment again. But his lips had no sooner touched hers than George's voiced called out to them from the porch.

"See you later!" he yelled. "And don't forget about me bowlin'! And those cookies, too!"

"I wonder if he means you or me," Vickie whispered.

Marcus gave the boy a wave and quickly put the car in reverse. "He means you. And if I don't get the heck out of here, I'm gonna have to challenge him to a duel to protect your honor."

"Why, Marcus," she said, nuzzling her face against his shoulder, "I believe you're jealous."

"You bet I am. I saw him offering you his ice cream. No kid does that unless he's serious about a girl. I'm gonna have to do some quick maneuvering if I want to compete with that!"

They both broke up laughing as he backed the car out into the street. On the way back to her place, he tried to talk her into going somewhere else. It was still early, not even six o'clock, and he wanted to leave her with something more than a memory of being chased by an elephant. "I know of a great place up by the lake," he told her as he drove into her parking lot a few minutes later. "The sunsets are beautiful by the old lighthouse and there's a theater in town so we could catch a movie, too. It's only a half-hour drive." He pulled the car up next to the back door of the apartment house and put it in park.

She sighed. "That sounds great, but I better not. My parents should be getting home soon and my mom will be calling me with all the latest family gossip. I wouldn't want to disappoint her. Besides, I've got work tomorrow…" And she paused and started giggling.

He asked her what was wrong.

"Nothing. But I sounded exactly like my father just then and it gave me shudders. Maybe my friends are right, I am becoming too conservative. Gee, Greg would be so happy to hear that."

He felt a glimmer of hope. "Does that mean you'd like to go to the lake after all?"

She tugged on his arm, acting concerned. "I'd like to say yes, but what about you? Aren't you tired? I mean, it's not every day you're chased by an elephant. I'd think you'd be exhausted after something like that."

"Oh, that's no problem, I'm used to being chased—" He stopped in mid sentence, realizing that he'd almost let the cat out of the bag. He made a quick mental note to be more careful in the future. "Uh…" he said, trying to cover his tracks. "I mean I'm used to running around. I sometimes do it all day at The Crystal."

"Marcus?" she said, staring at him inquisitively.

"What?" he said, avoiding her gaze and busying himself by playing with his keys. He'd seen the look too many times. She was formulating the questions in her head and wanted answers to them.

She grabbed his chin and made him look at her. "I'm your friend," she whispered. "You know that, don't you?"

"Of course."

"And you know you can be honest with me..."

He nodded, not sure what she was getting at.

"Is there anything you'd like to tell me?" she whispered, as if she was waiting for him to reply.

He searched her face, trying to figure out if she knew something, for instance, something about him. He tried to think of a careful way to word it. "Uh, what exactly are you referring to?"

She started to say something, but a wave of panic flooded over him. "I have been honest with you," he said, acting as if it was a joke. "I mean, I told you I run a bowling alley and that I'm single. I'm not hiding any forgotten wives or kids anywhere, if that's what you're worried about..."

"Oh, I know," she said, staring down at her hands like she was uncomfortable. "I only meant that you can be honest with me...about anything."

He observed her carefully, trying to figure out what to do. It was obvious she'd heard something and was now expecting him to fill in the blanks. But he couldn't. He might lose her if he did. "I'm not sure what you're talking about," he told her, his pulse racing with worry. He could feel his face turning red and his mouth going dry. He knew he was on the verge of an all-out panic attack and suddenly felt trapped.

"You can ask Ben and Jack..." he stammered. "They'll vouch for me. I'm no menace or anything..." He stopped himself as the panic level went right off the scale. *Jesus Christ*, he thought, mentally kicking himself in the ass. What was he doing? Deliberately spilling his guts? If she hadn't heard anything before, he'd sure as hell given her reason to suspect something now. "Uh, I mean..." he said, clearing his throat. "I'm not dangerous to anyone's health or welfare. You can ask anybody in town..." He bit his lip and silently cursed at himself. What the hell was he doing? Why not advertise it on a billboard for Chrissakes? Marcus Kerr, a.k.a. *The Famous Kirklin Klutz*!

She reached and out took his hand. "Marcus...it's okay. I know you're a good man. No one has to tell me that." She paused and looked up at him. "I only meant that...if something was ever bothering you, you could talk to me about it. I want you to feel you can trust me."

The soulful look in her eyes said it all. She really did care about him. He swallowed hard and tried to speak, but couldn't. He finally uttered a quick "thanks" a few seconds later even though it was completely inadequate. How could *thanks* even begin to tell her what he was feeling?

She wrapped her arms around him and pressed her face against his chest. He smiled and laid his head down onto hers. It was his fantasy, coming to life. He buried his face into the soft strands of her hair, letting it surround him. If only he could tell her. If only he could be sure she wouldn't run away if he did.

"I wish…" he whispered, nuzzling his face against her hair.

"What?" she replied softly. "Go ahead and tell me."

But he couldn't. There was too much at stake.

"Never mind," she said, hugging him tighter. "There's no big hurry. We've got time."

He started to ask her what she was talking about when someone tapped on the passenger side front window shield. It was the same Oriental man he'd seen that morning with Vickie.

"You hokay?" the man asked Vickie, at the same time glaring menacingly at Marcus.

"I'm fine, Sanun," she said, letting go of Marcus and scooting across the seat. She got out of the car and led the man over to the driver's side. She introduced him to Marcus. "And, Sanun, this is my friend Marcus Kerr. He lives in Kirklin."

Marcus and the man nodded to each other but from the icy demeanor in the man's eyes, Marcus knew it was useless to try and act cordial.

"Sanun's originally from Thailand," Vickie said. "He's been trying to teach me some Thai words but I'm still having trouble pronouncing some of them. I've also learned how to cook some great Thai dishes. You'll have to come over some night and try one."

Marcus started to reply that he'd love to when Sanun cut in. "Some people not like Thai, too spicy! Maybe not good idea come over."

Vickie began making excuses, promising not to put too much spice in the food.

"I like spicy," Marcus replied, narrowing his eyes at the man. "I'd love to come over sometime."

Vickie turned and whispered something to Sanun and from her body language it looked like she was asking the man to give them some privacy. The whole time she explained it, Sanun glared in Marcus's direction, acting like he was her personal watchdog.

"Hokay," the man told Vickie. "But you call me if you need anything." And he glared in Marcus's direction, silently communicating a warning message of "hands off."

Vickie thanked him and the little man walked over to the back door of the building. As he opened the entrance door, he turned and called back to Marcus. "You be sure to call before come. We don't like strangers in building. We keep good security." And with that the man gave Marcus a last long glare and disappeared through the door.

Vickie leaned down on Marcus's window. "He's really very sweet," she said, acting apologetic.

"I could tell right away," he said, smirking sarcastically. "He's a real charmer. And he seems to like me. As a matter of fact, I think he'd like to bite me. What is the guy? Your building manager or your jailer?"

"I know he seems gruff, but it's because he's kind of protective of me. He's like an old mother hen sometimes."

Not the word I'd use, Marcus thought. *More like bulldog.*

"I'm sure that once you got to know him, you'd see what I mean," she added.

He nodded an agreement but it was only a gesture to make her happy. In truth, he hoped to never see the man again.

"Uh, about lunch," he told her, wanting to make sure the date was still on. "How should we plan for that? I could call you at the water department whatever day George and his mother show up."

She took a pad and pen out of her purse and wrote something down on one of the pages. "Here," she said, ripping off the page and handing it to him. "The number on the top is for the water department and the one below that is my home number."

As he took the paper she leaned down near his face. "But you don't have to wait until George shows up to bowl before you call me. I'm usually home every night by seven." And then she grabbed his chin and gave him a peck on the cheek.

He leaned out the window and smiled up at her. "How about something a little more personal?"

She began to bend down to him and he closed his eyes in anticipation of the kiss. But a mere second after her lips touched his, Sanun's voice interrupted them.

"Miss Vickie!"

As she pulled away Marcus opened his eyes and saw the man standing at the back door.

"Father on phone!" the man bellowed at them.

Marcus chuckled. "Uh, does he mean his father or yours?"

"Mine," she said. "He and Mom must have gotten back early from the reunion."

Marcus's eyebrows shot up in surprise. "So they called your building manager to let him know about it?"

Vickie explained to him that Sanum and her father were friends. "Daddy probably called my place first and when he found I wasn't home, he called Sanun. I'd better get going." She bent down and gave him another kiss on the cheek. "Don't forget to call me," she said, turning and hurrying off towards the back door. Her landlord opened the door for her and as she hurried past him, the man glared back over at Marcus.

"No kisses in parking lot, either!" the man exclaimed, giving Marcus another nasty glare before slamming the door shut.

Sheesh! Marcus thought as he started up the car and drove it towards the exit. *What's that guy's problem? Hasn't he ever seen people kiss before?*

He drove back out onto the street, trying to forget about the gruff landlord. Besides, he had more important things to occupy his thoughts. Like the fact that he now had at least two more dates with Vickie on the horizon. Possibly even more.

Now all he had to worry about was his *gift* getting in the way again.

The date Friday night should be okay since it was at the one place his *gift* never showed itself, the bowling alley. The Crystal would once again be a safe haven but this time it would be protecting Vickie from enduring another one of his *moments*. Instead of the zoo animals, she could see him in his natural habitat. He could prove to her that he wasn't a freak or someone to be afraid of. He was just a man. With the same needs and wants as any other man.

He stared out the front windshield to the interstate and began planning. His birthday was coming up, which meant hers was, too. He could buy her a present. Jewelry maybe. All women like jewelry. He could have Ben go with him and pick out something nice.

As far as the lunch date went, perhaps he needn't worry about that either. It was only lunch, two people taking an hour to enjoy a midday meal, sandwiches and conversation in a nice quiet place with no animals or jittery waiters. Someplace that only served simple things like hamburgers, fries and no combustible alcoholic beverages.

What could go wrong?

He drove towards home and let his worries float away with the gentle breeze blowing through the open windows. Maybe things were finally turning around for him. Maybe his *gift* was going to take a break for a while.

Just a little while.

Nothin' wrong with taking a break once in a while. A lot of people did it. Sometimes even animals did it. Even large animals that wanted to take a break from their daily routine and go out for a little popcorn.

Nope. Nothin' wrong with taking a little break now and then.

Just ask Benji.

CHAPTER SIX

Because it was Wednesday and the middle of the week, The Farthest Point wasn't very busy. A few regulars sat at the bar and the day bartender was busy bringing in boxes of bottled beer from the storage room in the back. The only other people present were two guys occupying one of the booths at the back of the room, near the dart boards.

Ben Hollinger sat laboring away on his mug of beer while he tried to think of a way to get Magic to talk. From the pronounced frown on his friend's face, it was clear that something else noteworthy had happened.

"Can't you even give me a hint?" Ben said, hoping to coax some information out of him.

"I'd rather wait for Jack," Marcus replied, frowning down at his beer. "He should be here any minute."

Ben decided to leave it alone. Magic wasn't about to disclose any details until all three of them were present. If it was bad news it would be better to say it once and not have to repeat it. *And that's what it sounds like*, Ben thought. *Bad news*.

Over the years, he'd seen his friend deal with his strange condition, not with fear or anger but with the courage of a champion. No matter how bad the *moments* got, Magic would endure them with humor and quiet acceptance. He never used them as an excuse to indulge in self-pity or melancholy. And on those few rare occasions when he did complain about his problem, he and Jack could always kid Magic out of his sulks.

AND THE BULL SAVED ME

However, this time it looked like their work was cut out for them.

Marcus checked his watch and asked Ben when he had to be back.

"Not 'til 4:30," Ben replied. "But it's okay if I'm a little late. It's with my best student, Paul. I always make him my last lesson. That way, we can keep going if we're working on something special."

"Paul. Isn't that the kid that's collaborating with you on the songs?"

Ben put down his beer, anxious to talk about it. "That's him. We've been working on several pieces and the kid's got real talent. I'm helping him get into Baldwin Wallace College, my old alma mater. Your dad would have liked hearing that. Especially after all the encouragement he gave me."

"It would make him proud," Marcus agreed.

"I had this dream..." Ben said, getting thoughtful for a second. "Someday...if one of the songs ever gets published and actually makes us some money!" And he threw out his hands for emphasis. "I'm going to take a share of the proceeds and set up a college scholarship fund for gifted music students. And if it's okay with you, I'd like to name the fund after your dad."

A smile slowly formed on Magic's face and Ben knew the news had pleased him.

"You bet it's okay," Marcus replied. "I think it's a great idea."

Ben started to give him some of the details about how he wanted the fund set up when Jack came walking up to the booth.

"Sorry I'm late," he said, setting his Coke on the table and taking the seat next to Ben. There was a newspaper tucked under his arm and he took it out and set it on the seat beside him. "I had to stop and get today's paper."

"Paper?" Marcus asked him, the frown deepening.

Jack didn't answer him. Instead he took out his tobacco pouch and pipe and began filling it. "You're on some kind of roll, ain't ya, Magic?" Jack said, expertly packing the pipe. "If you continue this pace, Ben and I are gonna need tally sheets to keep up. This is the second meeting in three days." He paused to light up. "Okay. Let's hear it. This one didn't involve any elephants, did it?"

"No," Marcus replied morosely. "This time it was horses...among other things."

"Wait a minute," Ben said, a light going off in his head. "Yesterday one of my students told me he saw some horses running along Cherry Street. I also heard rumors that the cops were out trying to round them up. That wasn't by any chance..."

"Yeah. That was me," Marcus admitted.

Ben couldn't help but laugh. Then he remembered the *among other things* remark and asked Magic about it. "Exactly what did you mean by that? Other what?"

"Animals," Marcus replied. "It seems to be my week for them." He then explained what happened, beginning with Vickie's promise to watch little George bowl. "George showed up yesterday morning with his mother, she's joined the mother's league, and the first thing he does is ask me to call Vickie so she can watch him bowl."

"And did you?" Ben asked, intrigued at how far Magic would go to please one little angel-faced Casanova.

"Sure. I promised I would."

Ben smiled. "But I thought Vickie was the one who made the promise?"

"She was," Marcus said. "But how could she keep the promise unless I called her first and let her know George was there?"

"Just asking," Ben replied, amused at his best friend's blindness to his own situation. People, especially people in love, were always making what seemed like "innocent" ties to the people they were dating, never realizing that after enough ties, a knot eventually formed. A knot that sometimes led to a lifetime commitment.

Marcus continued, telling them that Vickie took an early lunch and drove over to watch George. "And, man, was he trying to impress her, too. He may be little but what he lacks in size, he makes up in determination."

"That he does," Jack added. "You should have seen it, Ben. Betsy picked out a five pound ball for him and he was hefting it so hard that he looked like a miniature body builder. I thought he was going to end up down the alley, right along with the ball, he threw it so hard. He's going to be a world class bowler if he keeps it up. And what a little character! Betsy fell in love with him."

"Which was the plan," Ben said. "Right, Magic?"

Marcus confirmed that it was. "I asked Betsy to keep George occupied after he bowled so I could take Vickie to lunch. Betsy bribed him with Mavis's chocolate chip cookies."

"Worked like a charm," Jack remarked. "The kid saw that big plate of cookies and thought he was in hog heaven." Jack paused and glanced over at Marcus. "But Magic never came back after the lunch date so I assumed it went smoothly. At least I did until this morning."

From the look on both of their faces, Ben knew he was missing something. "Okay, you two. What's the big secret?"

"I think Magic should tell you," Jack said, puffing on his pipe.

Ben waited but Magic didn't say anything. "What gives?" he asked Magic.

"You never said anything about Vickie coming to The Crystal yesterday morning, when we were at the jewelry store."

"I didn't know then," Marcus replied. "George and his mom showed up after I went back to work."

Jack asked Ben what they were doing at the jeweler's.

"I was helping Magic pick out a birthday present for Vickie. Her birthday's this week."

"Sunday," Marcus added. "Two days after mine."

Ben prodded him to get back to the story. "You told me that if Vickie showed up at The Crystal that you were gonna take her to Compton's for lunch. Didn't you?"

Marcus nodded yes.

"And did anything happen?" Ben asked him, anxious to hear it.

"No. And I was hoping it wouldn't. That's why I picked the place. It's small and only a few things have happened there in the past."

"That's because you've only been in there a few times," Ben said.

Marcus complained that he didn't have much to pick from. "The manager at the diner's always giving me dirty looks because of all the accidents I've had in there and Kleary's on Main Street wasn't going to work, either. Almost every time I go in there something happens and all the waitresses gather around while I'm eating, waiting to see it. Makes me feel like some kind of floor show."

Jack remarked that he'd heard quite a few of the stories. "Especially from the women on the mother's league. You're one of their favorite topics."

Ben knew what he was talking about. When you lived in a small town and had little in the way of entertainment, a calamity prone resident was better than going to the Multi-Plex.

"So what happened?" Ben asked him.

Marcus shrugged. "Nothing. The lunch went great. She had a Caesar salad and I had a perch sandwich with fries. Nothing exploded into flames and I didn't even find one bone in the fish to choke on."

"When did the horses show up?" Jack asked, clenching the pipe in his teeth.

"Later that afternoon," Marcus said and then he told them that Vickie's boss sometimes let her use the company van to run his errands, like yesterday. "And her boss told her that she could take the rest of the day off after she got the errands done. So I volunteered to ride along with her, to help. That way, I figured we could get done quicker and then we'd have plenty of time to go out somewhere, like to a movie and dinner."

"But you never made it to dinner, did you?" Ben asked. After listening to ten years of *Magic moment* stories, he'd gotten used to some of the vernacular. Sort of like Magic's version of "Once upon a time" or "Don't touch that dial!"

Marcus told them that the errands involved posting some mail at the post office and dropping off some forms to a residence out on Meyler Road, just outside town. "And to get there we had to drive down Halfway Road, past Old Man Pelling's place."

"I've heard about him," Jack said, "from some of the customers. He's supposed to be a recluse with a bunch of cats, isn't he?"

"Not just cats," Ben remarked. "All kinds of animals. It's rumored that he's got a regular zoo out there. He owns an old farmhouse and about thirty acres of land and part of it is woods. The local hunters will sometimes trespass in other people's woods, trying to bag a deer. But nobody ever poaches in Old Man Pelling's woods. They're too scared. The hunters tell stories about spotting strange things in his woods."

"What kind of strange things?" Jack said. "You mean like Big Foot and Sasquatch?"

"That along with other things," Ben replied, smiling over at Magic. "The 'Yellow Eyes' legend was supposed to have originated in Pelling's woods." And he paused to grin at Magic. "But as you know, that local legend was recently spotted in the woods out by the hospital."

"Don't remind me," Marcus replied with a smirk.

"Anyway," Ben said, continuing. "Besides the strange creatures, people have also reported weird screeching and screaming sounds coming from Pelling's woods. One hunter swore he saw a unicorn but everybody figured the guy was drunk and probably saw a horse or deer. But there's real animals on the place that are plainly visible from the road. Horses, a few cows and some reindeer. He once even had a llama on the place that someone got rid of but the authorities hauled it away to some zoo in Cincinnati. And the neighbors have been complaining forever about the smell coming from the house and yard. Old Man Pelling's big on taking in strays and feeding them but he's not much on hygiene or cleaning up after them."

Jack asked if the old man mistreated the animals.

Marcus told him he didn't. "The animals love him. It's people he doesn't get along with. The city council's been trying to get him to clean up his place for years. But his house is outside the city limits so they can't touch him. None of the ordinances apply. There was even a story going around that he had a bear living with him. One that he raised from a cub. That rumor proved to be true."

AND THE BULL SAVED ME

Jack took the pipe from his mouth and frowned. "You're kidding!"

"It's true!" Ben exclaimed, understanding Jack's response. "And that was only discovered by accident. A couple locals got drunk one night, drove out to the place and tried to sneak in to see it. Turns out it was living right there in the house with Pelling. But the bear must have been protective of the old man 'cause when those guys tried to break in through one of the side windows, the bear went after them."

Marcus added that no one was killed or mauled. "But the guys did get some nasty scratches and a hell of a scare. But something else significant happened because of it. Town council claimed the bear was a safety risk and made Pelling get rid of it. And that's when he really got reclusive. He put padlocks on his fences and doors and never came out of his house again. Even his groceries get delivered in."

"But he kept collecting animals?" Jack asked.

"That's what's really bizarre," Ben said. "People kept taking animals to him, ones they didn't want anymore and he always took them in. I guess the townsfolk figured he was a necessary evil. They didn't mind him being around but wanted him to keep his distance. Sort of like garbage collectors. Everyone knows they're there but no one ever talks to one." He then told Jack how the police had tried continuously to get on the place to see exactly how many animals were housed there. "But the old man won't let anyone near the place." He paused and glanced across the table. "But I have a sneaking suspicion we're about to hear someone who's seen a few of those animals, aren't we, Magic?"

"Some of them," Marcus replied. "Including six large and mangy looking horses."

Jack asked him what happened.

"Vickie's friend John has been telling her stories about Pelling," Marcus said. "So since we were out there, she wanted me to show her the house. I didn't think it would hurt anything…you know…just pulling in the drive and looking at it."

Ben's eyebrows shot up and Jack took the pipe from his mouth and let out a low whistle.

"You did what?" Ben asked, not sure he heard him right. "With your condition acting up the way it's been the last week?"

"I know. I know," Marcus said, waving them off. "I was asking for trouble and should have known better. But she really wanted to see it and I didn't want to disappoint her."

"Plus you were trying to impress her. Right?" Ben asked, knowing the question would needle the hell out of him.

"Oh, she was impressed all right," Marcus said. "But not with me or the stories about Old Man Pelling." He paused and sighed heavily. "I've only got myself to blame. We never should have got out of the van."

Jack smiled and told him to go on.

"We were driving by real slow when Vickie noticed a couple of reindeer back behind the house. So we pulled into the driveway, to get a better look. The drive's pretty long and there's a fenced-in area to the left of it so I figured we could take a quick look at the reindeer and then we'd book out of there. But when we started to get back in the van Vickie noticed something dark running around in the fenced area near the back of the house. She finally talked me into checking it out."

"Uh-huh," Jack snickered, "and curiosity killed the cat."

"I know now it was a foolish judgment call," Marcus griped. "But hey, after all the rumors I've heard over the years, I was pretty damn curious, too. I knew Pelling would sometimes threaten people trespassing on his land but he never minded us doing it when we were kids. Ben and I went out there plenty of times when we were growing up."

"Yeah, but that was back before the town council started giving him trouble," Ben said. "And don't forget. Back then you weren't having to deal with your *Magic moments*, either."

"Yeah. My *Magic moments*," Marcus sneered. "They were in true form yesterday all right." He then told how he and Vickie followed the fence to the back of the house and that five or six horses came walking up to them. The animals looked well fed but kind of dirty, their manes and tails were matted and they looked old. "But they were friendly, too. One of them even let Vickie pet him. But that was the last nice thing that happened. Because a few seconds later the horse got spooked by a shotgun blast."

"Cripes!" Jack said, acting alarmed. "Was it the old guy, shooting at you?"

"Not at us," Marcus replied. "He was standing on his front porch, firing the gun into the air. He must have been trying to scare us off but it wasn't only us that got scared. The horses started rearing up and racing all around the paddock in a panic. I never thought old horses could move that fast. But they were bookin'! Then they all started crowding over in one corner of the fence and knocked part of it down. Well, that was all it took. All six of them escaped. And that's when the fun started. Turns out there wasn't just horses held back by the fence. The old man had also been keeping a couple of ostriches and an emu."

"An emu?" Ben said, chuckling with gusto. "You sure?"

"I'm sure," Marcus nodded. "Vickie and I saw one just like it at the zoo the other day. Although this one looked a bit rattier."

"No wonder Old Man Pelling didn't want anyone sniffin' around his place," Ben said. "He was probably worried the authorities would take all the animals away."

Marcus got a strange look on his face and Jack asked him what was wrong.

"I think I just figured out why Old Man Pelling tried to scare us off. The van, the one Vickie was driving, it had the Water Department logo on the side. The old man must have seen it and thought we were with the police or health department. No wonder he shot off the gun."

"Sounds like Mayberry," Ben smirked. "He assumed you were revenuers, trying to break up his furry family."

"That must have been it," Marcus agreed. "Once the horses and other animals got out, the old man started rushing around, trying to herd them back into the paddock. Vickie and I felt responsible for their escape so we tried to help him catch them. He gave me some rope to use but let me tell you something, catching animals that don't want to be caught ain't easy. First I tried roping one of the horses but I ain't much of a lasso artist, so that was a bust. So I decided to go after the birds. But that was a mistake, too. I followed one of the ostriches over to the neighbor's house across the road but the damn thing kept bobbling its head and pecking at me, so trying to get the rope around it was a bust, too. Then the owner came out and started yelling at me, telling me to get the damned bird out of her flowerbeds. Apparently, ostriches are partial to begonias or whatever it was the bird was grazin' around in. I finally gave up and ran back across the road again."

"Why were you running?" Jack asked, tapping his pipe into the ashtray. "Did the ostrich chase you?"

"No. The woman did. She kept hitting me with a broom and yelling at me to come back and get the damned bird out of her flowers." Then Marcus rubbed his shoulder and complained that he was still sore from where she hit him with the broom.

"And where was Vickie while this was going on?" Ben asked, mesmerized by the tale. Magic's tales were always fun to listen to. It was like having a best friend who was a stand up comedian and the jokes never ended.

"She was helping with the horses," Marcus said. "She told me later she used to ride when she was younger so she wasn't afraid of them. She and Old Man Pelling managed to get three of them back into the paddock by the time I was chased away by the neighbor woman. At that point I was feeling pretty damn useless."

"Why?" Ben remarked. "You're no zoo keeper."

"No. But I wasn't much help, either. So right after that I spotted the emu over in a bunch of bushes on the other side of the fence and decided to give it one more try. I snuck up behind it, hoping to get the rope over its head. I'm not much of a cowboy but I made a half-assed lasso and threw it into the bushes at the emu."

"And did you get him?" Jack asked, his eyes large with excitement.

"No. But I did manage to rope another animal."

Ben tried not to smile. "I'm almost afraid to ask. What was it?"

"A skunk."

"Oh shit!" Ben muttered.

Jack asked if the skunk was one of Pelling's animals, too.

"It couldn't have been," Marcus said. "Otherwise what happened never would have happened."

"And what happened?" Ben asked, felling like he was talking to Peter Piper who picked a peck of pickled peppers.

"I didn't know what it was at first," Marcus said. "And I had to pull the rope hard to drag it out. Vickie saw what it was before I did. She and Old Man Pelling were behind me. So she whispered to me to drop the rope and started pulling at my arm, trying to get me away from it. She told me later she didn't want to yell at me to drop the rope because she was afraid she'd scare the skunk."

Jack stuck his nose in the air and whiffed. "Well, I don't smell anything so you must not have got sprayed."

"We didn't," Marcus agreed. "But someone else did."

"Old Man Pelling?" Ben asked with a snicker.

"Not just him," Marcus replied. "The skunk also sprayed the emu. It must have seen us running away and got scared. It started stompin' around and squawkin' like crazy, flapping its wings. The skunk must have thought it was being attacked and let the emu and Old Man Pelling have it, full force. And the sad part is that Pelling might have gotten away if not for the fact that the emu came running at him and knocked him down. You should have heard the cussing after he got sprayed!"

"Who?" Ben asked. "The emu or Old Man Pelling?"

"From all the squawking after that, neither one of them was happy," Marcus quipped.

"Probably a little hard for a guy his age to run very fast," Jack commented, finishing off the last of the tobacco in his pipe. "Especially with an emu in the way."

"No kidding," Marcus agreed. "And you should have seen the cops when they showed up a couple minutes later. They're trying to ask the old man questions but none of them wanted to get anywhere near him. Vickie and I told them what happened and right after we gave them our statements they told us to vacate the premises PDQ. We didn't argue."

Ben suddenly thought of something. "Yeah, but what happened with the rest of the horses and the birds?"

"This is what," Jack said, grabbing the newspaper from beside him and unfolding it on the top of the table. "It made the front page."

Ben joined Magic looking at the copy of the *Kirklin Gazette*. The headline read *Washington Announces Tax Cuts* and right below the article was another, smaller headline that read, *Kirklin Round Up!* Below the feature line was a drawing of a policeman crouched on the hood of his cruiser, swinging a lasso. An ostrich and couple of horses were out in front of the cruiser, trotting away from the car.

"Nice drawing," Ben smirked, trying not to sound too sarcastic. "It looks like the birds and the rest of the horses found their way into town. Not too surprising, really. It's only a couple miles from Old Man Pelling's place and no one was about to stop an emu reeking of skunk spray."

Jack bent his head down, trying to cover up the grin.

"Do they mention me or Vickie?" Marcus asked, peering closer at the article.

"No," Jack replied. "They only mention Paul Pelling. You're simply referred to as 'two people trespassing.'" And he pointed to the part in the article that referenced it. "And listen to this," Jack said, reading some of the highlights out loud. "The article says, 'It took four police cruisers and ten policemen, along with some help from the local humane society, to round up the animals.' Then it mentions that several dozen citizens complained about the animals running through their yards and properties. Some guy on Maple said one of the horses knocked down his lawn ornaments and a woman on Main reported that one of the ostriches kept trying to eat her lawn sprinkler."

Ben couldn't hold back the laughter as Jack continued. "Then it says they captured the emu on the front steps of the library after a woman came out of the building and fainted when she saw it. Makes you wonder whether it was the sight of the bird or the smell that knocked her down. Probably both."

Jack joined Ben laughing as he finished the article. It was how the *post moment* meetings usually ended, with all three of the laughing about it and Magic seeming to garner some humor and release from living through another goofy episode in his calamitous life.

But right now he wasn't laughing. He was staring hard at the article with a scared look on his face. And as soon as he noticed it, Ben stopped laughing. "What's the matter, Magic?" Ben asked him. "Are you worried she's gonna find out about you?"

Marcus leaned on his elbow, still reading the paper. "It's going to be hard to keep it from her after this."

Jack tried to reassure him. "Oh, I dunno. She lives way over in Barberton. She may not even get the Kirklin paper."

A glint of hope flashed in Magic's eyes and Ben nudged Jack under the table, signaling that the ploy had worked. "Sure," Ben told him. "She probably hasn't even seen the paper. Stop worrying."

"Besides," Jack added. "What if she does find out? She's going to eventually anyway. Why not tell her now?"

"But, I'm not ready yet," Marcus whispered.

Ben could hear the hesitation in his voice and tried to kid him through it. "Hey, Magic. Lighten up. Look at it this way. If you ever decide to change careers, you can always get a job at a circus. Look at all the experience with animals you have?"

"Not to mention reptiles," Jack added.

But Ben could tell by the sour expression that Magic wasn't in a kidding mood. He was running scared. "So what's next?" Ben said, trying to cheer him up. "Where you taking her on the next date?"

"The Crystal."

"Smart move," Jack remarked. "Nothing's ever happened there."

"At least not yet," Marcus said, frowning down at the paper. "She and her sister Marty are coming up Friday night." He then explained about his plan to help Vickie's sister.

"I wanna see that," Ben said. "I think Sue and I'll come up and watch."

Jack got back to the subject of Vickie's sister Marty. He asked Marcus if she knew the truth about him.

"That's the only thing I can figure," Marcus replied. "Otherwise Vickie would be asking me a million questions and so far, she hasn't. She didn't even seem upset about the elephant or the mess yesterday."

"And after The Crystal?" Jack said. "What then?"

"I don't know. I'm going to take it one step at a time."

"Maybe you could take her to a movie," Jack suggested. "That should be safe."

Ben shook his head no, prompting Jack to ask why not.

"Because I've been banned from the Pinnacle Theater uptown," Marcus said.

"One of your *moments*?" Jack asked, stifling a smile.

"Sue and I accompanied Magic and his date one night a few years ago," Ben said. "Magic's date was…uh…a very friendly type, if you get my drift."

"Melanie Hilander," Marcus said, finally cracking a smile. "She was friendly all right."

"What are you saying?" Jack asked them. "That she was loose?"

"And how," Ben replied. "Her dates never went home disappointed." He continued the story, telling Jack how he and Magic let the girls choose the film. "We knew they'd pick a chick flick but that was alright with us because we had a few plans of our own."

"Like talking the girls into sitting up in the balcony," Marcus added. "Nice place to neck. And we sat in the front row so we'd have plenty of leg room."

Ben explained that when the girls started crying over the sad parts, he and Magic could console them. "Also enjoy some light or even heavy petting."

"It would have worked out fine," Marcus said, "Except there was some loudmouthed asshole behind us making snide comments all through the movie. I mean, how stupid was this guy, anyway? He was at a chick flick with an audience full of women. He was just asking for trouble."

"I take it the women weren't very happy with the man?" Jack asked.

"Especially the woman right behind the guy," Ben said. "She was mad as hell. Who could blame her? After listening to him for over an hour, I wanted to kill the guy."

"And who'd have thought that little woman could land a punch that hard?" Marcus commented.

Jack blinked, surprised. "She hit the guy?"

"She not only hit him," Ben said. "She punched him so hard that he went flying forward, slamming into Magic and sending him over the balcony rail."

Jack asked Marcus if he saw the guy coming at him.

"No. I was busy nuzzling Melanie's neck when I felt something like a freight train slam into my back, sending me flying. I managed to grab the metal bar at the top of the balcony with one hand but I was dangling like a worm on the end of a fishing line. Ben tried to help me back up but my hand slipped. I landed right in this big guy's lap. Brother, did he get mad."

Jack put down his pipe. "Why? Surely he could see that it wasn't your fault."

"He didn't seem to give a damn," Marcus said. "I think the reason he got mad was because when I landed in his lap, he was crying."

"Crying?" Jack asked, giving them both a puzzled raise of the eyebrows.

Ben decided to fill him in. "The guy was crying about the movie. You should have seen it. Here's this three-hundred-pound yokel, wearing coveralls, sitting there, weeping into his popcorn when Magic plops down in his lap. Everybody turned around to see what the ruckus was and saw the guy crying like a baby. And then there was the other thing…"

"What other thing?" Jack asked.

"Uh, my jeans were unzipped," Marcus replied.

"Like I said," Ben explained. "Melanie really likes dark places."

"Oh," Jack said. "No wonder the big guy got mad."

"Not just mad," Marcus said, "furious. He took one look at me with my pants unzipped and hurled me like a damn discus across the top of the seats. I landed in a heap in front of the screen, my ribs aching like hell. Then he comes at me like a runaway freight train and butts me like a ram into the screen."

Jack asked him why he didn't fight back.

"I didn't have a chance. I was busy trying to zip up when the guy rushed me. I went flying into the screen and the guy jumped on top of me. It's hard to breathe with that much weight on top of you, let alone try and fight back. He might have killed me but the manager and a bunch of ushers showed up and finally got him off me. They made both of us leave and the manager told me I was barred from ever coming back. He said he'd heard about me and didn't need a jinx hurting business."

"That's asinine," Jack said, his voice turning angry. "That kind of thing could have happened to anyone…" And as soon as he said it, Marcus and Ben began smiling.

"Oh, you know what I mean," Jack said.

The three of them got off the subject of animals and began discussing Jack's upcoming fishing trip out on the lake. Marcus finished the rest of his beer and remarked that he had to get back to work.

"You two coming?" he asked Jack and Ben as he got up from the booth.

"I'm gonna have another Coke first," Jack said. "I haven't had my daily quota of caffeine yet."

Ben replied that he'd stay and keep Jack company. Marcus headed for the exit and Ben waited until he was all the way out the door to talk to Jack again.

"Is he gone?" Jack said.

"Finally," Ben replied. "How's the project going?"

"Good. I'm almost finished with the banner and Betsy and Mavis are making the cake. How about you?"

"The kids have been practicing all week. They're really excited about it. This will be their first gig. I hope this cheers him up. He's pretty depressed."

"I know. He's been moping around at work all day. I was a little surprised that you called me for the meeting and not him. Usually he's the one to tell me."

Ben thought about it. "To be honest, I don't think he was going to meet with us at all."

Jack asked him what he meant.

"I already knew about the animals running loose. All of my afternoon students were talking about it. What surprised me was that he didn't call us last night, to meet with him, like he always does after one of his *moments*. I asked him when he first got here, why he didn't call. He told me he forgot. Since when does he forget about something like that? He never did before."

"Well, it does fits with the way he's been acting lately," Jack said, stowing the pipe inside his vest pocket. "He's not himself. I've never seen him so worried before. That's why when you called me today to come up here, I figured we were in for an 'Alamo' meeting."

Ben asked him what an "Alamo" meeting was.

Jack explained it was a term used by the workers at the plant where he used to work at. "It's what they'd call it whenever the management would call the workforce together. Our plant threatened to close up a couple of times and the looks on the employees' faces were always the same before each meeting. One of the guys said it must have been the same expression on the American's faces at the Alamo when they found out they were surrounded by two thousand of Santa Anna's soldiers. Thus we always dubbed the get-togethers 'Alamo' meetings."

"And you were afraid Magic was being surrounded?" Ben asked him, enjoying the fact that Jack was admitting to a heroic effort on Magic's behalf.

"Let's just say that he's had me a little worried lately. Especially since he's been going out with Vickie. He really seems to like her."

"I'll say," Ben replied. "You should see the necklace he's having made for her. I helped him pick it out and it wasn't cheap. He also paid a hefty rush fee on top of that so he could have it by Friday."

"So you think he's fallin' for this girl, too?"

"Yep. But if she ends up leaving him or leaving a 'smoke trail' as Magic puts it, I'm not sure he'll recover. He's really set himself up for a fall this time."

"What can you expect?" Jack said. "Look what he's dealing with. Most people would have given up a long time ago. You've gotta give him credit for trying." He paused and picked up the newspaper. "But he's right. Having one of his *moments* plastered on the front page isn't going to help any."

"But they didn't mention him name."

"They didn't have to," Jack said. "Everybody already knows it was him. That's all they were talking about at the coffee shop and the morning leagues."

Ben sighed and felt the realization kick in. "Sure as shit. Something like that isn't going to get shoved under the rug and forgotten. I'm always telling him it's no big deal, but the truth is, it is, at least to the people in Kirklin. The kids I teach think he's cool but unfortunately, some of their parents don't. He can't help the things that happen to him and he's the one who has to suffer the aftermath, not them. Why can't they see that? He's not a freak. He's the same as the rest of us, doing the best he can to get through life and hoping he can find someone to be with. What's wrong with that, anyway? Why can't they just leave him alone? Ever since it began happening, people have treated him like a sideshow attraction, something to stare at and be afraid of. Why can't they look past the rest and see the man, not the strange things that happen to him?"

Jack agreed that people let fear get in the way, of many things. "But eventually they see the truth. It always has a way of coming out and no one can blind themselves to it forever. Magic's gonna come through this fine. Besides, he's got friends who care about him and I've been around long enough to know that's half the battle. I'll keep an eye on him at The Crystal and if I see any trouble crop up, I'll give you a call. If something does happen, we can put our heads together and come up with some ideas."

"Sounds like another Alamo meeting," Ben snickered. "And in case things get too dicey, I'll see if the armory has some spare troops we can call in for reinforcements."

"You might want to check the area zoo personnel, too. Magic seems to be keeping *all* the area wildlife busy lately."

Ben told him that he'd keep it in mind. "And you never know. With any luck, Magic will not only have a great birthday, he'll find the girl of his dreams. Or at least someone who doesn't mind dodging emus and elephants."

"Or skunks," Ben reminded him. "Even Pepé Le Pew never gave up finding his true love so there's still hope for Magic, too."

Ben laughed and pictured Magic dressed up as a giant skunk. One thing was sure, it would be an improvement over the werewolf costume. A giant werewolf named "Yellow Eyes" was bad enough. Giant skunks would definitely cause the townsfolk to react like Santa Anna and then it would be an Alamo confrontation for real. Not a pleasant thought. He finished the last of his beer and decided that a check on the armory reinforcements might not be a bad idea after all.

CHAPTER SEVEN

The Crystal boasted twenty-four lanes and had a bar that drew a large crowd every other weekend whenever area bands were featured. There were two access doors on opposite sides of the lanes and a ball locker area next to the west exit. Two offices, including Marcus's, were located by the east entrance and a small carpeted hallway across from the offices led to the restrooms and rear parking lot.

A popcorn machine, a miniature version resembling the one Marcus and Vickie had seen at the zoo sat near the west entrance, across from the ball lockers. But no one had to "man" the cart. For fifty cents a box full of popcorn was automatically dispensed. In front of the lanes were concourse areas containing tables and chairs for customers and people watching the games or taking time to enjoy a snack. The lanes contained seats for both the bowlers and the scorekeeper and one of Marcus's first official duties, as manager was to put in electronic scorekeepers. They were the electronic ones that reflected the score sheets on the walls above the lanes and tied in with a main computer that tallied the totals. It made record keeping for the leagues easier and even the old-timers eventually got used to the new technology.

The bar was polished wood and shaped like a "U." It extended out almost to the rental counter and back to the kitchen and storage rooms at the rear of the building. The left side of the U was for the regular bar where mixed drinks and alcoholic beverages were served. There was also a bar area adjoining it with tables, chairs, a bandstand and a small dance floor with a jukebox.

AND THE BULL SAVED ME

The other half of the U was the snack bar and adjoining game room area with pinball machines and video games. Because the kitchen was centrally located between the "U" it allowed easy access to serve both the bar and snack bar customers. Mavis, Jack's wife, ran the kitchen, which served the typical short order fare, pizzas, burgers, fries and various fried foods. But lately she'd been on a health kick so fresh fruit and grilled items had been added to the menu. The place was busy, typical for a Friday night and better than two-thirds of the tables in the concourse and bar were already occupied.

Marcus was busy behind the bar, filling beer coolers and listening to Tyler's, his regular bartender, latest "drunken customer" story. Tyler was one of the employees who'd worked for the former administrator and had survived the change in management. He was a family man in his mid-thirties and had a great sense of humor.

"Get this," Tyler said, handing a beer and change back to a customer. "Sunday night this guy comes in plastered to the gills. He's staggering so bad that he can hardly stand up so naturally, I refuse to serve him. I figured he'd get mad and leave but he doesn't. He orders a club soda and starts hitting on all the female customers."

"And what did they do?" Marcus said, shutting the cooler door and pushing the empty beer box to the side.

"They ignored him. There were only a few of them left anyway because it was almost closing time. So the guy finally gives up, drifts over to the corner booth and I forget about him. Then, a few minutes later, one of the customers tells me some guy is fondling one of the video games. I go over to the game room to investigate and here's this guy, groping the Wonder Woman pinball machine. He's got his face plastered to the glass picture on the back panel of the machine, whispering to it. He's so drunk that he thinks it's a real woman and he's trying to pick her up."

Marcus chuckled, enjoying the story. "What'd you do?"

"I show the guy that it's only a picture and then he gets this really hurt look on his face, like he's going to cry. I almost felt sorry for him. He kept saying, 'But she was smiling at me, she was smiling at me.' It was pathetic. So I called him a cab and helped him out to the parking lot to catch it. But his wife pulls in, right in front of the cab. Turns out she was driving around to all the watering holes looking for him. I help the guy into the passenger seat and then tell her about him trying to pick up the pinball machine. You know, trying to take the edge off any violent tendencies she might be harboring."

"Against him or you?"

"Either one of us," Tyler replied. "But I was worried for nothing. She wasn't even upset about it. She says he goes out and gets drunk every weekend. He claims it's the only way to deal with his job stress."

"Did she tell you what his job was?"

"No but she did tell me that he tried to pick up a coat rack last winter. Apparently he saw some woman's coat hanging there and thought the same thing."

Marcus laughed. "Makes you wonder what the hell he'd do if he picked up a real woman."

"Or at least one that didn't flash the word 'tilt' when you leaned on her," Tyler replied.

A couple more people took their seats at the bar and Tyler went over to wait on them. Marcus picked up the empty box and took it back to the storage room, next to the kitchen. After stowing away the box he headed over to the kitchen to talk to Mavis. But as he neared the doorway, Betsy stepped up and blocked his way.

"Whatcha doin'?" she said, acting like she didn't want him to pass. Her short permed hair and dimples in her cheeks when she smiled always reminded him of Tinker Bell from the Disney cartoons. But this particular Tinker Bell had a mischievous twinkle in her eyes and was holding a sizable knife. She was wearing a light blue, short-sleeved pullover and a pair of blue skorts. The dimples showed in her cheeks when she smiled and she was holding a knife in her right hand.

"I wanted to see if Mavis needed anything," he said, peering over Betsy's arm, blocking his view. "Looks like we're going to have a big crowd." He could see Mavis, with her back to him, a few yards away. She was standing at one of the kitchen tables, working on something. It was then that he noticed that she was wearing one of her "Sunday best" dresses that was protected by a starched, white apron tied around her waist. She paused and brushed a few locks of her graying hair back into place and as she put her hand down, he saw a knife in her other hand.

"What's going on?" he asked Betsy. "Why's Mavis dressed up? And what's with all the knives?"

"Oh, it's nothing," she said, waving him off, swinging the knife absent-mindedly as she did, causing him to jump back. She giggled and leaned over and put the knife on the sink, next to the door. "I was helping Mom cut up some vegetables and fruit. She wants to make sure there's plenty of food for tonight's crowd. Now, stop worrying about things." She grabbed his arm and

AND THE BULL SAVED ME

began leading him back along the bar. "So? How's it going with Vickie's present? Did you wrap it up yet?"

He told her he didn't. "I wrapped it twice and both times it came out looking like hell. Even that ribbon you gave me didn't help. So I got Sue to do it for me. She and Ben should be here any minute."

"Fine. Fine. Now what about the other thing we talked about?" she said, using her *big sister lecturing little brother* tone. "Have you decided about telling Vickie?"

"Telling Vickie?" he said, avoiding her gaze and trying to avoid the subject as well.

"You know what I'm talking about, Magic. Telling her the truth. About yourself."

He suddenly felt like he was put on the spot. "Well, no. Like I said, I'm not ready yet. I want her to get to know me better first."

"But you're bringing her here, aren't you?"

He stared at her, not sure what she was getting at. "Yeah. She's coming here with her sister…"

She pulled on his arm and motioned him closer. "You know what I mean," she whispered. "You're bringing her here, to your home. And you're introducing her to Mom and Dad. It's the same thing as taking a girl home to meet your parents."

His started to protest but stopped himself as he realized she was right. Jack and Mavis *had* become like surrogate parents to him. And The Crystal was more of a home than even his apartment. A wave of fear gripped him. If Betsy had come to that conclusion, then maybe Vickie had too. And if she was having any reservations about him, she might not be showing up at all. "Uh…" he said, checking his watch, the fear building with each second. "Maybe I should call her and tell her not to come." His mind started scrambling, tying to think of a good excuse. "I could tell her that the leagues went over and that there were no lanes available."

"Oh, my God," Betsy whispered, a look of astonishment filling her face.

As soon as she said it, Marcus's face turned red with shame. "I wouldn't really be lying to her," he said, trying not to make it sound so bad.

"I was only kidding about the parents thing. It was a joke, Magic." She paused and smiled sadly. "But you didn't laugh so that tells me something very important."

He told her didn't know what she was talking about.

"Oh yes you do. You're in love with her, aren't you?"

The question took him completely by surprise. "Uh...I..." he said, stammering and trying to come up with a believable answer. But he couldn't concentrate. The question was still swirling around inside his head, blotting everything else out.

She took his hand and squeezed it. "Never mind, Magic. You don't have to explain anything. I understand." Then she let go of him and took off back to the kitchen.

He stood there for a second, letting the question take root. In love with her? He hadn't really thought about it. Could he be? But how was that possible? He'd only known her for a short time.

"Magic?"

It was Sue. She was standing next to one of the barstools, holding a small package. He came out from behind the bar and led her over to one of the empty tables. She took a seat and he asked her where Ben was.

"Out parking the car," she replied, handing him the box. She asked him if it looked okay.

"It looks great," he told her, surprised at how nice it looked. She'd wrapped the box in a pretty pink print paper and finished it off with Betsy's ribbon. "But I better put it away before Vickie gets here." He went over and stashed the box underneath the register for safekeeping. After that he grabbed a bottle of Coke for himself and a Sprite for Sue, her favorite, and headed back to the table. As usual, she looked stunning. Her auburn hair accented the tan dress pants and white, embroidered blouse that was open at the top and showed off her tan.

"So? Have you told Ben yet that he's going to be a daddy?" he asked, setting down the drinks and filling up his glass.

"No. I'm not sure if I'm ready," she whispered.

"Gee, that sounds vaguely familiar," he mused. "I just said the same thing to Betsy."

"You mean about you and Vickie, right?"

"Yeah. You and I are nothin' but a couple of big cowards."

She put her arm around his shoulder and hugged him. "It's only because both of us have a lot riding on the outcome."

"Me?" he said. But he'd no sooner uttered it than she gave him a look that mirrored Betsy's statement a few minutes earlier.

Evidently his friends could see something he did not.

"Tell you what," she said. "We'll make a pact. Both of us will come clean by the class reunion. Deal?"

He thought about it. The time frame was in his favor. The reunion was still two weeks away. Plenty of time to come up with a nice gentle way to break the news to Vickie. Also time for a few more dates and a chance for her to see that he wasn't someone to be afraid of.

"Deal," he said.

Sue sighed. "That's a relief. I've been having anxiety attacks, just thinking about telling him."

He admitted that he too, had been experiencing a healthy dose of anxiety, trying to keep his secret from Vickie. "But I'm safe for tonight at least. This is one place my *Magic moments* never show."

"You mean they haven't yet," she reminded him. "Better not say it too loud."

Amen to that, he thought.

Ben showed up a couple minutes later with Vickie and Marty in tow. He'd spotted them in the parking lot and was giving them the cook's tour of The Crystal. Marcus hurried over to the three of them and volunteered to take over.

"Sure thing," Ben said, giving him a salute and then making his way towards the bar.

Marcus observed them. They were both wearing jeans, different colored cotton tees and tennis shoes. Marty had a French braid in her hair and she'd applied some makeup but it was overshadowed by the frightened look on her face.

"Hi, Magic," she said, glancing around nervously. "The place is a lot bigger than I imagined."

He went over and put his arm around her shoulder, hoping to dispel some of her anxiety. "It just seems that way because of all the noise!" he said, louder than he had to, trying to make his point. "An atom bomb could go off in here and you wouldn't know it. I'm not kidding. Go ahead. Shout." He waited while she smiled and considered it.

"Go ahead. Try it," he told her.

"Really?" she whispered, glancing over at Vickie like she was waiting for permission.

"Here. I'll show you," he said, cupping his hands to his mouth. "Hellllooooo!" he called out across the building. "Is anyone there?" He paused and pointed to the people on the concourse, still busy with what they were doing and oblivious to his shouts. "See? They didn't even hear it. It never ceases to amaze me." He prompted her again to shout.

"But what should I say?" she asked sheepishly.

He laughed. "Anything but 'Free Food at the lunch bar.' Otherwise we might start a riot."

Marty giggled. "Okay. Here goes," she said, cupping her hands over her mouth. She called out a weak "Hello."

"That's good," Marcus told her. "But let's do it once more and Vickie and I will do it with you." He put his arms around both of them and told them to yell out as loud as they could on the count of three. Then he winked at Vickie and mouthed the words "don't say anything" where Marty couldn't see.

"Here we go," he said. "Ready? One…two…three!"

He listened closely as Marty's voice called out a loud and hearty "Helloooo!"

This time it was loud enough to get several people's attention and they turned and yelled "hello" back to her.

"Whatcha doin', Magic?" one of them called out. "Havin' a yodelin' contest? Where do I sign up?"

Marty's face turned red and she laughed. "That was cool, Magic! I've never been to place where you could just shout out something."

"That's what I love about this place. You can yell, stomp, crash into things and no one gets mad. At least not unless you drop a bowling ball on someone's toe. Then they might get mad."

"We'll try not to do that," Vickie said. "But I better warn you. I haven't bowled in quite some time so anything's possible."

He took them over to the rental counter for shoes and then showed them where the balls were kept, in a long rack behind the concourse. Marty finished lacing up her shoes and hurried over to the racks to pick out a ball. Vickie stayed behind, to talk to him.

"I want to thank you for being so nice to Marty," she said. "She was really worried about coming. She didn't want to at first but changed her mind after I told her you'd invited her personally." She paused and smiled at him. "I think she has a crush on you."

He wasn't sure how to respond. No female had ever admitted to having a crush on him before. However, more than a few of them had run away from him, fearing that they might be the ones getting crushed. "I'm sure it's nothing," he said, making light of it but at the same time enjoying the admiration. "And it isn't going to matter. Because if all goes well, by the end of the night she's going to end up with someone she really cares about."

He got back to initiating his plan and went over and helped Vickie pick out a ball. He then escorted her and Marty over to the last two lanes against the

AND THE BULL SAVED ME

right wall, where two girls about Marty's age were setting up, getting ready to bowl. He introduced Vickie and Marty to them. "This is Barb and Sarah Johnson. They're going to be your teammates and will explain the rules to you."

"But I don't bowl very well," Marty quietly protested.

He could see that she was worried about it so he took her aside and tried to reassure her. "I know you're gonna do great," he whispered to her. "And do you know how I know?"

She shook her head no.

"Because I put you with a couple of ringers, sure things."

"You mean Barb and Sarah?" she said, her eyes growing large with excitement.

"Yep. Barb was teen champion in her league last year and Sarah came in runner up. The boys won't know what hit 'em."

She giggled and began smiling like mad.

"Now go gettum!" he told her.

She hurried back to the lanes and started talking excitedly to Barb and Sarah. Vickie got wind of the conversations and came over to ask him about it.

"What's going on? I thought you wanted the boys to win?"

"I do," he said. "But I have to make it at least *look* like it's a fair game. And you're gonna need all the help you can get. Tim and his friends are damn good bowlers. But we're covered no matter who wins. If we win, I'll pick the song and if your team wins, you pick the song."

"But Marty doesn't know Tim is one of the boys bowling against us. What if she backs out?"

"She won't. Barb and Sarah will see to that. They're going to convince her that it's a grudge match between them and the boys and ask Marty to help them get even. If she's the trooper I think she is, she won't let them down."

She wrapped her arm around his and smiled up at him warmly. "You're a genius, did anyone ever tell you that?"

"All the time," he replied, the pride bursting inside his chest. He heard someone calling him from the bar area and saw Ben and Sue, waving to him. Mavis, Jack and Betsy were sitting next to them. *Uh-oh*, he thought. The moment of truth. "Come on," he told Vickie, taking her hand. "I want you and Marty to meet someone." He took them over to the table and began introducing them around. Betsy was grinning with glee, seeming to enjoy the show and he knew she was still holding strong to her beliefs that he was seeking his surrogate parents' approval. He got a chance to tease her about a few minutes later when he introduced her to Vickie and Marty.

"This is Betsy," he told them. "George's new girlfriend."

"George?" Marty said, acting confused. "You mean that cute little boy Vickie told me about?"

"That's him," Marcus replied. "But Jack and Mavis are against the marriage until George can at least reach the pedals on Betsy's car. She's a terrible driver, you see. She almost killed me driving us to Columbus a couple of weeks ago."

Everyone started laughing and Betsy shook her finger playfully at Marcus. "You think that was bad. Just wait until the next time you're out riding with me. Man, will you be sorry."

"I can't wait," Marcus said, giving her a wink.

Marty asked Vickie if she could go back over with Barb and Sarah.

"Sure. Go ahead. And I'll be right there."

Marty had no sooner taken off when Ben got Marcus's attention and pointed to the other side of the room. "Uh, Magic. Here comes the rest of your team."

Marcus watched as three teen-age boys carrying bowling bags came walking towards them. He turned to Vickie and grabbed her arm.

"You better get back over with Marty. She might panic once she sees who she's bowling against. I already told Barb and Sarah that you're gonna be the one to put the names in order on the tally sheet. Don't forget. Put your name first and hers last."

"And if she gives me an argument?" Vickie whispered.

"Barb and Sarah are ready for it if she does. They'll tell her that the other two guys are their boyfriends and that they wanna dance with them. Marty won't want to spoil their fun so I'm hoping she'll go along with it."

"And if Marty wants to dance with you, instead?"

He leaned down close to her face. "Then you're gonna have to talk her out of it. I don't want my fun spoiled, either."

"Hope this works," she said. "Meet you on the dance floor." Then she gave him a quick peck on the cheek and took off towards the lanes. He reached up and touched the lipstick on his cheek when someone behind him started laughing. It was Tim.

"Hey, Magic. You're not supposed to do the kissing thing until after we win the match and dance with them. Remember?"

Marcus felt his face flush red and wiped off the lipstick. "Uh...I forgot," he said.

"Which lane we on?" Tim asked him.

"Twenty-four," Marcus replied.

The boys took off for the lanes and Marcus went over and grabbed his bowling ball and shoes from behind the counter. As he slipped on the shoes, a burst of excitement welled up inside his chest. If he was lucky and all went well, Marty wasn't gonna be the only one having a memorable night. So was he.

A few minutes later Ben, Sue, Mavis, Betsy and Jack moved over to one of the tables along the concourse, behind the last two lanes to get a better view of the games.

"But I don't get it," Sue said. "What does Magic's plan involve?"

Ben told her to look at the scorecard, reflected up on the wall above the lane where Magic was sitting. "See what he's doing? He's putting his name first then the others and Tim's last. Now look at the scorecard in the next lane. The one Vickie's written the names on."

Sue observed it. "Vickie's name is first on the girls' list and Marty's is last. Is that what you mean?"

"That's right. Remember the rules of the dance game? No matter which side wins, the boy number ones have to dance with the girl number ones and so on. And the team with the overall highest pins at the end of three games gets to pick the song they dance to."

"Oh. So Magic gets to dance with Vickie and Tim will dance with Marty, right?"

"That's the plan," Jack added. Then he turned to Ben and asked him how his own plan was going.

"Pretty good. The rest of my 'team' should be here any time now. And you should see how Paul decorated my and his guitars."

"He's the one on the bass guitar, right?" Betsy asked.

Ben replied that he was. "And my other students are on drums and sax. Paul found some of those thin glittery streamers at the novelty store and stuck 'em on all the instruments. It should look great along with the glitter. Speaking of which…" He asked Sue if she remembered to bring the glitter.

"It's out in the back seat of the car with your guitar. Should I go get it?"

Jack suggested she wait until the games started. "It was already hard enough keeping Magic out of the ball locker area this afternoon. We don't want to make him suspicious now. He already spotted that sheet over the drums a couple hours ago. I told him someone tore a hole in the carpet so I covered it up with a chair and sheet so no one would trip over it."

Mavis laughed. "And he believed that dopey story?"

"Sure," Jack replied. "He's a businessman. The last thing he'd need is someone suing him after taking a fall on a piece of faulty carpet. Lyin' to him about that was easy. What was hard was keeping him out of the pits, in back while I worked on my part of the plan. I had to keep sticking the stuff away whenever he'd show up so he wouldn't see it. I ain't worked that hard in years."

Betsy told them how Magic was also snooping around the kitchen earlier. "But I got his mind off it by reminding him about Vickie's present."

"Yep," Jack said. "That would do it all right. He's really looking forward to giving it to her."

"What he's really looking forward to is a night that's *Magic moment* free," Ben reminded them.

"Well, let's hope that he gets it," Mavis said, getting up from the table. "But if he doesn't, that wouldn't surprise me either. Especially considering what's been going on lately. And now if you'll all excuse me, I've got some things to check on in the kitchen."

"I'll help you, Mom," Betsy said, taking off behind her.

After they left Sue asked Ben what Mavis meant.

"I'm not sure," he said.

"No but I am," Jack volunteered, clenching the pipe between his teeth. "She's talking about how Magic's *gift* has been acting up the last couple of weeks, since he's been seeing Vickie. It's almost as though it's fighting to be seen."

"But he's had streaks of *moments* like this before," Sue argued.

"True," Ben said. "But not on this level of magnitude. He's ended up in the paper more than a few times over the last ten years because of the backlash from his accidents. But the last two weeks he's been highlighted in print twice."

"It would have been three," Jack added. "But the zoo thing never made the papers. The park board did some serious spin control and kept it from the public. Probably worried that it would scare people away and hurt ticket sales. Same as the amusement parks do whenever there's an accident and someone gets hurt."

"Yeah but the stories still leak out to the locals," Ben said. "And the zoo thing did too. I heard it from some of our customers who have friends in Mayer." He then noticed a strange look on Sue's face and asked her if something was wrong.

"I'm not exactly sure," she replied. "Earlier tonight Magic was talking about how he didn't have to worry about one of his *moments* making an appearance tonight because nothing's ever happened here."

"So?" Ben asked her, not seeing her point.

"So," Sue replied. "I said to him 'No, nothing's ever happened here yet.' I was only teasing him but now, after hearing you and Jack talk about how the *moments* have been escalating lately…you don't suppose…"

"That one might show up tonight?" Ben said. "Shit. I hope not."

"Me neither," Jack added. "That really would upset him. Not exactly the reaction we were hoping for."

"Then we better keep our fingers crossed that it doesn't happen," Ben said, suddenly experiencing a sinking feeling in the pit of his stomach. "But just in case, you better check to see if Mavis has any smelling salts back in the kitchen."

"Sure thing," Jack said and then he smirked. "Who are you planning to use them on? Magic or Vickie?"

"Maybe both," Ben replied.

Marcus finished writing the names on the score sheet and turned around to his fellow team members. The three of them were putting on their bowling shoes and trading quips back and forth, going through their usual routine. The only thing not usual was the content of the banter. It wasn't as raunchy as it normally was; no doubt they'd toned it down a bit because of the female presence in the next lane. It was always fun to watch how the groups of guys and girls would act during the dance game. The boys would strut, flaunt and tease the girls and the girls would return the barbs and taunts with the same kind of fervor. Almost like a volleyball or tennis game. Except in this case the balls were twelve to sixteen pound Brunwicks and if thrown hard enough, could put a respectable hole in the wall.

Tim was like the unofficial leader of his group of friends. He was also known among his peers as the class clown. Always had a clever retort and could see the humor in any situation. He was a stand up comedian in training, using the area youth and high school faculty as his audience and victims. Stories had circulated about how he'd turned his desk into a "bucking bronco" during a discussion of the old west in history class and how he'd recited Shakespeare in rap during English lit. It exhibited his desire to leave no stone unturned in his quest for laughs. He was five feet seven inches tall, medium build and dark brown hair that no matter how much he combed it, always looked mussed.

Sitting next to him was Kip, the tall, silent type or at least the quietest of the three. He came from a family whose main hobby and love was bowling. His parents were in two leagues a week and his younger brother Scott had won the area tournament in his age class a year earlier. Kip had light brown hair, a fair complexion and wore glasses and a perpetual grin. Whenever Tim would come up with a practical joke to be played, Kip was always the first one to volunteer to help with it. His sense of humor matched Tim's but he did things more or less from the wings, not center stage. Not taking the credit but always involved.

Rob was the inventive one of the three. He was also a top student but didn't admit to it. He was blonde and had a baby face that duped people into believing he was incapable of anything devious. Truth be told, he was the mastermind behind Tim's group of friends. Always coming up with ideas for the pranks and jokes they would play on their friends or anyone else they thought worthy of doing good-humored battle with.

Part of the fun of the dance game was the constant communication going on between the male and female teams, a battle of wits, trying to wear each other down psychologically. And tonight was no different. The trio of males had no sooner finished putting on their shoes when the verbal game commenced.

"Hey, Barb, you're getting stuck with Kip," Rob chided. "If you don't want your feet stomped on dancing, you better hurry up and change your name on the list."

"And get stuck with you, again?" Barb called back. "The last time I danced with you, all you wanted to do was kiss."

"I thought that was the point," Rob whispered, causing his friends to snicker.

Marcus glanced over to Vickie's lane and watched Marty's reaction, afraid that the remark about kissing might have upset her. But the frightened look she'd been sporting earlier had disappeared and she was huddled together with Barb and Sarah, giggling. Vickie was sitting a few feet away, in the scorekeeper's chair and turned away from the girls and mouthed the words "It's working" to him.

Great, Marcus thought. Now all they had to do was to keep it up.

"Hey, Sarah," Tim called out. "Rob just rigged his walkman to his new fillings so you may want to make sure you've got accident insurance before trying to kiss him. It could be hazardous to your health."

Sarah replied that she would keep it in mind and another round of giggling from the girls followed.

"I didn't hook anything up to my fillings," Rob whispered.

Tim nudged him in the elbow. "Yeah, but this way, she'll be checking and you're almost guaranteed a kiss."

"Oh yeah," Rob replied, smiling large.

Marcus chuckled. "I should take lessons on love from you guys. My way, simply asking for a kiss, seems outdated."

Kip went over and patted Marcus on the back. "Sure thing, Magic. Any time you want help with your love life, just ask."

Marcus thanked him for the offer and tried not to laugh.

"Get a load of Dr. Love there," Tim smirked. "Thinks he's Kirklin's version of Dr. Ruth." Tim stood up, crossed his eyes at Kip and snapped his wrist guard onto his hand. "First you make sure you've got the proper protection," Tim said, using a voice that resembled an old woman's. "And then you place your fingers thusly." And he put his fingers into the ball and held it up in front of him. "Then you carefully pull back and *thrust* the ball forward, making sure not to injure your partner or anyone else in the general vicinity. You release and if you are a very, very good boy, you *score!*"

Marcus joined the others and laughed at the display. The girls had also observed the show and Marty seemed to be enjoying it more than anyone.

"Come on, Dr. Ruth," Tim told Kip. "Let's bowl."

The contest began and the kids went into their usual gaming mode, trading barbs and insults in between bowling frames. Marcus's team started off well, helped along by Kip throwing a turkey (three strikes in a row) in the fourth frame. The girls were watching the score closely and every time one of the boys would throw a strike or spare, the girls' taunts would get louder, trying to throw off the guys' concentration.

Marcus got up to bowl the second half of his sixth frame when Vickie came over to him, still holding her ball.

"Uh, it's against the rules to drop your ball on my feet to stop me from trying to make this spare," he said, teasing her.

"Oh, I wouldn't do anything like that," she said, switching the ball to her other hand and out of way of his feet below. "I only wanted to give you an update on your plan. It's working out fine. Marty's really taking to Barb and Sarah. She seems to be having a lot of fun."

"She's going to have even more after we win," he whispered. "Tim's been checking her out and he was smiling when he did it."

Vickie got a worried look on her face and Marcus knew what she was thinking. "It's all right," he told her. "Tim and his friends like to talk big but when it comes right down to it, they're perfect gentleman. Besides, they're gonna have chaperones when they dance. Remember? Me and you."

She started to say something else when Kip yelled over at him. "Hey, Magic. You're holding up the game!"

Vickie went back over to the girls' side and Marcus got back to finishing up his frame. Afterwards he took his seat and Kip kidded him about Vickie.

"Hey, Magic. Who's the hottie? The one talkin' to you just now?"

"Yeah, and who's the girl you got Tim hooked up with?" Rob whispered. "She's not bad, either."

"The young lady's name is Marty Garrett and her older sister's name is Vickie," he told them. "Vickie also happens to be my girlfriend so you're not allowed to drool over her."

Kip and Rob made a few catcalls and Tim gave Marcus a hearty thumbs up as he went over and grabbed his ball to bowl the next frame.

"Okay," Rob said. "But we *are* allowed to drool over Marty, right?" At which point Tim tipped his ball at Rob and warned him.

"No drooling. You'll end up drowning her. Besides, she's dancing with me, not you."

They went back to the game and Marcus noticed that in spite of the boys' easygoing banter, they were bowling competitively. The girls also seemed to be making a respectable showing and Marty's score continued to improve with each game. They were halfway through the third game when Ben motioned Marcus back to his and Sue's table.

"How goes it?" Ben inquired. "From here it looks like the score is pretty close."

"It is," Marcus agreed. "We won the first game but Barb's turkey won them the second game and added a lot to their pin total. We're ahead by ten pins so far this game but it's definitely up for grabs. How's everyone else doing?" He paused and glanced around at the other lanes. Usually he was the observer, not one of the participants.

"It looks like the girls are the big winners tonight," Ben remarked. "We've heard more fast songs than slow ones coming from the jukebox."

Marcus noticed Betsy, standing with a group of people over by the ball lockers. He asked Jack what she was doing.

"Oh," Jack said, clearing his throat and taking his pipe from his mouth. "She's handing out free passes to anyone who bowls over two hundred."

"Must be a lot of people bowling over two hundred," Marcus said, watching closer as Betsy talked to a group of seven or eight people. "The lanes must be generous tonight." A few people saw him looking in their direction and stopped to wave at him. He waved back, wondering what was going on. "Everyone seems to be in good spirits," he remarked.

"Must be something in the air," Mavis said.

Marcus noticed that Mavis had gotten rid of the apron and was also wearing some makeup, accenting the Sunday best she was wearing. He asked her what she was so dressed up for.

"Oh, that," she said, acting like it was nothing. "Jack's promised to take me out to a fancy dinner later. So I thought I'd dress up." She paused and looked down at herself. "Do you like it?"

He told her that he did. Then he glanced over at Jack and smiled. "And I hope you're going home to change before you take your pretty lady out."

Jack gave him a *what's wrong with the way I look* shrug and replied that he wasn't doing any such thing. "Besides, I gotta stick around in case I have trouble with the pinsetters and I can't do that in a suit."

Marcus turned and looked at the lanes. All of them seemed to be working fine. "Why?" he asked Jack. "Do you expect some trouble with one of them? I wondered why you were spending so much time in the pit today." It was then that he noticed more than a few people from the other lanes, staring and smiling at him. He asked Jack what was going on.

"Nothing, Magic. They're just curious 'cause the Boss Man is playing the dance game with the kids. That's all."

"Not nervous, are you?" Sue asked him. "Knowin' you've got an audience?"

"It wouldn't be the first time," Ben whispered.

"Yeah but I'm not used to being stared at while I'm at work," Marcus noted. "It usually only happens when…" But he stopped himself from saying it; worried that repeating it out loud would put a hex on what had so far been an event-free evening.

"What's that, Magic?" Ben asked him.

"Never mind," he said. A second later Kip called to him, telling him he was up. "Gotta go," Marcus replied, hurrying back to the lane area. A lot of times, before one of his accidents or *moments* would happen, he'd get a prickling feeling at the back of his neck, almost as though his subconscious was warning him. But so far he'd gotten no such feeling or premonition. As he stepped up onto the lane he paused and ran his hand against the back of his neck. He took his hand away and waited. Nothing. Nothing at all. He breathed a sigh of relief and picked up his bowling ball.

The game remained close for the next few frames and the comments between the kids escalated proportionately. Marty joined Barb and Sarah in egging on the boys, who seemed to revel in the attention. The girls finished their game first and after bowling his last frame Marcus tallied the total pins for both teams and announced the results to everyone.

"The girls are ahead but Tim's got one more frame to bowl. His tenth."
"Then can we still win?" Kip asked excitedly.
"Only if Tim bowls two strikes and four pins," Marcus replied.

Right away the girls started whooping and hollering like they'd already won. Everyone that was, except Vickie who was sitting in the scorekeeper's chair, smiling at Marcus. To them, it didn't matter which team won because the fix was already in. If the girls' team won, Vickie was to hurry over to the jukebox and pick a slow song before Marty or the other girls could protest. If the guys won, Marcus would pick a slow song which is what the guys wanted anyway. Either way, the girls were going to slow dance with the guys. But only Marcus and Vickie (and a few friends sitting at one of the tables behind them) knew about it.

"Okay, Tim," Marcus told him. "It's all up to you."

Kip and Rob started patting Tim on the back, giving him words of encouragement. Tim picked up his ball and as he got into his stance, Marty and the girls started yelling, making noises to distract him.

"Please, ladies!" Rob exclaimed, holding up his hands in protest. "At least give the man a sporting chance!"

The girls' chanting was immediately replaced with rounds of giggles. Tim threw his first ball and the noise level in the place dropped to nothing more than a hush as the ball rolled down the alley. Marcus glanced around, surprised at the lack of noise from the other bowlers. They'd all finished their games and were now sitting at their lanes or tables on the concourse, staring in his direction, or more appropriately, at Tim.

What's going on? he thought to himself but the question was pushed aside as he heard the ball hit the pins and the sounds of Rob and Kip, yelling with triumph behind him.

"Strike one!" Kip hollered. Then he immediately put his fingers to his mouth and shushed everyone as Tim got into position to throw the next ball. Marcus temporarily forgot about the rest of the customers as he was drawn up in the action. Tim released the ball and Marcus immediately worried that he'd thrown it with too much English, causing it to miss the head pin. But at the last minute it curved into the pocket and once more, Tim scored a strike.

The entire place erupted with applause and Marcus turned and saw Jack,

AND THE BULL SAVED ME

Ben, Sue, Mavis and Betsy joining the rest of customers, yelling their support.

Once again, it got quiet as Tim got into his stance.

"What's everyone looking at?" Rob whispered.

"They're watching Tim, you idiot," Kip scolded. "Now pipe down."

Tim took a minute and glanced around at all the people watching him. "What's going on, Magic?"

Marcus knew he was feeling the pressure so he went up and talked to him. "Don't worry about it. I think they're all staring because the girls' teams have been winning all night. Jack told me they've been playing nothing but fast songs on the jukebox. Every guy in the place is waiting for you to get even for them. You up to that? Striking a blow for the male of the species?"

Tim grinned. "You betcha."

"Then go gettum!" Marcus said, giving him a last pat on the back. "Four pins, Tim. That's all we need." Marcus backed up a few feet to give him room. Tim stood straight and tall, the ball poised motionless in his hands as he stared down the alley, seemingly oblivious to everything around him. He swung the ball back and as he released it, a few of the spectators gasped with excitement. A stilted silence ensued as the ball rolled down the alley. It was as if everyone in the place was holding their breath, waiting for the ball to strike the pins. The ball began to curve over, towards the head pin and a few seconds later it hit, the pins crashing every which way, leaving only the number seven pin standing. The place exploded in applause and Kip and Rob started dancing around, whooping it up.

Tim simply turned to the crowd, gave them a toothy grin and took a dramatic bow.

"Nice job, Tim," Marcus said. "Tell the guys to grab their partners 'cause we're picking the music." He dug into his pockets for a quarter and headed for the bar. A group of kids had just finished a fast dance and was leaving the floor. He wove through them and went over to the jukebox in the corner. He had the selection number memorized. M26. He put the quarter in the slot and as he made the selection, Tim came up behind him.

"Something slow, Magic. Remember?"

Marcus turned around and couldn't help but smile as he saw Tim holding on to Marty's hand. Marty, on the other hand, wasn't only smiling, she was beaming.

"This one's perfect," Marcus told him as he spotted Vickie walking towards him. He took her hand and led her out onto the floor. Kip, Sarah and the others had already taken their places and in spite of the fact that they were being forced to dance slow, the girls were all smiles.

The couples started dancing as the song "I Knew I Loved You" filled the air. Vickie gazed up at Marcus, a look of such love and warmth in her eyes that it made his heart ache.

"I told you the plan would work," he told her, nodding over to where Tim and Marty were dancing together.

"It's not that," she whispered. "That song..."

"Yep. It's the same one you were singing that first day I met you."

"It's Savage Garden's song," she said, her voice cracking with emotion.

"Not any more," he whispered, taking her into his arms. "Now it's our song."

She hugged him so tight that it took his breath away. But he didn't mind. He loved it. They danced, holding each other close. He closed his eyes and laid his head down upon hers, the soft curls pressing against his cheeks.

He was finally getting to live out his fantasy. His dream.

They swayed to the music and he felt himself drawn away, just as in the dream. It was a sweet, sensual place where only their love for one another existed. Where she would always be with him, always love him. He wouldn't be alone any more. He enjoyed his personal reverie as the music played softly in the distance. The melody seemed to melt away as if it too, was floating further and further away. But the feeling of having her close remained. And his happiness with it. It was as if they'd *become* the music, their bodies pressed close together and sharing the same blissful sensation.

He saw another image form in his mind, a vision of the not too distant future. They were dancing together but it wasn't at The Crystal. It was somewhere else. A ballroom maybe. And they were dressed differently, too. He was in a tux and she was in a floor length dress. A wedding dress. He smiled and let the picture in his head blossom. A few seconds later he heard a voice, whispering to him.

"Marcus?"

He smiled as he recognized her voice, calling to him. He hugged her tighter and pushed his face down against her hair, the warmth surrounding him.

"Marcus?"

This time her voice was louder and he could feel the vibration as she said it. He knew he should open his eyes but didn't want to leave this warm, wonderful place. She started giggling and called his name again.

"Marcus?"

He opened his eyes and lifted his head, his heart aching from being torn from his fantasy. But he was jolted back to reality as he saw Kip, Tim, Marty and the others sporting huge grins and staring at him. What's more, his audience wasn't confined t to the dance floor. Ben, Sue, Mavis, Jack and everyone else in the bar and some of the nearby lanes were smiling at him, too.

"The song's been over for a while," Vickie whispered. "But you seemed to be enjoying yourself so I didn't say anything until everyone started staring at us."

He felt his face flush red and nodded, signaling that he understood. The rest of the audience broke into applause and Marcus bent down and whispered "sorry" to Vickie.

"I'm not," she said. She threw her arms around his neck and kissed him, passionately. A bunch of catcalls and whistles commenced and even though he was still embarrassed, he let himself get drawn away again by the soft warmth of her lips. She let go of him a moment later and his head started spinning, making him dizzy.

"Hey, Magic!" Rob yelled. "If you really want to impress her, then dip her!"

"Dip her?" Marcus said, but he never got to finish the question. Vickie grabbed him around the waist, placed her left foot behind him and bent him backwards. He let out a "whoa!" of surprise, thinking he was going to fall but she held on to him tight. She leaned down, gave him a quick kiss on the lips and then pulled him to his feet again.

"How's that for a dip?" she said.

"Way to go, sis!" Marty yelled. She and Tim were standing off to the side with the others, laughing. Vickie took Marcus by the hand and led him off the dance floor as their audience of onlookers applauded. He knew it must have looked silly but somehow, it had made him proud, too. It felt nice having her act as if he belonged to her. No woman had ever done that before. It gave him a sense of belonging and security.

A sense of being loved.

They went over to the bar and Marcus asked Tyler for a couple of soft drinks for him and Vickie. After Tyler left to get the drinks, Vickie apologized to Marcus for startling him. "But after hearing your teammates tease you about dipping me, I knew you'd never do it because you're such a gentleman. So I thought 'what the heck?' and did it myself."

"What shocked me was how strong you were. What are you? A bodybuilder?"

"Nope. Just a girl whose ex-boyfriend was. I used to spot for him sometimes and I still work out with a set of my own twelve pound weights." Then she paused, a faint glint showing in her eyes. "I like to be prepared for whatever emergency might crop up where a little extra strength might be needed."

Like running from elephants and after idiots dressed up as werewolves, he thought. She was right. Anyone trying to keep up with his *gift* would have to be strong.

They took their drinks and went over and sat down at Ben's table. Everyone immediately began kidding him about Vickie's "dip." But he didn't mind the ribbing. It was only his friends' way of making Vickie feel welcome and he loved them for it. Even Betsy seemed to be going out of her way to make Vickie feel more comfortable; discussing everything from little George to exchanging make-up tips. By the time they got done talking a little while later, Betsy had arranged for another "bowling" date when Vickie could come and watch George and Sue had made plans for him and Vickie to come for dinner the following week. He couldn't help but feel a special pride for his friends and as much as he didn't want to admit it, Betsy was right. He *had* been seeking approval. From his "family," his friends.

As usual, they'd come through for him admirably.

A few minutes later he watched as his friends conspired, in his favor. First Ben asked Sue to dance; something he rarely ever did. Then Mavis and Betsy headed back to the kitchen, making an excuse that they had to check on how the new cook was getting along. Then Jack remarked that he had to go check on the pin setters, even though all twenty-four lanes seemed to be running smoothly. That's when Marcus knew what they were up to. They were giving him some time alone so he could give Vickie her present.

He took advantage of his friends' generosity and went over behind the bar to get it. He asked Tyler how it was going.

"Busy, even for a Friday night. But so far no one's tried to molest any of the pinball machines."

"Let's hope it stays that way," Marcus said, grabbing the box and heading back to the table. But Vickie was no longer alone. Marty had returned and was sitting next to her.

"Tim, Barb and the others asked me to help them with something," she told Vickie. "Can I?"

"But what is it?" Vickie asked.

Marty smiled at Marcus and he was stunned at the transformation. The frightened look was gone and her face was flushed pink with happiness. "I can't tell you. It's a secret," she told Vickie. "But don't worry, it's for something here. Magic's friend Jack is helping us with it."

Vickie asked Marcus what it was.

"Beats me. Could be anything. He's been acting kind of secretive all day. But I'm sure that whatever it is, it's okay. He'll watch out for Marty."

"Okay," Vickie said and as soon as she said it, Marty stood up and gave Marcus a hug.

"That's for inviting me to your place," she said. "I absolutely love it!" And with that she bounded away, back towards the counter where Tim and the others were waiting for her.

Marcus sat down next to Vickie and started to hand her the box when several people entered the bar and took the table next to them. They were laughing and talking loud, making it hard to hear anything else. So he took Vickie's hand and they went in search of a more private spot. The last few barstools at the back of the bar were empty so they took the last two.

"I have something for you," he said, handing her the box again. "I know your birthday isn't until Sunday but I thought I'd give it to you now, just in case."

"Just in case what?" she asked.

He cleared his throat, trying to come up with a good excuse. "Uh, I meant in case something happened and..." He closed his eyes and cursed his big mouth. What the hell was he doing? Deliberately trying to scare her away? He was thinking that just in case another one of his *moments* happened and she ended up leaving him, he'd still like her to have the present. But he was supposed to *think* it, not say it *out loud*. "I only meant..." he stammered, covering his tracks, "that I know you always have dinner with your parents on Sundays so I probably wouldn't see you then."

"Oh," she replied. "You sure there's nothing else that you want to tell me?"

He searched her face, wondering what she was alluding to. "No," he replied, feeling confused. "That was all."

"Oh, okay," she said, acting a little disappointed.

He asked her if something was wrong.

"No, nothing," she said. She put down the box and reached into her purse and brought out a similar looking box. "I've got something for you, too," she said, handing him the present. "Happy birthday."

"But how did you know it was my birthday?"

"The DMV clerk, remember? When I called her for your name, she also gave me your birthday." She asked him to open his first.

He peeled off the brightly colored paper and bow and opened the lid. It was a small tie tack, in the shape of an elephant with tiny gems of different colors embedded in the body.

"It's Benji," she said. "At least it looks like him. I saw it in a jewelry case at the mall and had to get it for you."

He felt a lump in his throat and tried to mask it. A present. No woman he'd ever dated had given him a present before. Extraordinary. "Thanks," he said, carefully taking the tie tack out of the box and holding it up to the light. "I like Benji this size better," he told her. "Much easier to outrun."

"You better keep him away from your popcorn cart," she added. "Otherwise you'll wind up with popcorn all over the bowling alley, like the zoo."

He thanked her for the present and gave her a kiss on the cheek. "Now open yours," he told her. She opened up the box and her face lit up like a light bulb.

"Oh, Marcus, it's beautiful. Wherever did you find it? It looks exactly like them."

"I saw it one day when I was out shopping," he told her, lying. He wasn't going to admit it took an hour of going through books at the jewelers to find it and order it special.

"It looks exactly like the dolphins we saw at the zoo," she whispered.

"Amazing coincidence, huh? I thought it would be a nice souvenir. Something to remind you of the aquarium."

She moved closer and put her arms around his neck. "What it's going to remind me of is that kiss you gave me." And she pulled him to her, pressing her lips against his. Once again he was propelled into sweet, sensual bliss, surrounded by her warmth and touch. She was like an emotion elixir, sweeping him away every time she kissed him. He'd known passion before but this was different. It was a whole new sensation. One that clutched at his heart and soul, leaving him breathless. He felt his head spin and slowly began to drift away when the sound of Tyler's voice echoed through the haze.

"Hey, Magic. You'd better look at this."

He felt Vickie pull away and opened his eyes, his mind and heart still lingering on the kiss. She was turned away from him, looking back at the lanes. A strange, prickling sensation began at the back of his neck and he stood up from the barstool, the panic quickly replacing the passion he'd been enjoying a few seconds earlier. A general quiet had settled over the place, causing his safety mechanisms to kick in automatically. The usual clamor of pins being knocked down was normal in a bowling alley. The absence of the noise was disquieting.

"What in the world?" Vickie said, coming out from between the barstools. The lights had all been lowered and an eerie glow shined out from the bowling area.

"Those are our Glow Bowl lights," he told her. "But they shouldn't be on tonight." He followed her toward the lanes, a sense of dread creeping over him like a shroud. It had all the earmarks of being one of his *moments*. "I'm sure it's nothing," he told her, wondering if he was trying to convince her or himself. He suddenly felt betrayed. It wasn't supposed to happen. Not here. Not now. Just when she was getting to know him better.

"Look at that!" Vickie whispered, taking his hand and leading him towards the concourse.

He followed alongside of her, keeping his head down. Whatever it was, he didn't want to see it. A sudden burst of applause erupted, startling him and forcing him to look up. He squeezed Vickie's hand tight, not sure what was going on.

"It's all right!" she said, trying to be heard over the noise. "It's for you! Your birthday!"

People started patting him on the back, congratulating him. That was when he saw what everyone had been staring at. Every single lane, all twenty-four of them had a banner hanging down over the pins. The banners contained one letter each and were made of some kind of shiny material that shimmered in the glowing lights. The banners spelled out the words "Happy Birthday Magic."

"My birthday?" he said, still stunned. "I'd forgotten about it." At least he had until Vickie gave him his present a few minutes earlier. But something like this, he'd never expected. The applause got louder as Jack came walking out from between lanes twelve and thirteen. The big smile on his face gave away who'd been responsible for the banners. Jack walked up and shook his hand.

"Happy Birthday, Magic. Isn't she a beaut? I've been working for a week on it, trying to get it in place without you finding out. Betsy helped me with the letters a little, but the rest I did myself."

Marcus could hear the pride in his voice as he said it and was overwhelmed by the gesture. All he could manage was a quiet "thanks."

"And speaking of Betsy…" Jack said, nodding towards the bar.

Marcus turned and saw Betsy and Mavis pushing one of the metal carts from the kitchen towards them. It was holding a large sheet cake with what looked like an exact replica of a bowling ball in the middle. There were two lit sparklers mounted on the sides of the cake, sending sparks out in every direction. Mavis came over and gave him a kiss on the cheek and wished him a happy birthday.

"That looks like a real bowling ball," he told her in between chuckles.

"It's chocolate cake!" Betsy gushed, coming over and giving him a hug. "Your favorite. Mom had a dickens of a time getting it to stay in one place while she frosted it."

People began to crowd in around the cake and Betsy handed him a knife to cut it. He finally let go of Vickie's hand and leaned down and whispered to her.

"Thanks for holding on to me. The whole thing took me by surprise."

"Glad to be of service," she said. "You're lucky to have such wonderful friends."

Lucky to be with you, too, he thought. Hope my luck holds.

He cut into the cake and had already handed out a few pieces when music began playing behind him. He turned and saw a group of people crowded around near the west entrance. Then he saw what they were looking at. A four-piece band, highlighted with baby spotlights positioned on the floor in front of them, was playing in the ball locker area. One of the members was on drums, another on sax, and two people on guitars. The guitars were decorated like magic wands, complete with streamers and glitter.

"It's Ben," Marcus said, recognizing the guitarist on the right. He took Vickie's hand and led her across the room. As they neared the band, he saw who the other guitarist was. Paul, Ben's best student and fellow song collaborator. And standing off to the side, in front of one of the spotlights was Sue. She was throwing handfuls of glitter into the air in front of the light, giving the whole scene a magic feel, which was only appropriate, considering the song Ben and Paul were singing. It was "Do You Believe in Magic?"

"Oh, my God," Marcus whispered. "I can't believe he did this."

Vickie began clapping in rhythm with the rest of the crowd. Within seconds the entire place was clapping in time. It was as if the building itself had come alive, announcing its existence to the world in rhythmic pulse.

"Come on!" Vickie said, having to shout to be heard over the noise. "Since Ben went to all this trouble, let's take advantage of it and dance!"

He readily agreed and they threaded their way back through the crowd to the bar. Several couples had already gotten the same idea and were up dancing, including Marty, Tim and the other kids from their teams. As he put his arms around Vickie and began swaying to the music, he couldn't help but smile. He was in his place, surrounded by his friends, people who cared about him. And best yet, she was there with him, sharing it.

It didn't get any better than that.

They danced nonstop for the next half-hour when Ben announced that the band was taking a break. Ben and Sue joined Vickie and Marcus at one of the tables near the dance floor. Some of the glitter was still clinging to Sue's hair and clothes.

"You're sparkling," Marcus told her.

She leaned closer to him. "So are you," she whispered. "And I'm happy for you." Then she gave him a hug and wished him happy birthday.

He started to ask what she was talking about when a voice came over the P.A.

"'Scuse me, folks," the voice said. "But we'd like to interrupt the festivities for a minute to make an announcement."

"Hey, that's Tim!" Ben said.

Another voice came over the mike, but this time it was female.

"We'd like to ask everyone to sing Happy Birthday to Magic."

"Why, that's Marty!" Vickie exclaimed.

Marcus looked closer and saw that she was right. Marty was standing behind the rental counter, holding the microphone with Tim. Barb, Kip, Rob and Sarah were crowded around them.

"Okay, everyone," Tim announced again. "This is for our fearless leader. One…two…" And then all the kids started singing Happy Birthday. Everyone joined in and the song soon filled the room.

"I can't believe she did something like that," Vickie said. She asked Marcus if he knew about it.

"Nope. But I have a sneaking suspicion who did." And he told Vickie to look at who was standing behind Marty and the other kids. Jack.

"So that's what it was she was talking about," Vickie said. "The thing she was doing with Jack."

The kids finished the song and came over and congratulated him.

"It was all Tim's idea!" Marty said. "He got Jack to help us with it."

"And now for the cake!" Kip hollered and he and the other kids made a beeline to where Betsy and Mavis were still handing out pieces of Magic's birthday cake. Marty stayed behind and Marcus thanked her again for the song.

"No. Thank you," she replied, giving him a look that communicated something closer to friendship. He gazed into her eyes, a sense of awe filling his heart. The Crystal had been a magic ball for her, just as it had for him. Sometimes, amazing things could happen.

Sometimes it really was magic.

"You better get over here, Marty!" Rob called to her. "Tim's going face first into Magic's cake!"

"Yeah," Kip added. "He's drooling over *it* instead of you, for a change!"

"Be right there!" she replied. She then told Marcus she needed to talk to Vickie alone for a minute.

"Sure thing," he said, turning around to talk to Ben, giving them some privacy. She and Vickie went into a whispering mode for a couple minutes and then Marty took off with her friends again.

"What was that all about?" Ben asked Vickie. "Or is it some kind of secret that you can't tell us?"

"No secret," Vickie said, smiling at Marcus. "Just a favor. Marty said the kids are going to Riverbend tomorrow, that water park in Summit. Tim and the others want Marty to go with them."

"That's great," Ben said. "So, what's the problem?"

"My parents," Vickie replied. "I know Tim, Barb and the others are nice kids but my parents will never allow Marty to go out alone with them. However, if she had a chaperone…"

"Or two chaperones," Ben said, kicking Marcus under the table, trying to give him a hint.

"Water park?" Marcus said, his mind switching into high gear, trying to picture possible scenarios.

"You know you want to go," Ben said, slapping him on the back. "Go ahead."

Marcus suddenly felt pressured. He wanted to say yes but his safety mechanisms were telling him otherwise.

"Is it okay?" Vickie asked him, a worried look on her face. "Could you go with us?"

He knew if he delayed answering any longer, it would hurt her feelings. He swallowed hard, trying to ignore his fear and answered her.

"Sure. I'd love to."

She put her arm around his and gave him a smile that melted his heart. Whatever reservations he'd had a few seconds earlier suddenly seemed inconsequential. He just wanted her to keep smiling at him that same way.

"Okay, now that we've got that settled, let's get back to discussing a few other upcoming events," Ben said.

"That's right," Sue told Vickie. "Like when you and Magic come to dinner next week." She and Vickie put their heads together and began talking about menu selections.

"Come on, Magic," Ben said, prompting him up from his seat. "Let's leave the menu planning to the experts and go get some refills."

Marcus followed Ben to the bar, glad to get him alone for a minute. After giving Tyler the drink orders he told Ben about his concerns.

"You're getting upset for nothing," Ben told him.

"Yeah, Ben. But a water park? I don't like it."

"Calm down, Magic. It's only a bunch of swimming pools and water slides. There's no animals to chase you and if you start a fire, there's plenty of water to put it out with. And they don't allow any sea life, so you should be safe from squids and lizards."

"Yeah, Ben, but…"

"Relax, Magic. She still doesn't know about you and with any luck, she won't find out until you're ready for her to. Besides, she's already committed to coming to dinner at our place. And that should be safe."

"Jesus, I forgot about going to your place. There's another worry that's gonna keep me up nights."

Ben asked him why he was worried and Marcus rolled his eyes in frustration. "Have you forgotten about some of the other times when I had dinner at your place. Like last month when I caught the damn grill on fire?"

"Oh, that," Ben replied.

"I turned the damn thing into a fireball, for Chrisakes. And what about back in June when I helped you and Sue wallpaper and some of your students showed up to help? I turned your living room into a flypaper haven. How was I to know the paper already had glue on it and only needed water applied? I was only trying to make it stick to the wall."

"It stuck to the wall all right," Ben chuckled. "And everyone and everything else it came into contact with. Man, that was funny. The kids loved it, especially Paul. He said he never knew wallpapering could be so much fun. But my favorite part was when Sue's mom tried to help you and ended up getting glued to the stepladder. I thought we'd never get her off the damn thing. And, boy, was she pissed that her 'do' was ruined. I thought she was gonna kill you."

"See what I mean? It could happen again."

"Stop worrying," Ben said, giving him a nudge. "Besides, we're not wallpapering. Just having dinner. I'll make sure Sue doesn't serve anything potentially flammable or made with alcohol or sea animals. We can even make it completely vegetarian if you like. And as for the trip to the water park, you'll be fine. Sue and I would volunteer to go along for support but I've got lessons all day tomorrow. Plus, I've got to check on the bank loan."

"Hey, that's right," Marcus said, trying to forget about his own problem for the time being. "Have you heard anything yet?"

"Not yet. They're still working out the numbers and I've got to drop off some documents to them tomorrow. But I should know soon."

"Good luck," Marcus told him, meaning it.

"You, too," Ben replied. "But just in case something should happen, don't forget to give me and Jack a call, okay? We're your personal cheering section and moral support group, remember?"

"I won't forget," Marcus replied, picking up the drinks and heading back to the table with Ben. But as he took his seat next to Vickie, he said a silent prayer that he wouldn't have to make that call.

CHAPTER EIGHT

Marcus pulled into the parking lot at Riverbend Water Park at a little past ten the next morning. It was a typical, sunny, hot August day and the lot was already two-thirds full. He found an empty spot and had no sooner parked the car when Marty jumped out of the back seat, asking if she could go on ahead to meet Barb and the others, standing and waiting for her by the front gate. Vickie checked with her, to make sure she had enough money and some sunscreen and then let her go. Marty hurried across the lot, the sound of her flipflops echoing against the blacktop and the thigh-high cotton jacket covering her one piece swimsuit, flapping lightly in the wake.

"I don't know if I'm doing the right thing," Vickie said as she exited the car. "My father would have a fit if he knew I let Marty go off dressed like that. Even if it is the same thing everyone else is wearing. Do you think her suit's too revealing?"

As she asked him, Marcus turned around from locking up the car and noticed a couple of twenty-something girls walking by, dressed in string bikinis and thongs. "Not compared to some others," he replied, enjoying the view. Vickie came around the car and walked up to him, a peeved look on her face.

"I like that," she said, opening her own cotton covering and showing off what was underneath. "I go to all the trouble of wearing my best suit and here you are, looking at someone else."

He felt his heart jump into his throat as he stared at her. She'd been wearing the cotton covering back when she got into the car outside of her apartment so until now, he didn't know what her suit looked like. It was a bit conservative; a one-piece blue spandex but the slightly low cut front and high thigh design showed off enough skin to make any man's heart race.

"Uh, it's lovely," he said, trying hard not to drool.

"Why, thank you," she said, breaking into a grin as she noticed his reaction. She grabbed his arm and they walked together towards the entrance. "I like your suit, too," she added.

He glanced down at himself and snickered. "I haven't worn these trunks since last year when I went with my junior league to the city pool. They were faded and old then. I wanted to pick up a new pair but didn't have time. But they should do for today." He checked the string of the waistband. He discovered that morning that it was frazzled and worn, probably due to chlorine and age. But there was still enough left for him to make a good knot. He pulled on the string to check it and it still felt secure.

They paid for their tickets at the entrance and as they headed into the park, Vickie told him that Marty had signed up for the dance game the next two weeks.

"Then I take it you haven't told your father about it, right?" he said, suddenly seeing another opportunity open up. If they were still keeping it a secret from the man, someone would have to drive Marty to The Crystal and he hoped that somebody was Vickie.

"No," she replied. "And neither does my mother."

"Then does that mean you'll be accompanying Marty to The Crystal?"

She smiled at him. "Yes it does. Why? Did you have something in mind?"

He told her he did and quickly suggested they go to dinner somewhere while Marty was bowling.

"That's a great idea," she said. "But I wouldn't want to leave Marty alone too long so it would have to be somewhere close by. Any ideas?"

Somewhere far away from any animals, he thought, trying to come up with a place that would be suitable. He knew where he wanted to take her—his apartment. But to suggest something so bold after she'd made such a fuss about him being a "gentleman" would probably scare her off. And nowhere in town would do because his *Magic moments* might make an appearance. The only safe place was at The Crystal but having barbeque wings at the bar didn't seem very romantic.

"We could check on the movie times uptown," she said.

Uh-oh, he thought. *How do I say no without telling her I've been banned from the place?* "I'm not much of a movie fan," he said.

"How about the park?" she suggested. "That little one up near the courthouse? I always walk by it every day after work but never get a chance to stop."

Park, he thought. He'd taken Marilyn to a park and nothing had gone wrong. It only went wrong after going back to her apartment. "That's an idea," he replied. "We could grab some Chinese takeout from Noy's Place on the corner across from the courthouse and sit and eat it in the park."

Yeah, takeout, he thought. That was the ticket. You're in, you're out. Five minutes tops. No time for any *moments* to appear and cause any trouble or mayhem. And there shouldn't be an animal problem, either. Only an occasional squirrel and birds had been spotted in the park. No horses, emus or elephants. It might just work.

"It's a date," she said. "And don't forget. We're going to Ben and Sue's Thursday night."

That's two more dates for sure, he thought, experiencing a feeling of euphoria. He was still on an emotional high from the night before. The party at The Crystal had been the literal "icing on the cake" to a perfect date. No *moments* to have to explain away. No questions to answer. Only good times with Vickie and his friends. He couldn't help but smile as he followed her along the path towards the attractions. Perhaps he'd seen the worst of his "condition" and it had finally decided to take a much-needed rest. And why not he thought? It had been working overtime lately. It was almost as if...it was fighting him...fighting to let Vickie see it. He scoffed and quickly dismissed the idea. His condition wasn't the only thing working overtime. His imagination was, too.

It had been almost twelve years since he'd been to the water park and a lot had changed. Before it had been a mismatched bunch of small attractions consisting mostly of an old water log ride, two water slides and a small beach area. Now the place appeared to be three to four times larger, housing everything from a small, manmade waterfall inside one of the three large, Olympic size pools to a seven-foot mushroom that spewed out water. There were manmade beaches all around the wading areas and the sand was kept pristinely clean by the myriad park workers who went around with their dustpans and scoops, whisking up every tiny bit of litter. The older water rides had been replaced with new ones, including something called Thunder Canyon that sent round, boat like cars under three waterfalls and that almost assured the passengers of getting drenched. There was also a water log ride that had a large boat that could seat up to twenty people at a time. It went by conveyor to the top of a cut out, water-filled plume. From there it descended down, splashing water not only on the riders but the people standing on the bridge in front of the ride.

But the crowning pride of the place was the hundred-foot tower that sat in the middle of the park and held the water slides. The tower was concrete and had three metal staircases leading up to a main platform. At the top was an enclosure where people were seen filing in from the stairs. Six different colored water plumes extended from the building at different angles, making the structure resemble a giant octopus. Marty was standing on one of the staircases on the right, waving to Marcus and Vickie. Barb, Tim and the others were crowded around her and also waving.

Two of the slides were smaller to accommodate the pint-sized riders and all six plumes ended up in wading pools at the bottom where people could be seen splashing and playing in the water. The last twenty feet of the slide was open at the top, allowing spectators to view the sliders on their final descent before landing in the pool. From the repeat of the echoed shouts and yells coming from inside the plumes, quite a few people were using the slides.

A boy in blue swim trunks came sliding down the plume on the far right. He was flat on his back and didn't seem to have any control over his descent, simply sliding with the flow of the water. His body went off the end of the plume and flew into the air and he let out one great big whoop right before plunging into the water. His head popped up out of the water a second later and he started laughing like crazy.

"We've *got* to try that!" Vickie exclaimed, pulling Marcus towards the tower.

They stopped at the rental counter underneath the slides to get a locker where they could stash their belongings. They stowed away her purse, his wallet, car keys and a bottle of sunscreen, pausing long enough to apply a liberal coating of the lotion to any exposed areas of skin. She pinned the locker key to the inside strap of her suit with a safety pin and they headed up the stairs to the slides. For the next couple of hours they enjoyed the slides and other attractions in the park. Marty checked in with them from time to time and from the huge smile on her face, it was clear she was having a lot of fun.

At twelve-thirty Marcus and Vickie stopped for lunch at one of the concession stands. They munched on corndogs and fries and talked nonstop like a couple of magpies. She told him some of her friend John's funny jokes and he told her about growing up in Kirklin and different vacations he'd taken with his parents. They bought and shared a dish of ice cream as they strolled along the small beach and he felt himself relax in a way he'd never experienced before. It didn't seem like a date, somehow. It was more like two best friends, sharing time and enjoying each other's company.

His desire to be alone with her (in other words, spending the night) had been nagging at him. But he knew that there were a couple of obstacles he'd have to overcome first before it happened, the biggest one being her overprotective father. It was in the back of his mind to ask her more about the man and the opportunity came up a little while later when she told him about going fishing when she was little.

"It was at Forge Park," she said. "The place by Summit River that has the fishing areas and amusement park."

He told her he knew the place. "I sometimes go fishing there with Jack."

She said her father used to take them there all the time when they were kids. "It was his favorite place. He loved sitting on the bank of the river and watching all the people out fishing in their boats."

"Didn't he ever fish? Or you?"

She told him that her father fished every chance he got. "He doesn't have a boat. Just fishes off the piers over in Huron. As for me, I only did it once. He took me when I was about seven but I kept taking the fish he caught off the stringer and throwing them back in the water. He went home empty-handed that day. To be honest, I never saw the fun in it. Why? Do you like to fish?"

He replied that he did. "But it's not just catching the fish or going out on Jack's boat that I like. It's seeing the sunrise out on the lake. It's so quiet but spectacular at the same time. It's like listening to a symphony, but without any music. It amazed me that something so magnificent could happen so silently. It was the same with the dolphins we saw at the zoo. Watching all that power and grace exhibited but without any sound at all. It was humbling and at the same time inspirational." He saw her staring strangely at him and asked her if anything was wrong.

"No," she whispered, taking his hand. "I just happen to think you're a very special person, that's all."

He stared down at the sand, feeling his face flush with embarrassment. "Thank you," he said, suddenly feeling like a teenager again. It wasn't as though he'd never received a compliment from a woman before. But they usually came after the women had decided to leave him for greener and less dangerous pastures. Comments like "you're a nice man but I don't think we're compatible" were par for the course. But this was different. It was also encouraging. If she thought he was special then maybe it would be harder for her to leave him once she found out the truth.

Yep. Things were looking up.

They walked over to the main pool's wading area. A bunch of children were laughing, jumping in and around a circle of water spewed out by a seven-foot mushroom in the middle of the pool. Marcus and Vickie waded out near the mushroom to watch.

"I remember doing that when I was younger," Vickie shouted, trying to be heard over the noise of the falling water. She waded forward, joining in with the children, throwing her hands in the air, laughing and jumping around. It looked silly but also fun and Marcus soon found himself smiling at the sight.

"Come on!" she yelled, reaching out from the water and grabbing his hand. "This is so much fun!"

He followed her underneath the wall of water and before he knew what was happening, he was jumping up and down and yelling with her and the other kids. The mixed sensation of the flailing and water cascading everywhere made him laugh involuntarily. It reminded him of all the fun he'd had in the past with his parents. He splashed all around, throwing water every which way and yelling at the top of his lungs. He knew it must have looked ridiculous because a few seconds later some of the kids began laughing, not at the water but at him and Vickie. But it didn't bother him. He was used to people staring at him. Besides, he was having *fun*. It was an incredibly liberating and infectious feeling and he loved that she talked him into it.

He grabbed her hand and pulled her into the inner circle of the waterfall. Her face was flushed from laughing and the water droplets speckled her hair, making it sparkle when she moved. She was like something out of dream. A vision—smiling up at him with those lovely brown eyes. And that's when it hit him. That's when he knew. Just how incredibly special *she* was.

He took her into his arms, overcome by the moment. And as his lips met hers all his fears and doubts seem to wash away, cascading down into the pool along with the rest of the water. It was a deep, emotional cleansing of his soul. Almost as if he'd been waiting for her all those lonely years. Waiting for her to walk into his life and rescue him. From his loneliness. From his fear of forever being rejected. From himself. He wrapped his arms around her and let the image fill his mind and heart. They finished kissing and she gazed up at him with such of look of longing that it took his breath away. He began to lean in to kiss her again when a little boy's voice interrupted him.

"See? I told you they was kissin'!" he yelled to the little girl standing next to him and then both of them began laughing.

Vickie took Marcus by the hand and led him back out into the sunlight. The noise of the water beating down finally stopped and he saw a group of six small children ranging in age from six to ten years old, standing in the water a few yards away, staring at them. A rather large and stern looking woman in a tight, black swimsuit exposing all her bulges stood next to the children, her arms folded, glaring daggers at him and Vickie.

"That's improper behavior in front of small children!" the woman barked at them.

Marcus pulled at Vickie's hand, trying to lead her away in the other direction but she resisted. "We were only kissing!" Vickie told the woman. "Kissing is not improper behavior, for your information. There's nothing wrong with showing affection to the people you care about. For heaven's sakes! You do the same thing when you kiss your children!"

Marcus saw all six sets of small eyebrows shoot up in surprise, indicating that apparently, their mother didn't believe in kissing, or showing affection either, by viewing the scared looks on their faces.

"You young people act like dogs in heat!" the woman spat at them. One of the kids gasped in shock and Marcus pulled at Vickie's hand again, trying to coax her to leave.

"Come on," he told her. "Let's get out of here."

"She can't get away with that," Vickie grumbled. "Who does she think she is, anyway? We're decent people and deserve to be treated so."

He leaned down and whispered to her. "But we *were* kissing."

"But that's all we were doing. It's not like we were fondling each other or making love."

"Yeah, but on the other hand, the thought did cross my mind..." And as soon as he said it, she began smiling.

"Hey, Magic!"

Marcus looked up and saw Tim waving to them. He was wading in the pool towards them, Marty at his side. The woman turned and grunted disapproving in Tim's direction and Marcus knew why she was upset. Tim was holding Marty's hand, apparently handholding was against the woman's rules of morality, too.

"We're all going to try out the inner tubes," Tim said. "You guys wanna come with us?"

Marcus started to tell him yes, when Vickie took Marty aside and whispered something to her.

"What's going on?" Tim asked Marcus.

"Nothing. Let's get over to those inner tubes," he told Tim. He wanted to add that they were on the brink of trouble but thought better of it. Voicing his opinion might escalate things even more. He started to reach out for Vickie's hand when Marty let out a groan and whispered, "She what?"

Uh-oh, Marcus thought. *This doesn't sound good.*

Tim asked Marty what was wrong and she quickly turned and whispered to him.

"What?" Tim said, acting insulted. "What's wrong with kissing?"

Too late, Marcus thought with a sigh.

"What is she? Weird?" Tim said, almost shouting. He then waded over to the woman standing with her children. "These all yours?" he said, nodding to the children.

She gave him a stern glare full of pride and nodded yes.

"Well, then," Tim said, acting like he'd already made his point. "You must have done some kissing a few times yourself."

One of the little boys snickered and his mother yelled at him to shut up.

Tim turned to the woman's children. "What's matter? Didn't your mom ever tell you about how you got here?"

"You mean about sex?" one of the older girls exclaimed. "Heck no!"

Her mother yelled at the girl, causing her to cower down, acting like she'd just revealed a family secret. The woman then turned her anger towards Tim.

"If my children need to know the facts of life," she shouted at Tim. "Then I'LL tell them. I don't need any smartass young punk telling them!"

"Why not?" Tim asked her. "Sounds like maybe you forgot some of the more important points. You don't even remember the kissing part. Don't you want your kids to get it right?" Then Tim knelt down in the water and raised his hands up, like he was about to give a lecture. "Okay, kids," he said, directing his attention to all six eager faces. "First, you've got your basic female anatomy..." And he turned and motioned to Marty, who let out a giggle. "Then you got your basic male anatomy..." He paused and looked down at himself. "Now here's the most important part..." he said, slowly pulling the waistband of his shorts away from his skin and then letting go so it snapped back into place. "And when you want to add to the species you put the male anatomy and the female together—"

But he never got to finish it. The woman let out a howl of disgust, grabbed two of the youngest children's hands and jerked them beside her as she hurried away through the water. She barked at the others to follow her but had to yell twice at the two oldest children, both girls, who were standing with smiles on their faces, acting like they were expecting Tim to continue the lesson.

"Looks like we'll never find out!" the first girl grunted to her sister as they turned and hurried behind their mother.

Tim started laughing and Marcus, Vickie and Marty joined him.

"You givin' sex ed. lessons now, Tim?" Marcus asked.

"You weren't really going to show them anything, were you?" Marty asked, her eyes widening with interest.

"Course not," Tim said. "Besides, I would have needed a volunteer to demonstrate. I was hoping you would." And then he laid his head on Marty's shoulder and grinned up at her.

"Very funny!" she replied, pushing him off of her.

Tim shrugged, acting not the least put off by her dismissal. "So, what about it?" he asked Marcus and Vickie. "You guys want to go with me and Marty and try out the inner tubes? Looks like I'm not gonna get to demonstrate on Marty. May as well console myself and try and have some other kind of fun."

Marcus patted him on the back and reassured him that in spite of the setback, he'd probably survive.

"But Marcus and I haven't tried all the water slides yet," Vickie said. "How about we meet the two of you in about an hour?"

Everyone agreed to meet at the picnic area by the concession stands and Marty and Tim took off hand in hand towards the other side of the park. Marcus began walking toward the water slides with Vickie when she commented that his back looked pretty red. They made a pit stop at the lockers and she helped him put another coating of the sunscreen on his back to keep him from burning any more. It seemed like she was applying more than he needed but he was enjoying the sensation of her touch so much that he kept silent. After she did his back he rubbed some more of the lotion on his legs, stomach and face, making sure every part exposed to the sun was covered. Then they stowed the lotion back in the locker and headed for the slides.

They went up the metal staircase nearest the locker area and once they reached the top they saw how crowded it was. The afternoon had warmed up considerably and lines had formed at every slide. Park workers were stationed in chairs at every slide entrance to make sure no one cut in line and that the sliders went down at safe intervals. He and Vickie walked past the children's slides and got in line for one of the adult slides on the other side of the platform. His back was starting to sting from the sunburn but the cooling affect of the lotion helped alleviate the pain. He reached down and adjusted his trunks when he saw that another piece of the string near the knot had broken off. He inspected the rest of the string but it seemed to still be intact and secure. Vickie was standing in front of him, her head tilted forward as if listening to something so he asked her what she was doing.

"You can learn a lot by eavesdropping," she whispered. Then she put her finger to her lips and motioned for him to listen in. The source of her interest was two teenage girls in line in front of her. Both looked like they were sixteen or seventeen, had slim builds and were wearing two-piece suits. The girl on the right was better endowed in the bust and wore a thong, which upon further inspection, at least from the back, left nothing at all to the imagination. He was just beginning to enjoy the view when he felt Vickie smack him lightly on the arm.

"I said listen, not watch!" she whispered.

"Sorry," he said. "I promise I'll only stare at you."

She got back to listening to the girls and he joined her, trying hard not to stare. The discussion was about a male teacher from the girls' school and the girl on the right said she caught the teacher staring up her skirt, trying to see something. Marcus smiled and thought that if the man were smart, he'd make a trip to the water park to see his dream girl exposed instead of leering at her during class.

The girl on the left began telling a similar story and Marcus leaned forward to listen when he noticed something pull at his trunks. He glanced down and felt the waistband loosen. The string had broken off. The trunks began to slide down so he quickly gathered up the slack with his right hand to make sure they didn't come off.

"Whoops," he whispered, causing Vickie to turn around and ask him what was wrong.

He told her what happened.

"Try this," she said, unpinning the locker key from her suit and handing him the safety pin. But the pin was too small.

"It's okay," he told her. "I'll go and get a bigger one from my car."

"You carry safety pins in your car? You must be very organized. I'll bet you even have an emergency kit and extra set of clothes too, don't you?"

He wasn't sure what she was getting at and said nothing. She tilted her head at him, like she was expecting him to reply. His heart began racing, wondering if maybe she had found out about him. "What do you mean?" he asked, suddenly not sure he should have asked it.

"Never mind," she said, acting disappointed. "I only meant you're more organized than most men, that's all."

"Oh," he replied, somewhat relieved. He told her he'd be right back and took off across the platform for the exit. He'd only gone a few feet when a commotion broke out in the line next to them. Two teenage boys began arguing, calling each other names and pushing one another. People in both lines began backing up, giving the boys fighting room. A crowd quickly gathered and Marcus held on tight to his trunks as he shouldered his way through the throng. A couple of the park workers had noticed the scuffle and abandoned their posts to try and help break up the fight.

The argument had escalated to the shouting stage and the boys began grappling with each other, pushing their way towards the front of the platform. The workers, both muscular men in their twenties, tried to pull the boys apart but their efforts were hampered because the boys were wet and hard to grab hold of. The larger of the boys suddenly swung at the other but missed and landed the punch on one of the park workers jaw. The man reeled backwards and Marcus jumped back, trying to get out of his way. But he was facing the fight and hadn't noticed that he was backing into one of the empty chairs. The man crashed into him and Marcus felt his feet go out from under him as the seat of the chair cut into the back of his legs. He threw his arms out, trying desperately to grab hold of something to stop him from falling. At first he thought he would simply fall against the chair but it was wooden and collapsed beneath him, veering his body slightly to the right. A second later his hands hit dead air as his body fell back into a void. Something bright green flashed in front of his eyes and the echoing sound of rushing water surrounded him.

He'd fallen backwards into one of the children's slides.

His body skimmed down the slope and he threw his hands out to his sides, trying to stop. But it was no use. He was picking up momentum with each passing second. He hit a bump in the tube and his trunks slid down to his thighs, the slippery cool of the plastic hitting his naked butt cheeks. He grabbed at the trunks, trying to jerk them up but the sunscreen now mixed with the water made his skin too slippery to do it. He jerked at the trunks and tried pulling them up again or more appropriately, down since he was now sliding headfirst, down the slide. He managed to get them halfway up his thighs when his body slid halfway up the wall, negotiating the first turn in the tunnel. The angle of the turn caused him to lose grip of the trunks so he laid his hands beside him, trying to stay flat as the tunnel straightened out. The maneuver worked but the movement caused the trunks to slip down further, past his thighs.

He bent his knees, trying to keep the trunks from sliding down any further but an instant later his body swerved violently, entering the next turn. As he came out of the turn, the trunks slid down around past his knees towards his ankles and he cursed aloud at his useless attempts to retrieve them. The cuss words echoed throughout the tube as he reached down and tried to grab hold of the material again. He saw another turn coming up but this time he used it to his advantage and bent his knees slightly to one side, causing his body to curl up in a fetal position. As he came out of the turn he reached down and managed to grab the string trailing out from the trunks. He uttered a quick "yes!" and pulled hard on the string to pull up the trunks. But he'd forgotten that the string was broken. All he ended up doing was pulling the string the rest of the way out of the waistband.

His body glided over another steep slope and the trunks slipped off his feet completely, trailing behind him in the tunnel, no longer hampered by the considerable momentum from their owner. The light in the tunnel began to brighten, signaling that he was approaching the end. He suddenly remembered the boy in the blue trunks sliding down the tube earlier in the day and how the tube had opened up at the end, the plastic circle becoming half.

The upper half would have an edge, something he could grab onto and possibly stop himself.

He wrapped the string around his left hand and shoved it against the tunnel wall. He spread his legs and pushed them against the walls, the sides of his feet skimming along the inside of the tube. He then extended his right hand against the top of the tunnel, above his head, getting ready to grab hold of the edge of the tube when he slid out into the open part of the slide. The added grip of the string caused him to slow down considerably and was helped by the tunnel, whose angle was starting to straighten out. He saw sunlight stream into the tunnel, tensed his body and tilted his head back as far as it could go, riveting his eyes on the tunnel roof. He'd only have a second once he saw the tunnel edge and he'd have to react quickly. The adrenaline rush pushed his body into full alert mode and he braced himself. A couple seconds later he spotted the tunnel edge and threw his other hand above his head and against the tube. He clenched his hands and grabbed for it. His right hand slid past it but the string around his left hand gave him enough grip to catch it. There!

Since he'd gone down headfirst in the tube, his face hit the sunlight first and made him wince. His hold on the edge was shaky so he quickly reached up with his right hand and got a second grip on it. He had slowed down but was still sliding and the centrifugal force pushed his body down the tube, causing his legs and torso to bend in half so that now he was now facing downward. His private parts made contact with the cold water and plastic on the tube bottom and he scrambled, trying to get to his feet. The water was still rushing out of the tube so at first all he managed to do was get to his knees. He gripped the tunnel edge harder and groped around with his right foot, trying to feel for the side. He glanced behind him enough to see the small one-inch wide slide edges and planted his right foot securely one of them. He slowly lifted himself up, out of the water. He was now in a football line of scrimmage stance, spread eagle and hunched slightly, holding on to the to edge of the tube. He stared down at the tube opening, waiting for his trunks to slide past so he could grab them. They should be coming now…any second…

A child's voice suddenly cried out. "Mommy! Look at that man! He's naked! And his thing's showin'!"

Immediately the air was filled with screams. Marcus stepped down onto the slide and turned towards the commotion.

"Oh, my God!" someone else screamed. "What's he doing? Cover your eyes! Don't look!"

Another volley of screams filled the air and he instinctively cupped his hands over his exposed family jewels. Something slid over his right foot and caught on his big toe. His swim trunks. He bent down to grab them but as soon as he let go of his privates, the screams commenced again. He covered himself with both hands and bent his toes, trying to hold on to the trunks. He gave the problem some thought. Even if he only used one hand to grab at the trunks, part of him would be exposed and the screaming would start again. He suddenly got an idea and slowly but carefully raised his right foot towards his torso. If he could raise the trunks up high enough, he could grab them without exposing himself. He stuck his tongue out the side of his mouth and concentrated as he raised his right leg a few inches higher.

"What's he doing? Someone call the police! He's a PERVERT!"

Another few inches…almost there…

His left foot faltered slightly from the contortionist action and his body began listing backwards. He put his right foot down and threw his hands out to his sides, trying to regain his balance. Another round of screams came from the pool area and his body plopped down hard onto the slide, his rear end making a wet, slapping noise as it hit. He began to slide toward the tube end and offered no more resistance. A second later he was hanging in midair and a couple more angry shouts followed him into the pool. The water felt refreshing against his skin, which was starting to sting again from the sunburn. He opened his eyes underwater and tried to catch sight of his trunks. He spotted them a few yards away, floating next to what looked like someone's legs. He started to swim towards them when he noticed a couple more sets of legs. His lungs began burning and he decided to give up the quest. His head broke the surface and he welcomed the fresh air into his lungs. He wiped the water from his face and stood up in the waist high water.

It was then that he noticed he was surrounded.

Three women were standing in the water a few feet away and had strategically positioned themselves so that he couldn't move in any direction without confronting one of them. The woman to his right was blonde, thirtyish and wore a black swimsuit that clashed with her fair skin. The woman on his left was short and looked Asian from her dark skin and facial features. The woman directly in front of him he immediately recognized. It was the woman with the six kids from the mushroom, the one whose kids were waiting for a sex ed. lesson from Tim.

All three women's faces were portraits of fury and the little Asian woman was holding a sand shovel in her hand. His defense mechanisms quickly kicked in and he covered his exposed private parts hanging carefree under the water. The hair on his skin tingled with panic at the thought of his already sunburned skin being preyed upon by fingernails. He tried to think of a way to diffuse the situation but only managed an "I lost my trunks in the tunnel" remark that even HE thought sounded stupid.

"What were you doing in tunnel to begin with?" the Asian woman asked him, her voice full of venom.

"He's a sicko!" the woman with the kids barked, not waiting for him to answer. "I caught him earlier in the big pool, trying to have sex with someone right in front of my kids! And one of the men with him tried to attack my kids and talked dirty to them!"

Marcus started to open his mouth to correct the woman and explain that Tim was only making a joke but he never got that far. The Asian woman hollered "pervert" and the plastic shovel came down hard across his back. Within seconds, all three women were upon him, hitting him and jerking at the hair on his head. He kept his left hand cupped over his sensitive areas, not wanting to expose them even for a second to the onslaught being inflicted to his back and head. He took his right hand and covered his head, trying to shield it from the worst of the blows as he slowly pushed his way through the water, trying to get away from the irate women. A couple seconds later the shovel made a direct hit upon his right knuckles and he let out a piercing howl.

He suddenly heard Vickie's voice, shouting at the women to stop hitting him. He became concerned for her safety and lifted his head to warn her to stay away. But the shovel hit him hard on the head and he momentarily saw stars. He threw his arm back across his head and Vickie screamed at the women again to leave him alone. A second later someone grabbed at his hand and he jerked away, thinking it was one of the women.

"It's me!" Vickie yelled. "Hold on!"

He did as she asked and the blows finally ceased. She began to lead him through the water past the angry women and he could feel their glares burning a hole in his now aching and scratched back. The women formed a kind of gauntlet, standing in an almost military stance with their arms folded in front of them. The Asian woman was smacking the shovel against her arm like she was waiting for him to make a wrong move. He suddenly had a strange urge to let go of his privates and jump into the air, exposing himself to all three of them. But he quickly dismissed the notion. Any hint of sarcasm or defiance could result in further attacks and since Vickie was with him, she'd be included in the onslaught.

They crossed over to the side of the pool, next to the steps and she told him to stay there. She hurried up the stairs and over to a group of people lying on chaise lounges a few yards away. He snuck a look behind him and his heart sank as he saw the three women edge their way towards him. He cupped his hand tighter over his balls and hunched down, waiting for it. His back and shoulders were still stinging from the earlier attack and his skin began prickling in anticipation of another round.

"Marcus," Vickie called him. "Come on up."

He turned and saw her standing on the steps with a large beach towel open in her hands. He hurried up the steps and she quickly wrapped the towel around him. The women began to come up the steps behind him and he whispered to Vickie that they should leave. *Or more appropriately*, he thought, Run.

"No," she replied. "They had no right to treat you that way." And with that, she turned and faced his attackers. He tried to get in between her and the women but the Asian woman crowded in front of him and began to raise the shovel again to strike him. He started to duck when Vickie grabbed the woman's arm and got in her face.

"There's no need for violence," Vickie told the woman. "We're adults here. We should act like civilized human beings."

The woman let out a "hmph" and put down the shovel.

"Thank you," Vickie told her. Then she directed her attention to all three of them. "If you'll please let me explain, I can clear this up."

The blonde told her to continue and Vickie proceeded to tell them what happened up on the platform. "So you can see," she said, finishing up. "It was not his fault."

"But he was acting like a pervert in the fountain," the woman with the kids griped.

"We were only kissing," Vickie told her. "Besides, he didn't initiate the kiss. I did. I thought it was harmless and I certainly didn't mean to offend anyone. So if you want to blame anyone, blame me."

The explanation seemed to diffuse the women's anger and they began to calm down.

"It was nothing more than an accident," Vickie said.

Marcus figured it was time to help explain and held up the string he was still holding in his left hand to show them. He started to tell them about it breaking when he heard Rob's voice behind him.

"Hey, Magic! We found your trunks!" Then Rob walked up with the lost piece of clothing and held it out in front of him. "We found them over by the waterfall. The string's missing. What'd you do? Pull it out and decide to go skinny dipping in the kiddie pool?"

A round of laughter came from behind Rob and Marcus saw Tim, Marty and the other kids walk towards them. He knew the remark about pulling the string out wouldn't go over well with the irate women and sure enough, a few seconds later he heard the reaction.

"That's the man who was talking dirty to my kids!" the woman with the kids grumbled, pointing to Tim. "I told you they were perverts! All of them!"

Sarah and Barb began protesting vehemently and within seconds everyone was yelling at each other. The two park workers that had been breaking up the fight on the podium came running up, asking what was going on. One of the workers got in between the angry women, trying to get them to stop yelling and Tim pulled the other worker aside and started whispering to him. Marcus had been keeping a close eye on the little Asian woman with the shovel and was genuinely happy when the park worker asked her to please put down it down, which she reluctantly did.

"Now would someone please tell me what's going on?" the man said.

Immediately all three angry women started yelling again and it took the worker another couple minutes to get them quieted down. Vickie offered to give him the details and had just started to explain when the guy interrupted her.

"I know," he said. "I saw him fall into the tube. It was my fault. One of the kids took a punch at me and knocked me backwards." Then he turned to the angry women and pointed to Marcus. "This man did not go down the tube on purpose. It was an accident and he could have been seriously hurt."

"What about that?" the woman with the kids yelled, pointing at Marcus's trunks in Rob's hands. "He purposely took off his swim trunks!"

Marcus held up the string and told the worker about it breaking.

"And what about him fondling that girl in the pool?" the blonde said, pointing at Vickie.

"He was NOT fondling me!" Vickie shouted at the woman.

The women resumed the shout fest and the fight was on once again. The second worker finished talking to Tim and walked over to the other one still trying to break up the fight, pulling him aside. It was then that Marcus noticed the strange smile on Tim's face and asked him what was going on.

"I've got it all worked out," Tim said. "The guy I was talking to is a friend of mine and he's going to help us out. Just go along with whatever he says." And then Tim gave him a wink. The group was still in yelling mode and the two workers broke from their huddle and held up their hands, signaling everyone to be quiet.

"We'll take care of this," the second worker, Tim's friend, said, grabbing Marcus by the arm. "If you'll just come with me, Mr. Cousteau, we'll find you some clothes."

Marcus tried not to smile as he heard the woman with the kids ask, "Cousteau? Like the ocean guy on TV?"

"That's correct," the first worker replied.

The blonde woman remarked that Jacques Cousteau was much older.

Actually, he's dead, Marcus thought, keeping the remark to himself.

"He's not Jacques," Tim piped up. "This is Marcus Cousteau, one of his sons, also known as Magic to his friends."

"Magic?" the Asian woman asked.

"That's right," Tim replied. "It's the nickname his father gave him when he was little."

The Asian woman pursed her lips and raised her eyebrows like she understood.

"His father called him his little Magic Marcus," Tim elaborated, "and it was his father's wishes that Magic follow in his footsteps."

The worker holding Marcus arm turned to the women. "Mr. Marcus Cousteau is visiting our park at his company's request. They are considering putting in a new marine wild life section." Then the man directed his attention to Marcus. "I only hope this unfortunate incident won't deter you or your company from continuing with the new project. It would be a great loss to the people of northern Ohio to lose a chance to enjoy something on the magnitude of your company's visions." And the man glanced at the irate mothers, almost prompting them to agree. All three of them eagerly nodded and Marcus saw Barb and the other kids turn their heads to keep from laughing.

"So if you'll follow me," the worker said, leading Marcus away.

"Uh, Mr. Cousteau!" Tim called out, hurrying up beside Marcus. "We'll get everything taken care of here and join you shortly!" Then he leaned in and whispered, "Just follow Ted to the lockers, Magic. I'll take it from here."

"And Vickie?" Marcus asked, turning around to see where she'd gone.

"Right here!" she said, coming up and grabbing his free arm. "Let me help escort you, Mr. Cousteau," she said, quietly snickering. He gave her a grin and let them both lead him away.

After retrieving a spare set of clothes from his car trunk, pair of boxers, cut-off shorts and tee shirt he ducked into one of the restrooms to change. He then went over to the concession area to meet Vickie and the others. Next to the vendor's shops was an open area with chaise lounges, tables and chairs with large umbrellas offering plenty of shade. Marty, Tim and the others were sitting at a table a few feet from where Vickie was sunbathing on a chaise. He still had the towel Vickie had used to cover him and asked where he could find the owner.

"She told us to keep it," Vickie said. "I tried to pay for it but she wouldn't let me. She said she was honored to have one of Jacques Cousteau's son use it."

She offered him the chaise lounge next to hers and he sat down, stashing the towel behind him. He looked over at Tim and smiled. "I still can't believe you got away with a story like that." He then asked Tim to fill him in on the rest of the show that he'd missed. But before Tim could open his mouth, Marty volunteered the rest.

"It was so funny!" she said. "Tim told those women that he was your assistant."

"He also told them he was a marine biologist," Sarah added with a cackle.

"And they believed that?" Marcus asked.

"They sure did," Tim said, his head held high with pride. "That lady with the kids started to complain that I was too young to be a biologist, so I told her I was a prodigy."

"You also told her you won the Nobel Prize last year," Kip added with a smirk. "I couldn't believe she bought that one, either."

"You *were* layering it on pretty thick," Rob added.

"Ted was a big help in convincing them," Tim said, standing up and acting like he was making a speech. "But I did pretty good myself, I must say."

"I take it Ted was the guy escorting me," Marcus said, now seeing the complicity.

Tim confirmed he was. "He's a friend of mine. He thought it was a real kick. But the real convincing came from me. I had them eating out of my hand."

Marcus couldn't resist having the future academy award hopeful enjoy his moment and asked him to go on.

"I told them that I was your new rising star prodigy and that you and I were business partners looking into franchising our own sea life parks."

"He also told them that we were all part of your team," Kip added. "And that Vickie was your wife."

Marty and the girls started giggling.

"Thanks, Tim," Vickie chuckled. "I've always wanted to be married to someone famous."

Tim shrugged and turned to his friends. "Hey, I gave them that excuse so that lady with the kids would stop bitchin' about Vickie kissin' Magic in the fountain. She seems to think kissin' is against the law."

"I can see them believing that fib," Marcus said. "But the franchising idea is way out in left field. Sea World already has the franchise."

"I know," Tim said. "And one of those nice ladies pointed that fact out to me. So I told her our idea was to have an interactive park, one where the guests would put on wet suits and get right in the water with the dolphins and sharks."

"Sharks?" Vickie exclaimed.

"Those ladies reacted pretty much the same way," Tim replied.

"They sure as hell did!" Rob added. "That Oriental lady thought you were crazy."

"That's why I explained to them," Tim said, acting like he was ignoring Rob's critique of the performance. "I told them that we would have shark cages the guests would be put in, for their safety."

"That never worked in *Jaws*," Kip commented. "The shark still got the guy."

Tim tilted his head at Kip and rolled his eyes. "Hollywood, my good lad. Besides, the other women like the idea."

"I'll say they did," Marty piped up. "They asked Tim when the new addition was being built. He had them *totally* believing it. Even that woman with the kids!"

"That was a pretty good trick," Marcus told Tim, equally impressed. "Especially after you tried to give that woman's kids a sex ed. lesson this morning."

"Yeah. We heard all about that," Rob said. "And after Tim pulled his stuff about being your assistant, a couple of those kids started asking Tim a whole bunch of questions about mating habits."

"You're kidding!" Marcus said, not believing his ears.

"Just the mating habits of dolphins," Tim said, acting as though Rob had insulted him.

Vickie asked why dolphins.

"Because," Marty replied with a giggle, "Tim told those ladies that he specialized in mating habits of dolphins and sharks."

Marcus joined Vickie laughing. "And that woman with the kids bought that lie?"

Tim smiled and made a gesture resembling someone reeling in a fish. "Hook, line and sinker. She even forgave me for trying to give her kids that sex lesson this morning. I told her it was a job hazard because I deal with fish anatomies all day long."

"I think she expected Tim to give her kids a lecture right there," Kip added. "She acted even more interested than her kids. It was *classic*!" And then Kip gave Tim a high five.

Tim retook his seat and started chuckling. "That was *so* cool, Magic. Acting out that farce was fun enough. But getting to be there during one of your episodes was awesome!"

Marcus felt his heart jump into his mouth.

"What do you mean?" Vickie asked Tim.

Marcus quickly tried to come up with an excuse. "Uh, I think Tim meant, uh…" But he couldn't think of anything. His mind had gone blank. He began to open his mouth again when Marty broke in.

"Oh, it's nothing, sis," Marty told her. "Tim only meant that he liked getting to act like he was a *real* Nobel prize winner." Then Marty grabbed Tim's arm and whispered to him.

Marcus waited to see what Marty was up to and heard Tim reply a few seconds later.

"Uh, yeah. That's what I meant. It's not every day I get to act like a hero."

Marcus watched Vickie very carefully and hoped she bought it.

"Oh. Is that what you meant?" she said, smiling at Tim. "Okay. I get it, I guess." She then leaned toward Marcus and whispered. "I think the kids thought hanging around us was going to be kind of dull. Guess we showed them, didn't we?"

He nodded yes and sighed inwardly with relief. Vickie lay back on the chaise and put on her sunglasses, acting like it was no big deal.

Whew! he thought, sitting back in his own chair. Another possible disaster had been diverted. He then remembered who'd been responsible for the diversion and glanced over at Marty. She and Tim were in a huddle together, whispering to the others. They finally broke apart and all six faces began grinning at him. He wanted to ask Marty what she told them but was afraid to arouse Vickie's curiosity any more. The explanation would have to wait.

The kids got up and announced they were heading back into the park and Marty told Vickie she was going with them. Marcus stayed behind with Vickie, under the shade. He was still hoping to talk her into spending the night at his apartment and now seemed as good a time as any to bring it up.

But how would he approach the subject?

He sat back in the chaise and thought about it. He was used to having his dates enter into a sexual relationship quickly (his condition sometimes aided in that endeavor) but with Vickie it had been different. This was the first time he'd enjoyed a formal courtship with a woman and he was ready to take it to the next step. She'd already admitted to being intimate with her last boyfriend and he hoped to enjoy the same privileges. However, there were a few things he'd have to consider first. She still didn't know about his condition and since his *moments* had made appearances at other times when he would have dates spend the night, the risk increased of her finding out his secret. There was also the problem of her father, who seemed determined to keep a close eye on her whereabouts. She might agree to spend the night but then change her mind about any further intimacy if her father found out. And lastly, there was her. It was clear she wasn't promiscuous and engaging in a relationship that was both sexual and emotional could have costly results, for both of them. But as he rationalized it in his head, he knew he was only kidding himself. The truth was he'd been hoping she'd fall in love with him so she wouldn't leave like all the others.

He pushed his head back against the chaise and sighed. It was going to be a real struggle to get her to fall in love with him before she discovered his secret. And with love came intimacy so the next logical step was to get her to spend the night with him. He closed his eyes and began to think of excuses to get her to go to his place. He had nothing in particular to show her, no collection of rare books or anything that might give him an excuse to invite her up. The only thing of interest that came to mind was some mildew he'd recently found in his shower that was formed in the shape of a man's head. But as a rule, women didn't find that kind of thing fascinating. She suddenly interrupted his deliberation and asked him how his sunburn was.

He opened his eyes and told her it was still stinging. "But I think it's okay."

She got up from the chaise and motioned for him to move over. She sat down next to him and told him to take off his shirt. He pulled it slowly over his head and she touched his back gingerly, remarking that it was still pretty red.

"Here," she said, reaching for her purse on the little table between the chairs. "I brought some sunburn lotion along, in case Marty got burned." She then began applying some to his back. It felt cold at first but it wasn't long before he was enjoying the touch of her fingers against his skin.

"You should probably reapply it again before you go to bed," she told him, putting the cap back on the bottle.

He leaned against her, ignoring the pain from the burn. "Who's going to help me apply it?" he whispered to her, seeing an opportunity open up. "I can't reach back that far."

She handed him the bottle and winked. "You'll manage. If you get stuck, you can ask Ben to come over and give you a hand."

"I'd rather have you do it," he told her, leaning his head against hers. He felt a ray of hope, as she kept silent, considering it. But an instant later the hope was dashed as a sad smile filled her face.

"I better not. Besides, Marty is staying with me tonight."

"Oh. Okay," he said, not bothering to try and mask his disappointment.

"I'm sorry," she said, taking his hand and squeezing it. "Bad timing thing. But I'll make you a deal. I'll cook for you. My place one night next week. What night is good for you?"

He quickly ran his schedule through his head and told her Tuesday night.

"Great," she said. "I'm a pretty good cook, although I can't make anything as exciting as calamari."

His stomach did a small flip-flop at the mention of tentacles. "Anything would be fine," he told her. "Besides, we're going to Ben and Sue's on Thursday night and she's making Cajun, so I'll get two home cooked meals in the same week. My stomach won't know how to act. It's used to TV dinners or whatever the special is at the snack bar."

She told him it was a date and gave him a quick kiss on the cheek. She then began to get up but he put his arms around her and pulled her close, giving her a long, passionate kiss. She started to put her arms around him but stopped herself and pulled away.

"I forgot about your burn," she whispered.

"So did I," he said, pulling her close and prompting her to hug him again. He kissed her again, no longer giving a damn about the burn. If he was going to spend the night alone in his bed he at least wanted something to dream about. She finally let go of him a few seconds later and sat back, smiling and catching her breath. She didn't have to say anything else. The look in her eyes said it all. She really did care about him.

"Come on," he said, taking her hand and pulling her up from the chaise. "Let's get something to eat."

They ordered some food from the vendors next door and went over to one of the picnic tables with their selections. He couldn't believe how hungry he was and quickly wolfed down two foot long Coneys and fries to her one. Afterwards they went for a walk along the midway and ended up at the arcade, where they spent the rest of the afternoon. All in all it had been a pretty good date and with some help from a few friends, hadn't ended in disaster or Vickie running away in a fright.

By the time he got them home around 7 PM, the sunburn had graduated to the "full burn" stage and it was becoming uncomfortable to even sit in the car. He pulled into the lot behind their building and parked near the back entrance. They both got out and Vickie walked over to his side of the car.

"I could tell your sunburn is hurting you," she said, leaning down to his window. She took the sunburn cream bottle from her purse and handed it to him. He wanted to tell her he already had some in his arsenal of first aid items at home and in the trunk but he kept silent, appreciative of her concern for him.

"See you Tuesday night," she said, leaning in and kissing him on the cheek. "Make it about six."

He replied that he'd be there and she took off towards the door. Marty began to follow her but turned and hurried back to his window.

"Can you wait a minute for me?" she whispered.

He told her he'd be glad to and she ran back over to Vickie and followed her through the door. He wasn't sure what was going on but decided to give her the benefit of the doubt. He was still remembering all the whispering going on between her, Tim and the others and hoped she'd shed some light about how much, if anything, she knew.

As he waited, he saw Vickie's Super—Sanun—clipping some of the hedges near the side of the building. He waved at the man and expected a wave back but all he got was an angry glare. The man resumed clipping but it seemed as though he was working harder at the task than before and an occasional grunt could be heard in between the scissors motions of the shears. Marcus decided to forget about it and sat forward a little, trying to keep his back from making contact with the vinyl seat. Marty re-emerged from the back door a few seconds later and sprinted over to his car.

"Thanks for waiting," she said, a bit out of breath from running. "I told

Vickie I was going down to the store. I didn't want her to know I was talking to you."

Marcus became quite intrigued.

"I know all about you," she told him. "I guess you know you're a legend at Kirklin High. All the kids talk about you. Most of the people in town, too. At least that's what Tim says."

His heart jumped. "Does Vickie know?" he asked, his mouth suddenly going dry.

"No. And I'm going to make sure it stays that way."

He stared at her, not sure how to respond. He finally muttered a "thank you" to her.

"That's okay," she said. "I figure you've got your reasons for not telling her and I respect that. I can tell you really like Vickie and she seems to like you a lot, too. So if you can make her happy, I'm all for it. The last guy she was with was a jerk. She deserves to be treated better than that. When she first told me about going out with you, I thought it was funny. I figured she'd see one of your disasters happen and drop you like a hot rock."

He decided to be honest with her. "So did I. Actually, I was quite surprised at how tolerant she was about my accidents."

"I thought so too," Marty said. "After she told me about the restaurant and you catching fire, I figured you were history. But she kept talking about your parents and how much you loved them. She was moved by that. I think that's why she went out with you again." She paused and glanced back at the building. "She still doesn't suspect anything and as far as I know, she hasn't said a word to my parents about going out with you either. I guess she told you about how protective our father is."

"Uh…yes. She did mention it."

"Well, don't worry about them. I'll make sure they don't find out about it and I'll keep working at Vickie in case she asks too many questions. I'm pretty good at it. Like after that 'Yellow Eyes' thing I kept reminding her that a lot of people are allergic to latex. I'm allergic to a few things myself. I told her something like that could happen to anyone. So don't worry. If any more of your 'adventures,' as Tim calls them, happen, I'll keep telling her not to worry about it. I told Tim and the others about it and they're gonna help out, too. Tim's got some ideas about how to keep Vickie from finding out. He's got me checking the Barbertown paper every day before Vickie reads it to make sure she doesn't see if one of your adventures makes the paper. He's coming up with a few other ideas to help us out. He has great ideas."

"He does," he agreed with her. "He's quite a character and somebody I'm glad to have on my side."

"I know. He's great, isn't he?" she said, beaming. "And so is Vickie. She deserves to be happy and if she decides that you make her happy, I want to do everything I can to help her get it."

He stared at her, overwhelmed. For someone so young, she had incredible compassion and insight. "I appreciate it," he told her, feeling the words completely inadequate.

"No problem," she said, giving him a warm smile. "And thanks for introducing me to Tim, Barb and the others. It's great having friends!" She turned and took off down the street, pausing to wave goodbye.

He was genuinely happy for her. She'd changed from a timid wallflower into a beautiful rose, beaming with happiness. And best of all, he was partially responsible for it.

He drove out of the lot and smiled at his good fortune. Having Marty on his side was a definite plus. Not to mention finding out about a few friends he hadn't even known about, especially a certain assistant who claimed to be a prodigy and Nobel Prize winner. Marcus Cousteau for crying out loud. What an imagination!

A thought suddenly occurred to him.

Tim had mentioned a couple of times about looking for a part-time job. Maybe he could oblige him. Having a Nobel Prize winner, even a fictitious one, helping at The Crystal could prove interesting, not to mention entertaining. It would also give Marty (and therefore Vickie) another reason for visiting. *Hmm*, he thought. Marty was right. It *was* nice having friends.

It was late Monday afternoon when he finally met Ben and Jack for his usual *post moment* meeting. Finding out recently about some new friends had made him realize how much he'd been neglecting his other friends. Ben got to the Point first and while they waited for Jack to show up, Marcus told him about hiring Tim to work at The Crystal.

"You hired Tim?" Ben said. "But when? We were just there Friday night!"

"Yesterday. I called him up and offered him a part-time job. He started today."

"I can't believe it," Ben said. "The trip to the water park must have been something special to make you hire Tim so quick."

"It was. But I'll wait 'til Jack gets here to give you all the details."

"Okay," Ben replied. "And since we've got a minute, I've got some news, too. I got the bank loan. As of today, Cromwell's music store is mine."

They both sprang from their seats and began hugging each other, whooping and hollering and drawing stares from the patrons sitting at the bar.

"Uh...sorry," Ben said, letting go of Marcus as he noticed the customer's stares.

"No need to apologize," Marcus said, taking his seat across from Ben. "Any of them would be celebrating too with news like that." He asked Ben for the details.

"I took the rest of the insurance papers into the bank this morning and they told me the loan was approved. I don't know who was happier, me or Frank. He was so excited that he closed up the shop at noon so we could finish cleaning out the back room. He's deciding what he's taking with him and leaving behind." For the next ten minutes Ben relayed all the intricacies that came with financing and buying a business. Marcus listened with great interest, enjoying not only the finance lesson, but also the fact that his best friend had achieved one of his dreams.

"Oh, and something else," Ben added. "I haven't told Sue yet. I'm taking her to dinner tonight and breaking the news. But if she asks, let her think that I told her first, okay?"

"Sure thing. When's Frank moving?"

"He figures about two weeks. He's not taking much with him, only his violin and his new Baldwin. He'd be lost without that. The rest of the instruments and stuff in the back room he's leaving for me to get rid of. I need to clear everything out because I'm converting the area into a couple more music rooms for my students."

Marcus asked him what he was going to do with the stuff.

"The smaller instruments I can sell easy but there are a couple of older pianos that won't be so easy to get rid of. They're still in good shape but I don't have the room and we only use the new Spinets to teach with. I can probably run an ad in the paper and make a few calls to the music stores in Cleveland and Columbus to try and get rid of them." Ben suddenly acted sullen and Marcus asked him what was wrong.

"I called Dad and told him about getting the loan but his reaction wasn't what you'd call positive."

"What do you mean?"

"He acted worried. Said I was foolish to be investing all my savings in something so risky."

"Didn't you tell him your ideas? About what you want to do with the shop?"

"You mean your ideas."

"They were *our* ideas," Marcus reminded him. "We both came up with them. Besides, what difference does it make? They're good ideas and could make you a lot of money."

"I told him that. But you know how he is. Unless it's a sure thing, he wouldn't approve of it." Ben frowned down at his beer. "But your dad would have. He'd have been happy for me."

Marcus understood what he meant. Since he was a boy, Ben and his father had always been at odds with each other, disagreeing on everything from religion to the NFL draft. One of the main reasons Ben spent so much time at his best friend's house was because he was trying to get away from his father and the constant fights.

"Don't worry about it," Marcus told him. "He'll come around once he sees your plans for the place pay off."

"Hope so," Ben replied.

Marcus decided to get back to his own problem and told Ben about the upcoming date at Vickie's.

"So? She's still with you, huh? That's great, Magic. Is the date tonight?"

"No. Tomorrow night. I was hoping to take her out to a club or somewhere last night but she always has dinner with her folks on Sundays. It's one of the ways her father keeps tabs on her. She doesn't like that he's so protective but she wants to keep him happy. It sounds like he's pretty conservative."

"That doesn't sound good. Do her parents know about her dating you?"

"No. And her sister Marty said she'd make sure they didn't find out." He then told Ben about Marty's revelation and promise to help him.

"You're kidding! That's terrific, Magic!"

"Yeah, but eventually her parents are going to find out," Marcus reminded him. "And then I'll be in trouble."

"Why?"

"Think about it, Ben. You're considering becoming a parent yourself. What if you had a daughter who started dating someone like me, and my stupid problem? Would you approve of her going out with him?"

"Sure."

"No you wouldn't," Marcus grumbled. "You'd give him his walking papers the minute you found out. Anybody would."

"And you think you're history as soon as they find out about you. Right?"

Marcus didn't answer him. Saying it out loud would only reinforce the notion.

"Magic?" Ben asked him again. "Is that what you're figuring?"

Before he could answer, Jack came up and sat down next to Ben.

"Tim's gonna work out great," Jack said. "He may be a bit of a comedian but he ain't afraid to work. I showed him how to oil the lanes and he had 'em done in no time. And funny, the kid's like a joke bag. He's got a million of them. He should be one of those stand-up comics like on TV. Kept me in stitches all morning." Then Jack paused and pulled out his pipe and tobacco. "He also told me a little about what happened at the water park Saturday but we got busy and he didn't get to finish. So what's this about you losing your swim trunks, Magic?"

"What?" Ben exclaimed, sitting forward, anxious to hear it. "You lost your trunks? Was anybody watching when it happened?"

Marcus nodded yes and Ben and Jack started laughing.

"That ain't even the best part," Marcus said. "You'll be surprised to find out that our future stand-up comic is also a prodigy marine biologist and Nobel prize winner." And he paused for effect and added with a grin. "Oh, and I almost forgot. I'm one of Jacques Cousteau's sons."

"How's that?" Ben asked him.

Marcus proceeded to fill them both in.

CHAPTER NINE

Marcus smoothed down his tie and checked to make sure the elephant tie tack was showing. It looked silly wearing a tie with shorts and a tee shirt but he knew it would make her laugh. He switched the bottle of wine to his left hand and opened the back door of the apartment building. To the left was an open staircase going up to the second floor and to the right was a hallway with three doors for the lower floor apartments. The hall was carpeted in light brown hues and the walls were painted in a cream color that matched the carpet. There were decorative lamps dotted along the walls in between the doors. The lamp by the third and rearmost apartment was apart and being worked on by none other than Vickie's prickly Super, Sanun.

Marcus sighed and headed for the staircase. He'd been hoping to avoid the grouchy little caretaker but as he started up the stairs the man barked at him.

"Who you here for?"

Marcus stopped on the stairs and tried not to get annoyed. The man knew exactly whom he was there for. "I'm here to see Vickie Garrett," he said, keeping his tone civil as he leaned over the banister. "She told me her apartment is on the second floor."

Sanun was holding a large screwdriver in his left hand and began gesturing with it. "Miss Vickie not home. Went out little while ago, not back yet. You wait outside."

Marcus checked his watch, five after six. He then observed Sanun. The man's expression was angry but he was periodically glancing down at the floor, as if he was avoiding his gaze. *Hmm,* Marcus thought. Sure sign of someone lying. He decided to find out for sure.

"She told me to be here by six," he told Sanun. "She was expecting me. But if she ran to the store or out on an errand, I could sit here with you and wait for her." He walked back down to the bottom stair and sat down, placing the bottle of wine next to him. "So," he told Sanun, getting comfortable. "I see you're fixing one of the lights. I've become a bit of an electrician myself over the years. What kind of wiring does that have?" He knew that if he needled the little man enough, he'd get mad and give up his "second degree" routine.

"Regular wiring," Sanun grumbled as he got back to working on the light.

He asked Sanun how long he'd been an apartment manager.

"Four year," Sanun replied, keeping his eyes on the fixture.

Marcus smiled to himself and continued the inquiry. "Do you enjoy that line of work?"

"It okay."

Marcus could hear the irritation in the man's voice and knew the ploy was working. "Have you always been an apartment manager?"

Sanun let go of the fixture and grunted. He then walked over to Marcus, gripping the screwdriver in his hands like a vice. "Miss Vickie might be home," Sanun said, motioning up the stairs with the screwdriver. "We check." He took off up the steps and Marcus followed after him, trying not to laugh. Sanun led him to one of the apartments at the end of the hall and knocked on the door. As they waited for an answer Sanun noticed the wine in Marcus's arm. The man's eyes immediately narrowed and a disapproving scowl filled his face.

"Told you. She not home," Sanun grumbled at him, "you go now."

"Maybe she didn't hear you," Marcus said, reaching up with his free hand and rapping on the door again. A second later the door opened and Vickie smiled at him. She was wearing a white apron decorated with flowers over a sleeveless light blue shirt and dark blue shorts. Her face was flushed as if she'd been near a hot stove.

"Marcus. I was getting worried," she said. "I was afraid you forgot about dinner tonight." She then noticed Sanun. "Sanun. How nice of you to show Marcus where my apartment was." And she gave the man a hug. "Isn't he an angel?" she asked Marcus.

"Yes he is," Marcus agreed, at the same time thinking of another word to describe the man. She invited Marcus into the apartment and he waited for Sanun to graciously leave. He should have known better.

"I here. I look at toilet," Sanun said, pushing past Marcus.

"You don't have to do it right now," she told him. "It's not leaking that bad. I wouldn't want you to miss your dinner."

The man turned and gave Marcus the once-over again. "Dinner not ready yet. I go ahead and look now."

Marcus knew the man was using it as an excuse to keep an eye on him and decided to needle him some more. "Uh, what about the light you were working on downstairs? Don't you think it's unsafe to leave those electric wires exposed like that?"

The man's frown became more pronounced. "It okay. No one bother it."

"Oh," Marcus replied, trying to keep his tone pleasant, "then I guess you must not have any children living in the building who might tamper with it. That's good. Otherwise, one of them could get hurt."

Sanun's face suddenly went blank and Marcus had to bite his lip to keep from smiling.

"'Scuse me, Vickie," Sanun told her. "I need wrench to work on toilet. Be right back." The man hurried toward the door, grumbling under his breath. As soon as he left, Marcus couldn't help but grin.

"He's such a hard worker," Vickie said. "And he's so considerate. Did you see his face when you reminded him about the exposed wires? He really cares about the people who live here. We're all very lucky to have him for an apartment manager." She suddenly noticed the wine he was holding. He told her it was the house wine from Richetti's.

"How sweet of you," she said, reaching up and giving him a kiss on the cheek. "Here. I'll put it on some ice."

He'd been holding the wine so it covered up most of his tie. He handed her the bottle and waited for her reaction.

"Oh, my God!" she laughed, reaching out to touch the tie and tie tack. "I can't believe you did that!"

"I wasn't going anywhere formal to be able to wear it. So I had to improvise."

She threw her arm around his neck and hugged him. "I love it!" she told him. "I never cooked a formal dinner before. This is gonna be great!"

He followed her into the kitchen and helped her put ice in the sink for the wine. The kitchen was tiny but efficient. It had a large, old-time metal sink and adjoining cupboard that contained the only counter space. To the right of the sink was the fridge and craft type wooden potato and vegetable bin. On the opposite wall was a conventional stove and next to that, a small cart containing a microwave oven. A space saver wooden table and four matching chairs sat in the middle of the room, taking up almost all the spare space. He decided to find out a little more about the Thai watchdog and asked her how long she'd known him.

"Since I moved in here. He's originally from Thailand but moved to the States about twenty years ago. He manages the building for my father and he and his family have the apartment down the hall from mine." She pointed to the kitchen cupboards and told him Sanun had remodeled them. "He's an excellent carpenter. That's how my father met him. Sanun did some work at my parents' house. He'd just moved here from Michigan and was looking for a place to live. He got laid off from one of the big auto plants. So my dad talked him into managing the apartments." She paused and gave him a sly grin. "He also keeps an eye on me for my father but I'm not supposed to know that."

A light went off in his head. "Oh, that explains it."

She asked him what he meant.

"He's been glaring at me since the first time he saw me. I didn't say anything because I figured he had a thing for you."

She scoffed. "Oh, he's not like that at all. He's only a friend. Besides, he's very much in love with his wife."

"How do you know?"

"Because he told me so. He admitted it one night when we both got drunk together."

"Uh-huh," Marcus said. "I knew it. So he *has* tried to put the moves on you."

"It's not like that at all," she protested. "He didn't get me drunk, I got *him* drunk."

His mouth dropped open and she began giggling. She motioned for him to take a seat at the kitchen table and she sat down next to him. "I moved in here right after I broke up with Greg," she explained. "I wanted to find my own place but my dad kept suggesting I move in here. He owns the building. He kept telling me how safe the neighborhood was and how he would give me a break on the rent. I got tired of arguing with him so I took it. But what I didn't know then was that my dad asked Sanun to keep an eye on me and report back to him."

He asked her how she found out.

"As soon as I moved in here I noticed how protective Sanun was of me. My girlfriends would stop by and no matter what he was doing, he'd come over and talk to us. It was never obvious. He'd ask the girl's name and make conversation with us but I noticed he never did that with any of the other tenants, only me. That's when I suspected my father had him watching me. So one night, about a month after I moved in, Sanun came over to work on the cupboards. I was feeling sorry for myself and missing Greg, although I didn't want to admit it. I was into my fourth glass of wine when Sanun showed up and I knew he'd be reporting back to my father that I was drinking. So I figured that if I got Sanun drunk…"

He started laughing. "You could blackmail him! He couldn't report on you without implicating himself! That's quite a revelation. Who'd ever thought you could be so devious?"

Her face blushed with embarrassment. "Well, I wouldn't exactly call it devious. I just wanted to know the truth."

He asked her for all the details and she told him she had another reason for getting Sanun drunk. "I was lonely. I wanted someone to talk to."

He told her to go on.

"When I was living at home I always had Marty to talk to or my parents. Here I've got no one. I wanted my independence but I soon found out how lonely living by myself could be."

Been there myself, he thought.

"That night, when Sanun got drunk with me. I didn't plan it that way. It kind of just happened. He could tell how depressed I was. I sat here in the kitchen while he worked on the cabinets and I started telling him about all my problems with Greg. He agreed with me, too. About breaking up with Greg. I guess I needed someone else's reinforcement. I was grateful to Sanun for letting me cry on his shoulder so I offered him a glass of wine. I only think he accepted because he felt sorry for me."

"But it didn't stop at one glass, did it?" he mused.

"No. And after his second glass he started telling me his own troubles."

"Hard to believe someone as formidable as he is, has troubles."

"I was surprised, too," she said, scooting her chair closer like she was about to reveal a secret. "He told me he hates it when his teenage son corrects his English. It drives him crazy. He also told me that he gets insanely jealous when men flirt with his wife."

"Is his wife Thai?"

"No. She's American. He met her at the factory where he used to work. She was his boss."

"Probably still is," Marcus replied, picturing an angry little woman yelling at the Thai bulldog.

"She's the nicest person. And she's really pretty, too. Sanun said the men at the plant never complained about her being their boss, at least, not until she went out with Sanun. All the other men wanted to ask her out but figured she wouldn't go out with them since she was their boss."

"But Sanun did."

"Yep. He told me he fell in love with her the first time she yelled at him for doing a job wrong. She fell in love with him and the rest is history. But they both lost their jobs when the plant closed down a few years ago. Sheila, that's his wife, went for retraining and now she works for an accounting firm on Main Street. But it was hard for Sanun to find work and he was doing odd jobs when my father met him. He was very grateful to my father for giving him the job. I think that's why he didn't mind filling my father's request to watch over me."

Marcus smiled. "I can't believe you got Sanun to admit it. He looks like he's hard as nails."

"He kind of scared me at first, too," she said. "He's usually not very talkative, probably because he's so self-conscious about his broken English. But that night, after he'd had some wine, he began chattering and laughing like crazy. He started telling me about growing up in Thailand and all the places he's been to. I loved hearing about that. I've only been out of Ohio once and that was when my family drove to Missouri for my grandmother's funeral when I was ten. Talking to someone who's actually seen some of the world was fun."

"It sounds like you two have become friends."

"We did after that night," she agreed. "Now we're really close."

"Do you think he still reports back to your father?" he asked, not trying to sound too anxious. He'd hoped to spend the night but now it looked like it might not happen.

"I know he does. He's my friend but he's still loyal to my father. Besides, he has a son himself and probably thinks he's helping my dad protect me." Then she paused and gave him a coy smile. "And I'm sure he'll be telling my father about you being here tonight."

Not good, Marcus thought. "Your father knows about me?" he said before he could stop himself.

"Not yet," she told him. "But I have a feeling that's about to change." She paused and tilted her head thoughtfully. "Actually, I'm surprised he didn't find out about it before now."

He asked her what she meant.

"I was sure Marty must have mentioned it to my mom by now and what my mom knows, my dad knows."

He felt his alert button go off. "What makes you think Marty told your mom about me?"

"Because of the way she was acting the night of the dance game. She was so excited about it and you."

"I think what she was excited about was dancing with Tim."

She reached out and took his hand. "She wouldn't stop talking about that, either. But what really impressed her was you. She loved your place and all the fun she had and she always shares those kinds of things with my mom. I kept waiting for Mom to bring it up the other night at dinner but she didn't."

He felt the worry kick in again. "So your mom knows about me? Uh, I mean…that you and Marty were up at The Crystal?"

"No, and that's what was so strange. I kept waiting for Mom to mention it but she didn't. So I got Marty alone later and she said she never told mom about it." She paused and smiled at him. "And I'll bet you know why she never told her."

"Me?" he asked her, his mind going into panic mode and his throat going dry. "Why should I know?" He swallowed hard, afraid to hear the answer.

"Why else?" she said. "Marty didn't tell because she's afraid my parents would find out about Tim."

"Oh, oh yeah!" he exclaimed; almost dizzy with relief.

She told him she had to check on dinner and got up and went over to the stove. He sat back in the chair and silently sighed. Marty was still keeping her promise to him. Now all he had to do was keep from having a heart attack from the constant panic. Oh yeah. And keep the disasters at a minimum.

"Speaking of Marty," she said, taking off her apron and laying it across one of the chairs. "There's something I want to show you." She led him into the living room and over to a fireplace against the far wall. The room was small but the light brown carpet, spacious tan couch and accent tables made it look bigger than it actually was. The room had all kinds of feminine touches including a large collection of country crafts that occupied almost every spare space.

"Gonna start a fire?" he asked, teasing her.

"It's not a real fireplace. It has those revolving lights that give it a 'roaring fire' look. But I don't care, I love it." Then she picked up an object from the mantel and showed it to him. It was a Mason jar with a glass votive on the top containing a small candle. There was a painting of a snow scene on the jar underneath. He looked closer at it and was impressed by the detail the artist had put in it. Unlike some of the crude craft paintings he'd seen at area flea markets, this depiction was more like a miniature oil painting. He asked her where she got it.

"Marty made it," she said, going over to the coffee table in front of the couch. There was a similar looking jar sitting next to a magazine on the table and she picked it up. "Marty made this one, too," she said, handing it to him.

This one was a summer scene with children running through grass chasing bubbles. The detail was so vivid that the scene looked almost 3D. "These are excellent," he told her, not able to take his eyes off of the work.

"I know," she said. "I keep telling Marty how talented she is. My mother sells out every glass Marty makes. I'm trying to talk her into going to art school."

He carefully replaced the jars on the table and mantel. "Do you paint?"

She sighed. "No. I've always wanted to do something creative but I never took the time. Although…" And a wistful smile filled her face. "I've always wanted to play the piano. I even sent away for one of those 'teach yourself at home' kits. It was only a cardboard cut out but it was fun."

"Ben teaches music. You could take lessons from him."

"I'd feel silly taking lessons with all the kids."

He told her that Ben also taught adults. "One of his students is in his late fifties. Ben's teaching him to play the trumpet. And because you're a friend, I'm sure he'd give you a good rate."

Her face lit up and he could tell she liked the suggestion. They sat down together on the couch and discussed her love for music. He'd just put his arm around her when a knock came at the door. She got up to answer it and he knew it had to be Sanun, back to finish fixing the toilet. As soon as the manager stepped into the living room, the icy glares commenced again. The man was now holding a sizable pipe wrench in his right hand and slapping it against his other hand. For Marcus, the message came across loud and clear.

He was being scrutinized.

Vickie ushered Sanun into the bathroom and came back a couple minutes later. "I hope you don't have to use the bathroom for the next few minutes," she said, apologetically.

He told her he was fine but also wanted to add that he was feeling a bit intimidated. No doubt, if he was caught stealing a kiss from Vickie, the Thai watchdog would bury the pipe wrench in his skull.

"Come on," she said, reaching out for his hand and pulling him up off the couch. "Now for the cook's tour."

He followed her across the living room and down a small hallway to a room at the end. The room had two large windows and the window facing the west was lit up from the late afternoon light. There was a blue print loveseat against the far wall and to the right of that was a cabinet sewing machine. Baskets of material and yarn were lined up beside the machine and a small closet sat to the right of the sewing machine.

"This is Marty's room when she comes to stay with me," she told him. "The loveseat pulls out into a bed. I know it looks kind of bare but I'm working on a few ideas to finish it."

She led him back down the hall. "This is the bathroom," she said, motioning to the small room across from her bedroom. Sanun was knelt down next to the toilet working. He let go of the pipe wrench, got up and walked over to them. Vickie asked him if he was done.

"Mostly," the man grumbled.

Marcus looked around; trying to avoid the man's gaze which he knew was burning a hole in his head.

"Great," Vickie said. She then grabbed Marcus by the arm and escorted him into the bedroom. "I've got to show you this."

Marcus could see Sanun from the corner of his eye, standing in the hall, watching them. It was clear that the little man wasn't going back to his task until he was sure no hanky-panky was taking place. Marcus glanced around at the objects in the room, trying hard not to stare at the bed.

"My grandmother made the quilt," she said. "Isn't it beautiful?"

He knew she'd consider it an insult if he didn't look at it and glanced down at the bed. The quilt was light yellow with blue flowers along the edges and running up the middle. He could see the look of pride on her face and knew it meant a lot to her.

"You're right," he whispered. "It is beautiful."

That was all it took. A second later Sanun stepped into the room and the suspicious expression on the man's face had gone up more than a few notches. Vickie ran her hands across the tiny blue flowers on the quilt and prompted Marcus to touch them. He bent down and did as requested, knowing full well he was being closely observed. She then walked over to the wall and pointed up at the blue and yellow flowery border surrounding the room. The border brought out the colors of the pale blue paint and quilt, giving the room a cheery feel.

"I did the border myself," she said, her voice full of pride. "I also redid the woodwork borders in all the rooms, although Sanun helped me quite a bit. I'm not much of a carpenter."

"You do fine," Sanun replied, not taking his eyes off Marcus.

Vickie led the way back out of the room and Marcus followed, the little Thai bulldog just a step behind and watching his every move. They'd no sooner re-entered the hall than Sanun pulled the bedroom door shut securely.

"Air conditioner work too hard," Sanun said. "Best keep doors closed during day."

Marcus tried to keep from smiling at the man's obvious attempt to get his point across. The opposing camps went their separate ways, Sanun back to work in the bathroom and Marcus went with Vickie to the kitchen. As soon as they entered the room, Marcus wrapped his arms around her and pulled her close. "Your friend thinks that all I'm here for is to have my way with you," he whispered to her. "I don't need a bed for that. I could just throw you up on the kitchen table." He pushed her against the table and began to bend her backwards. He leaned in and kissed her but had no sooner got started when she giggled and pushed him away.

"That sounds like fun but let's have dinner first, okay? After all, I *did* spend a lot of time preparing it."

"Okay," he said, cackling lecherously. "Guess I'll have to settle on sex for dessert." He let go of her and turned around. Sanun was standing in the kitchen door, glaring murderously at him. It was apparent he'd heard the "sex dessert" reference and wasn't happy about it. Marcus cleared his throat and sat down on one of the chairs, trying hard not to laugh at the man's incredible timing.

"Have to shut off water for few minutes," Sanun said, his voice tinged with anger.

Vickie told him it would be fine and Sanun turned to go, pausing long enough to dole out another round of glares at Marcus. He ended with a final "hmph" of disapproval and left, letting himself out.

Marcus let the smile come. "Jesus! Does he do that with every guy you have over?"

"Actually, you're the first man beside my dad that I've had visit me here."

"You're kidding!" As soon as he said it, he felt stupid. He was afraid at how she'd take it and immediately apologized.

She came over and gave him a kiss on the forehead. "No need to be sorry. I thought it was a nice compliment." She then handed him a couple of napkins from the decorative holder in the middle of the table. "And since you're the first, you get the honor of setting the table." He took his cue and helped her with the rest of the preparations. She put hot rolls and a large bowl of salad on the table while he opened the wine. He finished pouring a sampling in their glasses and she handed him a pack of matches.

"I bought the candles today," she said, turning to grab a pair of pewter looking candle sticks from the counter and placing them on the table. "I thought it would be a nice touch."

As he lit the candles she put on a couple of oven mitts and went over and pulled a large platter of spaghetti from the oven. He stashed the pack of matches in his shorts pocket, grabbed a dishtowel and helped her carry the platter to the table.

"I wanted to keep it warm," she said, her face flushed from the heat of the oven. "I know it's your favorite."

He smiled. She'd remembered. He leaned over and gave her a quick peck on the cheek. "I'll try not to get it all over me so you have to hose me down," he told her.

"Oh, don't worry," she said. "I pride myself on being prepared. I don't have a garden hose but my tub is plenty big and I've even invested in an extra fire extinguisher in case you catch fire again."

He stared at her, not sure if she was serious or only kidding. There was a curious smile on her face so he assumed it was a joke. It was in his head to ask her if she had any other handy items around, like perhaps something to defend himself against a Thai watchdog wielding a pipe wrench. But the aroma of mushrooms and garlic filled his senses and he put the thoughts out of his head and sat down to enjoy the savory treat.

The dinner went without incident (much to his delight) and he enjoyed the conversation as much as the food. They talked all the way through dessert (ice cream cake) and even Sanun couldn't dampen the mood. He finished fixing the toilet in between grumbles and it was clear he wasn't happy Vickie was entertaining a male visitor. After Sanun turned the water back on, Vickie offered him a glass of wine. He declined the invitation, making an excuse that his dinner was waiting for him. But from the angered expression and dirty looks Sanun was still doling out, Marcus knew the reason for the refusal was because he was there, a usurper, an upstart trying to take advantage of Vickie. The angry little man headed for the exit, still clutching the pipe wrench in his fist like a footnote final warning. After he left, Marcus let out a low whistle. "Jeez. He's better than any home security system. Your father should hire him out."

"Who are you talking about? Sanun?"

He could see the worried look in her face and quickly changed the subject. In spite of his own observations, she still regarded the man as a friend and wouldn't take kindly to someone disparaging his character.

"So, what are your plans for your extra room?" he asked, wanting to get off the subject of angry apartment managers. She filled his glass with a little more wine and he chuckled. "Are you, by any chance, trying to get me drunk like you did Sanun?"

"No. But I *am* trying to get you more relaxed so I can talk to you about something."

He felt his heart race. *Here come the questions*, he thought to himself. He braced himself and asked her what she wanted to talk about.

"Well, since you mentioned about Ben giving me piano lessons, it got me to thinking. I've been saving up for over a year to buy a piano for my spare room. That way I'd have a real one to practice on instead of the cardboard. I was wondering if Ben would happen to know where I could get one at a reasonable price."

"Oh," he said, feeling his adrenaline level go back to normal. He'd been temporarily reprieved, again. "As a matter of fact," he told her, suddenly remembering his conversation with Ben, "Ben's got a couple of pianos for sale." He told her about Ben getting the loan for Cromwells and having to get rid of the pianos in the back room. "They're in good shape but he doesn't use them anymore. He'd probably give you a good deal on one of them."

Her face lit up like a light and she got up from her seat and came over and hugged him tight. "That would be so great!"

"No problem. I'll call him about it tomorrow."

She sat down in his lap and put his arm around his shoulder. "If you don't mind, I'd like to call him myself. That way I can talk to him about the lessons, too."

He simply nodded, happy as a clam. Having her so close was once again having a hypnotic effect. He nuzzled his face into her hair, hoping she'd take the hint that he'd like a kiss. She put her arms around his neck and began to kiss him when she abruptly stopped.

"Did you hear that?" she whispered.

He shook his head no.

"It was like a humming noise," she said, pausing to listen.

He listened with her. All he could hear was the sound of the air blowing through the floor vents. She shrugged her shoulders and got back to the kiss. He wrapped his arms around her and got back to business. They'd only been kissing for a few seconds when she stopped once more.

"There it is again," she whispered.

This time he heard it too. A humming noise.

"It sounds like it's coming from over by the microwave cart," she said, getting up from his lap.

He sighed inwardly and got up with her. With any luck, they could find out what it was and then get back to more entertaining pleasures. "Maybe it's coming from your refrigerator," he told her.

"I don't think so," she said, walking over by the fridge and pausing to listen. "It sounds more like it's coming from the microwave."

He walked over to the microwave and listened carefully to the humming noise. It was louder but still sounded muffled. It didn't seem to be coming from the microwave itself, but behind it. He carefully rolled the cart out and looked at the wall. It was made of plasterboard that extended from the ceiling down to about four feet from the floor. From there the wall was consisted of wooden boards, which looked newly varnished. Cut into the boards was a three-foot door with a latch. She told him the door led to an attic. He pulled the cart out as far as it would go, undid the door latch and peered inside. All he could see was roof rafters full of cobwebs and a floor made up of exposed wooden beams. He asked her if she'd ever been in inside.

"Only to put in some empty moving boxes."

He stuck his head into the dark alcove, trying to place where the sound was coming from. The humming was decidedly louder but it was too dark to see anything. He asked her if she had a flashlight. She took off across the room and came back a few seconds later with one of the candles from the table.

"Will this do?" she asked.

He took the candle and crouched down in the door. "I can't tell from here exactly where the humming noise is coming from," he told her. "I'm going to have to go in and look around." He put the candle in his right hand and carefully entered the attic. There wasn't a regular floor, only beams spaced every few feet with rolls of insulation in between. A musty, stale smell filled his nostrils as he crawled to the right of the door along one of the beams. Some of the cobwebs brushed across the bare skin on his legs and he reached back and wiped them away, hoping no spiders were still occupying them. He held the candle up and observed the attic. The floor ran some fifty yards to the left from where he was and the area was vacant except for a couple of leftover rolls of insulation in the far left corner and a group of empty boxes a few yards in front of him. He moved along a few more feet when he spotted a metal power box against the right wall.

He pushed the candle forward to get a better look when some of the hot wax dripped onto his hand. He whispered a couple of expletives and switched the candle to his other hand so he could wipe it away.

"Are you okay?" she asked him, leaning in the door.

"Yeah. Just got a little clumsy with the candle. But I think I found where the noise is coming from. There's a power box here against the wall." He moved towards it, listening carefully. There was a slight hum coming from the box but as he got closer, he realized it wasn't the same sound they'd heard earlier. He began to turn around when he heard the noise again. It was a loud humming and came from somewhere near the empty boxes. He could now make it out more clearly. It was more of a buzzing than a hum and the closer he got to the boxes, the louder it got. Something suddenly flitted in front of his face.

An insect.

He held up the candle and watched the bug land on the side of one of the boxes. He couldn't quite make it out because it was below one of the box flaps. He moved the candle closer and lifted up the flap. A bee. But the wings weren't quite the right shape. They were too thin. A jolt of adrenaline kicked in as he recognized what it was.

A wasp.

His safety mechanisms went into overdrive and he immediately began to back up. His mind was abruptly flooded with all the stories he'd heard as a kid about wasps being able to sting many times. The hair on his legs and arms started prickling as he thought about how much of his skin was exposed. He wanted to turn around but was afraid to take his eye off the wasp. He carefully retreated, placing one foot in back of the other. The buzzing slowly surged louder and he glanced around, knowing the nest had to be close by.

A sudden, stinging sensation pierced his right hand. He cried out in pain and dropped the candle. He quickly examined his hand, expecting to see a wasp sting but all he saw was another drop of hot wax. He glanced down at the candle, still burning bright in spite of lying on its side. It had landed on the foil exterior of the insulation in front of him, right below the box flap. He reached out to pick it up when the flap suddenly burst into flames.

"Shit!"

The instant heat hit him in the face and he instinctively took off one of his sandals. Vickie was yelling at him from the door but he had no time to answer. He had to put out the fire. He thrashed at the box flap with the sandal, causing the box to flop across the floor. The box landed on top of the candle and put it out. He finally managed to extinguish the flame but was now plunged into virtual darkness. He started to ask her for a match to re-light the candle when he remembered the pack in his pocket. He pulled it out and picked up the candle. But even before he lit the wick, he noticed that the buzzing had increased dramatically. The candle flame flared yellow and illuminated the attic, which was now full of angry, winged insects probably not happy that their nest had been attacked with fire.

He had to get his ass out there. Quick.

He threw his sandal into the burned box and made a dash for the door. Vickie saw him coming fast and screamed at him, asking what was wrong.

"Wasps!" he yelled, making a lunge for the door. She backed up enough to let him out and he stumbled out onto the floor, still holding the box and lit candle. He dropped both on the floor and scrambled to his feet.

He had to get the door shut.

By the time he was upright, it was already too late. A black, moving assault force gushed from the door, pouring into the room at an alarming rate.

"Aaaahhh!"

Vickie's scream filled the room and he yelled at her to make a run for it. She didn't have to be told twice and made a dash for the kitchen door. He stomped on the candle with his remaining sandal, putting out the flame. The bugs were now all around him, buzzing in his face and blocking his view. He grabbed the candle and burned box and scrambled over to sink, throwing them in. He ran some water over both, fearing they would flame up again. But just as he shut off the spigot one of the wasps personally let him know the consequences of invading their home.

"Owww! Goddamn it!"

He reached down to where the stinger had penetrated his left calf. A second later another sting pierced the skin on his neck and he cried out again. A third penetrated his left arm by his elbow and he ducked down, trying to protect himself. He turned around to flee when something large and yellow came flying at his face. A second later a heavy cloth surround his head and upper body.

"Follow me," Vickie yelled, wrapping her arm around his waist and guiding him across the kitchen. He could see the green, kitchen floor linoleum down by their feet. The green was then replaced with the brown of her living room carpet as they made their way toward the front door. Their legs were still partially exposed and they wasted no time escaping out into the hall. She slammed the door behind them and he came out from under the covering with her. It was then that he noticed the tiny blue flowers. It was her grandmother's quilt from the bed.

She let out a sigh of relief and bunched the quilt up in her arms. "Whew! That was close! I once saw a movie where people were attacked by bees. I never thought I'd be in a situation like that!"

"Are you okay?" he asked, worried that she'd been stung.

She smiled at him. "I'm fine! Not even one sting! How about that?"

He was amazed that she wasn't upset or at least scared. He suddenly felt a pang of guilt for putting her into another precarious situation.

She noticed the sting on his arm and became concerned. "I didn't get stung, but you weren't so lucky. How many times did they get you? Do you feel okay? You're aren't allergic to bee venom, are you?"

"No," he replied, doing a quick inspection from head to toe. "I think they only got me in a couple places, although they sure do hurt."

"I think you can put that back on now," she said, giggling softly.

He glanced down at his hand. He was still holding on to the sandal. "Holy cow! I never even noticed I still had it." He began to put it back on when he heard someone come up behind them.

"What going on?"

He didn't have to turn around to see who it was.

Sanun.

The little man walked up to them and the surly expression was still present on his face. He glanced first at the quilt and then at Marcus holding the sandal. The glare turned to outright hostility as the little man jumped to the wrong conclusion.

"You no good!" Sanun barked, shaking his finger in Marcus's face. "I saw from start. You get out, now!"

"What are you talking about?" Vickie asked the man. "We had to get out the apartment because of the wasps."

Sanun's eyebrows shot up. "Wasps?"

"Yes," Vickie said.

Sanun shook his head no. "Can't be. No wasps in apartment."

Marcus wasn't sure if he was calling Vickie a liar or simply not believing her story.

"I check everything," Sanun said, acting insulted. "No bugs of any kind."

"But Marcus found a nest in my attic," Vickie protested. Then she handed the quilt to Marcus and repeated slowly, "There's wasps in there, Sanun!" And she pointed to the door.

Marcus watched the man glare again at him and the quilt.

"It's not what you think," he told Sanun. "We had to get under the quilt to protect us from the wasps." As soon as he said it, the man's eyes narrowed in anger. Marcus sighed at his own poor choice of words. Sanun was assuming that he simply made the story up to get Vickie under the covers. "The quilt wasn't on the bed," he told Sanun. "We used it in the kitchen." The man grunted angrily and Marcus suddenly remembered his remark earlier about throwing Vickie up on the kitchen table and having his way with her. And from the look of fury showing on the man's face, Sanun had also recalled the comment.

"No wasps!" Sanun growled.

Vickie began to protest again but Marcus could see it was useless. The only way to convince the man was to give him proof. He motioned towards the door. "See for yourself," he told the man.

Sanun muttered an "I see'" and began to open the apartment door. Marcus pulled Vickie to the side as Sanun entered the apartment, slamming the door shut behind him.

"Hmph!" Vickie grunted. "I can't believe he didn't believe us…"

"Shhhhh!" he whispered, leaning in and listening at the door. Sanun's shouts came through loud and clear through the wood and Marcus jumped back not a second too soon as the door came crashing open again.

"Aaarrrhyyyaah!" the little man yelled as he rushed out into the hall at full steam. Several of the wasps were in hot pursuit and Marcus slammed the door shut to make sure no more got out. Sanun was frantically waving his arms around his face and head, yelling something in Thai. Marcus didn't know the language but assumed it had to be Thai cuss words. He glanced down at the sandal still in his hand and a wave of conscience swept over him. He handed Vickie the quilt and took off after one of the wasps, swatting it away from Sanun's head. The wasp landed on the wall under one of the decorative lamps and he quickly nailed it with the back of sandal, ending its buzzing existence. He then went after the other wasp. It was dive-bombing Sanun's head like a crazy kamikaze. He yelled at Sanun to duck and swung the sandal at the airborne target. He missed it, but caused the wasp to swoop close to the wall. As it came to within a couple inches of the flat surface, he swung the sandal and scored a direct hit.

"Got it!"

He turned the sandal over and showed the squashed remains to Sanun. "Man, he was a pretty big one!"

"Yes! Yes!" Sanun said, catching his breath. "He big one, alright. But I was lucky, he not sting me!"

Marcus smiled at him. "Good thing, 'cause he was sure trying hard to get you." He wasn't sure how Sanun would take the remark and waited for his reaction.

A smile crept across the man's face. "He was! He was uh...what do you call it?" And he made swooping motions with his hand.

"Dive-bombing," Marcus said, finishing it for him.

"That it!" Sanun yelled, almost giddy. "Dive-bombing! Like planes! Like King Kong!" He then began laughing with glee and Marcus joined him. Up until that instant, he'd never seen the man smile and was surprised to find that he had a sense of humor after all. Another voice came from down the hall and a boy about sixteen ran up to them. He had Asian American features and was wearing Reeboks and loose fitting clothing that was standard dress for kids his age.

"What's up, Pops?" the boy asked Sanun.

Sanun took the sandal from Marcus and showed the boy. "Wasp. In Miss Vickie's apartment."

"Wasps, huh?" the boy said. "No shit!"

"Watch mouth," Sanun said, correcting him. The boy automatically apologized as if it was a built in response. Vickie then introduced the boy as David, Sanun's son.

"And this is Marcus," Vickie told David. "He's a friend of mine."

"Mine, too," Sanun added. "He save my life—almost got stung!"

Marcus started to open his mouth to correct Sanun but thought better of it. Then he watched Sanun whisper a quick explanation to David, although it was hard to follow because some of it was in Thai. But he didn't have to hear it all to know that he was now enjoying hero status in Sanun's opinion.

"Wow! That's cool!" David said, inspecting the sandal again. "And you say they're all over Vickie's apartment?"

Vickie told him they were and then showed David the stings on Marcus's arm and legs. The sight of the puffy, red skin seemed to make the boy happy. "I heard they can sting up to twenty times," the boy said excitedly. "Do you think it was one wasp that got you or was it a bunch of them?"

Marcus mused, appreciating the boys' morbid curiosity. "I didn't really take time to check. I was trying to get away from them."

Another "Wow!" poured from the boy's mouth. "Hey, Pops! Can I get a look at them?"

Vickie immediately protested that no one else should venture into the apartment again.

"It okay," Sanun told her. "I get rid of wasp. Get big bug bomb tomorrow. Poof! Bugs be gone in no time."

"Bugs *will* be gone, Pops," David said, correcting his father.

"Right," Sanun replied, giving David a fatherly glare. "Bugs *will* be gone." Then he turned to Vickie. "But won't be able to sleep in apartment tonight. You find place to stay?"

"Oh, I'll be fine," Vickie told him. "My parents are out of town at a conference and I have a key to their place. I can stay there."

Sanun told her he would have her place ready by the next afternoon. Then he asked her if there was anything she needed out of the apartment that night.

"I don't think so. I've already got extra clothes at my parents'. The only thing I'd like is my purse and car keys. But I don't absolutely have to have them tonight and I can get Marcus to drive me over to my parents' place."

David grabbed Sanun's arm. "Hey, Pops! I can get all my hockey gear on and go in and get Vickie's purse!" And before Sanun could offer any objection, David ran down the hall towards their apartment.

"Should you let him do that?" Vickie asked Sanun.

"He be okay. I borrow your quilt and go in with him to make sure. Beside, he like bugs. He have to see. That his way."

Vickie handed him the quilt. "I'm still going to have Marcus run me out to my parents' place," she told him. "I want to make sure Marty doesn't use her key and try to get in before you kill the wasps."

Sanun nodded. "Okay, and I call your papa and let him know."

"Oh, you don't have to," she said. "I'll have Marty call him. She's got the number for his and mother's hotel room."

Sanun thanked her and requested her father call him if he had any questions on what happened. Marcus then helped Sanun clean the dead wasps off the wall aided by a couple of work rags that Sanun had in the pockets of his overalls. A few minutes later David came lumbering out of the apartment in full gear including hockey mask, gloves, guards and stick. Marcus was impressed with how fast the kid had managed to suit up.

"Ready!" David exclaimed, pulling what looked like a shower cap over his head. "Let's go!" He then hunched down into a goalie's stance in front of the door. Vickie told Sanun that her purse and keys were on the coffee table in the living room. He began to pull the quilt over his head. "You better stand down hall," he warned Vickie. "In case wasps come back out with us."

Marcus reached down and took off his other sandal. "I'll stand here by the door," he told Sanun, turning the sandals with the bottoms facing out. "That way I can get any stragglers that follow you and David out."

Sanun replied a quick "Good" and finished putting the quilt over his head, positioning himself behind his son.

Marcus tucked one of the shoes under his arm and went up to the door. "Here," he told David, "you won't be able to open the door with those gloves, so I'll do it for you."

David nodded an affirmative and replied that he was ready. Marcus opened the door and father and son went charging in like two men on a mission. As soon as they cleared the threshold, Marcus slammed the door. He only got to glimpse in for an instant but it was time enough to see that the air was heavy with the winged invaders. He and Vickie waited in silence for a few seconds and then Marcus leaned near the door to listen.

"Do you think they're okay?" Vickie said, the concern showing in her voice.

"They're both covered up pretty good. Wait," he said, backing up, "here they come."

The door flew open and David and Sanun rushed back out into the hall with five or six wasps in their wake. Marcus slammed the door shut and yelled to Vickie to get back. David was holding on to Vickie's purse and went crashing down onto the carpet, his father almost stumbling over him.

"Holy shit!" David yelled, scrambling to his feet.

Sanun came out from under the quilt and Marcus noticed he was clutching a rolled up magazine that he'd seen earlier on Vickie's coffee table. Sanun began swatting at the stragglers and Marcus grabbed his sandals and joined him. David let out a whoop, grabbed his hockey stick and entered the fight. David got a little careless with the stick and ended up smacking the wall a couple times, making small dents in the paint, something that under normal circumstances would upset his father. But this wasn't normal circumstance.

They were three men, united, fighting a dive-bombing menace.

Within a few minutes, all the wasps had been expurgated and the three victors were congratulating and patting each other on the back.

"That was classic!" David exclaimed. "Can we go back in again?"

Sanun chuckled and put his arm around David's shoulder. "No more tonight. Tomorrow we bomb them all."

"Bug bombs?" David yelled. "Oh, boy! Then we'll really annihilate them!" He hurried back down the hall, whooping it up.

Sanun handed Vickie her purse and she hugged him. "Thank you. You're very brave."

He blushed with pride and picked up the quilt from the floor. "I keep Grandmother's quilt safe until bugs cleaned up."

She thanked him and told him to call her at work when the apartment was livable again. Then she reached into her purse and took out a pen and small notepad, jotting down the number for the water department. He took the paper and headed back to his apartment, a big smile on his face.

Marcus escorted Vickie out to his car; a little sorry she was going to her parents' and not home with him. But he consoled himself when she got into the car and slid over next to him. Perhaps he could talk her into going somewhere to park before taking her home. Carswell Point was out, but there were a few other places in the area. Maybe the old mill. It was secluded and had a nice view of the reservoir.

"What are you thinking about so hard?" she whispered, putting her arm through his.

"Nothing. I was only waiting for you to give me directions to your parents' house."

"Oh. That," she said, sidling closer against him. "Uh… I'm not going to my mom and dad's house. That was a little fib I told Sanun."

He asked her what she meant.

"I lied because he'd expect me to go home to my parents' house."

"So?" he asked, not seeing her point. "Wouldn't your parents put you up?"

"Of course. But I don't want to go there. I want to go home with you."

He couldn't help but smile at his good fortune.

"Besides," she said. "I want to put something on those stings of yours. You don't by any chance, have anything for bee stings at your apartment, do you?"

"As a matter of fact…"

"Thought so!" she replied with a chuckle.

"What do you mean by that?"

As soon as he said it out loud, he mentally cursed himself. He was supposed to be keeping it a secret, not performing inquires to make her suspicious.

"I'm talking about how organized you are," she said. "It's no wonder you made The Crystal such a success. You always manage to plan for every contingency, don't you?"

"I try," he said, thinking that the way his *gift* was working overtime, even the entire local pharmacy might not be able to keep up with the pace.

After making a quick stop at her parents' house to warn Marty about the wasps and pick up some clothes, they headed back to his place. He was still concerned about her parents finding out about him and began quizzing her about it a little while later in his bathroom as she applied some ointment to his stings. "And you say your parents aren't getting home until tomorrow?" he asked her, wincing as the ointment penetrated the sting on his left calf.

"No. And Marty promised me that she wouldn't tell them about me staying with you so you don't have to worry about my father showing up at your door with a shotgun or anything."

"Uh, I wasn't worried about that," he said, lying through his teeth. "I just didn't want them to get the wrong impression about me, like Sanun did."

She stopped applying the lotion and smiled at him. "Well, you don't have to worry about Sanun anymore. You seemed to have won him over." She carefully applied the ointment to the sting on his neck and he looked at it in the bathroom mirror; surprised it wasn't swollen more.

"You should reapply it in the morning," she said, putting the bottle back in the medicine cabinet.

He grabbed her around the waist and pulled her close. "I don't think it's working," he whispered. "I'm still in pain. But the pain seems to go away every time you kiss me." And he leaned down and kissed her, trying to exhibit his undying passion for her.

Her lips began vibrating as she giggled. "I'm sorry," she said, pulling away, "but you made me laugh."

"I was hoping for a different reaction. Bordering more towards romance than comedy, if you know what I mean."

She went into his arms again and squeezed him tight. "I know," she said, "but I tend to giggle when I get nervous."

"Do I make you nervous?"

"Yes, you do. But you also make me happy, too. I can't explain it. I've never felt this way before. I'm experiencing all these different emotions every time I'm with you. It's like riding a roller coaster."

He pulled away from her, the anxiety coming back with a jolt. He knew what she was talking about. Like a roller coaster, the fire, the water park, the animals chasing them, the wasps. She was figuring it out.

"Marcus?" she whispered. "Is something wrong?"

"No. Nothing," he said, heading back to the living room, trying desperately to think of a few evasive maneuvers as she followed behind him. He glanced around the room. His apartment was bigger than hers and had three large windows in the living room, bringing in a lot of light in the early morning and late afternoon. His furniture consisted of two large, comfy upholstered chairs and state of the art entertainment center, complete with twenty-six inch TV, X-box, CD player and stereo set. The place was devoid of any carpet but a few choice throw rugs showed off the sheen of the polished, hardwood floors. The kitchen and bathroom were larger than Vickie's but unlike her place, he had only one bedroom. However, it was spacious enough to not only have room for a large dresser but a desk for his PC, allowing him to do some of The Crystal's bookkeeping at home.

"Marcus?" she asked him. "Where are you going?"

He walked over to the small wooden table between the upholstered chairs. On the table, beside the cordless phone was a framed photograph. It was just the diversion he needed. "Here," he said, picking up the photo and handing it to her. He sat down in the chair and pulled her onto his lap.

"Is this them?" she asked. "Your mom and dad?"

He put his arm around her waist and looked at the picture with her. "Yeah. That was taken when I was about twelve. It was at Hershey Park. I'm the one in the middle with the giant Hershey Kiss on my head. The reason I wanted you to see the photo was because you mentioned roller coasters. They had one there that my dad, mom and I loved. It was called the Sidewinder and it not only went forward, it also went in reverse. We must have ridden it ten times, we loved it so much."

"It sounds like fun," she said, putting the picture back on the table. She wrapped her arms around his neck. "What's it like?" she asked.

"What?"

"Riding roller coasters?"

He smiled at her. "You mean you've *never* ridden one?"

A look of shame filled her face and she shook her head no.

"But you said going out with me was like riding a roller coaster. So I naturally assumed you knew."

"No. I only meant that I *imagined* it was like riding a roller coaster. I've never actually been on one. My parents never let me. They believed in educational vacations and Mom is scared to death of roller coasters. She always gets so upset when she hears of someone getting hurt in an amusement park. She can quote statistics on accidents in fun places like some men can quote you baseball and football statistics. She's a sweetie but she worries way too much about things sometimes."

"But that was when you were younger," he told her. "You're all grown up now. You could have gone without them knowing about it. Don't your friends ever go to those places?"

She nodded bashfully. "Yes. And I sometimes go with them. But I only ride the smaller rides like the Scrambler or Dodgems. To be honest, I'm scared to try the larger rides. I know it sounds silly but I think I waited too long to try them. Maybe I'm too old now."

He chuckled and squeezed her tight. "Oh, no you're not. You should see some of the older people riding those rides. Mom, Dad and I would meet the nicest people. I used to complain about having to wait in some of the long lines but Dad loved it. He'd talk to everybody. We once met this guy celebrating his seventy-fifth birthday. He was there with his grandson and told us he rides the coasters all the time."

"You're just teasing me," she scolded.

"No, I'm not. I'm serious. There's a lot of older people who like to ride. They love it. And you'd love it too, if you'd give it a chance."

"But I'd be scared," she sighed. "I don't know if I could do it."

"I'd go with you. You could hold my hand the whole time. Besides, it's more fun to have someone to share it with."

"Do you really think I could?" she asked excitedly.

"Sure. We could go next weekend."

He felt her body tense up again. "But I wouldn't want to try anything as scary as that Sidewinder thing you talked about. At least not the first time."

He suddenly got an idea. "Hey. We could go over to Forge Park. They've got an old wooden coaster that's just the thing for beginners. We could borrow Jack's boat and go fishing early and then take in the park. They've also got a huge ballroom above the arcade and the bands on Friday and Saturday night are pretty good. And I could get Mavis to pack us a lunch to take out on the boat. We could make a day of it." She hugged him hard and he could tell she was excited about the idea. She lay against his chest again and a feeling of happiness filled him.

"Marcus?"

"Hmm?" he answered, still working out the details in his head.

"Do you think anything will happen at Forge Park?"

He stopped smiling and stared at her, dumbfounded. He wanted to ask what she was talking about but the fear wouldn't let him. He croaked out a weak, "What do you mean?"

"Well," she said hesitatingly, like she was broaching a touchy subject. "It's only that so far, our dates haven't been what you would call normal."

The panic gripped him like the cold hand of death and he pushed her up off of his lap and got to his feet.

"Marcus..." she said, taking his hand. "I only meant..."

"What?" he asked, scrambling for an excuse. "I don't know what you're talking about." He pulled away from her and hurried across to the kitchen. She asked him where he was going.

"I need something to drink," he lied. He suddenly felt trapped. He looked around for somewhere else to go but there wasn't any. He went over and opened the fridge. He could hear her walking up behind him and reached down for a soda.

"Marcus?"

He grabbed another soda and handed it to her, hoping she would drink it and stop asking any more questions.

"I only meant that our dates have been a bit unusual, don't you think?" she asked, picking at the tab on the can like she was waiting for him to answer.

He took a quick swig of his soda and put it down on the kitchen table. "I don't know what you mean," he replied, glancing around nervously. He had to get away from her. He had to get away from all the questions. He fled back to the living room, hoping she wouldn't follow him. But of course, she did. He tried to change the subject. "I'm gonna call Jack right now and ask him about the boat for next week." He walked over to the phone and hastily picked it up and dialed the number. She came over and stood beside him, waiting for him to finish with the call. But no one answered. The line kept ringing.

"Isn't he picking up?" she whispered, putting her can of soda on the table next to the photo.

"No," he told her, hanging up the phone. "I guess they're not home."

"Oh well," she said. "Maybe you can try him later."

He just stood there, not turning around to her.

"Marcus?" she asked him. "Is there something you want to tell me?"

He couldn't answer her. He knew what she wanted. Answers, answers he didn't want to give her. Why all their dates ended up in calamity? Why so many strange things happened to him? He bit his lip as the regret announced itself through every fiber of his being. It was no use. He couldn't win, no matter how hard he tried. He stared at the empty chairs. Why in the world had he bought two of them? Two chairs. Two people. It was never going to happen. He closed his eyes and cursed his existence. From the first time he saw her, he'd wanted to get her alone and here she was, in his place, alone with him at last.

Now all he wanted to do was get away from her.

He suddenly felt the warmth of her hand on his cheek.

"Marcus?" she said, pulling at his arm and making him face her.

He opened his eyes and gazed down at her, his heart breaking in two. "I can't..." he told her. "I can't..."

"It's alright," she whispered, gently stroking his cheek. "We don't have to talk about it. We don't have to talk about anything..." And she closed her eyes and kissed him.

The last of his resistance dissolved as the warmth of her lips touched his. She was like a wonderful warm breeze, floating into his lonely life and giving him hope. He finished kissing her and looked at her lovely face, smiling so sadly at him. His heart opened up to her. "Vickie…" he said, wanting to tell her everything.

"Shhh," she whispered. "Don't say anything else. Just kiss me."

She wrapped her arms around him and kissed him, her lips exhibiting a passion that until that time, he never knew existed. The world seemed to melt away and once again he was swept back to that sweet place where only her love and caress existed. He wished with all his heart to stay there, forever, with her. Nothing could touch them. Nothing could hurt them. He opened his eyes a couple seconds later and saw her gazing lovingly up at him. She opened her mouth and even before she whispered it, he could read it in her eyes.

"I love you, Marcus."

He took her in his arms as his heart and soul cried out with happiness. The rest of the world suddenly disappeared. It no longer mattered if she knew about him or not. Nothing mattered, the future or the past. The only thing that mattered was that she was with him. Right then, in that single moment.

And in that moment, he lived a lifetime.

He picked her up in his arms and she laid her head against his chest. No other words were necessary. Only her love and touch. He carried her down the hall to the bedroom, leaving all his doubts and regrets behind. He was going with her to that wonderful place he'd only imagined in his dreams. A place where only their love for each other prevailed and nothing else mattered. And being with her in that place and in that moment was enough for any lifetime.

Enough and more.

He awoke the next morning to the sunlight filtering in through the breaks in the blinds. The slow, rhythmic sounds of her breathing as she lay next to him were a soft, comforting sensation that lulled him back to sleep. He closed his eyes, experiencing an overwhelming sense of peace. He pushed his face against her hair and smiled. She was the center of his universe, the sound of her breathing filling his once empty life and existence, leaving him with an indescribable feeling of joy such as he'd never known, or ever would again.

He was happy.

He was loved.

He began to drift back to sleep when he suddenly remembered something. He opened his eyes and carefully raised his head up off the pillow, making sure not to wake her. He glanced around the room. The sunlight had illuminated it enough to afford him a good view. He checked the walls, floor and dresser. He then gave the covers and bed a quick once over. Nothing.

No wasps.

No elephants.

And best of all, no lizards.

Not a single intruder anywhere.

He lay back down on the pillow and sighed. It was going to be all right. Somehow, some way he would make it right. He pushed his face back into her hair and closed his eyes, letting the soft curls and her love surround his soul once more.

CHAPTER TEN

It was a little over a week later. Ben sat in a booth at The Point, discussing the latest developments with Jack. "I told you about the wasps, right?"

Jack replied that he did. "And Magic finally got around to telling me about it, too. He apologized for not meeting with us lately but I told him we knew how busy he's been and not to worry about it."

"He doesn't know you're meeting me now, does he?"

"No. I told him I had to run an errand for Mavis and then I was stopping off for lunch. You didn't say much on the phone. What is it? An Alamo meeting?"

"I'm afraid so," Ben replied. "But I'm not exactly sure how bad it is."

Jack pulled the pipe out of his mouth and told him to go on.

"Vickie phoned me. She asked to meet with us."

"She called you? When?"

"This morning, at the store," Ben said, pausing while the waitress set down his sandwich and Coke. He started on his burger while Jack placed an order for the lunch special, Reuben and fries. "And give me a Sprite," Jack added.

The waitress took off and Ben washed down the burger with a couple of swigs of Coke, anxious to get back to the subject at hand. "She's due here in about fifteen minutes. I needed some sustenance before we faced her. Did Magic say anything when you left The Crystal?"

"No. He was busy showing Tim around the Snack Bar." He paused to take a drag of his pipe. "Tim's getting to know all the ins and outs of The Crystal.

He learns fast and doesn't have the same cocky attitude some of the other kids seem to have nowadays. I was showing him how to run one of the pinsetters the other day and he sat there and paid real close attention. He likes to have fun but he knows the difference between that and getting the job done. He's a great kid. He had me in stitches the other day, telling me things that go on up at the high school."

"Magic tells me that Tim thinks you're pretty funny, too."

Jack clenched the pipe in his teeth. "Tim thinks everything is funny. That's what's great about him. A good sense of humor can get you through a lot of things."

"You mean like Magic's little problem?"

Jack nodded, as if he was giving it some thought. "Magic's always relied on his sense of humor when it came to dealing with his 'gift.' It's only here lately that it's been worrying him some."

"It's because he's in panic mode right now. He called me last night, really late, from The Crystal."

"I wondered what that was all about," Jack replied, expelling out a sizable puff of smoke. "He told me he stayed late working last night but I couldn't figure out what the heck he was doing. The leagues get done by eleven and he said he was there until after three AM."

"He was on the phone with me for two hours," Ben said, rubbing his eyes and still feeling the effects from the lack of sleep.

Jack asked him why Magic didn't use the phone at his apartment.

"Vickie's been spending nights at his place off and on the past week. He called me from The Crystal, wanting to talk where she couldn't hear him. He was nearly frantic."

"Why? What's wrong?"

"Vickie's invited him to meet her parents," Ben replied through a mouthful of burger. "He's supposed to have dinner with them Sunday, at their place in Jackson Manor."

Jack acted amused. "Snob Hill, huh? At least that's what Tim calls it. That also explains why Magic was acting so strange today. He tried to get me alone a couple of times but we were busy all morning with the mother's league and two of the lanes breaking down. I was going to find him to talk when I got your call." He paused, the smoke billowing like a cloud around his head. "He's afraid something will happen at her folk's place, isn't he?"

"Afraid? He's petrified!"

"Can't blame him. It's bad enough having to go through the usual third degree, answering questions like 'What do you want with my little girl?' and 'Are your intentions good?' or 'How do you expect to support her playing pool and shooting craps?' stuff."

Ben grinned. "Mavis's father?"

"None other. Man reminded me of a guard dog, growling at anyone who set foot near her. He and I ended up becoming friends but I'll never forget that first meeting. Magic *should* be scared. Meeting the parents is bad enough without having the added pressure of possibly setting their house on fire or having her family attacked by emus."

"Don't forget elephants and squids," Ben added with a chuckle.

"Exactly. That's why I feel for him. He seems to have it bad for this girl. God help him if he's in love with her, which I happen to think he is."

"Has he told you that?"

"No," Jack said, taking the pipe from his mouth. "But he has all the signs. It doesn't take a genius to see it."

Ben remarked that Vickie's call surprised him. "At first I thought it was about the piano lessons Magic set up for her. She's supposed to start them tomorrow."

"Then I take it that its not piano lessons she wants to meet us about?"

"No. She wants to talk about Magic. I didn't know what else to do so I suggested she talk to you, too."

Jack stopped puffing on his pipe. "So that's why you called me. I'm here for moral support, right?"

"That's only part of it. You're always telling me what a 'people watcher' you are. I want you to observe her and see if you can get a good read. If she's gonna end up breaking his heart, maybe we can do something to help soften the blow."

"So she still hasn't figured out the truth about him?"

"Not from him, anyway. Every time she brings up the subject, he says he dodges her questions or changes the subject. But the girl's not stupid. She must have heard rumors and she has to know *something* is going on."

"I shouldn't wonder," Jack replied, putting the pipe back in his mouth. "Magic's never gone this far in a relationship before, has he?"

"No. By this point, they're usually gone, or to quote him, 'leaving in a cloud of dust.'"

"So you think she's going to break up with him?"

"I think Magic thinks so. He figures that once she finds out about him, she's gone. That's why he's been avoiding all her questions."

"And you think she's meeting us to get those questions answered," Jack said, smiling like he was enjoying himself. "This *is* an Alamo meeting, isn't it?"

"That's what I'm afraid of. I'm not sure what to say when she starts asking questions about him. I mean, what or how much should we tell her?"

Jack sat back and puffed on the pipe, giving it some thought. "I've done a lot of lying in my days. And it's been my experience that the lies I told took more of a toll on me than the person I was directing them at."

"You mean you were lousy liar?"

"No. I was very good at it. So good that I almost always got away with whatever scheme or problem I was telling the lie for. But the one who suffered most because of it was me, my conscious, something I never knew I had until I met Mavis. Sometimes love can make you see things you'd never noticed before. It's a great teaching experience. If love taught me nothing else, it made me realize that it's okay to be imperfect, to make mistakes and stumble once in a while on life's path. It's real, it's human. It's also honest. Lying doesn't fit into that picture."

"So you're telling me to tell her the truth?"

Jack shook his head like he wasn't sure. "I know you're instincts will be to protect him but sometimes you have to let nature take it's course. Besides, lying will only postpone the inevitable and if she was going to break his heart anyway, isn't it better to end it quick?"

Ben stared down at his Coke, thinking about it. Protecting and defending Magic had become such a habit over the years that to do otherwise seemed unnatural. But he knew Jack was right. Lying wasn't going to help. It could even make things worse. "Okay," he told Jack. "I'll tell her the truth. Can I count on you to help me?"

"Just try and stop me," Jack replied, giving him a wink.

The waitress brought Jack's lunch a few minutes later and the two of them finished their sandwiches and talked about Magic's most recent *moments*. The last couple hadn't made headlines but the town rumor mill had been churning overtime with the details. They also discussed how lately the *moments* seemed to be occurring with more frequency, another fact that the local gossips were discussing and clucking over.

"A few people have even speculated that something bad is about to happen," Jack said, pushing his empty plate aside.

"What do you mean? Like some kind of natural disaster?"

Jack shrugged, as if dismissing it. "You know how some small-minded people get. They try to blame someone else for their rotten lot in life. But the people who know Magic don't buy into those theories. They know better."

"Of course they do," Ben agreed. "They see Magic as a man, not some kind of monster."

"They also see him as a friend. It's hard to think of anyone being a jinx or monster when it's also one of your friends. There's a great power that comes with friendship and love. Most people take it for granted. Someone like Magic knows what a special thing it is."

Ben snickered. "Yeah, but most people don't go through life running from elephants and lizards. Magic's no jinx. He's simply what some people would call 'an adventure in dating.' In my book, that's an asset. Any girl going to dinner with him not only gets a meal, she also gets a free show, too. What more could you ask for?"

"Uh, and speaking of dinner," Jack said. "How did it go Thursday night when you had Vickie and Magic over?"

"Good. After the wasp thing, Sue and I were prepared for anything. I've told you about the *Magic moments* that have happened at our place over the years."

"Yeah. My favorite was right after you and Sue moved in. When Magic got his arm caught in the dryer vent and the kids in the next yard thought your building was eating him and called the police."

Ben recalled the sight. "It was easy for them to come to that conclusion. He was jammed up so tight against the vent that it really *did* look like the building was eating him. Sue kept complaining about the dryer not putting any heat out and Magic and I checked the fuses and the lint guard but they were okay. Then I remembered how sometimes the lint would fall back down into the trap and the only way to get it out was to clean the pipe. Magic volunteered to do it but stuck his arm in too far and got it caught on the elbow joint of the shaft. I poured some dish soap on his arm and we finally managed to get it free just as the fire truck pulled up."

Jack laughed. "I know. You told me."

"The neighbor kids thought they were doing the right thing," Ben said. "Can't fault them for that. After that they got used to things happening when Magic was around. Shit! They started looking forward to it. They kept bugging me all the time, asking me when he was coming over."

"Sounds like my grandson, Brett."

Ben asked him what he meant.

"Brett is a member of Magic's fan club, like your neighbor kids."

Ben suddenly remembered. "Oh yeah. Brett's the one who had the lizards that Magic babysat that time with Wanda. And isn't he the one that always goes fishing with you and Magic?"

Jack replied that he was. "As a matter of fact, Brett and I just went out on the lake the other day. Magic was supposed to join us but he and Vickie had other plans. Did you hear about Magic borrowing my boat to take her out fishing this weekend?"

Ben almost spit up his Coke. "Jesus! That sounds like an accident waiting to happen! He never mentioned it when he called me this morning. What's he trying to do, kill her?"

Jack waved him off. "I know what you're thinking. But weird things don't always happen when he goes out with me on the boat, or anywhere else for that matter, only some of the time."

Ben let out a sarcastic grunt. He knew Jack was deliberately downplaying the incident ratio. More often than not Magic's "gift" would make an appearance, turning a leisurely excursion on the lake into an "Irwin Allen" adventure. "Uh, what about the time your boat got capsized?" he asked Jack, trying to throw it in his face.

"Which time?"

Ben laughed out loud. "Well, I only heard about one time! Do you mean to tell me that it's happened twice?"

"Hey, the first time some drunken idiots cut across our path and we got caught in their wake. You've seen how small my boat is. That could have happened to anyone."

"And the second time?"

Jack made a face like it was no big deal. "That wasn't his fault, either. I was trying out a new stringer and we were putting a fish on it. It was a big one. A bass. Real beauty. Anyway, the fish kept flopping around and the other end of the stringer came loose and the bass managed to flop right over the side, taking the rest of the fish with it. That new stringer was pretty stiff and when I tried to grab it, the dang thing jerked right out of my hands. I guess Magic felt bad about me losing a whole day's catch so he lunged across the boat, trying to grab it before the end of the string went into the water. He tipped the boat and the next thing I know, all three of us are in the water."

Ben asked him if his grandson was all right.

"Sure. I always have him wear his life jacket whenever he goes out with me and he's an excellent swimmer, like his old granddad."

"How far out were you?"

"Not far. Both times when it happened there was always someone there to help us. The drunks in the speedboat that capsized us the first time came back to pick us up and they even tied up my boat and towed it in. And the other time, with the stringer, a coast guard cruiser happened to be passing by and picked us up. We were only in the water a couple of minutes."

"That was lucky."

Jack told him that it was more than luck at work. "His *Magic moments* seem to be exactly that. Magic. Everyone that sees them or goes through them with him ends up walking away smiling or feeling enlightened by them."

"Not everybody," Ben reminded him. "I'm sure that lady who fainted after seeing that emu didn't feel enlightened."

"No but she didn't get seriously hurt, either. Only frightened. And even that didn't last for long."

Ben asked him what he was talking about.

"Haven't you heard? It's all the customers at The Crystal have been talking about lately. Uh…that is…besides *Magic's moments*. The lady came to The Crystal, looking for Magic a couple days after it happened."

"That sounds like trouble," Ben said. "Was she carrying any weapons?"

Jack told him she wasn't. "She was nice as pie, actually. She asked Magic to take her out to Paul Pelling's place so she could get a better look at the emu."

"Now I know you're pulling my leg," Ben said but Jack assured him he wasn't.

"She'd never seen one before and told Magic that after she woke up and someone told her what it was, she realized how silly it was to be scared of it. To quote her 'It was only a big bird.' So Magic did as she asked and took her out to Pelling's place."

"But I thought the authorities took the ostriches and emu away."

Jack told him the birds weren't taken away until a week later, when the authorities finally found an animal park willing to take them. "Until then, Pelling kept them on his place. Where else were they gonna put them? In a paddy wagon or the town jail?"

"Never thought of that," Ben said. "So what happened after Magic took the lady out to Pelling's? I didn't hear anything about another animal stampede."

Jack explained that the trip to the old man's place was *moment* free and that the lady not only got to see the birds but all of Pelling's other animals. "And Magic said that Pelling's even got a nest of baby bunnies living in his attic that the lady went crazy over. Pelling ended up giving her one. Now she's going out to his place a couple times of week and helping him care for the animals. And the rumor is she sometimes spends the night."

AND THE BULL SAVED ME

"No way!" Ben laughed. "You're making this up."

Jack shook his head no and smiled. "A couple of our customers live out by Pelling's place and told us that's what's going on. I kid you not."

"Incredible," Ben said, still finding it hard to believe.

Jack told him that the whole episode merely proved his own theory about the *moments*.

"You mean that a higher power is behind it, right?" Ben asked, trying not to smile.

Jack eyed him carefully. "I see that smile Ben, and know what a cynic you are. But I'm telling you. There's something special going on and I'm not the only one who sees it. So do a lot of people at The Crystal, especially the kids. That's why they idolize him. They see what some of the adults fail to, that something mysterious and spiritual is going on. It's nothing to be afraid of, it's an honor to witness it. And I know my grandson Brett feels honored every time it happens. He's becoming Magic's number one fan."

"Brett? Why?"

"He was with me all the times Magic went fishing with me. After that first time, when the boat got capsized, I thought Brett would be turned off fishing or going out in the boat. Turns out he *loved* it. So much so that he insists on going every time Magic goes with me. And Brett never comes back disappointed." Jack paused and grinned. "Neither do I. Hearing about his *moments* afterward is entertaining enough, but experiencing them with him firsthand, even the little ones, is…like Brett says, 'pretty sweet.'"

"Uh-oh," Ben replied. He could see exactly where this was going. "This must be a few of his *moments* he doesn't always tell me about." He told Jack to go on.

"Oh, it's never anything as dramatic as elephants or emus. Just little things. For instance, the second time we went out Magic snagged a branch and pulled in a cottonmouth."

"Snake? Isn't that poisonous?"

Jack held up his hand in protest. "Yeah, but none of us got bit. We didn't even know it was there until Magic tried to pull the hook from the branch. I let out a yell and jumped on top of Brett, in case the snake got any ideas."

Ben shook his head in disbelief. "What did Magic do?"

"He was kind of wrestling with it at first. He kept turning the branch every which way but the snake kept slithering around at him."

"Why didn't he throw the branch back in the water?"

"He couldn't," Jack replied. "The hook caught on his sweater. He was connected to it. I let go of Brett long enough to help Magic get loose from the hook but by that time the snake was slithering close to Magic's arm again. So we threw the branch back in the water but Magic lost his balance and fell in right after it. You know that scene from Jaws when the swimmer is in the water, trying to get to the boat and away from the shark? Well, that was Magic and the snake. The damn thing was zigzagging through the water at him and me and Brett are grabbing at Magic, trying to drag him back in the boat before the darn thing bit him. It got pretty darn exciting there for a while."

"I've no doubt," Ben said, stifling a chuckle.

Jack folded his arms on top of the table, getting comfortable. "The rest of the incidents were similar, although not quite as dangerous. Things like Magic getting his foot caught in the planking and falling on top of my tackle box. It took us over an hour to get all the hooks out of his clothes. And then there was the time he threw out his line and accidentally got it snagged on a speedboat."

"A speed boat? Now that's one big fish!"

"It dragged us a couple hundred yards before Magic had the presence of mind to let go of the pole. He's hanging on to the pole and Brett and I are hanging on to him, trying to keep him from being dragged off by the boat. Another time I put Magic in charge of handling the outboard and we ended up bogged down in a swampy area with what looked like a million frogs."

"Yeah. He seems to have a special rapport with the animals, doesn't he?"

"It's true. But those frogs didn't seem too friendly. And the noise! I finally caught a few dozen and threw them in my minnow bucket before I steered us out of there. Mavis hates them but Brett and I love them fried. Brett thought it was some kind Wild Kingdom Adventure, especially when the frogs started jumping in the boat."

Ben started to open his mouth to ask when Jack held up a finger and explained it. "It got dark on us, we were stuck in the bog all afternoon. Magic turned on one of two lanterns I have stashed in the boat. But the one he grabbed was a kerosene type that I keep for pier fishing. I don't use it on the boat, only on land, but I keep it stored with all my other fishing gear on the boat. Magic didn't know that and tried to light it while I was groping around trying to find my battery-operated lamp. He spilled some of the kerosene on the planking and when he tried to wipe it up, the lantern got knocked over."

"I see where this is going," Ben said. "Another fire, right?"

Jack confirmed it. "But Magic didn't set the boat on fire. Although later, he told me he thought he was going to so he threw the lamp out of the boat. Unfortunately, it crashed and exploded on the biggest mass of frogs and then all hell broke loose. The dang things were flying through the air and jumping helter-skelter all over the place, trying to get away from the fire."

"Holy shit! Smokey Bear wouldn't enjoy hearing that."

"Oh, he didn't set any of the woodland on fire. The lamp, or what was left of it, sunk into the swamp after it exploded. But the frogs weren't waiting around for any other similar missiles to show up so they abandoned ship and elected to jump in ours. We were throwing frogs out hand over fist. The whole boat was crawling with them. Brett still talks about it."

"Jeez!" Ben said, seeing what Jack was talking about. "No wonder Brett likes going out with you and Magic on the boat. Every time is a new adventure."

"Yep. The only problem is that Brett enjoys himself too much. When he found out that Magic wasn't going with us the other day, he was pretty disappointed."

"Poor kid," Ben remarked. "He had to spend the day with Grandpa and just fish."

"Well, I may not be as entertaining as Magic but Brett still managed to have a good time. He caught his first big catfish. It wasn't as exciting as a boat load of frogs but we both thought it was pretty sweet."

Ben snickered. "Maybe you should have capsized the boat to make him feel better."

"It crossed my mind a couple of times," Jack replied with a gleam in his eye as he tapped the last of the pipe ashes into the ashtray in front of him. "But I was afraid we'd end up at the bottom of Lake Erie with my new stringer."

"Bottom of the lake, hell!" Ben laughed. "It's probably being dragged to Canada by that escaped fish, right along with the rest of your day's catch. That fish ain't stupid enough to come back to this side of the lake again. What next? Whales? If that's the case you're gonna need a much bigger boat, Captain Ahab."

"Strange you should mention it," Jack said. "I happen to have my eye on one." Then he told Ben that he was looking to buy a larger model.

"Why? The old one worn out from all your adventures with Magic?" Ben quipped.

"No. It's still in great shape. I'm simply ready for a trade in." Then he smiled at Ben. "Speaking of adventures, what about you and Sue? Did anything happen Thursday night at dinner?"

Ben replied that it did. "And it was almost as funny as the frogs. I call them his *mini moments*, ones not worthy of making headlines but still amusing, like the ones you told me." He told Jack that Sue made a Cajun dish to serve Magic and Vickie. "So I tried to think of possible scenarios that could happen in case one of his *moments* showed up. I stocked some syrup of Ipecac in case he developed a sudden allergy to pepper or anything else and I even went out and bought another fire extinguisher."

"Good thinking. Hope you didn't have to use it."

"I didn't use either of them. What I ended up using was a videotape."

Jack finished filling his pipe and lit it. "This I gotta hear."

"The dinner went fine but right after we ate, Magic developed the worst case of hiccups I've ever seen. They wouldn't stop. Vickie, Sue and I carried on a conversation for almost an hour while Magic sat on the couch and hiccupped. It was comical. Vickie would make a comment about whatever we'd be talking about and Magic would open his mouth to ask her something and all that would come out is this huge hiccup! Sue and I were bustin' up laughing and so was Vickie. The only one who didn't enjoy it was Magic. His face kept getting red from frustration. So I decided to have some fun…"

Jack narrowed his eyes at him. "Okay, Ben. What'd you do? Knowing the two of you, I imagine it was pretty good."

"Nothing," Ben said, trying to act innocent. "I simply cured his hiccups. That's all."

"Knowing you, you probably tortured him. Come on, Ben. Fess up."

"Okay. You know how Sue and I have been trying to get Magic to go to the reunion with us?"

"Uh-huh. And he seems determined not to."

"Well, he's going now. And better yet, Vickie's going with him!"

"How the hell did you talk him into that?" He paused and pointed his pipe at Ben. "He couldn't talk, so you tricked him into it, didn't you?" Ben nodded his head yes and Jack put down the pipe and laughed. "I was right! You did torture him."

"Yeah and it was great! You should have seen it. I started yakking about the reunion and how I was on the organization committee. I told Vickie about the DJ we'd lined up and about all the kids Magic and I used to go to school with. She seemed quite interested so naturally, I suggested she go with Magic to meet them."

"And of course, Vickie thought it was a great idea."

"She did, but Magic didn't," Ben said, trying to keep from laughing. "He kept trying to say 'no' but every time he opened his mouth, this giant hiccup would come out instead. Then he starts shaking his head no but Vickie thought he was only reacting to his frustration over the hiccups. So then I have a little more fun. I offer to show Vickie the video of the last reunion."

Jack's mouth dropped open. "You mean the one you gave me a copy of? The one showing him setting the gym floor on fire?"

"Yep."

"Jesus, Ben. Magic must have had a coronary! You didn't show it to her, did you?"

"I only got as far as putting it into the machine. Magic lunged across the room and started wrestling me for it. He's got some pretty good moves for someone who never wrestled and he should. I practiced plenty on him in the old days. Then Sue yelled at us to stop acting like a couple of kids and we called it a draw. So I made up some excuse and told Vickie that it was the wrong tape and that I must have lent the other one out."

"What'd she think about the two of you wrestling? Wasn't she suspicious?"

Ben came up from taking a swig of his Coke. "She did at first but Sue helped out and told her that Magic and I never grew up and still sometimes use the living room floor as a wrestling mat. She told Vickie we were a couple of juvenile delinquents."

"That's the truth."

Ben ignored the sarcasm and got back to the story. "Anyway, the point of the whole thing is that Vickie didn't find out about him and the scare tactic worked."

"What do you mean 'scare tactic'?"

"I mean the plan worked. It got rid of Magic's hiccups. That's why I did it."

Jack shook his head in disbelief. "Sue *was* right. You *are* a juvenile delinquent!"

"Who's a juvenile delinquent?"

Ben looked up at Vickie standing beside the table, holding what looked like a root beer. Jack offered her a seat and she sat down next to him, placing her purse and drink on the table. She was wearing a knee length denim jumper, white cotton shirt and sandals. The dolphin necklace Magic had given her was around her neck. Ben commented on how nice it looked on her.

"I never take it off," she said, touching the necklace. "I love it. Marcus is helping me look for a pair of earrings to match it."

Ben glanced down at his Coke, trying not to smile. He knew that Magic had already bought the matching earrings and was no doubt waiting for an opportune time to give them to her.

She asked Ben if dinner was still on for Saturday night.

"Saturday night?" Jack asked.

"Magic and Vickie are coming to my place for dinner again," Ben told him. "Sue is on a domestic kick and decided to use us all as guinea pigs for one of her new recipes. You and Mavis should be getting an invitation, too."

Jack nodded, sat back and puffed away on his pipe. He asked Ben what the recipe was.

"Some kind of French dish, loaded with lots of eggs and cheese. Not exactly what the American Heart Association would recommend."

"Sounds like my kind of food," Jack replied.

Vickie turned to him. "Do you like French food, Mr. Kinderbrook?"

"Absolutely," Jack told her. "And please…call me Jack."

"Marcus seems to be able to eat anything," she said, smiling like she was enjoying a personal joke. "I could never eat anything like calamari or eel."

"Me neither," Ben agreed. "But Magic's always had a cast iron stomach. I even saw him eat rattlesnake once when we took a trip to Texas. Of course, he was drunk at the time…" He cleared his throat and cut the story short, realizing he wasn't helping Magic's case any. "Uh, I've seen Magic eat weird things when he was cold sober, too."

"So have I," Jack added. "Although what some consider weird is normal for other people."

She asked him what he meant.

"Turtle, for instance. Lots of people eat it. My grandson and I go turtle hunting and a couple years ago we talked Magic into going with us. He helped us catch the turtles and then we showed him how to cook them."

She acted intrigued. "I've always wondered. How *do* you cook them?"

"Usually I just flour it and fry it in oil," Jack told her. "Magic really liked it that way. I've also taught him how to fry frog legs but he won't eat 'em. I think it bothered him when he saw them move around in the hot oil."

Vickie's eyebrows shot up and Ben grinned. He'd heard this story before.

"But aren't they dead?" she asked with a look of revulsion.

Jack tapped the ashes into the ashtray. "Sure. But frog legs are mostly muscle and sometimes when you fry them, they'll contract in the hot oil, making it look like they're still alive."

"Which is a pretty good trick considering there's no body or head," Ben added with a cackle.

"Magic didn't want anything to do with them once he saw that," Jack said. "But my grandson Brett loves them. He thought it was cool to eat something that moved around when you cooked it."

"Your grandson sounds adventurous," Vickie told him. "I wish I could be more like that."

You will if you stay with Magic, Ben thought with a smile. He decided to kid Jack. "Uh, if you ever get a notion to try some, Jack knows where you can get some nice juicy frogs. He and Magic found a spot burning up with them." Jack kicked him under the table and Ben snickered. Vickie noticed the reaction and asked if something was wrong.

"Nope," Jack replied with a wink. "Just disciplining a juvenile delinquent."

Ben decided to get down to business. "You said you wanted to talk about Magic," he told her. "I'm not sure what you were referring to but I thought Jack and I could explain a few things." He paused, not sure what to ask next or how to approach whatever issue she was concerned with. Maybe he could throw out a little bait. "I know Magic said he's supposed to meet your parents and they may have some concerns over his finances. But Jack can tell you that the bowling alley is doing very well, so your parents don't have to worry about you dating a deadbeat."

Jack's eyebrows shot up in shock and Ben knew he'd overplayed his hand.

"I think what Ben meant…" Jack said, giving him a warning glare. "Is that Magic is quite stable, financially. He's by no means a rich man but with his imagination and drive, I think he's on his way to being one of the leading businessmen of the community."

"Oh, I wasn't worried about his finances," she said. "Although my father would be. No, I only wanted to ask a few questions about him, that's all."

Ben felt Jack kick him under the table again and knew what he was thinking. *A few questions, that's all.* Questions no doubt involving elephants and wasps.

She'd finally found out about her boyfriend.

He decided to find out exactly how *much* she knew. "What kind of questions did you mean?" he asked her.

She pushed her soda aside and sat forward, her expression turning serious. "A couple of things have been bothering me. I've tried to talk to him about it but every time I bring up specific things, he acts…I don't know…uncomfortable talking about it."

"What kind of things?" Ben asked, knowing very well which things she was referring to.

She put her hands in her lap and frowned down at them. It was clear she was trying to find the words. "Things have been happening since we've started dating. Like the first night we went out. His pants caught on fire."

"We know," Ben told her.

She gave him a bewildered look and he tried hard not to smile. He always loved the fact that although women told each other everything, they were nonetheless shocked whenever they found out that some men did the same thing.

She composed herself and continued. "At the zoo, an elephant chased us. That happened on our second date."

Jack and Ben both nodded and a look of revelation filled her face. Undoubtedly, she was beginning to see that Magic's best friends were informed about certain things.

"Then at the water park..." she said, her face flushing with embarrassment. "I assume you know about that, too."

"Not only by Magic," Jack told her. "Tim Prentiss also filled us in."

"Oh, that's right," she said. "Tim was there." Then she opened her mouth to say something else but thought better of it and stayed silent. Ben knew she was feeling uncomfortable and tried to reassure her.

"Take your time. We're in no big hurry."

She gave him a sad smile. "Thanks. I rehearsed this whole speech. I even wrote it down, making notes. But when I read it back it sounded a bit...bizarre...you know what I mean?"

"Yes we do," Jack told her. "We've been there, too. You're among friends so feel free to talk."

She sat up in her seat like she'd suddenly made a decision. "Okay," she said with an air of conviction. "It's like what happened with the horses, and the wasps. I know those kinds of things happen sometimes but with Marcus, it seems to happen *all* the time. Take last night, it happened again when we went to Burger Haven for dinner."

Ben tried hard not to smile. Obviously one of the *moments* had made another appearance but Magic had failed to mention it during his pre-dawn call. The panic of being invited to her parents must have blotted it out. And why not? When strange things happened to you every few days, what was one more?

Jack asked her what happened.

"It was kind of late, just after eleven. Marcus was at The Crystal until after the leagues finished but I wanted to have dinner with him so we stopped there for a sandwich. We noticed someone locking the door while we were ordering our food, you know how they sometimes do that at closing, so no other customers come in? So we got our food and took a seat. While we were eating we noticed a couple of the workers, teenage boys, go into the playroom to clean it up. The playroom is one of those with slides and a big container full of plastic balls that the kids jump around in."

"I know the place," Jack said. "I take my grandkids there sometimes."

"After the boys got done cleaning," she said. "Marcus noticed that one of them had dropped his car keys on the playroom floor. We looked around for the boys but they'd gone in the back. It was past closing, so no one was behind the counter, either. We finally decided to go get the keys ourselves so we went into the playroom. But the door shut behind us, locking us in. They told us later that they keep it locked for insurance purposes, so no one can get in and get hurt."

Jack took a puff on his pipe. "Did someone unlock the door and let you out?"

"No," Vickie said. "We were pounding on the windows and kept waiting for someone to come out from the back but they never did. So Marcus got into the container of balls and banged on the glass, trying to get someone's attention in the drive-thru line. The drive-thru is open later than the restaurant and we could see cars going through it."

Ben asked if someone saw them.

"Yes. But they must have thought Marcus was a burglar or that he'd broken in because one of the people in the drive-thru line started dialing on his cell phone. A couple minutes later three police cars with their sirens and flashers going full blast come roaring up!"

Ben watched Jack take the pipe from his mouth and smile. He knew what he was thinking. It was almost like one of their *post moment* meetings with Magic. But in this case it was Vickie telling it.

"The police almost broke down the front door trying to get in and that's when everyone runs out from the back," Vickie said. "They let the police in and then they see the two of us locked in the playroom and try to get us out but no one can find the keys. They only have one set of keys to the playroom, if you can believe that. So it turns out that the keys we saw on the playroom floor were the set of keys to the door."

Jack began grinning larger. "So you could have let yourselves out the whole time."

"Not exactly. When Marcus went through the container of balls, he accidentally dropped them."

"Uh-huh," Ben said, seeing all the familiar signs of one of Magic's *moments* forming. "What did the cops do?"

Vickie told them that they wanted to break down the playroom door. "But the manager kept complaining about the damage that would be done to the property and how she wasn't authorized to okay something like that. So while all of them are arguing about it, Marcus and I decided to jump into the balls and try to find the keys. I found them a few minutes later and we got the door unlocked before the police knocked it down. The manager was very grateful and kept apologizing to us for being locked in."

"I bet you were glad that was over," Jack remarked.

"But it *wasn't* over," she said. "When Marcus and I were looking for the keys, we found some other things, a wallet, a change purse and another set of keys. The manager told the police the wallet and change purse would be returned to their owners and the police took the other set of keys. But then the manager started wondering what other stuff was hidden down in the balls. She was worried some child would get cut on any other keys or sharp objects that still might be lurking there. She wanted the whole container searched for other potentially harmful objects but her employees were busy making burgers for the drive-thru customers. So Marcus and I volunteered to help and so did the policemen." She paused and began grinning.

"You should have seen it. There we were, me, Marcus and four police officers, rummaging through the balls. Marcus and I were trying to be careful but the policemen were getting the balls all over the floor and they started spilling out into the main restaurant area because the door was still open. Then after we searched the container, we all started running around, picking up the balls and throwing them back. It was some sight! The policemen were laughing, having a great time and so were we. Even the manager was laughing until she saw the other things we found in the container."

Ben asked what else they found.

"There were some little kids' toys and a couple of used disposable diapers...those were only wet, not soiled, thank goodness. But one of the policemen found a couple of used condoms."

Jack started chuckling so hard that he had to take the pipe from his mouth. "Condoms?"

"I know," she said, chuckling herself. "I'll bet the manager had a meeting with the employees about that. Marcus and I weren't the first ones in the playroom after dark!"

Ben was happy to see that her latest adventure with Magic hadn't dampened her spirits any, just the opposite. The expression on her face as she told them about the incident had been pleasant, almost cheerful. It was strange seeing someone involved in Magic's incidents act so receptive to the experience. And today he'd found two people who seemed to enjoy Magic's *moments* as much as he and Jack did. First there was Jack's grandson Brett, and now Vickie. He was suddenly happy for Magic. It was about time people saw him for what he really was, an honest, hard-working, good-natured human being, not a freak. He stared across the table at her. Maybe she was exactly what Magic needed, someone who could love him and wouldn't mind getting caught up in a whirlwind of adventures. He decided to take a chance and tell her the truth about his best friend.

"Has Magic ever told you about his parents?"

The smile abruptly left her face. "Yes. He said they died when he was seventeen. He's told me all about them, the wonderful things they used to do together. He loved them so much. He talks about you, too, and when you were kids together." Then she turned to Jack. "He tells me about you too, Jack. You'd be surprised what I know about you and Ben."

Ben cleared his throat and decided to forge ahead. "Uh, Magic has a unique problem. Some people would even call it a gift." And he glanced over to Jack who gave him a nod of approval.

"Go ahead, Ben," Jack whispered. "Tell her the truth."

Vickie asked them to continue and Ben knew they'd reached the point of no return. She'd have to hear it all.

"Things happen to him," he told her. "Things like what's been going on during your dates the last few weeks. It's been happening to him since his parents were killed."

"So you're telling me that this happens to him all the time?" she said.

"That's right," Jack replied.

Ben saw the concerned look on her face and tried to reassure her. "Of course, the incidents vary on different levels. It's not always as big as say…"

"An elephant," Jack said, putting the pipe back in his mouth with a smile.

Ben tried not to smile. "Exactly. A lot of times it's merely little things, like when he got the hiccups at my place the other night or when he lost a couple of teeth out of his plate last year."

"Well, that can happen to anyone," she commented.

"That's right," Ben said, glad that she was taking an optimistic view.

"Yeah, that was funny," Jack remarked, "Magic and I just finished setting up the new sandbox in the daycare center and were trying to get some of the kids to try it out. Magic was sitting on the side, holding one of the kids when two of his front teeth popped out of his partial plate. The kid saw it and thought it was so funny that he laughed his head off. Then the other kids started jumping up and down, wanting Magic to pop out some more of his teeth for them, too. But the best part came when we started digging around in the sand, looking for the teeth. All the kids jumped in and helped us, acting like it was a treasure hunt. They thought it was great fun."

Vickie asked Jack if they found the teeth.

"Yep. And this was right about the time the mother's league was finishing up and picking up their kids. You should have seen the looks we got from some of the mothers when the kids told them they'd been fishing around in the sand looking for someone's teeth. I thought it was hysterical."

She frowned. "How awful for Marcus."

"Yeah, but he doesn't let the things that happen get him down," Ben told her, trying to make his point. "He accepts them and deals with them the best way he can."

"Magic keeps his sense of humor about the whole thing," Jack said, adding to Ben's point. "That's what puts him a step way ahead of others. He doesn't wallow in self-pity, feeling sorry for himself. Anyone else who had to deal with something like that might fall apart or give up. But Magic doesn't. He approaches life like all of us should, with a great hope for every day to be better than the day before. But in his case, he knows it's highly likely that it ain't gonna be."

Ben was proud of Jack for saying it. Knowing what kind of man Magic was could help her make up her mind about him. And with any luck, stay with him.

Her expression suddenly changed, as if she'd figured something out. "You've been honest with me so I'd like to do the same."

Here it comes, Ben thought, *another one leaving in a cloud of dust*. But at least this one had the decency to talk to his friends before doing it. She began acting like she was hesitant to continue, so he decided to give her a nudge. "You're dumping him. And you've come to ask us our advice on how to do it without hurting him too much, right?"

Her eyes widened in surprise. "Is that what you think?" she turned to Jack, directing the question to him as well.

They both nodded their heads yes.

"I'm not dumping him," she whispered. "On the contrary. I only wanted to know more about him and thought you could tell me."

"So why all the honesty talk?" Ben asked her, suddenly confused. "You said you wanted to be honest with us. Honest about what?"

"I haven't been honest with him, with Marcus," she said, as if it hurt her to say it out loud.

Ben glanced at Jack and saw the same question on his face. Exactly what was it she wasn't being honest about? He had to find out. "What are you trying to tell us?"

She slowly leaned forward, acting embarrassed. "I know all about him," she whispered. "About him being the 'Kirklin Klutz.' I knew even before our first date."

Ben stared at her, not quite sure he heard her right. "You already knew?"

She nodded and Jack began chuckling so hard that he had to put his pipe down. Ben couldn't hold it in any longer and laughed out loud, enjoying the irony to no end. She'd known. The whole time. Magic had been scrambling around, trying to keep his secret for nothing. He stopped laughing long enough to ask her how she found out.

"My friend John. That I told you about."

"Oh, yeah," Ben said, recalling the conversation. "He was the elderly man who had the wrong kind of meter on his house."

"That's him," she said. "He's lived in Kirklin most of his life and knows everyone in town. After I told him I was going out on a date with Marcus, he started laughing like mad and so did everyone else in the office. I didn't know what was so funny so I asked John to explain it to me. He did."

Ben tried to keep from laughing again. "Uh, and what did you do when you found out?"

"I thought John was pulling my leg at first, you know, teasing me. But then when he began telling me one story after the other, I knew he had to be telling the truth."

Ben made the next obvious deduction. "So Magic doesn't know that John's talked to you about him?"

"No. I lied and told him that John's never heard of him." Then her face turned solemn. "But I don't *like* lying to Marcus. It's dishonest."

Jack asked her why she didn't come out and tell Magic the truth.

"I've tried!" she said, sagging back against the booth. "But every time I bring it up, he gets upset and goes all cold on me. It's like he's afraid that if he talks about it, something bad will happen."

"It will," Ben replied. "At least in his mind. He's afraid you'll leave him if you know the truth."

She stared blankly at him.

"It's true," Jack told her. "Magic's been killing himself, trying to make sure you don't find out about him."

Ben knew it was time to lay all the cards out on the table. He and Jack explained everything to her, including Magic's involvement with Marilyn and the trouble at the business school. "He never told me everything that happened there," Ben told her, trying to downplay it. "But from the way the other students acted around him, it wasn't much fun for him."

"No," she said. "It can't have been easy for him." She bent her head, like she was avoiding their faces. Ben asked her if she was okay. She slowly nodded yes but he could tell she was visibly upset.

Jack noticed her distress and put his arm around her shoulder. "You care very much for him, don't you?"

"Yes, I do," she whispered, a tear running down her cheek.

Ben grabbed a couple of the napkins from the holder and handed them to her. She thanked him and wiped her eyes. He suddenly felt awkward. Dealing with crying females had never been his strong suit and more than once Sue had accused him of being insensitive. Nevertheless, he decided to make the effort.

"Magic is very lucky to have someone as nice as you care about him," he told her. He watched her face, hoping she'd take it the way it was intended. She wiped her eyes again and gave him a hopeful look.

"Thank you," she whispered.

"No problem," he replied, rather happy with himself.

"Magic cares a great deal about you, too," Jack told her. "Ben and I can tell."

"Really?" she said, seeming to regain some of her resolve.

"Sure," Jack said. "That's why he's been running scared lately, trying his best to hold on to you."

"Oh," she replied. "I wondered why he's been avoiding all my questions."

"It's not the questions he's worried about," Ben said. "It's the answers." He then told her about the meetings he and Jack would have after every *Magic moment*.

"You're kidding!" she said, perking up with curiosity. A small smile began to appear. "Could you tell me about some of them?"

"Why not?" Jack said, tapping the last of the ashes into the ashtray. "You may as well know it all."

Ben tried to think of where to begin. There were so many of them. He quickly tried to categorize them, putting them into some kind of order. Perhaps some of the more amusing ones, little ones that wouldn't scare the shit out of her.

Jack went first. "I haven't known Magic as long as Ben has but I can tell you about some of the things that have happened since I've known him. For instance, Magic went with me and Mavis to the Ice Capades a couple of years ago and we took my two grandsons, Brett and Joey. They had these cartoon characters on the ice and they also had one of those super heroes the kids are all crazy about. A lot of the parents were taking their kids down to the fence next to the ice so they could see the super hero up close. So Magic took Brett and Joey down to the fence, too, so they could shake the guy's hand.

"But so many people were pressing against the fence that when Magic leaned against it with Brett and Joey, it collapsed. No one was hurt but everyone at the fence went sprawling out onto the ice. Most of the parents were having trouble getting to their feet but the kids weren't. They thought it was a holiday and started running across the ice. They were everywhere. So the parents and other skaters start chasing the kids all over the ice. It was really funny, kids sliding every which way and parents slipping and falling trying to catch them. The management finally had to call out the rest of the skaters to scoop up the kids. A bunch of maintenance men put the fence back up but the show was kind of dull after that. Brett and Joey, me and Mavis loved it. I used to think the Ice Capades was kind of dull, but not that night!" Jack chuckled and stashed his pipe in his inside vest pocket.

Ben studied Vickie's face, wondering what she'd made of the story. She didn't look too worried so he assumed she hadn't yet been scared away. But they'd have to be selective about which stories they told her. For that, he'd first need Jack's input. He thought of a way to get Jack alone and put his hand under the table, switching his wallet from his back pocket, to the front pocket of his trousers, so it wouldn't show. He then acted like he was reaching for the wallet in his back pocket. "Damn!"

Vickie asked him what was wrong.

"I forgot my wallet. I must have left it in the car. Uh, Jack. Can you lend me a couple of bucks?"

Jack replied "sure" and reached for his own wallet.

Ben got up from his seat. "Why don't we go up to the bar and you can pay the bill there? That way I can get a refill on my Coke." He asked Vickie if she'd also like a refill.

"No thanks. I'm good," she said, getting up to let Jack out.

The two of them headed up to the bar and Ben asked Terry, the bartender for the check. Jack grabbed for his wallet but Ben stopped him.

"Never mind," he told Jack, pulling his wallet from his front pants pocket and retrieving the money. "I just needed an excuse to get you alone for a minute."

"Oh. You want to discuss with me which stories to tell her, right?"

"You guessed it," Ben said. He handed a twenty to Terry and told him to add Jack's bill to it.

Jack started chuckling. "Thanks, Ben. But you didn't have to bribe me."

Ben hunched down on the bar and motioned Jack closer. "We might have to bribe her to stay with Magic if we end up telling her the wrong kind of *moments*. I wanted to lay some ground rules before we started shooting off our mouths."

"Good idea," Jack replied. Then he gave Ben a sly grin. "So I take it we're not going to bring up Wanda, and the lizards?"

"No. And that means eliminating any of the ones that happened while Magic was…uh…naked or in a compromising situation with a girl."

"Even though some of those were the funniest?"

"Right. We want to put Magic in a good light. If she ends up staying with him, he can decide himself whether to tell her all the stories or not. And since we're trying to make him look good, we've also got to eliminate the scary ones. For instance, the episode with that girl in Summit when he blew up that transformer and caused the blackout. And when he caused that disturbance at the Tiffin police station and all those prisoners escaped."

"Yeah, but no one got hurt and they caught the prisoners a few hours later."

Ben glanced behind him to make sure Vickie wasn't getting suspicious. "I know," he whispered to Jack. "But the whole town went into a panic for those few hours and Vickie doesn't have to think that the man she cares about is…"

"Typhoid Mary?"

Ben blinked, amused at the comparison. "Exactly. So let's keep more to the *mini moments* where it only involved a few people. The animal stories should be okay. She's already lived a couple of those herself."

Terry handed them their refills and Ben his change.

"Got it," Jack said, grabbing his soda. "No sex and nothing too scary. Let's do it."

Terry asked them what the hell they were talking about.

"Trying to save a friend," Ben replied, grabbing his drink.

"Right," Terry said, nodding like he understood. "Magic."

Terry wished them luck and Ben and Jack headed back to the table to get started. Ben thought it was best to start from the beginning, which meant stories from high school. He thought of a few innocuous ones that were probably safe.

"All the kids in high school made fun of Magic when the things began happening," he told her. "Especially when the incidents started occurring regularly."

She asked him to continue.

"I think the first one happened when he was helping the art teacher put supplies away one day after class. He accidentally dumped some of the paints on himself. He had an allergic reaction and his face swelled up like a balloon. They had to rush him to the hospital, but he was okay after a couple of days. Then about a week later he got his hand caught in a tuba in band class and it took three teachers to get it out."

Jack chuckled and pulled out his pipe. "I never heard this one. How did that happen?"

"Magic and I were throwing paper wads at each other while the band director was out of the room. One of the wads ended up in the tuba and when Magic tried to get it out his arm got stuck. Little things like that. Then there were others, like when the pull out bleachers where Magic was sitting during wrestling practice folded up and sent all the mat maids and parents flying." He saw a concerned look on her face and quickly added that no one was hurt. "And then there was the time when he was practicing at the senior play and the curtain against the back wall caught on his jeans. He didn't know it and as he walked across the stage, the curtain pulled back and exposed a couple of teachers naked, putting on their own personal play."

She smiled coyly. "Goodness. That sounds like a big scandal."

"Not really," he told her. "The teachers were married to each other and simply finding time in their busy schedules to be with each other. A lot of the parents squawked and the teachers were given a severe warning but no one made a big deal out of it. Besides, it got to be old news after the play went on and Magic did some exposing himself."

Her brow furrowed with worry. "What do you mean?"

He told her about Magic's emergence from the volcano sans the loincloth.

"Oh," she said, blushing. "He must have been so embarrassed."

"No doubt," Jack added, taking a puff on the pipe.

"It looked to me like he turned ten shades of red," Ben agreed. "But that color was nothing compared to what happened at graduation."

"Why?" Jack snickered. "What color did he turn?"

"Green," Ben said, taking a second to wet his whistle. He put down the glass and got back to the story. "The school colors are green and yellow and so were our graduation caps. We had our commencement outside because our class was so large and the new gym hadn't been built yet. It rained and most of our caps got wet but Magic's cap was the only one whose color ran." He saw the inquisitive look in her face and added, "It was because his cap was manufactured by another company. His first cap got pulverized after an incident with a meat slicer so he bought another one from some costume outfitters. He got up to accept his diploma and his whole face had turned bright green. Everyone in the audience had noticed by then and was snickering. Magic was so embarrassed that he took his diploma and hurried across the stage. But he got in such a hurry that he ended up slipping on the stage edge and fell right into the principal's lap. Then everyone in the audience cracked up laughing. Some of the teachers thought he did it on purpose but I knew he didn't. It was one of his *Magic moments* happening."

"Magic moments?" she asked Ben.

"Uh…yeah. At least that's what I call them," he replied, noticing Jack grinning with glee in the corner.

"Hmm," she said, acting like she'd just figured something out. "Did one of those *Magic moments* happen to involve him getting locked up in the biology closet all night?"

"It did," Ben replied, exchanging a knowing glance with Jack. "How did you know that?"

"Marty told me about it. It's something of a legend at the high school. But of course, I didn't know it was Marcus that was the one involved."

"Tim says that Magic stories are still circulating through the school," Jack said. "And not just the old ones, all the new ones, too. Probably why all the kids flock to The Crystal so much. Magic's something akin to their local super hero. Too bad the adults don't hold him in the same esteem."

"Neither did the teachers back when his *moments* first started happening," Ben added.

"But I don't understand," she said. "Didn't any of the teachers try and help him? Or try to figure out why this was happening to him?"

"No," Ben told her, understanding her frustration. "I think they were as mystified about why it was happening as Magic was. And since so many of the teachers complained about the *moments*, they seemed quite relieved to get him out of there."

She asked which teachers complained about him.

"The band director for one. He got pissed after Magic dropped his bass drum during the spring parade. The harness came loose and the drum rolled at some woman in the crowd. She was screaming bloody murder and threatened to sue the school. It didn't hurt her, only scared the hell out of her. And then there was the football coach. He tried to get everyone in town to sign a petition to force Magic from coming to the games."

"What?" Jack said. "When did that happen?"

"In the fall of the same year Magic's parents died. He was in business school then and came home for the weekend. We were both spectators one night at a home game and one of his *moments* showed up with us. It happened in the first quarter when Magic and I were standing on the sidelines. Our team was driving down the field and one of our receivers had just caught a short pass. It was pretty spectacular considering the receiver was completely surrounded by the defensive line. And as soon as the guy made the catch, the entire line tackled him but not before they ended up tackling Magic, too. They drove him right into the ground."

"That's not so uncommon," Jack said. "Players sometimes go off the field a little when they're trying to tackle someone."

"Yeah but when they tackled Magic he was up at the snack counter, getting a drink and the snack counter is at least twenty yards from the sideline.

"Holy cow!" Jack laughed. "How the heck did that happen?"

Ben explained that the players got a little overzealous trying to bring down the receiver and pushed right through a hole in the people standing on the sidelines and ended up at the snack bar. "Hell, I was standing in their way too but they went right past me and nailed Magic. There were six or seven people standing with Magic at the snack bar but he was the only one who ended up at the bottom of the pack. I sometimes think they would have gotten him even if he was in his car in the parking lot."

"Well, I'm sure something like that's happened at other football games," Vickie remarked, acting like it wasn't that extraordinary.

"That's true," Ben agreed. "But when it happens to someone who'd recently been branded as the *Town Jinx*, people assumed it was Magic's fault."

"That's asinine," she replied, acting indignant.

"It is," Jack said. "But a lot of times people let their fears rule over their common sense. Sad but true."

"No wonder he's been avoiding telling me about himself," she whispered, frowning down at her root beer.

Jack mouthed the words *you're doing fine, keep going* at Ben. He gave Vickie a few seconds to collect herself and then asked her if she was okay.

"Yes, thank you for asking," she said, glancing up at Ben and giving him such a look of compassion that it made his heart jump. "It must be very hard for you, being his best friend and seeing him go through all that."

"Oh, I don't know," Ben replied, trying to act humble. "It wasn't so bad. Magic's got an inner strength that could get him through almost anything. Besides, his *moments* aren't always so dramatic or upsetting, sometimes they're a lot of fun."

Jack sat up, acting like he was now ready to join the explanation. "Ben's right. Some of Magic's episodes are really funny." He told Ben to tell her about the "snipe hunting" episode.

"Snipe hunting?" she said. "What's that?"

Jack explained that it was a ruse that had been going on since the beginning of time. "It's a classic practical joke played on unwary teenagers. You take some naïve kid into the woods, send him out with a burlap bag and tell him to catch as many snipes as he can in an allotted time. The only problem is that there is no such thing as a snipe."

She acted puzzled. "Then how does the kid know what to look for?"

"You make up any description you want," Ben told her. "And the more bizarre the better. That way the kid ends up searching for nothing and that's what he finds, nothing. The kid gets terrified and battered from falling down all over the dark woods, looking for 'snipes' and the guys that sent him in get a big laugh. The kid ends up feeling like the world's biggest sucker."

"And someone sent Marcus after these so-called 'snipes'?" she said.

"Ben, too," Jack added with a chuckle.

Ben told her that Jack was right. "Magic and I both fell for it."

"So you didn't find anything and ended up feeling foolish," she said, coming to the logical conclusion.

"Not exactly," Ben said, "I came out with an empty bag and pretty cut up from the branches and trees I ran into in the dark. But when Magic got back, not long after I did, he had something in his bag."

Jack started snickering and Vickie acted confused. "I thought you said there were no such things as snipes."

"There aren't," Ben replied. "That's why all of us were understandably curious about what Magic had in the bag. We asked him and he claimed it was a 'snipe.'"

Vickie told him that she didn't understand.

"It turns out," Ben said, "that while Magic was stumbling around in the woods looking for snipes, he ran into some good ol' boy farmer who was out hunting for real animals. Magic told the farmer what he was looking for and the farmer said he knew exactly where a snipe could be found. He took Magic back to his house and helped him get it in the bag. The old man said he was glad to get rid of it and how he was tired of the damn thing rummaging through his trash cans."

"Naturally," Jack added.

"So the two guys that sent us in the woods asked Magic what it looked like and he said it was hairy and had beady eyes, the same description the guys gave us of the 'snipe.' I tried opening the bag to look at it but the bigger guy jerked it out of my hands. He and the other guy opened the bag but it wasn't a snipe they found, it was a groundhog."

"A groundhog?" she said. "But didn't Marcus know it was a groundhog?"

"Uh, no," Ben said, trying not to make his best friend sound stupid. "Magic and I are city kids. Neither one of us had ever seen a groundhog. Raccoons and rabbits, sure."

"And the guys that sent you into the woods," she said. "Didn't they know what a groundhog looked like?"

Ben replied that they never found out.

"What do you mean?" she asked.

"Because of what happened next," he told her. "When those two guys opened up the bag to look at it. Magic had dragged the bag back across the woods, bouncing that groundhog up and down so it wasn't in a very good mood."

"Heck. Who could blame him?" Jack remarked with a snicker. "Disturbing his nice garbage dinner like that."

Vickie asked Ben what happened when the men opened the bag.

"They got bit. Then both of them started jumping around and yelling like they were dying. The little guy kept crying that he was sure he got rabies. The groundhog ran off into the woods and Magic and I did the same and lit out, too. I heard later that those two ended up at the hospital screaming they had rabies. They didn't but they did need a couple of stitches. And they never tried taking anyone snipe hunting again after that."

The smile returned to her face and Ben knew she was starting to get the picture. "So you see, his *moments* are basically all like that," he told her. "It's similar to things you see happen to people sometimes that are kind of goofy but never really harmful. Like you'll see a guy drop his keys on the ground and he and his wife bend down to pick them up and hit each other in the head. It's funny, and it doesn't hurt anyone but the man and woman. That's kind of like what happens to Magic."

But with Magic it's always on a much larger scale, Ben thought; keeping the comment to himself.

"It really makes you wonder, doesn't it?" she asked them.

Ben asked her what she was referring to.

"Him, Marcus. Having to put up with something like that and being branded a jinx. It's a wonder it doesn't get to him or make him feel great despair."

"There's a reason for that," Jack told her. "Magic has a theory about the things happening to him. But I think Ben can explain it better."

Ben knew it was his cue to continue but he took a few seconds to study her face. He, Jack and Magic were the only ones who knew about the theory and most people would consider it even more fantastic than the *Magic moments*, so he proceeded carefully, hoping she was open-minded enough not to dismiss it so quickly.

Jack kneed him under the table. "Go ahead and tell her, Ben. It'll be okay. Trust me."

She was now staring directly at him, waiting to hear it.

"Okay," he said, resigning himself to tell it. "To understand the theory, you have to know a little something about Magic's parents. They were very special people. I used to call them the king and queen of practical jokes. If they weren't playing a joke on me, Magic or one of their friends, they were helping someone else play one. They lived for it. And they always seemed so proud of me and Magic when we'd pull off a good joke on them or one of our friends. Sort of like the teachers watching their students succeed."

"They sound like a lot of fun," she remarked.

"They were," he agreed. "Anyway, after they were killed and the things began happening to Magic, I was scared that he would sink so far into depression that I'd never get him back. Losing his mom and dad was already hard on him, and me, too."

"Marcus told me how much you loved them," she said. "It's no wonder you worried about him."

"That's a pretty rough ride to go through at that age," Jack said. "But you were lucky you and Magic had each other to talk to."

"But that's just it," Ben told Jack. "Magic wouldn't talk about it after it happened, about the accident, them getting killed or anything else. He clammed up and wouldn't say anything, to me or anyone. That's why I got so worried."

Vickie asked Ben what he did about it.

"Nothing. I didn't have a clue what to do. But the day after Magic got locked in the biology closet he told me he *knew* why the things were happening to him. It came to him during the night, while he was singing to himself."

"Singing?" she said.

"Yeah. He said he did it to keep his mind off being locked in. But then he started hearing someone singing with him." He paused as he watched her figure it out. "That's right," he told her. "He said it was his parents' voices. He was absolutely convinced that it was their spirits and that they'd come back and were singing with him."

She asked Ben if he believed it.

"I didn't know what to think. After I found him that morning I thought for sure he'd be a blithering idiot or catatonic from fear."

"*You* found him?" she asked. "But how did you know where he was?"

Ben replied that he finally figured out what must have happened. "And that was only after half the town went looking for him. When I unlocked the door, he was staring up at me, with this look of complete calm on his face. It scared me at first, he looked *too* calm. But it turned out that he was fine."

Vickie tilted her head at Ben. "What made him think that his parents' spirits were making the things happen?"

"That's what I asked him. He said they were watching over him. That because they were both such jokesters, it was their unique way of telling him not to despair, that they were still with him."

"And he believes this?" Vickie asked. "Even now?"

"With all his heart and soul," Jack said. "I couldn't believe it either, once he told me. I thought to myself, hey, if that's what it takes for him to accept his *gift*, then why not? Who knows? Anything is possible. Besides, who are we to say it isn't real? He believes it. That's all that counts."

"But there are sometimes when I think he doubts his theory, although he's never admitted it to me," Ben told her. "After one of the more humiliating or painful 'accidents' happens, he'll kind of brood, clam up and won't talk to us about it. But he always seems to bounce back. He's a lot stronger than he gives himself credit for."

"That's for sure," Jack added. "He's a bit of a phenomenon, even though a few closed-minded people in town don't see it that way."

Ben looked directly at her, hoping to get through. "He's a good man. He's not a freak. He's simply dealing with an incredible situation the best way he can. Just trying to find his way, like the rest of us."

She got quiet and stared down at her hands, like she was lost in thought.

There it is, Ben thought. They'd given her all the facts and now it would be her decision what she'd do with the information, or if she'd abandon him, like so many others before. But he hoped she wouldn't. There was something different about her. She seemed to possess the qualities that would enable her to adapt to an existence that would be, to say the least, out of the norm.

"I know he's a good man," she said softly. "I knew that before you told me all of this. He's very special." Then she paused as if not sure how to continue. "And since you've been honest with me, I have to be honest with you. I think...no. I *know* that I'm in love with him."

Yes! Ben thought, trying hard not to smile.

"But now I'm in a bit of a dilemma," she said.

Ben asked her to explain.

"I don't want him to be afraid of me," she said. "Or to be afraid to tell me about himself. I want him to trust me, the way he trusts the both of you. I know I can't win his trust overnight but I'm going to try my best to get it. That's where I'm going to need your help."

"We'll be glad to help," Jack told her and Ben also assured her they would do anything they could.

"Then please don't tell him that you told me about his *moments*," she said. "I want to give him a chance to tell me himself, to trust me enough to share it with me. I know it may mean lying to him but it's very important to me. Would you do that for me?"

"Yes, we will," Jack said.

"Damn straight," Ben added. "And if there's anything else Jack and I can do to help, let us know."

She thanked them for the offer. "And I think Marcus is very lucky to have such good friends."

"There's always room for one more," Jack said, giving her a wink.

She seemed to relax a little more and the three of them got back to discussing *Magic's moments* over the years. He and Jack stayed with the ground rules, omitting any of the ones that didn't seem appropriate or that might scare her, although afterwards Jack remarked that after being chased by an elephant and emus, it seemed a bit redundant to leave them out. She reacted to each telling with great interest and excitement, almost as though she was listening to a good fable instead of her boyfriend's life. After about an hour, they'd covered most of the stories they wanted to tell so Ben asked her if she had any questions about them.

"No," she said. "But I do appreciate you sharing them with me." She checked her watch and remarked that she had to get back to work.

"Me too," Jack said, getting up with her.

"Uh, Jack," Ben said. "Can you stay for a few more minutes? I've got some things to tell you about dart league."

Jack nodded and sat back down.

"Thanks again for meeting me," Vickie told them. "And don't forget about your promise, will you?"

"We won't," Jack replied. "You can count on us."

She headed for the exit and Jack asked Ben what was going on with dart league.

"Nothing," he whispered, watching while Vickie went out the front door. He turned back around to Jack. "I wanted to talk to you."

"You mean about Vickie? Or the promise?"

"Both," Ben said. "What do you think?"

"At least she's willing to try and stick it out," Jack said. "That in itself shows a lot a character. Magic's lucky he found her."

"She's gonna need some luck to get Magic to trust her. He's been dodging the bullet so long; it's become second nature to him. He can be pretty hardheaded."

"So let's do what we can to improve her luck," Jack said. "We need a plan."

Ben agreed. "The first thing we'll have to do is lie. I'm gonna need you to back me up with that part. I've never been good at lying to him. He's known me too long and he can see right through me."

"You'll do fine. Even if he does find out she met with us, you can tell him you were discussing her piano lessons."

"Okay," Ben replied, seeing his reasoning. "That might work."

"See?" Jack said. "It's not that hard to lie. All you have to do is make yourself believe it first. Then you can make it sound feasible."

Ben smirked. "You mean like Magic's theory about his mom and dad watching over him?"

"Hey. Just because you don't believe it, doesn't mean it isn't possible. Maybe they are. Besides, what's wrong with having a little faith in something? You could do with a little more faith, yourself, especially now that you're considering becoming a parent. You can't experience something like that without it making you question your beliefs and faith. It humbles you and makes you question your own existence."

"Sounds kind of scary, if you ask me," Ben replied, trying to needle him. "Maybe I better reconsider doing it."

Jack got up from the booth and patted him on the back. "I'm sure Sue will have a thing or two to say about that."

"I'm sure she will," Ben agreed. "And in the meantime, I'll try to keep from laughing when Magic calls me up and tells me how he's managed to dodge Vickie's questions again."

"Especially if the call comes in at one AM," Jack replied as he walked away.

Don't remind me, Ben thought as he stared down at his empty Coke glass and felt the fatigue return. It was as if by mentioning it, Jack had summoned it to the surface again. He yawned and stretched, his muscles and joints reacting sluggishly. It was going to be a long afternoon. Frank had stepped up the pace cleaning the back room and his body ached at the thought of loading heavy instruments into trucks and buyer's cars. *Oh well*, he thought, getting up and heading for the door. If it meant Magic ending up with someone who loved him, then it was worth the extra effort.

He walked out onto the sidewalk and pulled the collar of his shirt up to protect his face and neck from the warm afternoon rain. *Maybe Jack was right*, he thought as he hurried down the street towards the store. Maybe there was something to Magic's theory. After all, no one had ever proven the existence of an afterlife or lack of it. Perhaps it *was* possible. Maybe they *were* behind it. It would be just like something they would do. A practical joke to end all practical jokes. The Bible said that God created Man in his own image and if that was true, then it was reasonable to assume that God must have a sense of humor, too.

He stepped through the front door of the store a few minutes later and put down his shirt collar. *Not too wet*, he mused as he looked down at himself and his damp clothes. He brushed the rain droplets off his shirt and pants and said a silent prayer that Magic be given what he wanted most, Vickie. *What the heck*, he thought. *Nothing wrong with a little prayer now and then*. Besides, you never knew who else might be listening. Like maybe a couple of playful spirits named Adam and Kathleen Kerr.

The same two sweet jokesters he'd had the pleasure of loving when they still inhabited the earth.

CHAPTER ELEVEN

As soon as he pulled into the drive, Marcus experienced a wave of anxiety. The house wasn't exactly a mansion but it was stately enough to be impressive. It was three stories high and had gabled windows on the second floor front, reminding him of some of the Gothic tales that were required reading in English lit. But that was where the comparison ended. Nothing about the rest of the place gave any indication of being dark or mysterious. The house had bright, white siding and every inch of the landscape was immaculate, giving a cheery yet rigid feel to the place. The lawn was lush and green and even the three elm trees in the front yard looked like they'd been symmetrically trimmed and shaped. The flowers and shrubs surrounding the home were blossoming and full, with not even a hint of a weed among the colored stone mulch. He got out of the car with Vickie and peered around to the large yard in the back.

"What? No swimming pool?" he asked her.

"Dad wouldn't hear of it and Mom agreed with him," she replied, coming over to his side of the car. "She saw some special on TV about how many children get killed in their own pools and that was the end of the idea. She and my dad wouldn't even let us use our friends' pools unless they made sure a lifeguard or someone with CPR training was present."

"I guess you were right," he replied, sighing inwardly. "They *do* sound very protective." He was also wondering what the hell they were going to do when they found out their daughter was dating a disaster magnet. He straightened the collar on his shirt and checked to make sure the shirttail wasn't sticking out of his jeans. Vickie was also dressed casual, jeans and a sweater but both looked ironed and she was wearing some makeup, making him wonder if maybe he was underdressed.

"Do I look okay?" he asked her, the nervousness announcing itself in his belly with a series of knots.

"You look great," she replied, taking his hand and leading him across the sidewalk towards the house.

The porch was constructed of different colored mosaic stones and two large Corinthian columns stood at opposite ends like sentinels, towering over any intruders foolish enough to dare enter. She asked him what he thought of the house.

"Very nice," he replied but in his mind he immediately thought, *Intimidating*.

He followed her through the large, ornate wooden door and into a small foyer (at least small compared to the rest of the house). The foyer was larger than the living room of his apartment and there were two decorative lamps on either sides of the wall. The foyer opened out into a hall area and a large, wooden staircase. The stairs were carpeted and the staircase itself looked like it was made of oak. There was a set of double doors to the right of the foyer, off the bottom of the stairs. One of the doors was ajar and he leaned forward and looked in to what appeared to be an office.

To the left of the foyer was a small sitting room furnished with two settees and a couple of upholstered chairs. It reminded him of a doctor's office waiting room except for the hardwood floors that were glossed to a high shine. Several round, brightly colored oriental rugs adorned the floors and what looked like cherry wood accent tables sat next to the upholstered chairs.

"Come on," she said, taking his hand and leading him down the hall, next to the staircase. "They're probably in the living room."

The hall led to a bright, large room that looked like it spanned the width of the house. It had cream colored carpet and six cathedral windows, three on either side of the room that let in the late afternoon light. On the wall opposite the hallway there was a large fireplace whose mantel was crowded with framed photographs. The room was furnished with several couches and matching accent chairs, along with two coffee tables that also looked like they were made of cherry wood. The draperies looked expensive and so did the furniture. It reminded him of the lobby of a four star hotel. The only thing missing was the check-in counter and bellhops. He glanced over at the far right corner and saw a familiar face. Sitting cross-legged with a set of headphones and a book in her lap in one of the accent chairs was Marty. She was barefoot and wearing a sweatshirt and shorts. As soon as she spotted them, she got up and came over to greet them.

"Hi, Magic!" she exclaimed. "Welcome to the mausoleum. They keep our coffins upstairs."

Vickie told her to hush and stop making jokes. "And do me a favor, will you, Marty? Be on your best behavior tonight. I want Marcus to have a nice time and I'm already so nervous I can't stand still."

Marty gave her a hug. "You should be. This is the first time you've dared to bring anyone home." She let go of her sister and turned to Marcus. "Did Vickie tell you not to mention Tim's name at dinner? My parents still don't know about him."

"Your secret's safe with me," he told her. *And why not*, he thought. Marty wasn't the only one keeping secrets.

"Thanks," Marty said. "Now I'm gonna do you a favor. You've still got time to escape. Otherwise my father is going to suck the soul right out of you." She grabbed his arm and began pulling him towards the kitchen. "Come on. I'll show you to the back door so you can get out of here."

Vickie scolded her and told her to stop kidding around.

"All right," Marty said, rolling her eyes and letting go of Marcus's arm. "Just trying to have some fun." She went back over to her chair and picked up the headphones.

"Here comes my mom," Vickie whispered to him. "She'll want to give you a tour of the house and I know she'll want to show you her collection. It's her pride and joy."

"Last chance!" Marty whispered to him. A moment later her mother entered the room and Marty called out "Too late!" in between snickering.

Marcus observed Vickie's mother. She was in her late forties and had short, dark brown hair that was smartly styled, accenting her high cheekbones and face. She was wearing a stylish, high necked, light purple dress and a string of pearls that matched her low, white heels. She wasn't as slim as Vickie and Marty; she was filled out a little more in the hips and waist, giving her a more mature appearance. Her legs showing out from beneath the dress were quite shapely and he tried not to stare as she walked up to them. Vickie introduced her.

"Hi, Marcus," she said. "I'm Ann Garrett."

As he shook her hand, he studied her face. After hearing about how protective they were, he figured to see someone with an angry or worried countenance. What he found was an expression full of life, smiling and cheerful. Not at all what he'd expected.

Ann became the perfect hostess, asking him if he'd like something to drink or if he'd like to sit down. He declined both and graciously thanked her.

"How long before dinner?" Vickie asked her.

"About a half-hour," Ann replied, carefully adjusting the clasp on the pearls. "And your father is on the phone with a client but he asked me to come get him as soon as you and Marcus got here." She turned to leave but Vickie stopped her.

"Please, Mom. Can you hold off going to get Dad for a few more minutes?" She grabbed Vickie's hand and patted it reassuringly. "Now, honey. Your dad isn't *that* bad." And she smiled at Marcus as she said it.

Hope not, Marcus thought to himself.

"I'm sure your father and Marcus are going to get along famously," Ann said. "Now stop worrying."

"I'm not worried," Vickie replied. "I only thought it would be nice if we could make Marcus feel comfortable before din…"

"You mean before Daddy gives him the third degree," Marty added.

Vickie and Ann both scolded her for saying it and Marty put her headphones back on and ignored them.

"How about giving Marcus a tour of the house before dinner, Mom?" Vickie said. "And your collection. You know how you love to show off that."

Ann quickly agreed and Marcus let them both shuttle him around the abode. They started upstairs; skipping the third floor, which Ann told him was mostly used for storage. She showed him the second floor, which had four large bedrooms and a bathroom that looked as big as his whole apartment. One of the bedrooms had been converted to a kind of workroom, with tables containing homemade crafts and supplies.

"This is my craft room," Ann said. "Now that Vickie and the others have moved out, I finally have the time and room to devote to my hobbies."

He told her how impressed he was of Marty's jars.

"I'm always getting requests for more," she said. "And Marty loves making them. She's sometimes in here working until the wee hours of the morning on weekends." She led them back down the hall towards the staircase and Marcus pulled Vickie aside for a minute.

"Do your mom and dad always dress up for dinner?" he whispered. "They're gonna think I'm a bum showing up in jeans."

"No they won't. It's nothing formal. Mom's only dressed up because she had a meeting at church and Daddy wears what he always does, trousers, shirt and tie. Jeans are perfectly acceptable. And even if they weren't, I'd still want you to wear them. I want you to feel comfortable around my family."

He followed them down the staircase, still harboring misgivings about coming. He'd agreed to it because Vickie seemed to have her heart set on it and he didn't want to disappoint her, something that was becoming a fast habit. He had to admit. So far it hadn't been as bad as he'd thought it would be. Her mother was quite pleasant and friendly. There was also something about her that seemed familiar but that he couldn't put his finger on. He only hoped her father was as amiable.

They crossed the family room again and went through the dining room adjoining the kitchen. The dining area had a shiny, polished sectional table that looked like it could seat twelve. Two captains' chairs with decorative carved arms sat at either end. On one side of the room was an expensive looking wooden buffet, complete with fancy carved handles on the drawers. On the other side of the room was a massive, lighted hutch full of fine china. As Vickie led him through the room and into the kitchen, on the other side, he let out a low whistle.

"My mom would have loved something like this," he said, admiring the kitchen. It resembled a layout from *Better Homes and Gardens*. There was a large countertop island in the middle of the room, housing all kinds of small appliances. A hanging rack was located above the island, holding every conceivable pan and cooking utensil. Ann went over to the built in stove to the right of the island, picked up a couple of potholders and opened the oven door. He didn't have to see what she was looking at to know what it was. The aroma wafting throughout the room announced itself plainly. Roast beef.

"That smells delicious," he whispered to Vickie.

"Mom's a great cook. She also made one of her special Dutch apple pies for dessert."

His stomach began growling and he folded his hands in front of him, trying to mask the sound. He'd been so nervous about meeting her parents that he'd eaten next to nothing all day.

"It should only be about fifteen minutes," Ann said, poking around at the roasting bag. "Just enough time for us to show Marcus my collection. Go ahead and I'll be right there."

"She's very proud of her collection," Vickie said, taking his hand and leading him back towards the living room.

He squeezed her hand, enjoying how protective she'd become since they'd arrived. It was as if, by holding on to him, she was shielding him from some unseen menace. Or better yet, he thought, announcing to her parents that he belonged to her, no matter what objections they might have. He smiled and walked with her into the living room, reveling in the sensation. *So this is what it's like*, he thought. *To belong to someone. Nice.*

As they entered the room, Marty called out, "How's it going, sis? Did Magic get scared away yet?"

He laughed. "Not yet. Why? Is there something I should look out for? Your mom doesn't collect dead bodies or something, does she?"

"I wish," Marty said, putting the headphones back on and getting back to her book. Then she muttered, under her breath. "The only dead bodies around here are when we sit down at the dinner table and try and make interesting conversation."

He asked Vickie what Marty was talking about.

"Remember how I told you about how boring our dinners were? Well, that's what she's referring to. Daddy tries to get us to open up and talk to him at these Sunday dinners but it never works so he tries to tell us stories about his business, instead. In other words, really boring stuff. You'll probably fall asleep from boredom."

"Sounds okay to me," he quipped. "Besides, I'm gonna be busy enjoying your mom's home cooking." He let go of her hand and went over to a door to the left of the hallway. "Is this where your mom keeps the bodies?" he whispered, causing Marty to break out into peals of laughter. He asked Marty what was so funny.

"That's where Dad is," Vickie volunteered, coming up and standing beside him. "It's his office here at home. There's another entrance out by the staircase. You probably saw it when we first came in."

He nodded, remembering the double doors to the right of the staircase.

"Here," she said, leaning forward and cracking open the door a few inches. "Take a look."

He peeked in and saw someone sitting at a commanding looking work center. It was a cube dweller's dream, a huge desk that jutted out on either side from the main desk area and contained a file area on the right and bookcase on the left. The computer system looked state of the art and there was a fax machine and small copier on a table to the left of the workstation. A sizable file cabinet was located to the right of the computer system and a man whom he assumed was Vickie's father was sitting in a plush looking desk chair with his back to them, talking on the phone.

He scanned the rest of the room. There were several bookcases full of books on the walls and a sizable treadmill in the far left corner. The walls were filled with what looked like school diplomas and awards, along with a few mounted fish, including a large wide-mouthed bass that he knew even Jack would be impressed with. In spite of the extensive files and other office paraphernalia on the desks and next to the copier, the place was immaculately kept, with every item neatly stacked and in its proper place. Not a speck of dust was visible and even the potted fern plant in the far right corner looked properly trimmed and groomed.

"Dad works a lot at home," Vickie told him. "This is what Marty likes to call the DMZ."

"Demilitarized zone?" he asked, not seeing the connection.

"No," she replied, grinning. "Daddy's Mausoleum Zone." She shut the door and he followed her over to one of the couches. They sat down together and he decided to quiz her on her father.

"That's some office. What did you mean it was his office at home? Does he have another?"

She told him he did. "In Cleveland. At his firm. He's a financial analyst. But a lot of his clients kept calling him at all hours of the night so he set up this office here. He asks us not to bother him when he's conducting business…" She paused and sighed. "But no one seems to know exactly when that is. He treats his home office like his sanctuary. He doesn't even invite guests or friends in there, only clients, and that's not very often. You'd have to be someone important as the Pope or President to get an invite in."

"You mean your mom, you or Marty aren't allowed in?"

"We are but I only go in when I want to borrow a book and that's only on Sundays when I come to dinner. Marty hates it in there, so she's happy to leave it alone and Mom knows Daddy's eccentricities so she doesn't care. She goes in to clean and that's only once a week."

"She must do a heck of job cleaning. There isn't a speck of dust or book out of place."

"That's Daddy. He's meticulous about keeping everything neat and in perfect order." She leaned against him and added, "Kind of like the way he tries to keep me and Marty in line and living by his own code of ethics and rigid rules. That's why Marty hasn't told them about going out with Tim. She knows they'd overreact and forbid her to see him anymore."

He felt his heart quicken and tried to word the next question carefully. "Uh," he whispered. "Do your parents know you've been staying overnight at my place lately?"

"No," she replied. "Marty knows of course. And as far as I know, Mom still doesn't know either. But even if she did know or suspect, I don't think she would tell my dad."

"Why not?"

"Did you ever see a volcano erupt?" she whispered. "Well, that would be my father if he found out I was…" She abruptly broke off and gave him a nudge in the side. "Hi, Mom!" she said, getting up from the couch as her mother walked towards them. He got up with her.

"I was just about to show Marcus your collection," Vickie told her.

"Oh, let me show you!" Ann gushed, escorting them over to a small room on the other side of the sitting room.

Ann held the door open and Marcus followed Vickie into the room. But his heart almost stopped when he saw what it was. The collection wasn't dead bodies but it might as well have been. The afternoon light shone in through two octagon shaped windows on the right, illuminating the largest collection of glass he'd ever seen. There were long, wooden cabinets with glass display windows on the right and left walls, housing a collection of pottery and glass in every color of the rainbow. At the back of the room were two tall curio cabinets with display lights inside, spotlighting the contents, glass figurines and expensive looking collectibles. In the middle of the room, between the long cabinets was a sleek, thin wooden stand with a glass case on top containing a foot high sculpture of a swan. The swan was made of blown glass and shimmered as the sunlight shone through it.

Everything—every single thing in the room looked fragile, and breakable.

His pulse quickened and his heart jumped into his throat, making it feel like he was choking on it. Sweat beads formed on his forehead and his chest tightened up like a vice. If there was ever any invitation for one of his *moments* to make an appearance then this was it. From the start, from the very first date with her, it was almost as though it was duel, a race, between his *gift* and him. It had challenged him at every turn and it had taken all his strength and cunning to keep up. But now the playing field had changed and not in his favor. He was standing in the middle of the Holy Grail of all challenges. It was as if he'd slapped his *gift* in the face with a glove, daring it to show itself and from past history, his *gift* would not abandon such a challenge. He could almost hear the breaking glass…and the screams.

He had to get the hell out of there.

He slowly and carefully did an about-face as the panic attack clutched him. He took a step towards the door when Vickie asked him where he was going.

AND THE BULL SAVED ME

"Uh…" he said, clearing his throat. "I'll be right back. I need a glass of water."

She quickly circumvented him, placing herself between him and the door. His escape route was now cut off and his panic level rose another notch. He tried ducking around her but she cut him off.

"I *really* need that glass of water!" he told her, sucking in his stomach and trying hard not to come in contact with the cabinet to his right. He managed to finally get around her without bumping into anything and made a beeline for the door. She reached out and grabbed his hand, pulling him back.

"Marcus! Listen to me!"

He glanced back and saw her mother standing a few feet away, by the glass swan. She asked them if something was wrong.

"No, Mom," Vickie told her. "I just have to tell Marcus something." She grabbed the front of his shirt collar and pulled him down closer to her face. "Marcus. It's going to be fine," she whispered.

He swallowed hard and searched her face, knowing she couldn't understand. "I have to get out of here!" he whispered, hoping against hope she wouldn't ask him why. "I can't *stay* in here!"

He tried to pull away from her but her grip tightened on his hand and she pulled him down to her again. "Marcus!" she said forcibly. "Listen to me!"

But he couldn't hear her. His eyes kept scanning the room, cataloging all the breakables. It was gonna cost him a fortune to replace them once the catastrophe occurred. He started running scenarios through his head, wondering how the hell his *gift* would do it. Me. He thought with a pang of dread, *I'm gonna faint and crash into the Swan, starting a domino effect that will wipe out the whole room in a matter of seconds.* His legs started shaking as he saw the image take shape in his head.

Vickie placed her hands on his cheeks and forcibly jerked his head to the front, making him look at her. "Marcus!" she said. "Look at me! Focus on me!"

The room seemed to collapse towards him as the panic gripped him. "I have to get out…" he muttered, feeling like a caught animal.

"No! You don't!" she told him, pressing her hands harder against his cheeks. Her touch was comforting but he resisted it.

"I have to…"

"Shhhh!" she said. Then she gently blew into his face, much like a parent would do to get their child's attention. He blinked and focused in on her.

"You'll be all right," she whispered. "Trust me."

He gazed into her eyes, her voice and expression having a somewhat calming effect on him.

"Do you trust me?" she asked, her voice pleading.

He couldn't answer. He simply nodded yes.

"Okay," she said, letting go of his face and taking his hand again. "Then stay right beside me and you'll see, it'll be all right."

He stayed right next to her as she slowly led him over to where her mother was standing, next to the swan. The fear was still present and hovering over him like a storm cloud but holding on to her hand gave him a strange sense of security.

"Is everything all right?" Ann asked them.

Vickie told her it was nothing. "Marcus just had some trouble focusing with all the sunlight coming in through the windows. He's fine now. Why don't you tell him about some of your favorite pieces, Mom? I'm sure he'd love to hear about them."

The answer seemed to satisfy Ann and she began explaining how she'd acquired the different pieces, starting with the swan. He only heard parts of it, something about a master craftsman making original pieces at a craft show in Pennsylvania. She then took him and Vickie to the back of the room by one of the curio cabinets. He held tight on to Vickie's hand as she carefully guided him past the swan stand and glass display case against the right wall. Ann opened the door on the curio cabinet to the left and took out several delicate and intricately crafted pieces. She handed them, one by one to Vickie and she let go of his hand and took them, placing them on the top of the display case to the left.

"Here," she said, picking up one of the pieces and prompting him to open up his hand. He hesitated and she gave him a wink. "I told you. It will be all right. Trust me."

He held his breath and opened up his hand. She carefully placed the figurine, a dolphin, in the middle of his palm. He watched her face light up and suddenly realized the importance of that particular piece. He brought the piece closer to his face and smiled.

"I thought you'd like that one," she whispered. "Mom got it from the same craftsman that made the swan. It looks like one of the dolphins on my necklace." She then turned to her mother and showed her the pendant at the end of the necklace.

"It does look like it!" Ann whispered, her voice full of awe as she touched the pendant. "Wherever did you get it?"

"Marcus got it for me," Vickie told her. "For my birthday."

"You have very good taste," Ann told him.

"So do you," he replied, handing her back the dolphin figurine. "That's a beautiful piece."

Ann beamed with pride and thanked him for the compliment as she took the piece from his hand and put it back in the cabinet.

"See?" Vickie whispered to him, taking his hand again. "I told you it would be okay."

He nodded yes and suddenly felt better. It was as if all his fear had somehow, mysteriously evaporated. He couldn't explain it but there it was. No prickling sensation at the back of his neck, the usual prelude to one of his *moments*. No sense of alarm causing him to switch to "alert" status. No cold sweats or anxiety at all. Nothing. All he could feel was the warmth of her hand against his.

They spent the next fifteen minutes or so going around the room with Ann, viewing her collection. He continued to hold fast on to Vickie's hand as Ann talked about the history and value of each piece. A couple times she offered him one of the pieces to view up close and both times Vickie intervened and held the piece in her hands for him to examine. It was as if she'd sensed his fear and was making every effort to make the experience pleasant. It was only after he exited the room after the tour that he realized what had happened. Nothing. No broken glass. No screams. No apologies.

Somehow, Vickie had willed away the *moment* that he'd so dreaded would come.

She'd rescued him from his fear.

He followed her back out into the living room and only then did she finally let go of his hand. He looked down at it and smiled. It had been like a lifeline between them, his safe place. It was as if she *knew* how terrified he was of a calamity. But of course, she couldn't know, she still didn't know his secret. He glanced over at her, talking to her mother and felt both humble and awestruck as he recognized what an extraordinary person she was. She had somehow sensed his fear and reacted automatically—like a person protecting someone they loved.

It was the only explanation.

He went over and stood beside her, suddenly happy to be part of her world, to be one of the people she cared about. And at that moment he knew beyond any shadow of a doubt how much he loved her.

"I'm going to check on dinner," Ann said, retreating to the kitchen.

Vickie turned to him, giving him one of her disarming smiles. His heart swelled with love for her.

"See? I told you it would be okay," she said. "And there's nothing else to be afraid of here."

"Except Daddy," Marty remarked from across the room. She took off her headphones and came over to join them. "Have you shown Magic the mausoleum yet?" she asked Vickie.

"Yes I have. And kindly don't call it that at dinner. I want Dad in a good mood when he talks to Marcus."

Marcus told her that he wouldn't know what to talk about. "I don't know anything about big finance."

"Oh, don't worry," Marty said, snickering. "You won't *have* to. Daddy will do all the talking. Just smile and nod like you understand what he's saying, it always works for me."

Marcus replied that he'd give it a try and the three of them went out into the kitchen. Ann was standing in front of the counter island, removing a healthy sized beef roast from a plastic roasting bag. The air was full with the aroma of cooked roast and vegetables. He closed his eyes and took it all in. It reminded him of home…so long ago. Marty started giggling and he opened his eyes to her smiling face.

"Check out Magic," she said. "He looks like Daddy, going all gaga over his fishing magazines."

He leaned closer and whispered to her, "You mean like Tim going gaga over you." Which caused her to giggle even louder.

Ann asked him if he liked roast beef.

"Love it. Especially prepared that way," he replied, going over and standing next to her. "The last time I saw someone use a cooking bag like that was my mom."

"Vickie told us about what happened to your parents," Ann said. "You must miss them very much."

He told her that he did. "But it's nice to look back at all the great memories I have of them. For instance, that roasting bag."

She asked him what he meant.

"Mom loved the cooking bags because they were so easy to use and clean up. Dad would sometimes tease her that all we had to do was grab a fork and eat right out of the bag, that way she'd have no dishes at all. Then one night Dad and I sat down to dinner at the kitchen table and Mom brought over the roasting pan and put it down in front of us. The meat was sliced but still in the bag with all the vegetables and gravy. So Mom hands me and Dad a couple of forks and tells us to dig in."

Ann let out a gasp. "Was your father angry?"

"Shoot, no. He thought it hysterical. We picked up our forks and all three of us ate over the pan. It was great. Mom was a good cook but I don't think anything tasted as good as that roast..." He broke off, feeling suddenly self-conscious.

Ann noticed his discomfort and put her hand on his arm. "They sound like very special people."

"Yes they were," he replied, staring at her face, drawn to it somehow. She had soft, sculptured features and tiny wrinkles by her eyes. And there was a gentle exuberance in her eyes and the same kind of freckles by her nose that his mother's face had. It was almost as if she was standing there beside him, like so many nights when he was younger, helping her fix dinner.

Ann's expression turned to one of concern. "Marcus? Are you all right?"

He cleared his throat as her voice pulled him back from his thoughts. "Uh, yeah...fine."

"He's just drooling over the roast again, Mom," Marty said. "You'd better serve it up before he dives in headfirst."

Ann berated Marty for talking so to a guest.

"That's okay," he told Ann. "I know Marty's only kidding. But she's right. I am kind of hungry." He suddenly needed to get away from his memories and went over and grabbed Vickie's arm. "Let us help out," he told her. "How about we set the table?"

"Sure," she said. "Follow me."

"Uh..." Ann said, raising her finger as if she wanted to tell them something. A strange smile crept across her face and Vickie began giggling.

"Forget it, Mom," she said. "Daddy would die before he'd eat over the pan."

"Oh, well," Ann replied with a shrug. "It was just a thought."

"But I'd still love to see my dad's face if she did do it," Vickie whispered as he followed her into the dining room. "That would sure liven up the dinner conversation for once."

They went over to a large, lighted china cabinet in the far corner. She pulled out the appropriate number of cups, plates and dinnerware and handed him some. He stood there; holding the dishes as his mind was propelled back to another memory of his mother.

"Marcus?" she asked him. "Is something wrong?"

He couldn't answer her. The emotion was building up inside his chest with such speed that it took his breath away. She put the dishes she was holding on the table and took the others from his hands and did the same.

"Marcus," she whispered, taking his hands. "What's the matter?"
He stayed silent. He didn't want to talk about it.
She gently stoked his cheek. "You know you can trust me. Please tell me."
"It's nothing," he croaked, the emotion spilling out with the words.
She stroked his cheek softly. "It was Mom, wasn't it? She reminded you of your own mother, didn't she?"
He gazed into her eyes as his heart pounded harder, wanting so much to share it with her, to share everything…
"That was it, wasn't it?" she whispered.
He nodded, experiencing a sudden sense of release, as if the feelings that had been pent up had finally been set free. "It wasn't only that," he told her. "It's the china cabinet. We lived in a small apartment and there wasn't much extra space. Mom always longed to have a dining room and a china hutch, like this one. She and Dad always talked about buying a house or condo with a dining room but they never quite got around to it…" He swallowed hard and bit his lip, trying to push the emotions back down. She put her arms around him and hugged him tight, laying her head against his chest. He held on to her and it was as if her embrace was somehow holding him together, keeping the memories and grief at bay. He squeezed her tighter and lay his face down in her hair, letting the soft strands brush against his cheek.
It felt so good to be with her, touch her, have her close and in his heart. She tilted her head back and he gazed down at her, her eyes hypnotizing his very soul. It cried out to her, wanting so much to tell her, everything. To share it all with her.
"Vickie…" he whispered.
"Kiss me," she said, her eyes full of longing.
His heart swelled with love and he did as she asked. The warmth of her lips surrounded his mind and soul and he was whisked away once again to that sweet abandon, where she was the sun and he was the dark side of the moon. He had gone so many years without her light and love shining upon him. But now…at last…her love had finally found him. He wrapped his arms tighter around her and felt her moan softly as his lips and touch showed her how much he needed her. She was everything. He existed only for her love and caress. He finally finished kissing her and she took a step back, an expression of happiness and mild shock on her face.
"Holy cow!" she whispered.
His face flushed with both humility and pride. He opened his mouth to thank her for the compliment when she sprang forward and threw her arms around

his neck, almost knocking him off balance. She began to kiss him but he couldn't help but chuckle. She pulled away and giggled.

"Uh, if memory serves," she said, playfully shaking her finger at him. "This exact thing happened a few days ago."

"Yep," he replied, enjoying the joke. "Except it was *me*, complaining that I was expecting a more serious response to my advances."

"More romance and less Comedy Central," she said. "Now I know how you feel. Gee, I think I've just made a fool of myself."

He pulled her to him. "And if my memory serves right, I was also told that sometimes you laugh when you're nervous."

"You're not the nervous type," she stated, acting annoyed.

He wrapped his arms around her and laid his face against hers. "You make my heart flutter," he whispered in her ear. "Besides, you shouldn't give up so easy." And with that he covered her lips again, letting every bit of his passion came forth, wanting it to surround her and carry her away. She moaned and wrapped her arms tighter around him, the vibration alerting every fiber in his being. She responded to his passion and began running her hands through his hair. The world suddenly disappeared as her caress swept him away. He moaned with her, his body and soul silently crying out to her.

"Ahem."

He became aware of a faint sound, like a man's voice drifting into his sweet abyss. He ignored it.

"Ahem!"

This time the voice was more distinct. He tried to wish it away.

The room was filled with the noise of someone clearing their throat, quite loudly.

"Ahem! If you don't mind! This is not a bedroom!"

The sound of something hard hitting the table dragged him with great regret from his vision and Vickie's lips. He turned his head and viewed an angry looking man standing on the other side of the table, his right hand pressing against the top of a large book on the dining room table. The realization finally kicked in. Her father.

"Daddy!" Vickie said, noticing that they weren't alone.

Marcus pulled away from her, stood up straight and ran his hands across his shirt and hair, making himself more presentable. She took his arm and led him over to her father. Marcus bent his head down and rubbed his hand across his jaw, mouth and cheeks, hoping to rub off any of Vickie's lipstick that might still be lingering. He glanced up and held the same hand out to her father, introducing himself.

"Hello," the man said, glaring at Marcus's hand as if he'd just been insulted.

Marcus realized that her father must have seen him rubbing his face and quickly wiped his hand on the side of his jeans and offered it to the man again.

"Calvin Garrett," the man said, gripping Marcus's hand and grimacing with disgust as if Marcus had just pulled his hand out of a toilet bowl.

"Sorry," Marcus whispered. "I have a tendency for sweaty palms."

"Understandable," the man replied, wiping his hand across his sweater. "Considering you were also sweating all over my daughter."

"Thanks, Daddy," Vickie said, turning to Marcus and rolling her eyes sarcastically.

Marcus nodded an acknowledgement to her father, trying hard to be civil in spite of the snide remark. But the man wasn't having any of it. He just stood there, glaring hard at Marcus, almost as though he was trying to burn a hole through his head. The man looked like he was in his early fifties but had none of the usual signs of middle age. There was no paunch showing and he seemed in good physical shape. He was approximately six feet tall, had dark brown hair speckled with gray and was lean of stature. But he was by no means lean of character. His expression exuded strength and confidence and the striking blue eyes reminded one of a jungle cat's, gleaming and calculating, poised and ready to strike at the least provocation.

Vickie somehow sensed the animosity between them and pushed in between Marcus and her father. "Marcus is our guest," she told her father. "He's having dinner with us."

Calvin's angered expression didn't falter in the slightest and Marcus knew the man wasn't one to readily back down. Especially after catching the so-called guest fondling his daughter in plain sight. Marcus continued to glare at the man, letting his own determination signal that he neither, was about to back down. The man's eyes narrowed and Marcus half expected lightning bolts to shoot out of them.

"Guests who show up to dine with us," Calvin whispered angrily, "don't grope family members for dessert. No matter how good the food is."

Marcus fought back the smile. At least the man seemed to have a sense of humor. That was something, anyway.

"He wasn't groping me," Vickie protested. "If anything, I was groping him."

A shocked look came over Calvin's face as he switched his gaze from Marcus to Vickie. "You what?" he asked his daughter.

"I was only kidding," she said, giving her father a giant hug.

Marcus watched the man's expression turn on a dime and simply melt in the matter of a few seconds. He hugged his daughter back and his whole body seemed to relax. He leaned back and gave her a fatherly tilt of his head. "You know what I mean," he told her. "It wasn't appropriate behavior out in public."

"I know. But we weren't *out* in public," she told him. "We were in the dining room. I got a little carried away, okay?" And she rose up and gave him a quick kiss on the cheek, which brought a smile to the granite face.

Amazing, Marcus thought. The power of a hug from your children. It was more powerful than any weapon the military farms could design. It not only disarmed the body, it overwhelmed the soul.

"Besides," she reminded her father. "You're always asking me to bring my friends home to meet you and Mom, so I did." She walked over and stood beside Marcus. "Marcus is my friend."

Marcus waited for the man's response. He almost felt sorry for him. Vickie had drawn the lines, forcing her father to either accept the "friend" or take a chance in the future of her never bringing anyone home again. The man's cold, blue eyes glared at Marcus, signaling that he didn't appreciate being put in such a dilemma, especially with his own daughter. The seconds ticked on. It was clear that the man was not used to giving in, even to his own children. Finally, after what seemed like an eternity, the man's expression softened. He extended his hand again to Marcus.

Marcus glanced down at it, not quite sure if the man was welcoming him to shake it or challenging him to an Indian arm wrestle. He decided to give him the benefit of the doubt and shook his hand. The man's grip was firm enough to convey a message of warning, he was extending his welcome but also letting "the guest" know that he was being observed or better yet, scrutinized.

"Welcome to our home," Calvin said. The statement was neither friendly nor encouraging but Marcus respected his effort. He thanked him and Calvin picked up his book and held it firmly against his chest.

"Tell your mother to call me when dinner's ready," he told Vickie. He then headed towards the living room, adjourning back to his respective corner which Marcus assumed was the man's office.

Round one had ended.

"Well, that went pretty good," Vickie said, when her father was out of hearing distance.

He let out a sigh. "I didn't help matters much. Sorry."

She gave him a sweet smile and leaned against him, close enough to make his heart race. "Don't let Daddy scare you. He's all bark but no bite." She gave him a peck on the cheek and then went back to setting the table. He picked up the silverware and lent a hand, suddenly feeling as though he'd just missed getting mauled by a pit bull.

A little while later, the pit bull showed up again.

The dinner went smoothly, at least through the first course, salads and rolls. A couple of the leaves had been removed from the massive table so it seemed a little more like a family supper and not a banquet. Calvin and Ann were seated on opposite ends of the table and Marcus and Vickie sat in the middle, across from Marty. Ann passed around the platter of roast beef and Marcus piled a couple thick slices on his plate, followed by a good portion of vegetables and gravy. He dug in with zeal and listened to Calvin discuss with Ann the client he'd been talking to earlier on the phone.

"His son is looking for a place to live in our area," Calvin said. "He's going to college at Firelands and has two other kids rooming with him."

"Boys or girls?" Marty asked, picking at her food.

"Boys, of course," Calvin replied, giving his youngest daughter a glare of disapproval. "I said the boy could look at one of the apartments," he told Ann. "But I'm not sure it's a good idea to rent to college kids."

"Why not?" Marty asked. "They have to live somewhere."

"I'm talking about all the drinking and partying that goes on with college kids," her father said. "I suppose I could have him look at the apartment opening up in Vickie's building. Although I don't know what Sanun would make of three partying collegians."

"Sanun can handle anything," Ann said, passing the plate of rolls to Marcus. "He's very capable."

Marcus thanked her through a mouthful of roast beef and grabbed another one of the flaky biscuits. He took his knife and cut some butter from the dish next to his water glass. He applied it and shoved half the biscuit into his mouth. Ann asked him if he was enjoying the food. He nodded, not wanting to speak with a mouthful of food.

Marty began giggling. "He must really like it. He's been shoveling it in even faster than Tim does."

Her father looked up from his plate questioningly. "Tim? Who's Tim?"

Marcus watched all three women exchange worried glances and from the looks on their faces it was evident that Calvin Garrett hadn't yet found about his youngest daughter's new boyfriend. Calvin put his fork down and glared at Marty.

"*Who* is Tim?" he emphasized the question, making it sound like an ultimatum.

"He's a boy I know," Marty said, suddenly becoming very interested in her food. Her father asked her where she'd met him.

She glanced across the table at Marcus and smiled. "At The Crystal."

Marcus gave her a wink and bit into another forkful of mashed potatoes and gravy.

Calvin asked what The Crystal was.

"It's the bowling alley Marcus manages," Vickie volunteered. "Marty and I went up a couple weeks ago. Tim was bowling in the lane next to ours."

Calvin pushed his chair back like he'd suddenly lost his appetite. "Why wasn't I told this?"

Uh-oh, Marcus thought. *The man's just found out his daughters have been plotting behind his back.* He watched Calvin's face scrunch up in anger and it was obvious that the Garrett clan was about to approach Def Con 4 status, escalation to an all-out family dispute.

"It was no big deal," Vickie told him.

"Yes it was!" Marty exclaimed excitedly. "It was this big party and it was so much fun!"

"A party?" Calvin asked, acting slightly alarmed. "What kind of party?"

Marcus opened his mouth to tell him about the birthday party when Vickie beat him to it.

"It was a birthday party. For Marcus…"

"It was great!" Marty said, interrupting. "We got to bowl and dance and we even sang over the microphone!"

The alarm level on Calvin's face shot up a couple of degrees. "What do you mean dance? Who did you dance with?"

"Tim," Marty said, sitting up straighter in her seat and folding her arms in a huff like she was challenging her father to a duel.

"He's a friend of mine," Marcus added, hoping to help her out.

"A friend of yours?" Calvin asked, glaring daggers at Marcus. "And what kind of place is it where men are dancing with young, impressionable girls?"

Marty protested that she wasn't impressionable and Vickie interjected, telling her father that it was completely innocent.

"You never told *me* about dancing with a boy," Ann said, acting slighted.

Marty gave her a sad smile. "Sorry, Mom. I didn't say anything because I thought it would upset you and Daddy."

"No doubt!" Calvin replied, throwing his napkin next to his plate. "And what else haven't you told us?"

Here it comes, Marcus thought. *Moving to Def Con 3.*

Ann told Calvin to calm down but he only lowered his voice a few decibels and repeated the question to Marty.

"All she did was dance," Vickie said, trying to placate her father's anger.

Marcus tried to help Vickie explain it. "It's a dance game the kids play," he told Calvin. "They bowl against each other and the winners dance with the losers." He started to explain about the dance floor he and Jack built when Calvin cut him off.

"Dancing? Slow dancing?"

"Oh, Daddy," Marty said, impatiently waving him off. "It's just like the dancing you and Mom do at the club."

Calvin's eyes got wider. "But you're only sixteen!"

Marty put her hands on her hips defiantly. "I'm going on seventeen and I'm not a baby anymore. I can dance if I want or even…or even kiss a boy if I want!"

Calvin's expression turned to something close to fury as he leaned forward and regarded Marty. "Did you kiss this boy?"

Marty quickly clammed up and Marcus felt his heart go out to her.

"Martha Garrett," her father said slow and deliberate. "Answer my question. Did you *kiss* this boy?"

"Only a couple of times," she whispered, glancing over at her mother anxiously.

Calvin stood up from his chair and bellowed at her. "Leave this room right now! We'll talk about this later!"

Ann began to protest but Calvin held up his hand and shook his head no. "I know what you're going to say. We don't bring up family matters in front of guests. But guests don't usually influence my daughters into inappropriate behavior!" And he glared menacingly at Marcus. Marcus stopped chewing the roast beef in his mouth. Calvin once again ordered Marty to leave the table and she got up and trudged out of the room.

"But it was innocent," Vickie protested. "It was only part of the dance game." She then turned to Marcus. "Go ahead, Marcus. Tell him."

Marcus started chewing the meat again and tried to open his mouth to say something. Calvin didn't give him a chance.

"If I want information from *that* man, I'll ask him for it!"

Ann immediately yelled at Calvin for talking in such a manner.

"Why?" Calvin asked, rigidly folding his arms in front of him. "Do you actually think he'd tell us the truth?"

"Of course he would!" Vickie replied, throwing her napkin on the table with so much force that it knocked over her water glass.

"Really?" Calvin asked. "Then why doesn't he tell us all about you spending the last few nights over at his place?"

Marcus felt the roast beef in his mouth suddenly lose it flavor.

"Well?" Calvin asked Vickie. "Have him tell us all about that!"

Marcus chewed the last of the cardboard flavored chunk of meat and swallowed it. He hadn't chewed it quite enough and the wad gave him a bit of discomfort going down. But not as much discomfort as the angry man standing a few feet away. *Proceeding to Def Con 2*, he thought. *Time for defensive maneuvers.* He tried to explain.

"There were wasps in Vickie's apartment," he told the man.

"I know!" Calvin barked. "Sanun told me. He was also under the impression that Vickie was staying with us until her apartment was ready. I had to call the water department to find out where she was staying."

Vickie's mouth dropped open. "You called my job?"

Marcus saw the look of shock on her face and knew the news wasn't something she wanted to hear.

"How could you do that?" she cried.

"Calvin, you didn't!" Ann exclaimed.

"Damn right I did!" he replied. "And how do you think I felt when they told me she could be reached at *that* man's address?" And he shook his finger at Marcus.

Vickie jumped up from her chair, knocking it backwards. "I can't believe you would check up on me like that!" she yelled. "It's bad enough you bully Marty, making her feel like a slut for kissing a boy!"

"I did not call her a slut!" Calvin yelled back.

"No!" Vickie replied, her voice full of fury. "But you as much as called *me* one when you checked at my job and demanded to know where I was staying!"

Calvin plopped down into his chair so hard that Marcus was sure the man had hurt himself. "I did not call you a slut. But if you're going to act like one, what other choice do you give me?"

It was Ann who reacted first. "Calvin Garrett! How dare you say that to your own daughter! You apologize at once!"

Calvin gritted his teeth and ignored his wife's request. Marcus reached over and took Vickie's hand, hoping to diffuse the situation.

"Maybe we should be leaving," he whispered to her.

"Where?" Calvin growled. "Back to your apartment? For some more dancing, kissing and God knows what else?"

Vickie pulled her hand from Marcus's grip and shook a fist at her father. "Goddamn it! I'm not going to let you talk to us that way!"

Calvin stood up and yelled at her to watch her language, to which Vickie replied a rather loud "Go to hell!" A shout fest ensued and even the dishes in the china cabinet shook from the decibels as father and daughter voiced their opinions. Ann joined the melee, trying to calm them both down but it was useless.

"She won't listen to us!" Calvin complained to his wife. "Don't you care if she ruins her life?"

Ann jumped up from her chair. "Why should she listen to us?" she yelled. "When you call her names?"

Calvin protested that he was only calling it as he saw it and Vickie and Ann both responded with another verbal retaliation. Marcus stayed in his seat, fearing that if he stood up he'd get pelted by the missiles of words being hurled back and forth across the table.

It appeared that the family was now at Def Con 1. All-out war.

The three members of the Garrett family presented their respective opinions with great enthusiasm and noise. Marcus watched the demonstration, enthralled. An only child with parents who didn't quarrel much, he'd never gotten a chance to observe a family at war with each other. Even Ben's father wasn't one for shouting or voicing his views, his style was to brood and express his opinion through a series of grumbles and subtle body language. Watching the Garretts engage in a verbal altercation was not only fascinating, it was like watching the movie *King Kong* played out in front of him. With Calvin as the determined giant monkey, clinging to the side of the Empire State Building and Vickie and Ann the biplanes swooping down, trying to knock him off.

Marcus glanced down at the plate in front of him. There was still a lot of food left and being a bachelor, home cooked meals were far and few in between. It seemed a shame to let it go to waste. Slowly and inconspicuously as he could, he picked up his fork. He hunched over his plate a little and filled his mouth with the delectable selections. The verbal assault was still waging above him and he tried to keep his eye on it and his food. Over the next few minutes, he ended up learning a great deal about Vickie's family, due mostly to Calvin's reference to what he termed as "relationship disasters," resulting in two grandchildren. One was regarded in high esteem, Stephanie, Vickie's older sister Karen's girl. The other, a boy named Eddie, Vickie's brother David's child, was not, due mainly to the fact that the family never got to see the boy because David's ex-girlfriend chose not to have David included in the child's life.

At this point, Calvin included Marcus in the discussion. "And how many kids does *this* one have roaming around the countryside?"

"Daddy!" Vickie yelled. "Leave Marcus out of this!"

Marcus swallowed a mouthful of food and tried to help out in the discussion. "I don't have any children…"

"That's what they all say!" Calvin grunted, directly it more at Vickie than at him. "You'd just be another notch in his belt!"

"I don't wear belts," Marcus replied, hoping to clear up that point.

Calvin's expression turned to one of exasperated annoyance. "You know what I'm talking about!" he yelled at Marcus. "You're only using her for sex!"

Vickie let out a yelp and plopped back down into her chair. "How could you say that?" she demanded of her father.

"Well, just look at him!" Calvin said, pointing to Marcus. "He's like all the other males his age! Only interested in feeding his needs. He doesn't even have the courtesy to stop eating while we're talking to him!"

Marcus stopped chewing the next bite and quickly swallowed it.

"He's nothing but a pig!" Calvin added with a grunt of disgust.

Now it was Ann who responded. She slammed her fist down on the table so hard that Marcus had to hold on to his plate to keep it from bouncing into his lap.

"Ann!" Calvin exclaimed, acting shocked. "What are you doing?"

"I'll *TELL* you what I'm doing!" she said, her face contorted in anger. "I won't stand here and listen to one more minute of this! You've succeeded in alienating David and Karen and now you're doing the same thing to Marty and Vickie! You're driving everyone away!" And she paused to take a breath and then grumbled at him. "And you're driving me away, Calvin Garrett! You're tearing this family apart!" She then directed her attention to Marcus. "I'm so sorry you had to hear all of this. Please excuse me." With that she pulled a Kleenex from her pocket, put it to her face and fled the room.

Marcus put his fork down out of respect for Ann's departure.

"I better go after her," Vickie whispered to Marcus. She got up from her seat and her father asked her where she was going.

"Mother needs me," she replied defiantly.

"Your mother will be fine," he said, motioning at her to take her seat. "We're not finished talking yet, young lady!"

She grabbed Marcus's hand. "We're leaving! And right now!"

He got up from his seat and began to follow her when Calvin called out, "Please, Vickie."

She spun around to him. "Why should I stay? In your eyes, I'm nothing but a slut!"

"I didn't say that!" he protested. "At least I didn't mean to. I said it only in the heat of anger."

"You don't trust me!"

"Yes, I do," he replied, his tone apologetic.

She squeezed Marcus's hand and glared at her father. "Then why did you have Sanun spy on me?"

Calvin's face went blank. "Who told you that?"

"Sanun did. He's a good man and I know he didn't feel right doing it because he was my friend. Shame on you for doing that to me and shame on you for asking a good man like Sanun do something so deceitful!"

Calvin sighed heavily and sat down in his chair, acting like the wind had been knocked out of him.

"How could you do that?" Vickie asked him.

Calvin closed his eyes and rubbed his hand across his face. "I was only trying to protect you," he whispered; more to himself than to them.

Vickie's face scrunched up with hurt and Marcus knew she was on the verge of tears. It had been a trying afternoon for her. She'd vented feelings that must have been pent up for a long time. He nudged her in the arm and mouthed the words "talk to him" to her. "I'll make myself scarce so the two of you can have some privacy." He let go of her hand and took off across the room. As he entered the kitchen he saw Marty sitting on one of the stools at the counter island.

"Are they still at it?" she whispered.

He shut the door behind him and walked over and took the seat next to her. "Vickie and your dad are having a private discussion so we'll give them a few minutes alone." He glanced around the room and asked her where her mom was.

"She went for a walk out back. I think she wanted to cry but didn't want me to see her do it." She sighed, put her elbows up on the counter and rested her head on her hands. "Too bad Tim isn't here. We could all use a good laugh right about now."

"That's for sure," he agreed. "Sorry about your parents finding out about him."

"I've got my own big mouth to blame, making that comment about him. What the heck was I thinking?" She paused and sighed. "Well, it was nice while it lasted."

He told her not to take it so hard. "You never know. Your dad might change his mind, once he meets Tim."

"That's never gonna happen. After the way Daddy treated you tonight, I'm *never* asking Tim to dinner!"

"Too bad. I think your father might be impressed with a Nobel Prize Winner."

She giggled. "Watching Daddy buy a story like that would almost be worth going through a third degree like you and Vickie did tonight. But you're used to situations like that, aren't you? I mean...with all your *Magic moments*."

He told her he was. It was then that he noticed a strange smile on her face and asked her what he was missing.

"You shouldn't be afraid," she said. "You know. Of Vickie finding out the truth about you."

He stared at her, wondering if perhaps she knew something he didn't. "Why?" he asked her. "Has she said anything to you?"

Marty hesitated answering, causing him to experience a wave of worry.

"Has she?" he asked her again.

She reached out and put her hand on his arm. "No. But you still shouldn't worry about her finding out." She then leaned closer and whispered, "It won't make any difference to her. She's in love..." But she never got to finish the sentence. She was interrupted by what sounded like gunshots, coming from out back, behind the house.

"That sounds close!" Marty exclaimed, jumping down from the stool and hurrying towards the back door. "Mom's out there!"

Calvin and Vickie ran into the room and asked them what was going on.

"Shots!" Marty yelled, throwing open the door. "Out back! Where Mom went walking!"

Calvin ran over and stopped Marty before she went out the door. "Stay inside with your sister," he told her. "I'll check it out."

Marcus saw the frightened looks on Marty's and Vickie's faces and knew what he had to do. "I'm going with him," he told Vickie.

He hurried over next to Calvin and the man immediately protested.

"It doesn't matter how much you complain," Marcus told him, not backing down. "Like it or not, I'm going with you."

The man sighed. "Okay. But stay behind me."

The two of them went out the door and Marty and Vickie crowded in together at the screen door, behind them. There was a twenty-by-twenty foot brick patio directly behind the house and a large brick barbeque pit at the end of the patio, past the two umbrella topped table and chair sets. Four chaise lounges sat to the right of the patio and the outer perimeter of bricks was dotted every few yards with built in four-foot high citronella candles. Behind the patio was a half acre sized yard that went back to a wooded area. A line of young fruit trees stood between the patio and woods and a white gazebo sat in the middle of the line of trees. There was a row of shrubs to the right of the property that extended almost all the way back to the woods. The trees in the wooded area and to the left of the property cast off long shadows across the yard, adding an ominous feel to what was going on. Calvin put his hand to his forehead, blocking out the final, bright rays of late afternoon sunlight.

"There's Mom!" Marty cried.

As soon as Marty said it, Marcus spotted her. She was running across the grass past the gazebo, towards the patio.

"Everybody stay here!" Calvin whispered and then he took off after his wife. He caught up to her halfway between the gazebo and patio. He put his arm around her, in a protective gesture and led her back to the patio. Her face was flushed with fear and she was holding her shoes in one hand.

"Mom!" Marty cried, bolting from the back door with Vickie right behind her. They both went over and hugged their mother as Calvin kept asking her if she was all right.

"I'm okay," she said, catching her breath. "I was walking out by the woods when someone started shooting. I don't think they were aiming at me but it sounded close!"

Marcus looked back at the wooded area at the rear of the property. He asked Calvin if any of the neighbors owned guns.

"No. It's probably poachers. We've had trouble with them before. They come onto our land looking for deer." His expression turned angry. "But this has gone way too far. Taking pot shots right on our land! Someone could have been killed!" He reached out to Ann again and she went into his arms and hugged him tight. Calvin took her chin in his hand and whispered to her, "You take the girls and go back inside. I'm going to check it out."

Ann began pleading with him not to.

"Mom's right!" Vickie said, grabbing her father's arm. "I'm scared! I don't want you going out there!"

He leaned down and gave her a kiss on the cheek. "I'll be okay."

"But please, Dad! Don't go back there! Let's call the police!"

"Good idea," he told her. "And in the meantime I'll head out there and keep an eye on them."

Ann and Vickie began to protest again but Calvin held up his hand and stopped them. "I'm only going to watch them," he said. "I want to make sure they don't chase some deer into the yard and end up shooting at the house. This way I'll be able to direct the police right to them when they get here." He turned and told Marty to go dial 911. "Tell them what's going on and be sure to let them know that they're shooting firearms on our property, that way they'll know it's serious."

Marty sprinted towards the door and was out of sight in a second. Calvin told Ann to go back inside with Vickie but Vickie refused to go.

"I'm going with you!" she told her father.

"Don't worry," Calvin said. "I'm not going to do something stupid like get myself shot. I'm too devious for that. Just ask Sanun."

"Oh, Daddy!" she cried, hugging him tight. She sobbed "I'm sorry" several times and he told her there was nothing to be sorry for. He then took her hand and gave it to Marcus. "Go inside with Marcus and your mom," he told her. "Go on. I'll be all right."

"I'm not going back inside," Marcus told him. "I'm going with you."

Calvin started to give him an argument but Marcus cut him off. "If they see two of us, it might scare them away or at least get them to stop shooting off their guns. This way, I can watch your back. And don't try to talk me out of it. My mind's made up."

Just then three more shots came from the woods and this time they sounded closer. Calvin yelled at Vickie and Ann to get inside and they both rushed up the back steps. They were met at the door by Marty who told them that the police were on the way.

"All three of you stay inside," Calvin told them. "As soon as the police get here, show them where the shots are coming from but *don't* come out here. Marcus and I will go out and try to pinpoint where the poachers are so we can show the police. We'll be right back." With that Calvin ducked down and hurried across the patio. Marcus crouched down and followed behind him when he heard Vickie call after him.

"Marcus! Please be careful."

He took a second to blow her a kiss and then took his place again behind her father.

"We can follow the shrub line towards the back of the yard," Calvin whispered, moving almost silently across the grass to the right. "That way we can sneak up on them without being seen."

Marcus became the man's shadow and tried to mirror his every move.

They hurried over to the shrubs and ducked down behind them. The bushes were less than three feet high so they had to keep down while they made their way towards the woods. After a hundred yards or so Marcus felt the muscles in the back of his legs ache from continuously crouching down. But Calvin showed no signs of discomfort of any kind. For someone in his early fifties, he moved as agile as a man half his age. Calvin stopped at the end of the row of bushes and squatted down. Marcus took his place beside him and surveyed the woods.

The wooded area ran behind all the neighboring properties and went back as far as the eye could see. The late afternoon sunlight was partially blocked by the trees, giving the woods an almost twilight appearance. He squinted hard, hoping for some movement to reveal the poachers. But there wasn't even a twitch or sound of a branch breaking.

"I can't see anyone," Calvin whispered faintly with a tinge of urgency. "It's going to be dark in a little while and then we won't be able to see at all. We'll be a couple of sitting ducks."

Marcus was impressed with the quick way Calvin had assessed the situation. Apparently, the man was as fast in the brain department as he was with his feet.

"We've got to get in there now," Calvin said. "While the light is still with us." He'd no sooner said it than he began to skulk the few yards of open space and into the trees. Marcus hurried behind him, trying to keep up with the man's pace and hoping that they weren't accidentally mistaken for a couple deer by the poachers. They entered the woods without any trouble and Marcus crouched down next to Calvin and looked around. The light was only half what was in the yard and it took his eyes a few seconds to adjust. Calvin motioned for them to go a little deeper into the trees.

They started forward, carefully stepping on top of the underbrush. A couple of small branches crunched under Calvin's feet and they stopped and crouched down, waiting to see if they'd been detected by the intruders. A minute passed without any movement or noise from the surrounding area so they began to move forward again. They'd only taken a couple of steps when the silence was broken by the sound of branches breaking to their right.

They both crouched down again and Marcus peered over to a cluster of ferns to the vicinity where the noise had come from. A large buck deer with a sizable rack stood about ten yards away. It was standing erect with its ears perked back, trying to detect danger.

"I can't see it very well," Calvin whispered. "Stay here. I'm gonna get a

AND THE BULL SAVED ME

little closer." Then Calvin silently crept up a couple yards past a maple tree trunk, blocking his view.

Marcus stayed behind the ferns, a couple feet from the maple trunk and watched the deer. He marveled at the creature's defensive instincts. The animal's legs and muscles were tensed, ready to spring away from any possible sign of danger. And from the number of points on the rack, it was clear the animal had been around a long time and had honed those self-preservation instincts over the years.

The lack of sound among all that greenery and branches seemed almost disquieting and Marcus scanned the area and listened closely, for any noise or movement. The light was now beginning to fade and the images were getting harder to see. There was another faint sound of branches breaking as a smaller deer walked up beside the buck. It was a doe, about two-thirds the size of the buck and she too, was poised, listening for any sound of danger. A few seconds later another doe came into view but this one was being followed by it's baby, a little version only three or four feet tall. The little deer stayed close to its mother's legs and incredibly, seemed to be able to move as silently as its parent. Marcus smiled as he heard Calvin whisper a barely audible "Wow!"

The deer didn't seem to hear the comment and went about scrutinizing the area. Calvin slowly stood up, trying to get a better look and Marcus understood his curiosity. Baby deer, even in rural areas, were not a common sight. He too, began to stand up when something caught his peripheral vision. He glanced to his left. There, about fifteen yards away was a hunter walking towards them, carrying a rifle. The gun was still at the man's side so he hadn't yet spotted the deer but it wouldn't be long before he did. Calvin had his back to the man and was still standing, staring at the deer so he had no idea that the hunter was coming up from behind him.

Marcus crouched down again and tried to figure out what to do. If he yelled to Calvin about the hunter, the hunter would probably shoot at the deer first, possibly even shooting the baby. And if he spooked the deer, they might break to the left, directly into the hunter's aim. Not to mention that in the process, Calvin might get run over by the deer. He was still deliberating about what to do when he saw the hunter stop in his tracks and stare in the deer's direction. A second later the man raised the gun to shoulder level and Marcus felt his heart jump into his mouth. The hunter was going to shoot at the deer.

The only problem was that someone was in the way.
Calvin.
Either the hunter hadn't noticed Calvin was in the way or didn't care. But

whichever it was, the result was going to be the same if the hunter shot the rifle. Calvin would get hit.

The sound of a faint click filled the air and Marcus knew he had to act, now. He lunged, hurling his body forward with all the strength he could muster at Vickie's father. Right before making contact Calvin turned to him, an expression of horror on his face.

"Wha?" Calvin said just as Marcus crashed into him, spread-eagle, knocking him over. The sound of a gunshot pierced the air as they both crumpled down, upon the underbrush. Calvin started to raise his head but Marcus shoved it down again, against the brush, hunkering down on top of him, trying to make sure they were out of the bullet's path. The sound of dead branches being broken erupted from the right, signaling that the deer were fleeing the scene. Another shot went off, followed by several more a few seconds later.

"Jesus!" Calvin groaned beneath him. "We're at the goddamned OK Coral!"

Marcus felt a wave of relief that he was unhurt. Although from the way he'd driven him against the ground, his clothes were probably ruined. A second later the woods were flooded with light from flashlights as five or six policemen rushed towards them. Shouts ensued and a few of the men's voices were heard moving over to where the hunter had been standing. Marcus finally felt safe enough to let Calvin go and got up off him, offering him a hand to help him up.

"The cavalry's here," he told Calvin.

"Thank God," Calvin replied, taking Marcus's hand and getting to his feet. "How in the hell did you know about the shot? Are you psychic?"

"No," he replied with a smile. He told Calvin about the hunter and how he was afraid to say anything. "I thought if I made any noise the hunter would shoot first and ask questions later."

An expression of fright swept across Calvin's face. "Jesus. You're right. He probably would have."

Two of the police officers ran up and asked if they were all right.

"We're okay," Marcus replied, waiting for Calvin to explain to them what happened. But the man had become suddenly quiet, as if he was in slight shock. Who could blame him? Marcus thought. It wasn't every day you were mistaken for a deer and lived to tell the tale.

Another shot rang off in the area to their left and the first officer told the second he was going to check out the rest of the woods with the others.

AND THE BULL SAVED ME

"Go ahead," the second officer said. "And I'll get statements from these men." He then took a notepad and pen out of his front pocket as his partner hurried into the brush.

"And your names?" the officer taking notes asked, aided by his flashlight.

Marcus told the officer Calvin's name and then his own. The officer's eyebrows shot up, like he recognized it.

"And you and Mr. Garrett came out to the woods to investigate where the shots were coming from, correct?" the man said, making some kind of notation on the pad.

Marcus explained about Ann being frightened by the shots and about him and Calvin going into the woods. He then asked the officer if he wanted his phone number and address, in case he had any questions later.

"No," the officer replied, making another notation on the pad. "We already have that on file down at the station."

Uh-oh, Marcus thought, experiencing a wave of anxiety at the remark. No doubt on their *Most Wanted* or at least *Most Annoying Citizen* list. He glanced over at Calvin to see if he'd noticed the officer's remark. But Calvin wasn't paying any attention to them. He was busy mumbling something as he tried to get the worst of the dirt off his sweater and trousers. The officer noticed Calvin's mumblings and asked him if he had anything to add.

"No," Calvin whispered, glancing down at his clothes again. "Marcus can tell you better than I can. I was busy watching the damn deer."

Marcus finished up with the explanation and the officer closed up his notepad. "That's all very informative, Mr. Kerr," he said, stashing the pad in the front pocket of his shirt. "But you acted foolishly."

"What?" Marcus said, not sure he heard him right. "What's *that* supposed to mean?"

"You should have waited for us to show up."

Marcus felt his frustration flare. "We only wanted to get the hunter to stop shooting, for Chrissakes! We were protecting loved ones. What would you have done if it was *your* family?"

"I understand your reaction," the officer said. "But both of you could have been shot. Mr. Garrett still looks pretty shaken up."

"I'm not shaken!" Calvin grunted, seeming to come out of his trance. "I'm just not used to getting shot in my own goddamned back yard, that's all." He then marched up to the officer and glared at him. "This isn't the first time this has happened. And you can bet your bottom dollar that I'm going to be at the next city council meeting to complain about the lack of support by the local

311

authorities to do something about this menace!" Calvin paused and took the same authoritative stance that he'd exhibited earlier when he'd caught his older daughter kissing a strange man in the dining room. The presence was nothing short of intimidating.

"Now," Calvin grumbled at the officer. "Why don't you finish checking out my woods before the jerk with the weapon shoots the mayor…Or better yet…one of you?"

Marcus stifled the smile as the officer quickly replied that he'd see what the others had found out and took off into the woods.

"Assholes," Calvin muttered as the man hurried away. "It's a wonder the damn hunter didn't come back and shoot that idiot while he was taking all his stupid notes."

Marcus chuckled. "That officer might not mind going after an armed poacher after the way you told him off."

Calvin smiled. "Well, it's ridiculous what you have to do nowadays to get anyone to take any action. But the cops chasing that guy though the woods with Billy clubs isn't going to be much of a deterrent. I would have been happier if they came in shooting like Doc Holliday and the Earps. I don't own a gun. I'm a devout pacifist. But after this I might just keep my Tournament Spincast by the back door. It can't fire bullets but I can be pretty deadly casting out with a hook."

"I'd prefer one of those new graphic specials myself."

Calvin's face lit up. "You fish?"

He told Calvin about going out on Jack's boat. "I'm no great angler but I can cast almost as good as Jack can. And he's been fishing since he was a kid."

"I've only been fishing out on the water a couple of times but it was great! I caught a large mouthed bass, it's mounted on the wall of my office. Would you like to see it?"

Marcus replied that he would and he and Calvin set off for the house. Ann, Vickie and Marty were waiting on the patio and as they headed across the yard, Marcus gave them a quick thumbs up to let them know they were okay.

"Are you going to tell them what happened?" he asked Calvin.

"I know what you're thinking and I don't want them to worry, either. But we'll have to tell them the truth. It's been my experience that lying to them is an impossibility, they can see right through it."

He wanted to tell Calvin that he'd already found out exactly how inquisitive Vickie could be. But to do so, he'd have to reveal his secret so it wasn't an option. A few seconds later Vickie, Marty and Ann came running up, surrounding him and Calvin and talking all at once, asking them if they were okay.

"We're unharmed," Calvin said, giving them all a hug. "But only thanks to Marcus." He then explained in detail what happened. Marcus thought he was exaggerating a bit by calling him a hero but kept the comment to himself. Having the man praise him was a site better than the man acting like he was the hunter and Marcus the deer.

"The police, as usual, took their politically correct stance," Calvin said. "They made it sound like Marcus and I were the ones breaking the law. But everything's okay now. I've got my girls back." And he hugged all three of them again.

After Calvin let go of Vickie she went over and took Marcus aside. She whispered "thank you" at him and gave him a smile that made him beam inside. "Are you sure you're okay?"

"Absolutely," he replied, glancing over at Calvin, still being hugged by Marty and Ann. "Your dad's a lucky man," he told her. "Look how much he's loved…" He stopped himself as soon as he said it. He hadn't meant to tell her something so personal. But the thought had somehow escaped his mouth before he could stop it. "Uh…" he said, clearing his throat and looking down at the bricks of the patio. "I only meant that it was lucky that nothing happened to him."

She wrapped her arms around him and squeezed him so tight that it took his breath away. "I know what you meant," she said, her voice full of emotion. "And I love you for saying it."

He closed his eyes and lay his head down upon hers, his heart smiling as he experienced the same feeling of love that he'd seen Calvin enjoying. Being hugged by someone who loved and cared about you. It didn't get any better than that. But his reverie was short-lived as a few seconds later he felt a hand slap him hard on the back. It was Calvin.

"We haven't been very hospitable to our guest here," Calvin said. "What's say we all go back inside and finish dinner?"

Fine with me, Marcus thought. Enjoying Ann's home cooking beat being shot at any day.

They all adjourned to the dining room and after Ann heated everything up in the microwave, Marcus happily got to finish the roast beef and fixings with the rest of the family. The officers showed up at the back door a little while later and reported that although they hadn't caught the poachers, the woods were now free from any hunters bearing arms. Calvin seemed quite happy with the news and now that the situation had cooled down to the Def Con 5 stage, things were much more pleasant at the dinner table. And there was another unexpected consequence to the family's little adventure. Not only was Calvin Garrett not boring his family with his "work" stories or shouting at them. He was talking, telling jokes and laughing like he was having the time of his life. What's more, all three of his "girls" seemed to notice the change.

"What's with you, Daddy?" Marty giggled. "Since you came back from the woods you've been acting funny."

He asked her what she meant.

"She's referring to your attitude," Ann said. "And I've seen it too. It's almost as though you're happy that someone almost shot you."

Calvin stopped smiling. "Well, I wouldn't say it made me happy," he said, staring down at his empty plate. "But it did make me do some thinking." He glanced up at Marcus. "After Marcus saved my life..."

"Oh, I didn't do anything—" Marcus said but Calvin cut him off.

"I know your natural modesty will prevent you from admitting it, my friend," Calvin told him. "But the truth is...you *did* save my life. While you were holding me down, out of the bullet's path, I realized exactly how close I came to dying. That was a very sobering experience." Calvin then directed his gaze to his family. "I kept thinking about how I almost left this world and the last words I spoke to the people I love were in anger. That thought haunted me. No man wants to leave a memory like that behind." He paused and glanced down at the table. "At least I don't."

"Oh, Calvin," Ann whispered, overcome by the moment. She then mouthed the words "I love you" to him and he repeated that he loved her, too.

He then smiled at his daughters. "It also made me realize that no matter how much I try, you're still going to grow up and leave us."

"But we'll be coming back with our own families," Vickie reminded him.

"I hope so," Calvin said. "And that's why I've made a decision."

"That doesn't sound good," Marty whispered.

Calvin chuckled. "Don't be so pessimistic," he told Marty. "This is something good. It involves you and Vickie both." He then told Vickie that he would talk to Sanun and ask him to stop watching her. "Your mother and I have raised you with good, Christian moral values so we're going to trust your judgment when it comes to matters that are...uh."

"My own business?" Vickie said, smiling and finishing it for him.

He smiled back at her. "That's correct. Your own business. And I hope you continue to bring your friends out to meet us. We want you to feel at home here.

Not like it's a mausoleum." And he winked at Marty. "That's right," he told her. "I heard all those comments. You don't exactly whisper."

"Sorry, Daddy," Marty said.

He told her there was no need to apologize. "Besides, I plan to rectify things."

"How?" Marty asked him, folding her arms in front of her defiantly, like she was expecting him to list them right then. Marcus couldn't help but smile at her tenacity. Marty wasn't going to be fooled by empty promises. She was going to make sure those promises were kept.

"All right," Calvin said, smiling slightly like he was enjoying the challenge. "First thing on the list is the 'dating' issue. I'm going to overlook the fact that you've been doing it behind my back and give you permission."

"Yes!" Marty exclaimed, obviously happy with the decision.

"Just a minute," Calvin told her. "There's going to be some ground rules first."

"Oh, brother," Marty said, sagging down into her chair. "Like what?"

Calvin told her that he expected her to use her head when she picked the boys she went out with. "And since you seem to already be dating someone..."

"Tim Prentiss," Marty added.

"Tim," Calvin said. "Then I expect you to give your mother and I the same courtesy your sister Vickie has. We want to meet Tim and will expect him to come to dinner with us next Sunday."

Marty rolled her eyes at Marcus and he felt sorry for her. Now that Vickie had invited her beau to dinner, Marty would be expected to do the same with every boy she went out with.

"Great!" Marty whispered. "Maybe we can invite those poachers back and they can take a shot at Tim, too."

"Martha Garrett!" Ann yelled at her. "What a thing to say!"

Marty muttered a quick "sorry" and got back to picking at her food.

"And as for Marcus..." Calvin said.

Marcus held his breath and waited to hear it.

"He and I are going to my office," Calvin said, giving Marcus a wink. "We've got some important things to discuss. Like fishing. So unless the three of you ladies want to listen to me brag about my large-mouthed bass again, I'll understand if you don't want to join us."

"I'll pass," Marty replied.

"Me too," Ann added. "But what I will do is get us some dessert."

Calvin got up from his chair and told Ann he'd help her. "I'll grab a couple slices of pie and meet you in the office," Calvin told Marcus. "Vickie and Marty can show you the way."

As soon as their parents left, Marty and Vickie began laughing. Marcus asked them what was so funny.

"Daddy," Marty said. "You've worked some kind of magic on him, just like your name."

Vickie reminded him that her father never had anyone but clients visit in his office.

"That's right," he replied. "You said only someone as important as the Pope or the President would have the honor."

"Correct," Marty said. "And even *they* wouldn't be allowed to eat pie in there! Daddy's gone completely haywire!" Then she started laughing again.

"Come on," Vickie said, grabbing his hand and pulling him up from his chair. "I mean, if you'll allow me, Mr. President, I'll show you the way to my father's Oval Office."

Marty told them to go ahead without her. "I'm gotta call Tim and tell him the good news." Then she cupped her hand over her mouth and added, "Then the bad news about having to come to dinner next week."

"Don't worry," Marcus told her. "Tim can handle anything, even poachers."

"Hope so," Marty replied. "But just in case, I better check and see if he owns a bulletproof vest." And with that, she went bounding out of the room.

"You could have used a bulletproof vest yourself tonight," Vickie told him. Then she began smiling strangely.

"What is it?" he asked her.

"Oh, nothing," she replied, acting like it was anything but. "I was just thinking about what happened here in the last couple of hours. You went from being branded 'that man' by my father to 'hero.' That's some impressive accomplishment. Marty was right about your name. You really do have some kind of magical force behind you."

Sure hope so, he thought as he followed her into the living room. And with luck, that same magic would hold just a little while longer.

CHAPTER TWELVE

It was a few days later. Ben sat in one of the corner booths at The Point with Jack and Magic, laughing at Magic's retelling of what happened at Vickie's parents' house.

"At least this one didn't make the papers," Ben remarked, in between guffaws.

"It's a wonder," Marcus replied. "Especially after that cop did a double take when he heard my name. He made some kind of mark on his little pad, probably 'Public Enemy Number One.' Hope to hell it didn't get broadcast over the police ban."

"Uh...I'm afraid it did," Jack replied, reminding them about Mavis's penchant for listening in on her police scanner. "She said things really began buzzing on the scanner after your name was mentioned."

"I've no doubt of that," Marcus smirked.

"Well, what do you expect, Magic?" Jack said, puffing on his pipe. "Let's face it. Kirklin's a small town. Poachers taking pot shots at one of its residents is big news. Especially when someone of your notoriety is involved."

Notoriety, Ben thought, trying hard not to laugh at Jack's attempt to downplay it. More like "Kirklin Klutz Strikes Again." "One thing's for sure," Ben remarked. "You were damn lucky Calvin *is* a pacifist, Magic. Otherwise you might have found yourself at the end of his shotgun once he found out about Vickie staying at your place."

Marcus rolled his eyes and sighed. "Tell me about it. If I'd known he already knew about it, I never would have gone to dinner. I was walking right into an ambush and didn't even know it."

Jack gave Marcus a wink. "But if you hadn't walked into that ambush, you never would have made friends with Vickie's dad."

Marcus smiled, like he was thinking about it. "Yeah. How about that? Once we started trading fishing stories it was just like Vickie said it was. A magic wand, transforming her father from a suspicious tyrant into a human being. Pretty amazing."

Ben felt confused. "I thought you said her father changed his mind about you because you saved his life."

"He did," Marcus agreed. "But once we started talking in his office, I found out what a really nice guy he was. So I guess you could say it worked a little magic on me, too."

"You also reminded Calvin of a forgotten dream," Jack said, taking the pipe from his mouth. "That can be very moving."

Ben asked Jack what dream he was talking about.

"Calvin's always dreamed of owning a fishing boat."

"So why doesn't he buy one?" Ben asked, not seeing the problem.

"Sometimes dreams get pushed aside," Jack said. "You let your family and job get in the way. You make excuses and tell yourself that your family comes first and before you know it, you're too old to chase your dreams anymore."

"You sound like you've had personal experience," Ben mused.

"I have," Jack replied. "And talking to Calvin made me aware of that fact."

Ben's eyes widened with surprise. "When did you talk to Vickie's dad?"

Jack stuck the pipe in his mouth as he and Marcus exchanged grins. Ben suddenly felt left out of the loop and called them on it. "Okay, you two. Now that you've sufficiently tortured me, how about filling me in?"

"I asked Jack to call Vickie's dad," Marcus said. "Calvin told me that he's always wanted a small boat and I told him about Jack's and how he sometimes goes over to that boat place in Monroeville and drools over all the new models."

"I don't exactly drool," Jack said, correcting him.

"Anyway," Marcus said, "I asked Jack to call Calvin and invite him to go look at the boats."

"And did you?" Ben asked Jack.

"Yep," Jack replied. "Yesterday afternoon. That's why I had to put off our meeting here until today. First I swung by my place and showed Calvin my boat, which I might add he drooled over a little himself. Then we went over to the place in Monroeville and checked out the newest models, including the one I've had my eye on for quite some time. He really liked it, too."

Ben kicked Magic under the table. "How come you never mentioned this last night when you called me from Vickie's at one AM?"

"Jack told me he'd call Calvin but I didn't know if Calvin ever followed through with it or not. I'm just hearing about it now with you."

Jack got a strange look on his face and Ben asked him what was bothering him.

"Magic," Jack replied.

Marcus asked him what he meant.

"Ben said you were at Vickie's last night," Jack said. "But you told us that her father made her promise not to let you spend the night there anymore."

Ben smiled across the table at Magic. "Go ahead. Tell him."

Marcus turned to Jack, a mischievous grin on his face. "Vickie and I knew her dad might still be checking to see if her car was at my place so we had to come up with a way for me to stay with her."

"But what about the Thai watchdog?" Jack asked. "You said he still might watch her, even if her dad told him not to."

"Right," Marcus replied. "So I had to come up with an angle to get around that. Remember how I told you Sanun was crazy jealous over his wife?"

"Yeah?" Jack said, eyeing him carefully.

"I told a little white lie," Marcus whispered. "I told Sanun that there was a man obsessed with Vickie and that I was afraid he might be stalking her at her apartment."

"And he believed it?" Jack said, acting skeptical.

"He did after I told him who it was," Marcus said.

"Why? Who did you say it was?"

"John."

Jack took the pipe from his mouth and laughed. "The old man that gave Vickie the flowers? But he's in his seventies!"

"I know," Ben added. "I thought it was hysterical, too."

Marcus continued, telling Jack how he convinced Sanun of the lie. "Sanun doesn't know that John is in his seventies. Vickie's never told him the guy's age, only that he talks to her a lot. So then Sanun tells me that he was already suspicious of John, simply because of that fact. He said no man talks to a pretty woman that much without wanting something from her. That alone told me what I wanted to hear, that Sanun assumed John was a younger guy, like me."

"And you found no need to dispel his misconception. Right?" Jack asked.

Marcus replied that he didn't. "Besides, Sanun's the suspicious type already. Even if he does find out how old John is, he'd still think it was possible for John to stalk her."

"Why not?" Jack said, acting like he was enjoying the joke. "The guy may be old but he ain't dead. John might even be flattered to know someone thought that of him."

Marcus continued, telling Jack that Sanun was more than happy to help him with his plan to watch over Vickie in case John showed up. "Then I told him that I'd have to stow my car out of the way so Vickie wouldn't know what's going on and get scared."

Jack put the pipe back in his mouth and snickered. "That way, in case Vickie's dad showed up, he wouldn't see it either. Nice move, Magic. Where'd you end up putting it?"

"Sanun had me hide it behind the storage shed that holds the lawn equipment, at the back of the parking lot. So every night he and I take turns watching her. He takes the shift from five to ten PM, after Vickie gets home from work. He keeps an eye on the parking lot from his place. Then I show up at ten to relieve him and watch the building from my car."

"Yeah, but what the hell are the two of you watching for?" Jack asked. "Or does Sanun stop every young guy that comes near the building?"

"I made up a description of John and gave it to him," Marcus told him. "I also gave him a model of car and plate number to watch for."

Jack remarked that the guy with the real plate number might show up and accidentally get beat up by the Thai watchdog.

"No he won't," Marcus replied.

Jack asked him how he could be so sure.

"Because the plate, model and description are mine," Ben remarked, enjoying watching Jack's reaction as soon as he heard it.

"Yours?" Jack laughed. "You're kidding!"

"Nope. It was the only thing me and Magic could come up with," Ben said. "I'm not going to be doing any stalking at Vickie's place and Sue would kill me faster than Sanun could if I started showing up at Vickie's apartment. It was the perfect solution."

"Yeah, right," Jack replied. "That's what every famous criminal says right before he gets shot or ends up in jail."

Ben told him he was worrying for nothing. "Besides, it's been working great the last few days. Hasn't it, Magic?"

"And how," Marcus replied. "I've even got Sanun bringing me coffee in the morning, after my shift."

Jack nodded his head yes, like he'd just figured it out. "But you don't spend the night in the car, do you?"

AND THE BULL SAVED ME

Marcus shrugged. "Hey, can I help it that Vickie feels sorry for me and invites me up?"

"But what about Sanun?" Jack asked him. "Doesn't he come out and check on you, during the night?"

Marcus told him that he didn't. "I convinced him that doing that might make Vickie suspicious so he only comes out in the morning, after she's left for work about 8:30."

"And giving you plenty of time to sneak back out to the car," Jack said, finishing it for him.

"Exactly. And like clockwork, right after Vickie drives away, Sanun comes out to my car and brings me a hot cup of java. It's better than room service."

Jack sat back in the seat and chuckled. "You better hope he never finds out the truth. Otherwise you'll be looking at the wrong end of that pipe wrench of his."

"He won't," Marcus replied. "Besides, it makes him feel good that he's helping me watch over Vickie. It couldn't have worked out better. Her dad thinks she kept her promise and we still get to be together." He paused and finished the last of his Coke.

"Speaking of Calvin," Ben said, wanting to get back to Jack's revelation about taking Vickie's dad boat shopping. "What happened at the boat place? Did Calvin find one he liked?"

"He sure did. And he bought it."

Ben asked him what kind of boat it was.

"Mine," Jack replied with a grin as he took a sizable drag on his pipe.

"Yours?" Marcus exclaimed. "But why?"

"I never thought you'd get rid of your boat," Ben added, suddenly wondering what kind of persuasive powers Vickie's dad used to talk Jack out his "baby."

Jack told them that Calvin was the reason. "He told me how he's put off his dream of owning a boat for so many years and I realized that I was doing the same thing myself. So I decided not to wait anymore and neither did he. I made him an offer on my boat and he wrote me a check right then. I turned around and paid it down on the new boat. I'm picking it up tomorrow."

Ben reached across the table and slapped Jack on the back. "That's great, Jack! I can't wait to see it!"

"Me too," Marcus added. "And I can't wait to tell Vickie about her dad buying your boat."

Jack glanced at his watch. "You've still got time to call her before Tim shows up for his grilling lesson."

Ben chuckled. "Grilling lesson?"

"I'm teaching Tim how to run the grill," Marcus told him. "Now that Betsy and Mavis are working the morning shift in the daycare center, it put me shorthanded on the grill at night. Tim's going to cover for me." He checked his watch again and commented that he'd better get moving. "I need to stop by WalMart and see if they've got that new Savage Garden CD. I wanna get it for Vickie."

Ben asked him what the occasion was.

"Nothing, really. But I know how much she likes them. I also wanted to get a copy for myself, to play in the new CD walkman she bought me. I've been using it when I have to walk around uptown, running errands." He started to get up from the booth when Ben reminded him about Friday night.

"The shop said we could pick up our tuxes anytime after one."

Jack asked them what the tuxes were for.

Marcus made a face at Ben. "Ben tricked me into taking Vickie to our ten year high school reunion on Saturday. I still think it's a mistake."

"You'll be fine," Ben said, waving him off. "The only animal that's gonna be present is Ken Simmons and he'll be so busy getting drunk and passing out that he won't have time to pick a fight with you."

Marcus told him that it wasn't only Ken Simmons he was worried about. "You both know what I'm talkin' about. I'm not going to relax until it's over and no one has an 'America's Scariest' video showing me catching fire or causing a riot." He then muttered a quick "see you later" and headed for the exit.

Jack scooted down the booth across from Ben and asked him who Ken Simmons was.

"Remember the snipe incident?"

"Uh-huh."

"He was one of the jerks who sent me and Magic into the woods."

"You mean one of the guys the groundhog bit?"

"Yeah, and the damned groundhog should have bit him twice," Ben said, taking a second to take a swig of his Coke. "Simmons has hated Magic for as long as I can remember."

"Why? Because of his *gift?*"

"It started a long time before that. Although Magic's affliction only gave Simmons one more reason to hate him. It all started when we were twelve and went to a carnival over in Barbertown. Magic and I played one of those ring toss games and Magic won a goldfish. They gave it to him in one of those plastic bags with a twistex on it. But the bag started to leak so we put the fish in my empty drink cup so it wouldn't die. Simmons comes along and starts bullying us and knocked me down." Ben paused and thought about it. "You know, it was a few days later that I joined the wrestling team. It really pissed me off that someone could just come along and knock me down like that."

Jack took his pipe from his mouth and pointed it at him. "So basically, you have Ken Simmons to thank for you becoming a state champion wrestler."

Ben blinked at him, not sure he liked the sound of it. "I guess so. But I'd never thank the asshole for doing it."

"Inspiration and motivation come from both sides of the fence," Jack said. "It's not always a happy memory that drives you toward your destiny."

"Well, it wasn't a happy memory for Simmons that day, either. After he knocked me down, he demanded Magic give him his drink. Magic told him there wasn't any soda in the cup but Simmons called him a liar, jerked the cup out of Magic's hand and downed the contents, water, fish and all."

Jack asked him if the kid swallowed the fish.

"Yep. And it got caught in his throat and almost choked him. He was so mad he chased us all the way home. And Magic and I were laughing the whole way. It was classic."

"And are you sure this Simmons guy is going to be at the reunion?"

"I know he is. He's put himself in charge of the decorations. The committee and I figured it was the one thing he couldn't do much damage with."

"What do you mean?"

"Simmons," Ben said. "He's a jerk. He has a reputation for drinkin' and fightin' and reeking havoc wherever he goes. He's been banned from here because he showed up one night at a dart ball game, this was back before you moved to town, and picked a fight with Magic. Terry didn't blame Magic. He was here when it happened and saw that Simmons started it. Magic had just gotten a bull's-eye for our team when Simmons, he was sitting up at the bar, drinkin' and staring at us, starts calling Magic names and telling the entire bar about what a dirty son of a bitch Magic was. Magic tried to ignore it but then Simmons came over and got in Magic's face. Then he started swingin' and all Magic could do was defend himself."

"And did he?" Jack asked him.

"Sure. Simmons has at least forty pounds on Magic but it didn't make any difference. Magic easily put him out of commission. Like I said, all those years of me practicing my wrestling moves on him came in handy. And unfortunately, Magic's had to rely on those moves more than a few times over the years."

"But I've never seen him fight anyone."

"He doesn't much anymore. People are used to his *moments* now. But back when they first stared happening, he got in quite a few fights because of them. People would blame him for the calamities, like he purposely made them happen."

"That's stupid."

"You and I know that but others didn't. Besides, the people usually getting mad were the ones who were made to look stupid because of the *moments*. Let's face it, some of his escapades do tend to make people look bad or put them in situations they'd rather not be in."

Jack chuckled. "Yeah. I've noticed that myself. Kind of a 'personality magnification' effect. How you deal with his *moments* has a way of exhibiting your personality traits."

Ben smiled. "Gee. I never thought about it but you're right. Sometimes they do."

"Sure. Look what it did for Calvin. In that case, it had a positive response."

Ben reminded Jack that not all the responses were positive. "More than once it's happened when I was with him and we both ended up in a brawl because of it."

Jack tapped his pipe into the ashtray in front of him. "Can you tell me about a few of them?"

Ben thought about it for a minute. "Let's see. Some of them I've already told you about. Like the one that happened about five years ago when Magic went to pick up those new brochures for the daycare center that he'd ordered from Mike Cheeseman's printer."

"Oh yeah. The guy that runs the newsstand uptown. Is this the story when Magic picked up Cheesman's box of *Hustler* magazines by mistake?"

Ben told him it was. "The boxes were the same shape and sitting on the front counter but Mike didn't realize Magic took the wrong one until after he left."

"And after a couple members of the cross country team bumped into him outside the door and knocked the box over," Jack added. "Yeah, I do remember you telling me that one."

"It wouldn't have been so bad if the wind hadn't been blowing so hard and blew the magazines all over that school playground next door to the newsstand store. And as usual, Magic's timing was perfect. It just happened to be the exact time when the Catholic elementary school let the kids out for recess. Magic tried to get the magazines back but by then over fifty kids were grabbing them, laughing at the pictures. It took almost an hour to get the nuns to help

Magic round them all up and I heard later that Mike didn't get all of them back, either. Even though the nuns double-checked every kid's desk."

Jack smirked. "Leave it to the Catholic kids to hide something that good. Gotta applaud their determination. Some of the customers still talk about that particular *Magic moment*. A few have even made jokes about that being the only kind of sex ed. classes the Catholic church will ever have."

"The point is, Magic had a couple of rough weeks after that because some of the parents came gunnin' for him. Not to mention a few of the teachers. He never ended up fighting with anyone but I was sure he would. As far as the kids were concerned, Magic was like a hero but the parents didn't share that opinion."

Jack put down his pipe and pushed his root beer glass aside. "Must be why some of the kids call him the Kirklin Pied Piper."

Ben laughed. "No. He got that title after an incident with some birdseed uptown." He told Jack that it was not long after the *Hustler* fiasco. "Sue and I had just moved into our house on Trent Street and Sue was driving me crazy with all the yard work and landscaping. She went out and bought these two hanging bird feeders for the back yard and I was supposed to pick up twenty pounds of birdseed from the pet shop. I got stuck at work and asked Magic to pick it up for me. He did and since the pet store is only a few blocks from my store, he decided to walk it down to me. He had it slung over his shoulder and didn't realize there was a hole in the bag. He started dropping seed behind him as he walked and before long he had a trail of birds swooping down, picking it up."

"That must have looked cute."

Ben told him that what looked cute was the thirty or so kids trailing behind the birds.

"Kids?" Jack said. "What kids?"

"The two kindergarten classes from Kirklin Elementary school. The school is a block down from the pet store and they'd just had a fire drill, so the kids were out in the grass, next to the building."

Jack chuckled. "Magic's impeccable timing again."

"Right. Turns out the two kindergarten teachers were busy with a few kids that took off running towards the other side of the building. The rest of the kids, standing around noticed the flock of birds following this guy down the street and they decided to join them."

Jack laughed. "Too bad you missed seeing that one."

Ben told him he didn't miss it. "I was just leaving the store and saw it. I didn't know what the hell it was at first. Here's Magic, lugging this bag over his shoulder and a bunch of birds swoopin' down behind him and right behind that, thirty or forty kindergarteners. It looked like some kind of weird, half-assed parade coming down the street."

"Didn't Magic even know he had a following behind him?"

"He told me later that he couldn't hear anything because of all the traffic noise coming from the big trucks driving by. And he couldn't see that well because the bag was blocking part of his view. He didn't figure it out until I yelled at him to look behind him."

Jack asked him if the teachers or parents were upset about it.

"Not really. Everyone knew it wasn't Magic's fault. Not even Magic can control what a bunch of birds do. But there are few other times when they did blame him."

Jack told him to go on.

"For instance there was this *moment* that happened at the old pool, the one they tore down and bulldozed a few years ago. There used to a six-foot high fence around the pool and adjoining building. Sue's niece was taking swimming lessons and wanted us to stop by and watch so we did. Magic was with us that day too. So we're all three leaning against the fence watchin' and all of a sudden the fence breaks free and falls on top of the pool."

Jack asked him how big of a section it was.

"About ten feet or so. There was only a couple feet of concrete between us and the pool, so the top few feet of the fence ended up stickin' into the water. Sue and I managed to lean back in time before the fence fell but Magic didn't. He was stuck on it and started to crawl off it when one of the big flood lights, connected to the fence, gave way and fell on top of the fence."

"That doesn't sound good."

"It wasn't. Especially for Magic. The light started sparkin' and once the current hit that fence, it was like watchin' a cat on a hot tin roof. Magic was bouncin' across the fence like crazy, trying to get off it which he finally did a few seconds later. But it didn't end there. Because the fence was now electrified and sticking into the water…"

"Holy hell!" Jack exclaimed. "The whole pool was electrified, wasn't it? Jesus! Were any of the kids in there?"

"No. The class had already let out and everyone was outta the water, thank God. But the sparks were cracklin' and scaring the shit out of everyone there."

"It's no wonder," Jack said. "They were all wet. I'd be scared shitless too."

Ben told him that the cops and fireman showed up and finally shut off the electricity. "But that's when the trouble started. A lot of the parents were there and as soon as they saw Magic, they started accusing him of trying to kill their kids. Three or four of the fathers came after him so I had to jump in and help. I didn't much care for hitting those guys but they seemed determined to kill Magic. The cops stepped in, trying to break it up but by that time, the fight had moved over to where the fence was sticking in the pool. One of the fathers swung at Magic, missed and ended up losing his balance. He grabbed at one of the other fathers, who instinctively grabbed at one of the cops and before we know it, all four fathers and three cops are in the pool."

"But I thought you said the current was already turned off."

"It was," Ben said. "But those guys weren't taking any chances of it being accidentally turned back on. I swear to God, all six of them were out of that water in six seconds. I've never seen anyone swim that fast."

Jack started laughing and then acted like he was ashamed. "I shouldn't laugh. I'd be scared, too."

Ben told him that the fathers wanted to press charges against Magic.

"But they didn't, did they?" Jack said, acting amused.

"Nope. The cops wanted to haul us all in for disorderly contact but Sue and a couple of the mothers finally explained to the cops what happened so they changed their minds. And the parks department didn't want to press any charges. They were afraid of a lawsuit because of the faulty fence. There's been a few other incidents like that and Magic's always been able to hold up his end of a fight, which is strange when you consider that he's a pacifist, like Calvin. Strange how some people end up doin' the thing they hate the most."

"Not surprising," Jack added. "Considering Magic's *gift* and circumstances like that. And you say this Simmons character's always had it out for him?"

Ben replied that he had. "He's a drunk and a mean one at that. He was the one who spiked the punch that got dumped on Magic the last reunion. When Magic set the dance floor on fire."

Jack asked him if he expected trouble this time.

"From Simmons? Always! That's why we let him volunteer to help with the reunion. He's supposed to be on the wagon and we figured letting him do the decorations would keep him busy and out of trouble. But he's making a big production number out of it. He's a partner in that construction business out on route 20 and he's got his men working on some elaborate decoration for the party."

"What is it?" Jack asked, acting quite interested.

"He won't tell us. He's keeping it secret until the party. We figured it must be harmless, so the committee agreed. I'm hoping that it will keep him out of the way."

Jack chuckled. "You mean out of Magic's way."

"Right. Now that Magic's made friends with Vickie's father, the man doesn't need to read any headlines putting Magic in a bad light."

Jack got a gleam in his eye. "Calvin already knows all about Magic."

"What? But how'd he find out?"

"I told him," Jack replied.

"What? But why?"

Jack told him that after Calvin bought his boat, he offered to take him out on the lake to show him how to run it. "He's never used an outboard before. We did some fishing while we were there and the subject got around to Magic. Calvin said he'd been hearing all kinds of crazy rumors about him and wanted to know if they were true."

"Shit!" Ben exclaimed, seeing the parallel. "Just like Vickie, meeting you and me!"

"Exactly. So I figured rather than let Calvin listen to the town gossips, he should know the truth. So I told him."

"What did he think? I hope he's not shopping for a shotgun to go after Magic."

Jack laid his pipe in the ashtray and took a sip of his root beer. Ben knew he was deliberately prolonging the explanation.

"I can wait all day," he told Jack. "My next lesson isn't until four."

Jack grinned and put down his glass. "Calvin was shocked at first but he finally believed me. I told him the same thing you and I told Vickie—how Magic's no threat, just a guy doing the best he can in an extraordinary situation and how it's been going on since his parents got killed."

"Did you also tell him about Magic's theory about what's happening to him?"

"No. But I *did* give him my own theory on it."

Ben smiled, knowing Jack had probably given Calvin Garrett a pretty convincing argument. Jack wasn't only a master fisherman with sea life. He was also a pretty good angler when it came to people. He asked Jack what Calvin thought of the theory.

"He basically agreed with me. He's a good Catholic and Catholics know the importance and existence of things not easily explained by conventional science. He was quite open-minded and he's nobody's fool. He understands about things with a spiritual connotation."

Ben grinned inwardly at his clever choice of words. "Magic doesn't consider what's happening to him 'miraculous' and I'm apt to agree with him on that point."

"Not necessarily a miracle," Jack said, tilting his head to the side. "But it does fall into the realm of the supernatural and even you'd have to agree that it's exceptional. Calvin sees it that way, too." He paused to take a drag on his pipe. "And I believe that Calvin now considers his future son-in-law to be quite an extraordinary fellow."

"Son-in-law?"

"Calvin thinks so, anyway. He knows his own daughter and can recognize that she's in love. He figures it's just a matter of time and so do I."

Ben sat back and ran his hand across the top of his head as he thought about it. It now appeared that Magic was running around in circles for nothing. The girl that he was in love with *and* her father knew all about his secret. "I think we should tell him," Ben said, finally coming to the obvious conclusion. "He's runnin' around like crazy and makin' himself miserable for nothing."

Jack replied that they couldn't. "Vickie's right. Magic's got to learn to trust her. Don't forget. She's going to be living with Calamity James."

Ben snickered. "Calamity James? That's a new one."

"I know. That's what Betsy calls him. But the point is... if they're going to have any kind of life together, Magic is going to have to trust Vickie. That's why she's waiting for him to tell her the truth about his *gift*. I feel like you do. It would be a heck of lot easier if we came out and told him she already knows. But we can't. We're going to have to rely on her judgment, out of respect for what she's taking on."

"So you thinks she's ready for the big commitment with him?"

"I think she's already made up her mind," Jack said. "Now the only obstacle she has to overcome is Magic himself."

Ben threw out his hands in exasperation. "Exactly! So let's tell him and get this over with!"

"We can't. They have to learn to be honest with one another. Remember how I told you how I only learned about honesty *after* I fell in love with Mavis? It's the same thing with Magic and Vickie. Otherwise it's never gonna work out between the two of them, especially if they end up spending the next fifty years together. We're gonna have to hold our tongues and wait for them to work it out." Then Jack paused and got a queer smile on his face. "But that doesn't mean we can't nudge him a little from time to time to make sure he's pointed in the right direction."

Ben saw a problem with the plan. "As stubborn as Magic gets sometimes, it might take a good shove."

"It might just come to that. But one thing is for sure. If they do get together, the next fifty years ought to be damn interesting. Hope Vickie can survive it."

Ben snickered. "I hope to hell the town can survive it. I wonder if disaster relief would cover wasp or frog attacks." He suddenly thought of something. "Hey! This sounds kind of like that twelve Plagues of Egypt thing from the Bible, doesn't it? Maybe there *is* some kind of theologian side to this. I can see it now, biblical prophecies coming true, right here in Kirklin! Locusts and burning hail! Now that would make the papers!"

"God forbid," Jack said, motioning for him to lower his voice. "Let's not start any more rumors."

"Still might not hurt to check on the Internet to see if anyone sells asbestos umbrellas."

"You better hope you don't need one at the reunion. Speaking of the reunion, I wonder if anyone is going to be videotaping it. You know, just in case something does happen."

"I told you," Ben said, grinning slyly. "I'm on the organizing committee. And that was the first thing we made sure of."

Jack waved him off. "You are a juvenile delinquent."

"So are you," Ben replied, knowing damn well Jack would be requesting the first copy. Burning hail aside, *Magic's moments* had already made an appearance at the first and fifth year reunions. To expect them to skip this one wasn't only naïve, it was fool hearty.

Perhaps searching for the asbestos umbrellas wasn't such a bad idea after all.

CHAPTER THIRTEEN

The evening had turned out clear and the stars were just beginning to shine out in the milky light blue mass of sky above the high school parking lot. The complex had been built back in the 70s and at the time the architecture had been considered quite stylish. It boasted three long, one-story buildings for the classrooms and a large, adjoining structure housing the cafeteria and gymnasium area. Ben and Sue walked over to the side entrance of the cafeteria and joined the other couples entering the building for the class reunion. As soon as they went through the entrance, Sue let out a yelp of surprise.

"Oh, my God!" she said. "What is that?"

He knew exactly what she was referring to, the decorations. They were nothing short of bizarre. The walls were strung with multicolored streamers dotted intermittently with beer company paraphernalia and pictures, all leading up to a huge poster of the Clydesdale Horse team located above the empty lunch line steamer tables. Christmas bulb lights bordered the poster and there was an adjoining poster with the words: Welcome Back Class of 1992. Another group of streamers ran from the "Welcome Back" poster over to the two sets of double doors leading into the gym. Sue asked him who was responsible for the spectacle.

"Who else? Ken Simmons. I got a call from three of the organizing committee members while you were getting dressed, bitching about what he'd done."

"But it didn't look like this last night, when we decorated the tables."

"I know. Simmons snuck all this stuff in this afternoon. He kept telling us he had a big surprise for everyone and how he was paying for it himself. We figured it was harmless enough. We should have known better."

Sue tugged at his arm. "Well, at least it's not *too* bad. Only tacky."

"Better hold judgment on that," he told her, nodding toward the gym. "We haven't seen it all yet."

"How could it get any worse than this?" Magic said.

Ben turned and saw Magic and Vickie, coming up behind them. Magic was wearing a black tux and Vickie was in a light blue, knee high chiffon dress. "It gets worse," Ben said, taking Magic aside while Vickie went over to talk to Sue. "Wait 'til you see what's in the gym." He then lowered his voice and added, "See? I told you the black tux would work better."

"After the punch bowl thing last time, I'd have to agree," Marcus said, glancing over at Sue and Vickie. "Sue looks great."

"She should for what she paid for the dress," Ben griped. "But I have to admit, after I saw it on her, it was worth every penny. She was worried she'd be showing."

"Then she's already told you?"

"This afternoon. Looks like I'm finally gonna be a daddy. She told me how you already knew about it. That was pretty cute, the way the two of you kept it secret."

"Well, it sure as hell wasn't easy. I'm not good at lying to you."

Me neither, Ben thought. He suddenly remembered his promise to Vickie and decided to find out if the situation had changed. "Has Vickie found out yet?" he asked Magic. "About your *moments*?"

Marcus's expression turned solemn.

"No. And I already promised Sue that I would tell her tonight."

Ben couldn't hold back the smile. "What do you mean you promised Sue?"

Marcus explained about his and Sue's pact, making the reunion a deadline. "Sue kept her side of the bargain but I'm afraid I can't."

"Why not?"

"I got cold feet at the last minute. I was all prepared to tell her the truth tonight but when I got here, I changed my mind."

Ben tried not to make the next question sound too stupid. "But wouldn't now be the best time to tell her? I mean…in case…"

"In case one of my *moments* shows up? That's what I'm afraid of!"

Ben noticed a queer smile on Vickie's face as she watched them and grabbed Magic's arm, keeping him from seeing it. "Lower your voice," Ben told him. "Otherwise she'll hear you."

"I'm tired of lying to her, Ben," Marcus said. "But I don't want to tell her here, in front of the whole class. Or during one of my *moments*. I want to take her somewhere else, where we can be alone. Then I'll tell her."

Ben asked him where he had in mind.

"My place. But in order to do that, I've got to get her out of here."

"And how do you figure on doing that?"

"I've come up with a plan," Marcus said, leaning in to make sure no one else could hear. "I'm going to give it about an hour, time enough for Vickie to meet some of our friends and then I'm going to develop a bad case of diarrhea…"

"Diarrhea?" Ben laughed.

"Yeah. Diarrhea. Why? What's wrong with that excuse?"

"Nothing but I'd suggest something less…uh…disgusting. You're trying to get a little sympathy, not make her sick."

"Oh, I see what you mean," Marcus replied.

Ben suggested he use "nausea" for an excuse. "I'd say use 'stomach cramps' but then she'd think you were on your period or something. Better yet, just tell her you're sick to your stomach. We're gonna be eatin' in a little bit anyway so that excuse will play."

Marcus replied that he'd try it. "The important thing is to get her out of here before anything happens."

"Like one of your *moments*?" Ben remarked.

"Not only that. I have to keep her from hearing any 'Magic Marker' stories that might be circulating. I don't want someone else telling her before I do. So I'm going to need your help avoiding any run-ins like that. Can I count on you?"

"You know you can," Ben replied, noticing the desperate look on his friend's face. "And maybe your way is the best," he added.

Marcus asked him what he meant.

"I met Scott Akers, just now at the door and he said Ken Simmons showed up drunk. You know how he always goes after you when he's loaded."

"I thought he was on the wagon?"

"Apparently, he fell off. Probably after he got done setting all this up," Ben said, motioning to the tacky decorations. "And Scott warned me that the gym is worse."

"If it's as bad as this, I may not need that 'nausea' excuse," Marcus said. "I'll be sick for real."

They went back to join the girls. Ben smiled when he heard Sue excitedly telling Vickie the good news about her pending motherhood. By the time the night was over, even the cleaning crew would know about it.

The cafeteria was only a fifth as large as the gym and was connected to the hall by a set of double doors. The gym was one and a half times the size of a regular basketball court and the floor was always maintained with a high gloss shine. On the right of the hall were sets of wooden, collapsible bleachers, spanning the length of the gym. At present, they were folded up against the wall, allowing plenty of room for the many tables and chairs to accommodate the two hundred and fourteen graduates and their spouses or dates. On the left side of the gym was a long, stage that went two thirds the distance of the room. The curtains were closed and in front of the stage was a DJ, standing on a wooden platform, behind a couple of tables full of mixing boards and various revolving lights. A Garth Brooks tune came floating out of the two huge speakers, sitting on the floor in front of the DJ's display. Directly to the right of the entrance doors were five or six tables, close up to the wall. They were laden with steamer trays for food, being brought in by servers through the cafeteria kitchen. People were beginning to line up to enjoy the buffet dinner. In the far right corner, on the other side of the buffet tables were a couple of tables, set up to dispense beverages, including three beer kegs, packed in tubs of ice and sitting on the floor. There were over a hundred or so people occupying the fifty odd tables and a few couples were already up on the dance floor.

"Oh, my God!" Sue gasped.

"Is that what I think it is?" Vickie asked.

"It sure as hell is," Ben said, following their gaze across the hall to the largest beer mug he'd ever seen. It sat against the far wall and loomed close to eight feet high. There were baby spotlights on either side of the mug, shining up at the huge display. The "mug" had to be at least ten to fifteen feet around and was filled to the brim with a yellow mixture that bubbled like beer. There was a foot high foam mixture topping the mug. It was a monstrosity. "Scott told me about it," Ben said, still not believing his eyes. "But he left out the part about how big it was. Simmons told Scott that the mug is made of Plexiglas and it's lined with one of those pool liners to hold in the water."

"Then I take it that it's not beer inside?" Sue asked, her mouth hanging open in awe.

"It's water they colored yellow," Ben replied.

"I hope they used food coloring," Marcus snickered. "I hate to think they let the construction crew color it themselves."

"You mean *pee* in it?" Vickie asked, acting appalled.

"Let's hope not," Ben replied. "But maybe we better make sure." He grabbed Sue's arm and guided Magic and Vickie over to a table not far from the mug. As everyone took their seats, Ben noticed Scott sitting at the next table with his wife and Ben proceeded to introduce everyone.

"Scott's one of my old teammates," Ben told Vickie. "He now coaches the JV wrestling team at the high school." He then told Scott about Magic's speculation of how the mug was filled.

"Wouldn't surprise me none," Scott said. "But I was here when they filled it this afternoon. It's food coloring."

Sue whispered a quick "thank goodness."

"The bubbles are from a couple of aquarium filters," Scott told them. "And the foam at the top is marshmallows with a plastic liner separating them from the water. It took Ken's construction crew all afternoon to set it up. Ken calls it a symbolic summation of our class, if you can believe that."

"Maybe for him," Marcus smirked. "And that's only because he spent most of his high school years inside one of those mugs. The rest of us were busy trying to get an education."

"He's still in one," Scott whispered. "He's stumbling all over the hall, bragging about what a great job he did on the decorating. Watch out for him, Magic. You know how he's always got it out for you because of your mishaps."

Marcus glanced at Vickie with a worried expression and Ben knew he was afraid she would overhear Scott's remarks. Ben quickly tried to smooth things over and leaned over to Vickie and Sue. "Uh, why don't we get you girls something to drink?" He took their orders and then prompted Magic to help him. They got up from the table and Ben grabbed Scott's arm and asked him to join them. As soon as they were out of hearing range of the girls he explained the situation to Scott.

"Sorry, Magic," Scott replied.

"No problem. No way you could have known."

Ben explained to Scott about Magic making an excuse to leave. "He's only gonna be here for an hour, so if you could kind of spread the word not to talk about his *moments* it would be a big help."

"Consider it done," Scott replied. Then he smiled strangely at Marcus. "Do you think you can get your mishaps to hold off that long?"

Ben slapped Magic on the back. "We're sure as hell gonna give it the old college try. Right, Magic?"

Marcus nodded but Ben knew he wasn't going to relax until he was safely off the premises.

"Hey, you guys," Scott whispered. "Before you take off, you might want to check out Wendy Mathers."

"Our old wrestling teammate?" Ben asked. "Why? What's wrong with her?"

"Nothing. That's just it!" Scott replied. "She turned out to be a real fox! You ain't gonna believe it!" He began to break off in another direction when he called back to them. "Oh, and, Ben…you better keep an eye on Sue. Tom Kushman looks like he's on the prowl and just stepped out of one of his commercials."

Scott took off across the hall and Ben went with Magic to get the drinks, including a couple beers for themselves. They headed back to their table a few minutes later and Ben balanced Sue's Sprite in one hand while he took a quick swig of his beer.

"Hey, Magic," he said, coming back up for air. "I'd better warn you about something."

"You mean besides, Ken Simmons?"

"It's about me and Sue," Ben whispered. "We talked it over and we want you and Vickie to be the baby's godparents."

Marcus stopped walking as a look of shock filled his face. "Isn't that a bit premature?" he asked Ben. "I don't even know if Vickie and I are going to stay together."

Ben stuck out his arm holding his beer and motioned Magic back towards the table. "That's okay. Sue's sure. And you know how hard it is to talk her out of something once she's got her mind made up. I told her not to bring it up to Vickie yet, but I wanted you to know about it." He paused and regarded his friend. "Don't panic. Just give it some thought. Then you can decide later to ask Vickie." Ben watched him nod with the same worried look and for now that was enough. It was a nudge in the right direction, just like Jack suggested and hopefully, it would make Magic see himself with Vickie in the future. It was a lot harder for someone to give up a dream if their friends were helping them picture it.

"Uh-oh," Marcus whispered. "Scott was right. Kushman's honing in on Sue already."

Ben glanced up and saw what he was talking about. Tom Kushman was occupying his chair and had his arm around Sue. "That guy never learns," Ben grumbled.

"That's because he's never gotten over her," Marcus reminded him.

"She ought to give him a hard elbow in the ribs...no, that's okay. I'll do it."

Marcus started laughing. "I thought you were supposed to be helping *me* stay out of trouble. Sounds like you're brewing up some yourself."

As soon as they walked up to the table, Tom got up from the chair. *Smart,* Ben thought. *Don't let the husband catch you pawing his wife.* Ben sat down the drinks and Tom grabbed his hand and shook it, a little too enthusiastically.

"Hey! How you doin', Ben? You're looking good! Great to see you!"

Ben took his seat and felt his stomach turn as Kushman took a seat across the table and went into his usual oozy charm act, trying to endear himself on everyone within listening distance. The man immediately went into brag mode and for the next few minutes they got to hear the ratio success of his law firm and the details of his last case. Ben felt Magic kick him under the table and knew what he was thinking. Guys like Kushman gave lawyers a bad name, if that was even possible nowadays.

"And who's this pretty lady, Magic?" Kushman said, giving Vickie a wink.

Marcus introduced her and Ben felt his stomach turn again as Kushman kissed her hand.

"How very 'chivalrously medieval,'" Ben whispered under his breath to Sue.

She giggled and patted his leg.

Kushman got up from his chair and asked Vickie if she'd like to dance.

"Uh, that's okay," Marcus said, getting up and taking Vickie's hand. "We were about to try out the music ourselves." And before Kushman could say anything else, Marcus led Vickie out onto the floor.

Kushman glanced around nervously, acting like he was looking for somewhere to escape to. Ben decided to have some fun and asked him to have a seat.

"Oh, okay. But I can only stay a couple of minutes," Kushman said, pulling out a chair and sitting down on the other side of Sue. "So? Ben. You and Magic are still friends, huh?"

Ben replied that they were and always would be.

"And what about Magic?" Kushman said, smiling like a cat that'd just ate a canary. "Is he still doing his 'crash bang' thing and terrorizing the town?"

Ben bit his lip and tried not to show the asshole any anger, in spite of the fact that he'd like to put him in a headlock.

"Magic does not, as you put it, 'terrorize' the town!" Sue said, acting upset.

Nice move, Ben thought, struggling to keep from smiling. *Now you're gonna be sorry. No one puts Magic down in front of Sue.*

Kushman leaned over and put his arm around her. "You know I was only kidding!" he told her, hugging her playfully.

Ben took the man's arm and pushed it back at him.

"Still the jealous type, huh, Ben?" Kushman snickered.

"Always," Ben replied, suddenly picturing the man's head stuck in a vice. "Not only is Magic *not* terrorizing the town," Ben told him. "He's become one of the town's leading businessmen."

"He manages Crystal Lanes," Sue added. "He's made it a great success."

"Really?" Kushman said, putting his elbows up on the table like he was suddenly giving it his own expert examination. "What kind of numbers is he showing?"

"They're good," Ben replied, thinking that it wasn't any of the guy's damn business what Magic's numbers were.

"He's very popular with the teenagers in town," Sue remarked. "The Crystal is their favorite hangout."

Kushman shook his head, like he was agreeing. "Well, it's nice the kids like him. But he should be careful about that. He wouldn't want the wrong element in there."

Ben smiled as he heard Sue whisper a "hmph" of disapproval. Kushman noticed the reaction and tried to make amends.

"I'm not saying that all the kids are bad. But Magic should think about his reputation as a businessman."

"His reputation is stellar," Ben said, enjoying to no end Kushman putting his foot in his mouth. It was one thing to insult an ex-classman. But it was even worse insulting the woman you were still carrying a torch for.

"It's true," Sue replied, acting perturbed at the remark. "Magic is very active in the community. He's always organizing flea markets and fund drives for the kids, to send them to the bowling tournaments and camps. And last year he started a scholarship fund for Kirklin graduates. He got some of the other businessmen to do the same."

"Including Frank Cromwell," Ben added. "And I plan to continue that tradition."

Kushman asked Ben what he was talking about.

"Hasn't Ben told you?" Sue said. "He just bought the music store."

Kushman gave Ben his congratulations and Ben could tell the news wasn't welcome. No doubt the twerp had hoped to find him penniless and struggling so he could rescue Sue from a fate worse than death. He decided to make the guy's day. "Has Sue told you the news? She's pregnant."

"Oh…really?"

The man's expression suddenly went blank. He offered congratulations to them both but Ben knew the guy was secretly loathing the news.

"And how about you, Tom?" Ben asked him. "Any little Kushman's running around yet?"

"No. 'Fraid not. I'm a confirmed bachelor. You know that." Then he paused and glanced lovingly at Sue. "Guess I never got over my first love."

Sue gave him a smile and Ben knew the twerp would eat it up. He decided to let Sue see exactly what a jerk the guy really was. "That's not what I hear," Ben told him. "Someone told me you and Heather Morris are getting married."

Just then Marcus and Vickie came back to the table and Marcus asked them what they were talking about.

"Tom's getting married," Sue said, "to Heather Morris."

Ben almost laughed as Magic slapped Kushman on the back and congratulated him.

"But we're not…" Kushman protested.

"That's not what I heard," Ben added, still trying hard not to laugh.

"When's the big day?" Marcus asked Tom.

"Uh…we haven't set one yet…" Kushman said; twitching nervously like someone had just told him he'd soiled himself.

Ben leaned over to Scott and his wife at the next table and told them the good news. They, in turn, told everyone sitting with them and within a few seconds, all of them were calling out congratulations and well wishes to Kushman.

"Yes…yes…thank you…thank you," the man said, getting up and taking off in a great hurry to the other side of the gym.

"That was hilarious, Ben!" Marcus said, in between laughing.

Sue also began laughing and Ben joined her. He then noticed a confused look on Vickie's face and explained it to her. "Tom's a lawyer in Columbus. He does these really dopey TV commercials for his firm."

"Oh," Vickie said. "I thought I recognized his face."

Ben told her about Tom dating one of their ex-classmates. "Her name's Heather and she had a reputation as being the class nympho. She once bet someone she could sleep with every man on the volunteer fire department."

"She won that bet!" Sue added with a tone of disgust. "It was the class scandal. A couple of the guys ended up getting divorces because of it. I heard that she was still involved with a couple of guys on her squad. They think she's wonderful."

"And why not?" Ben said. "She's a one woman welcome wagon."

Vickie asked Sue what she meant by "her squad."

"Heather ended up joining the volunteer fire department," Sue told her. "Which only made sense since she had all that on-the-job-training."

"On the job training?" Vickie asked her.

"That's what the town gossips call it," Ben smirked.

"It's not gossip. It's fact," Sue said, correcting him. "Everyone in town knows all about Heather's frequent nightly trips to the fire station and it wasn't to learn CPR. It's no wonder they let her finally join the squad. It was much more convenient for her, to not have to do all that sneaking around, avoiding the wives waiting for her in the fire department parking lot."

Vickie laughed. "They didn't!"

"They sure as hell did," Marcus added. "And it was also reported that one of them always brought a gun with her. For a long time, anyone walking uptown at night would cross the street to avoid the fire station, worried they'd accidentally get shot by one of the wives staking out the parking lot."

"Tom doesn't want anyone to know about his involvement with Heather," Ben told Vickie. "He thinks he's the next F. Lee Bailey and is very image conscious."

"Are you sure he's involved with her?" Vickie asked.

"Oh, he's involved with her alright," Scott said as he leaned over from the next table. "The two of them have been seen together at a motel in Mansfield. It's also one of Heather's regular haunts. I guess Kushman figures none of us yokels ever goes to Mansfield and that we're all stupid."

Sue grabbed hold of her cup of Sprite and sighed. "I can't believe I actually had a thing for him once."

"He's still got a thing for you," Ben reminded her. He then noticed Scott and a few others get up and head over to the other side of the gym. He asked Magic if he knew what was going on.

"New arrival," Marcus told him. "See her over there by the DJ's table?"

Ben strained to see through the throng of men making their way towards a shapely woman standing near the DJ's platform. "You mean that woman who looks like Jacqueline Bisset?"

Marcus laughed. "That's not Jackie Bisset. That's your old wrestling teammate, Wendy Mathers."

Ben's mouth dropped open. "You're kiddin' me! Hey, I should go and say 'hi.'" He started to get up when Sue grabbed his arm and pulled him back down.

"Oh, no you don't," she said. "You're not going to be able to get within ten feet of her right now anyway. You can just sit here and keep me company."

He gave her a peck on the cheek, conceding her point. Ben changed the subject and they got back to discussing the news of the other classmates. A few minutes later Sue complained that she was hungry so the four of them went up to the buffet. By the time they got back so many people were crowding in around the giant beer mug that they had to move their chairs to the other side of the table to make room. As they finished eating, Sue remarked that maybe they should move to another table.

"I don't think there's an empty one left," Ben told her. "Besides, we've got our own spotlight sitting next to Ken Simmon's monstrosity. But it looks like some of those marshmallows on top are starting to roast from the rays. Reminds me of those two years I spent working at Carswell's Candy."

"You mean the factory outside of town?" Vickie asked him.

"That's the place," he replied.

She asked what it was like working there.

"Great at first. They let us eat whatever we could carry out in our bellies, as long as that's the only way we took it out. I loved the chocolate covered cherries."

"You sure did," Sue said, patting his belly. "But they didn't love you."

"That's for sure," Marcus told Vickie. "Ben put on twenty pounds. It took a few months of throwing me around on his living room floor, practicing his old wrestling moves to get him back in shape."

Ben suddenly recalled it. "Yeah, and I kept bribing you with those boxes of chocolate marshmallow hearts to do it, the irregular ones I got cheap from the factory."

Vickie asked him what made the hearts "irregular."

"Lots of things. Like if they weren't quite the right shape or if the chocolate wasn't covering the whole thing. And man, were those things a bitch to make. Especially that day the whole crew ended up face first in them."

Vickie laughed. "How the heck did that happen?"

Ben told her about the "enrober" lines, machines with moving belts that took the molded candy pieces from the kettles down the belt to where they were coated with chocolate. "But one day the line broke down so we had to put the marshmallow in plastic heart molds by hand. We used pastry bags and man, was it a sticky mess. No matter how hard we tried, the marshmallow ended up all over everything, our uniforms, shoes and the floor was covered with it. Then one of the cooks, a new guy that just started that day accidentally dropped a ten gallon tub of cleaning water on the floor next to the marshmallow machine. What most people don't know is that marshmallow doesn't mix well with water. The floor became so slippery that no one could stay on their feet. It was like an ice skating rink with no ice skates."

Vickie asked him if anyone got hurt.

"Just the cook that dropped the tub of water."

"Oh," Vickie said. "Did he get hurt when he fell down?"

"Nope," Ben added with a snicker. "The rest of us beat the shit out of him for screwing up. Needless to say, he didn't come back the next day."

Sue scolded him for telling such a story.

"Hey," he replied, not seeing the reason for the objection. "What else were we supposed to do? Thank the guy?"

"You know, Ben," Sue said, huffing impatiently. "Sometimes I think you've got a streak of bully in you." Then she turned her back to him.

"What did I say?" Ben said, confused. "I did what any guy would do, right, Magic?"

"Uh, be right back," Marcus said, avoiding answering the question as he got up from his seat. "Gotta hit the john."

Ben smirked at him. "Wuss!"

"I'm not upsetting a pregnant woman," Marcus called back to him. "And if you intend to, it's going to be a long seven months."

Ben waited until he was out of hearing distance and turned to Sue. "Have you told Vickie, yet?"

"Told me what?" Vickie asked them.

"Magic's uncomfortable here," Ben told her. "He's afraid of what might happen if he stays."

She got a strange look on her face. "You mean like what happened last reunion?"

Sue asked her how she knew about it.

"I've seen the video," she said, giving Ben and Sue a smile. "The same one you threatened him with at your place, Ben. When he had that bad case of hiccups."

I'll be damned, Ben thought. She knew what was on the tape all along.

"I saw a copy Marty got from the kids at school," Vickie explained. "That was quite exciting, wasn't it?"

Sue agreed that it was.

"That's why Magic wants to get out of here," Ben told her. "He's afraid something like that will happen again." He then paused and decided to be honest with her. "The only reason Sue and I talked him into coming was because we were hoping something *would* happen. And when it did, we could help convince him to tell you the truth. We figured if he had us with him, his friends, that it would easier for him." He paused and turned to Sue. "But it turns out he doesn't need us to be here."

"What do you mean?" Sue asked him.

He told them both about Magic's plan to leave the reunion early. "He wants to take you to his place so he can tell you in private," he told Vickie.

Her face lit up with happiness. "That's wonderful! It's what I've been hoping for!"

"His plan is to develop a bad case of stomach cramps in about a half-hour," Ben told her. "He'll probably ask you if you want to stay and ride home with us. But of course, he's hopin' you don't."

"And I won't," she said, acting excited. "I can't wait. I've been working at him from day one, that first date, hoping he would tell me the truth about himself. Now we can get past it and on to the rest of our lives."

"Then you do see a future with him?" Sue whispered.

"Of course," Vickie said, tears of happiness welling up in her eyes. "I love him! I think I'd die without him. I only hope he loves me."

"Don't worry," Ben said, happy for her. "He does."

"But he's never said it," Vickie whispered.

"It's hard for him to say," Sue told her. "Because he's so in love with you."

Vickie asked her what she meant.

Ben tried to explain it. "He's scared of losing you. Because of his *Magic moments*. He was in love with another woman but she couldn't face living with his uh...problem. If you get my drift."

Sue put her hand on top of Vickie's. "But you are, aren't you?"

Ben had to smile at the way Sue was applying her soft coercion. He should know. He'd been the recipient of that same method plenty over the years.

"I am," Vickie told her. "I don't care about his problem. As a matter of fact, I don't consider it a problem. I think it's more of...I dunno...a gift."

Holy shit! Ben thought. Jack had gotten to her. He decided to find out for sure. "Uh...did you talk to Jack lately about Magic's problem?"

"No. I talked to my father. He came over to see me after he went fishing with Jack the other day."

Bingo! Ben thought. The skilled angler was at it again. Reeling in not only Vickie but her father.

"I told my father that I was prepared to meet any problems that might come from Marcus's *gift*," she said.

Sue asked her what her father thought of that statement.

"He had some reservations at first but after I explained to him how much I love Marcus, he supported my decision."

"I'm so happy for both you and Magic!" Sue said, giving Vickie a hug.

Yes! Ben thought, even happier for his best friend. Now all Magic had to do was pop the question and he and Vickie would be all set. Of course, there was one other little obstacle to get past, namely Magic telling her the truth about himself.

Sue began to say something else when she stopped and let out a grunt of disapproval.

Ben followed her gaze and saw what she was looking at. Ken Simmons, standing or more appropriately hanging over one of the beer kegs in the far corner. His two hundred plus frame looked ridiculous in the soiled and rumpled tux he was wearing. He was holding on to the keg with one hand, as though it was supporting him. In his other hand was a large, plastic cup of beer that he would spill on the floor periodically whenever his balance would falter, which seemed to be every few seconds.

"Someone should throw him out and I mean right now!" Sue grumbled.

Scott, at the next table, noticed Sue's comment and got up from his chair. "I'll go and get to a couple of the other committee members," he told Ben. "We'll talk to him and see if we can get him to leave peaceably or at least find someplace to sleep it off."

Ben asked Scott if he wanted him to go along.

"No," Scott said, glancing around. "It'd probably be better if you kept on eye on Magic, to make sure he steers clear of Simmons. You know how the asshole always goes after him when he's drunk."

"Okay," Ben replied. "But if Simmons gives you any shit at all, just holler and I'll get the rest of the wrestling team and we'll throw his ass outta here."

"Don't worry," Scott replied. "I will." And he took off across the hall.

"What did he mean?" Vickie asked Ben and Sue. "About that man coming after Marcus?"

Ben reminded her about the snipe-hunting incident. "The one I told you that day when you met with me and Jack. Ken Simmons is one of the jerks that sent me and Magic into the woods. He tries to pick a fight with Magic every time he sees him. Wait," Ben said, seeing Magic heading back to the table. "Here he comes. Quick. Change the subject."

The three of them quickly got back into regular conversation mode.

"I'll make spaghetti. Magic's favorite," Sue said, acting like she was in the middle of a discussion.

"Another dinner date at your place?" Marcus asked Sue as he took his seat next to Vickie. "Sounds good to me. What night next week do you want us?"

As they began making plans, Ben snuck a peek over at the beer kegs and saw that Scott had taken his advice. He'd taken reinforcements with him to confront Simmons. One…two…no, three of his former wrestling mates stood on either side of Scott as he talked to Simmons. *Uh-huh*, Ben thought. *Simmons is drunk but he's not stupid. He's not about to take on three bruisers, especially the one on the far right, Clem Sommers.* Clem was presently the assistant wrestling coach at the high school and looked in better shape now than when they were in high school.

A group of people heading for the buffet blocked his view and Ben had to wait a few more minutes to find out what happened. Scott came back to the table and Ben got up and took him aside.

"Well, I didn't see Simmons' body flying out over the crowd so I assume he left peaceably," he whispered to Scott.

"He left but it wasn't what I'd call 'peaceable.' He started grumbling about how he deserved to be here like everyone else and that no one was gonna throw him out. I thought for sure he'd start something but once he saw Clem starin' him down, he backed off. Clem and the others escorted him to the exit and we offered to call him a cab but he wasn't havin' any of it. Kept callin' us all a bunch of ungrateful sons a bitches for not appreciating what a nice job he did on the decorations."

"Yeah, nice," Ben smirked, nodding to the beer mug monstrosity. "We'll put him up for a Nobel Peace Prize for decorating."

Scott then told him that Simmons was complaining about Magic. "He was squawkin' that we were only pickin' on him because we're all friends of Magic's and that we're protectin' him."

"Yeah, right!" Ben grumped. "What we're doin' is protectin' Simmons from the rest of the class. He's the one that always starts the fights with Magic and tries turning the reunions into a barroom brawl."

"Simmons wanted more than a brawl this time," Scott said and then he told Ben about how Ken threatened to drive his pickup right into the hall and run over Magic. "Once we heard that, we didn't have any choice. Clem got physical with him and took Ken's truck keys from him. Ken went ballistic after that but he didn't throw a punch or anything. He knows he'd never stand a chance against Clem, drunk or sober. Not to mention your other two teammates. He finally went over to his truck and crawled in the bed to sleep it off. We shouldn't have any more trouble from him tonight."

"Good," Ben said. "Magic is gonna be leaving in a little while anyway so hopefully we've averted any possible disasters."

"Magic's leaving?" Scott said, acting disappointed. "A lot of people are gonna be mighty sorry to hear that. Some of them only showed up because they were anticipating him having one of his adventures. I've got six people armed with video recorders, ready to film in case anything happens."

Ben quickly explained Magic and Vickie's situation and how Magic was about to spring the truth on her.

"You mean she doesn't know?" Scott said and then he started chuckling.

"She *does* know," Ben replied. "But Magic doesn't know that she knows."

"Jesus, Ben!" Scott laughed. "This is better than a movie!"

Ben told him about what was going on and after a good deal of laughter; Scott finally agreed to help him. "Clem and the others are taking turns watching Ken to make sure he stays put. I'll go and make sure it stays that way."

Ben thanked him and headed back to the table.

"Is everything okay?" Sue asked him, a tinge of worry in her voice.

"Fine," he replied, taking her hand. "Now how about we get in a couple dances before I have to take this monkey suit back to the tux shop?" As he helped Sue to her feet he suggested to Magic that he and Vickie do the same. The four of them got up from the table and Ben noticed a worried look on Vickie's face. He took her aside and tried to reassure her.

"Don't worry. It's all been taken care of. The guy's out in the parking lot, sleeping it off."

"You're sure?" she whispered.

"Absolutely. Now go up there and get dancin' with Magic. You've got much more important things to think about."

"But what if that guy comes back?"

"He won't…"

"But what if he does?" she implored.

He could see she was worried about it so he told her that if she even spotted the guy to come and get him. "And in case you're on the other side of the room if it does happen…and I don't think it will…just give me a whistle and I'll come runnin'. Can you whistle?"

"I was the loudest one in the neighborhood when I was growin' up. I've been known to crack glass with it."

"Great," he told her. "Hope I don't see any glass breaking."

"Thanks, Ben," she said, leaning up and giving him a kiss on the cheek.

"Hey! That's my date, Ben!" Marcus said, coming over and grabbing Vickie's hand. "You've already got one."

"Oh yeah. Sorry," Ben replied, guiding Sue out onto the floor.

The dance floor was pretty crowded but no one seemed to mind. The music choices were perfect, an eclectic mix that included not only selections from their era but some newer sounds that were recognizable and easy to dance to. Before long the dance floor was like a giant pulse, moving in rhythm with the lively sounds emanating from the two large speakers and the lights pulsating across the crowd, floor and walls. Ben and Sue had just started their third dance, a slow one when he felt someone tap him on the shoulder. He turned around and saw Wendy Mathers dressed in a striking white gown and looking like she'd just stepped out of a fashion magazine. The gown had overlapping straps that revealed an ample bosom and was cut up the side to reveal her long, lovely legs.

She gave him a perturbed look. "Weren't you going to say 'hello' to your fellow wrestling mate?" She then grabbed him, giving him a bear hug.

"Uh, you're still pretty strong," he said, trying hard not to enjoy the closeness of such a beauty. She let go of him a second later and he felt his face flush with embarrassment. He turned to Sue, waiting to see the all-too-familiar disapproving glare that would appear any time he was enjoying watching another female. But she wasn't frowning. She was smiling.

"Uh...this is my wife, Sue," Ben told Wendy.

"Oh, I remember Sue," Wendy said, shaking Sue's hand. "And I have a confession to make. I was always jealous of you because you were dating the guy I had a crush on." Wendy turned and gave Ben a wink. "You never knew, did you?"

He felt his mouth suddenly go dry. "No. I had no idea."

"Don't worry about it," Wendy said. "I finally got over you."

Too bad, Ben thought with a smile.

She then introduced the man she was dancing with as her husband, John. John looked like a wrestler himself and had the good looks to match the muscles. Wendy told them that she and John ran a gym in Columbus and that she was starting a girls wrestling team.

"Why don't we have a seat and catch up on old times?" Ben suggested.

The four of them headed back to the table and Ben glanced back, checking on Magic and Vickie. They were slow dancing and Magic had his head turned away so Ben mouthed the words "We'll be back at the table" to Vickie. She gave him a smile and thumbs up, signaling that she got the message.

"Are they okay?" Sue asked Ben.

He told her they were. Then he noticed Wendy again, walking in front of them. The soft curves of her shapely body showing through the dress as she walked made his pulse race. "You should get a dress like that," he whispered to Sue.

"Oh, sure. After all the trouble you gave me about spending money on this one? Besides, in a couple of months I wouldn't be able to wear it."

"You'd look great and I wouldn't care how much it costs."

She stopped and turned to him, a look of such love in her eyes that it made his heart ache. "Do you know happy what you just said makes me?" she whispered, taking his hand and squeezing it.

He pulled her close and kissed her cheek. "You've always made me happy," he told her. "Don't you know that?"

"I always suspected," she replied, giving him a hug. "But it's still nice to hear you say it."

He put his arm around her and led her back to the table, feeling pretty good about himself. So far the night had been shaping up pretty well. None of *Magic's moments* had showed up and now it looked like Ken Simmons had been put out of commission so the chance of a fight breaking out was quickly diminishing.

It looked like it was going to turn out to be a fun but uneventful reunion.

A first.

He and Sue got reacquainted with his former wrestling mate and her spouse and Ben soon found out he and John had a lot of the same interests. It wasn't long before they were making plans to go to Columbus to visit Wendy and John's gym. Ben temporarily forgot about Magic and Vickie. It was only after their second round of drinks with Wendy and John that he noticed they still hadn't come back to the table. He glanced around the room and finally found them, still out on the floor, dancing to a slow tune.

"Look at them," Sue whispered.

"I know," Ben said. "I guess Magic decided to stay."

"That's not what I mean," she said, acting annoyed. "Look at how they hold each other. They're both in love. It's so obvious."

Wendy asked them who they were talking about.

"Magic," Ben said.

Wendy began smiling excitedly and told John. "That's Ben's best friend, the one I was telling you about."

AND THE BULL SAVED ME

"The one that all the disasters happen to?" John asked, acting very interested.

Wendy prompted Ben and Sue to tell John about Magic. Ben was more than happy to oblige. Unlike some of the other kids from their class, Wendy had always treated Magic with respect and friendship, probably due to the fact that she too, was an outcast because of her wrestling abilities. He and Sue spent the next half-hour telling John and Wendy about some of Magic's more amusing *moments*—a top ten list from the last ten years. They laughed and enjoyed themselves so much that Ben didn't even notice the whistling noise coming from the dance floor a little while later. He stopped talking and listened closely.

There it was again.

"That's Vickie!" Sue said, her voice full of alarm.

Shit! Ben thought as he bolted from his seat and hurried towards the dance floor.

"Be careful!" Sue called after him.

Almost everyone in the hall was looking in the direction of the dance floor and a crowd was quickly gathering. Vickie was standing not far from one of the DJ's speakers, whistling and motioning at Ben to help. As he pushed past the people towards her he noticed a circle of observers on the dance floor. The scene resembled an old schoolyard fight, with two opponents grappling each other in the middle.

Magic and Ken Simmons.

Ben asked Vickie what happened.

"We were taking a break from dancing and went over to get something to drink when that Simmons guy started calling Marcus names. I think Marcus was afraid I'd find out about his secret so he ignored the guy. We went back out on the dance floor but the guy followed us. He couldn't get Marcus to fight him so he started making nasty comments about me."

"What kind of comments?"

She pulled him down and whispered into his ear, "He asked me if I liked fucking freaks. Marcus heard it and hit him."

"Oh," Ben said, understanding Magic's provocation. He watched the two of them trade blows. Simmons was too drunk to put anything on his punches but Magic was connecting with almost every hit. Simmons stumbled to his feet and began retreating to the right, trying to get away. The circle of people opened up to give him room and then it closed back up as Simmons neared the first row of tables, next to the dance floor. It was then that Ben saw Sue, standing near one of the tables in front of the giant beer mug. She hurried over and joined him and Vickie.

"Are you all right?" Sue asked Vickie.

"I'm fine. It's Marcus I'm worried about." She turned to Ben and pleaded with him. "Can't you stop it?"

"No need. It's almost over." He couldn't make her understand that with men like Ken Simmons, it wouldn't do any good to stop it. If Magic walked away now, Simmons would get up and go after him again. The only way to stop the jerk was to knock him out.

"You sum bitch!" Ken yelled, swinging wide at Marcus, missing him by a mile and causing Ken to lose his balance and almost fall. He regained his footing and took another swing at Marcus. Marcus easily ducked out of the way and landed another right hook to Simmons abdomen, causing him to double over and stagger backwards, to the right. He was now in front of the beer display and leaned back against the Plexiglas for support. He was breathing hard and looked close to passing out, but there was still some fight left in him.

"Fucking jinx!" he said, spitting the words at Marcus. He lost his footing again and crumpled to the floor like a marionette puppet whose strings had gone slack.

"Piss off!" Marcus said, lowering his fists and turning his back to the man. As he walked away a few of the onlookers patted him on the back and congratulated him.

"Nice job, Magic," someone called out. "You sure showed that drunken asshole what for."

Ben watched his best friend walk towards him, impressed with how calm he looked. His tux was devoid of any of the blood, in spite of the fact that Simmons' nose was bleeding profusely and Magic's hair didn't even look disheveled.

"You look like you just stepped out of GQ instead of coming from a fight," Ben told him. Then he leaned in and whispered, "But I think it's about time to develop those stomach cramps, Magic. Before anything else happens."

"To hell with the excuses," Marcus said. "Vickie and I had already decided to head home when that jackass started his shit. We're plenty ready to go."

Ben decided it was time for him and Sue to cut out, too. She was standing a few feet away, talking with Vickie. He started towards them when he saw Sue's face go ashen with fright.

"Ben! Behind you!" she screamed. "Lookout!"

He'd no sooner turned his head when a fist went flying past, an inch from his face. It was Ken. Ben ducked down, out of sheer instinct as Simmons's fist followed through and went towards Magic's face. Magic threw up his arms, easily avoiding the blow and once again Simmons staggered backwards, almost losing his balance. He found his footing again a few seconds later and threw up his fists, ready to fight again.

"Sumbitches!" the guy croaked, staggering forward towards Magic and Ben. "I'm gonna git both of yas!"

Ben started towards the guy when Magic put out his arm and stopped him.

"No, Ben," Marcus told him. "Leave the pleasure to me."

Ben did as he asked and watched as Magic turned to face the guy.

"Come on, freak!" Simmons yelled at Marcus. "Let's see what you got!"

Both of them began going for each other when Vickie jumped in front of Marcus, almost as though she was trying to protect him.

"Leave us alone!" she screamed at Simmons.

Simmons eyed her up and down and laughed. "Shurr, baby! Ish nobody's bushnis if you wanna fuck freaks like that! Guess that makesh you a freak, too!" Then he began laughing like it was a big joke.

Ben started to go for the asshole when he Magic grabbed his arm to stop him.

"Get Vickie out of here!" Marcus yelled and then he leapt at the drunken bully.

Ben grabbed Vickie around the waist and pulled her out of harm's way as Magic laid into Simmons with a vengeance. He'd never seen Magic so angry and the punches came fast and furious. Simmons began to resemble a used up punching bag as Magic pummeled his upper body and torso. The man had salvaged enough presence of mind through the alcoholic haze to throw his arms across his head and face, protecting himself from the worst of the blows. They were now grappling in front of the giant mug and the crowd had gathered again, watching the fight. Ben guided Vickie and Sue back behind the mug to make sure they were safely out of the way.

"You goddamned freak!" Simmons yelled, suddenly coming out of his defense mode and throwing a punch at Marcus's face. But the man's reactions were sluggish enough that Marcus was easily able to avoid getting hit. The fact that he missed seemed to infuriate the drunken brawler and he lunged at Marcus, stumbling over one of the aquarium cords, pulling it out of the mug and causing the filter to fall off the top of the Plexiglas rim of the mug.

"Watch out!" someone yelled and several people jumped back as the filter crashed to the floor, breaking apart upon impact.

Marcus landed a punch to Simmons gut and the man rammed into the side of the mug with such force that the lining on the top, holding the marshmallows, began to slosh around, shifting towards the rim. The lining slowly began to slide over the top of the mug and someone, trying to be funny yelled out a "Watch out! It's gonna blow!"

A woman standing near the mug, called out to Ken Simmons to look out for the marshmallows, about to fall on top of him.

"What fucking marshmallows?" Simmons bellowed at her. He'd no sooner said it when he threw another wide angled punch at Marcus's face, missing him.

"Goddamn it! Stand still so's I can hit ya!" he yelled at Marcus. He then somehow mustered up some energy and swung at Marcus again, doing it quickly enough so that he managed to hit Marcus in the right side. But because of Simmons's inebriated state, there wasn't much on the blow and Marcus reeled to the side a bit but quickly regained his balance.

"To hell with this!" Marcus muttered angrily, pulling back his right fist. He sent it forward, landing a huge upper cut to Simmons chin, causing the man to reel backwards, crashing into the seam of the Plexiglas making up the mug. The seam began to separate, causing the plastic lining behind it to bulge out between the cracks. Simmons, semiconscious but still hanging on, clung to the side of the seam, trying to stand up. But as he pulled himself up, he didn't see that he was opening up the seam wider. The liner bulged out, looking like a bubble about to burst. The marshmallow foam at the top sagged down dramatically into the mug as the seam split open wider. A man near Ken yelled at him to stop pulling on the seam.

"Wha' the fuck ya talkin 'bout?" Simmons yelled back at him, still acting dazed from the uppercut. An instant later he lost his balance again and reeled backwards. He was still holding on to the seam edge and the weight of his body caused the opening to widen a couple more feet.

"Look out, everyone!" Ben yelled at the bystanders as he saw what was coming.

The people began quickly backing up as the top of the liner sagged over, sending the water over the side. Ben grabbed Sue and pulled her back out of the way. He then reached out with his free hand to grab Vickie, but she escaped his grip and ran over to Marcus, standing in front of the split in the mug, with his fists up, waiting for Simmons to come at him again. She grabbed him by the shoulders, pulling him backwards, just as the liner collapsed. People took off in every direction, trying to get away as the Plexiglas gave way completely, the liner crumpling up, spewing forth the yellow liquid across the gym floor. Along with the water came the marshmallow foam, mixing and sliding across the floor like a miniature snow avalanche.

The hall was filled with the sound of people yelling and tables and chairs being knocked down from the throng of well-dressed couples making a mad dash for the exits. Ben watched with fascination as the marshmallow and water mix slid along the gym floor and out into the cafeteria. As the torrent slopped towards the DJ's display, the man jumped down from the foot high platform and shoved one of the two large speakers backwards, onto to the platform, trying to keep it dry. He then slipped and slid over to the other one and cursed as the water beat him to it, sloshing inside the huge speaker, sending sparks flying across the floor. He lunged at the speaker, yanking the electric cord from the back and throwing it onto the platform, the only dry item left in the area. He then shoved the speaker back, on top of the platform like a dead weight. He tried to stand back up but hit a spot of marshmallow with his shoe, causing him to fall down hard. He sat in the water, gesturing with his fist at the now empty beer mug, cussing at the top of his lungs. But his words were drowned out by the music, which somehow was still emanating from the rescued speaker.

Ben asked Sue and Vickie if they were okay.

"I'm fine," Sue replied, straightening out her dress.

"We're both okay," Vickie said. "But where's Marcus?"

Ben looked up and spotted him, a few yards away, by the split in the mug, helping Ken Simmons to his feet. Ben went over to help him. The task wasn't easy considering that the booze and slippery floor hampered the man's equilibrium. He was also having trouble focusing because one of his eyes was swollen shut.

"It washent supposed to cum apart like that," Simmons muttered as Ben and Marcus helped him to his feet. "I dunno how tha couda happent." Ken's footing started to falter but Marcus caught him in time and stopped him from falling down again.

"Darn nice of you," Ben whispered to Marcus. "Considering you're the one who beat the shit out of him."

"I just didn't want him to get electrocuted," Marcus replied. "Those lights are still plugged in and laying in the water."

Ben saw his point and helped Marcus lead Ken to the wall behind the mug, where the polished floorboards had somehow managed to stay dry. The man slumped to the floor like a rag doll and a beat up one at that. Ben and Marcus then went searching for the lights and any other electrical appliance that might be hooked to the display. As they finished checking everything out, Ben heard Marcus let out a slow whistle.

"Holy shit!" Marcus said. "You were right about a skating rink, Ben. Look at it!"

Ben felt his mouth fall open as he looked out, across the gym. It was just like that day at the candy factory. Everyone was slipping and sliding, trying to stay on their feet and most weren't succeeding. The women were getting the worst of it; probably because of the high heels most of them were wearing not being able to support them in such an environment. Women in formals were falling down everywhere and being helped up by their significant others, who were finding it extremely difficult to stay standing and also help their lady loves.

And as usual for one of Magic's *moments*, the reactions to the incident covered the entire emotional spectrum, ranging from laughter to outright hostility. In Magic's favor was the fact that a lot of the couples had consumed several drinks, making them more receptive to an adventure. If they still felt that way in the morning was another matter. Also in his favor was Magic's reputation. Because incidents had happened at the previous two reunions, a lot of their classmates showed up, *expecting* something to happen so it was no big surprise for a lot of them.

It seems they got their wish.

"Let's get out of here," Marcus said. "Before anything else happens."

Ben laughed. "Like what? Locusts? Burning hail?"

"Like someone coming up to Vickie and telling her about how the *The Kirklin Klutz* has done it again."

"Oh," Ben replied. "I see your point."

They went over and got Sue and Vickie and set off towards the exit. The floor was still treacherously slippery but a few of the overturned tables and chairs had blocked the marshmallow/water mixture in spots by the folded up bleachers, allowing fairly safe passage. The dry areas were very narrow so they had to travel single file. It took a few minutes but they managed to make it over to the cafeteria without anyone taking a spill. Quite a few of their classmates had also made it to safety and were standing around, trying to clean the sticky water mixture from their clothes.

The women, especially the ones wearing formals, were giving Marcus dirty looks so Ben knew it was best to avoid any confrontations.

"Uh, let's stand over here under the Clydesdale sign," he told the others, also giving Marcus a nudge in the side to alert him to the approaching hostility.

"No one's there and we'll be out of the way when the firemen get here."

"What firemen?" Vickie asked.

As if on cue, the sound of approaching fire engine horns filled the air.

"Oh," Vickie said.

One of the guys, cleaning off his clothes a few yards away, looked up and called to them. "Hey, Magic! This was the best reunion disaster yet! Can't wait to see the video!"

Marcus turned to Ben. "Oh Shit!" he whispered. "Here come the *Magic moment* comments, Ben! Vickie's sure to hear them now."

Ben knew he had to diffuse the situation and quick. He took off after the guy, to shut him up. But Scott beat him to it.

"I'll handle it," Scott told Ben. Then he put his arm around the guy and started whispering to him.

Ben glanced around and noticed quite a few people staring in Magic's direction and knew if they didn't leave soon, Magic's secret would be out for sure. It didn't matter if Vickie already knew the truth. Magic expected to tell her himself. Not have her learn it from someone like Ken Simmons.

"Come on," he said, going over and taking Sue's arm as he nodded to Vickie and Marcus. "Let's get going."

They headed for the exit but had no sooner got there than the fire truck pulled up to the curb, sirens blasting away. A few people were holding open the doors, to allow the firemen access. Five or six of the firefighters jumped down from the truck and came running in. Two of the men were hoisting a sizable fire hose and as they entered the hall, a man standing by the cafeteria counter yelled at them.

"We don't need any water. We got plenty already. The mess is in the gym!"

The six firefighters headed for the gymnasium and Ben edged his way out in front of Sue, trying to push his way past the crowd gathered at the door. But all the people that had been standing outside, about thirty of them, followed the firemen back into the building to see what was going on.

"It's too crowded here," Ben called out, trying to be heard over the noise. "And the fire hose is in the way. Let's try the exit over by the restrooms."

"Okay. Lead the way," Marcus told him.

Ben grabbed Sue's hand and began making his way through the throng of people. As they neared the cafeteria doors, the crowd thickened to the point where it was almost impossible to pass. He paused by the door and stole a glance into the gym. There were only about twenty or so people left and the firemen were helping them towards the exits. But in spite of their firefighters regulation boots, they too were falling victim to the slippery marshmallow mess. Every few seconds one of the firemen and whoever they were helping could be seen, their feet flying out from under them as they went momentarily airborne and then crashed to the floor.

"Reminds me of those Keystone Cop movies we used to watch when we were kids," Ben told Marcus. It was then that he noticed quite a few people, crowded around the two sets of double doors, leading in to the gym. All of them were laughing and seemed to also be enjoying the site.

"Now that alone was worth coming to the reunion for," a voice said behind them. It was John, Wendy's husband. The two of them were standing together, a few feet away. Ben took Marcus and Vickie over and introduced them.

"Oh, I remember Magic well," Wendy said, leaning over and giving him a hug. "He and I used to try and come up with wrestling moves to outsmart Ben."

Marcus let go of her and smiled. "And as I recall, we never did."

"Nope. Probably why he made the championships and I never did," she replied. One of their ex-classmates walked up and started to ask Marcus something when Wendy interrupted the man.

"Sorry, guys," she said. "But I really need to pee and can't remember the way."

The man immediately volunteered to show her and she grabbed hold of his arm and turned to Vickie and Sue. "How about you girls? You're pregnant, Sue, so I know you have to go. Wanna join me? It appears I now have an escort."

Vickie and Sue quickly agreed.

"And how about you, Magic?" Wendy asked him. "We're probably gonna need an escort back. Wanna volunteer?"

"Sure," he said, taking Vickie's arm and following behind them.

As the five of them disappeared into the crowd, Ben asked John how he was enjoying the reunion.

John laughed. "It's definitely not your usual boring reunion, is it? When Wendy told me all those 'Magic Marker' stories, I thought she was pulling my leg." He paused and glanced around the room. "Guess she wasn't kidding."

A few seconds later Wendy reappeared but without the others.

"That was fast," Ben commented.

"I ducked out of the bathroom when no one was looking," she said. "I only made up that excuse about having to pee to protect Magic. That guy that escorted me to the john and some of the others were making comments about what happened at the last reunion so I was trying to keep Magic's girlfriend from hearing it."

"She already knows about him," Ben said. He told her about his promise to Vickie and how Magic was finally going to tell her truth. "But he doesn't want to do it here. As soon as they get back, we're gonna leave." He paused and looked around at the people. "That is, if we can make it through this crowd."

Wendy and John quickly volunteered to help out by running interference. "Wendy and I will lead the way." John said. "And then we can stop anyone from asking Magic or his girlfriend any questions."

"Especially any of those people Tom Kushman's been talkin' to," Wendy added.

Ben asked her what she was talking about and Wendy told him that Kushmn had been going around the room, trying to start trouble for Magic.

"What kind of trouble?" Ben asked, his worry level returning.

"Legal trouble," Wendy replied. "Almost everyone seemed okay with what happened at first. Some of the women were upset about getting their dresses soiled but none of them acted like they were holding a grudge against Magic."

"One of the guys even laughed about," John added. "He told his wife she should have expected it, knowing Magic was coming."

"And they should have," Wendy added. "Look at me. I wore this old gown because I didn't care if anything happened to it or not."

Hmmm, Ben thought, admiring Wendy's shapely curves again. The gown didn't look old. But maybe that was because of what was in it.

Just then Scott came walking up to them. "You guys talkin' about Kushman?"

Ben told him they were. "Apparently, no one is upset by this latest *Magic moment* but him."

"I know," Scott said. "He's been griping to everybody that his suit is ruined beyond repair and that people should sue Magic for the damage done to the clothes and medical bills."

"Medical bills?" Wendy grumbled. "That's a crock! John and I talked to some of the firefighters and they said no one was hurt. Not even a scratch. That fact didn't seem to surprise them, either. One of them said no one ever gets hurt during his *Magic moments* so I guess you were right about that, Ben."

"Everybody in Kirklin knows that," Scott added. "And so do the few people complaining about Magic. The only reason they're making a stink is because Kushman is putting on his TV face, acting like he's holding court and promising them he'd help them file suit against Magic and get them a cash settlement."

Ben shook his head, not surprised. "Figures the jerk would try to capitalize on Magic's problem. He always was a little slime ball."

Wendy told them Kushman was also griping that the Reunion Committee should be compelled to ban "a certain known menace" from further reunions.

"In other words, Magic," Ben replied.

"What the hell's he talking about menace?" Wendy griped. "That jerk Kushman used to call me 'butch' behind my back at school, him and Ken Simmons both. More than once I wanted to get them out on the wrestling mat and show them exactly what a 'butch' could do to them!"

"You should have," John sneered. "Maybe then those same jerks wouldn't have tried hitting on you tonight."

Ben smiled and asked her if it was true.

"They did!" she said. "And right in front of John! First Kushman and then Simmons, not long after that. I had to hold John back from taking a punch at them. What a couple of goddamned hypocrites."

"Yep. That's our fine, upstanding ex-classmates for you," Scott quipped.

"Poor Magic," Wendy sighed. "How he's ever managed to put up with shit like that for ten years is beyond me. Why can't people leave him alone, for Chrissakes? Obviously, they have no idea how much it hurts to be branded an outcast."

Ben leaned over and gave her a kiss on the cheek. "Thank you," he told her, deeply moved. "It was nice to hear someone else say it."

She blushed and gave him a hug.

"Excuse me, he's taken."

It was Sue. She put her arm through Ben's and winked at Wendy. "You may be the belle of the ball but you can't have this one."

Ben gave Sue a peck on the cheek. "Nice having two gorgeous women fighting over me," he whispered to her. It was then that he noticed that Sue was alone. "Where's Magic and Vickie?" he asked her.

"Taking a tour of the classrooms or more accurately, the halls since all the rooms are locked. Actually, I think Magic's only biding time until people leave so Vickie won't hear any *Magic moment* comments."

"That may play to our advantage," Ben said and then he told her about how Wendy and John had volunteered to help them exit the building.

"Thank goodness," Sue said. "And we definitely need the protection. I had my hands full just going to the restroom with them. Three people came up to us and started congratulating him on what happened."

"About tonight's *Magic moment*?" Ben said.

"No, about him beating the shit out of Ken Simmons. Apparently, everyone in town hates the jerk. But you should have seen Magic's face when they started congratulating him. He was scared to death. He must have thought they were talking about his *Magic moment*. The sooner we get him and Vickie out of here the better."

"That may not be easy, considering what Tom Kushman is doing." And Ben explained to Sue about what Kushman was up to. "So it looks like getting out of here without a confrontation isn't an option any more. Any chance we can sneak out one of the classroom windows?"

"You may not have to," Scott said.

Ben asked him what he had in mind.

"Remember how uncomfortable Tom got when we asked him about his involvement with Heather?"

"Yeah?"

"Well, I was talking to Mark Schaeffer..." He paused and told Wendy and John that Mark was one of the firemen on Heather's squad.

"And also one of the guys Heather is still involved with," Sue added.

"Anyway," Scott said. "Mark said Heather's been telling all the guys on her squad that she and Tom really are getting hitched."

Ben smirked. "No doubt, promises Tom made while he was under the sheets with her. Everyone knows he's not about to jeopardize his TV image by marrying her. It'll never happen."

Scott smiled. "No, but nothing says we have to tell everyone that, right?"

Ben suddenly realized what he was getting at. "That might work," he told Scott. "And it would give us a long enough diversion to sneak Magic and Vickie out of here. Let's do it."

Ben took Sue's hand and had Scott, Wendy and John follow him over to the cafeteria doors. As he whispered to everyone what to do, he glanced in to where some of Heather's squad mates were busy in the gym. Three or four of the school custodians had been called in and were busy with mops and buckets, cleaning up the floor.

The only people left in the gym, besides the fire squad and custodians, were the DJ who was busy packing up his equipment and Ken Simmons. Ken was sitting in a chair near the catering tables and two of the firemen were trying to keep him in the chair while they examined him. But they were having a difficult time and not because of the slippery floor which the custodians had now rendered harmless. It was because of Ken's inebriated state and the fact that he couldn't sit in the chair without periodically weaving from side to side, trying to fall out of it.

The other four members of the fire squad were now heading towards the cafeteria and Ben quickly motioned them over to the door.

"What's up?" Mark Schaefer asked him, pausing to shake some of the marshmallow mixture from the helmet in his hand.

"Just thought you guys would like to hear the good news," Ben told him and then he nodded to Scott and Sue.

"It's about Heather," Scott said. "Tom Kushman announced to everyone tonight that he and Heather are getting married."

"Yes," Sue added. "We wanted to congratulate her. Isn't she on duty tonight?"

"No," the guy standing next to Mark said. "Tom told her she couldn't come to the reunion with him—"

"Uh…Never mind about that," Mark said, cutting the guy off. "Heather was feeling a little under the weather tonight. That's why she didn't come to the reunion." Then he started smiling full face. "But that's great! She's been telling us for weeks that her and Tom were gettin' hitched!" Then he turned to the others. "Isn't that great, guys?" And all of them nodded enthusiastically.

"We've all been congratulating Tom," Ben added. "Thought you guys might want to as well. He's right over there." And he pointed to Kushman, standing across the hall, talking to a group of people standing under the Clydesdale sign.

"We'll just do that!" Mark said, motioning to the others to follow him.

As they took off across the room, Ben joined Sue, Scott and the others and laughed.

"We're ready to leave," Magic said, walking up to them with Vickie on his arm. There was a strange look on Magic's face so Ben asked him if something was wrong.

"No, nothing," Marcus replied, acting like he didn't want to talk about it. Marcus asked Ben what was going on.

"We've come up with a diversion to get you and Vickie out of here," Ben said. Then he filled him in on what was going on. "Come on," Ben said, grabbing Sue by the arm and leading the way. "We're not gonna want to miss this."

The seven of them made their way over to where Kushman was holding "court." But it wasn't at all like his TV commercials. It was the man's worst nightmare. The four guys from the fire squad were not only congratulating Tom on his upcoming nuptials, they were also spreading the news to everyone in the vicinity, which included most of the graduating class. The results were nothing less than comical as more than a few of the women scowled disapprovingly at Tom. Comments like "How can he possibly marry that slut" and "That outta boost his TV ratings" could be heard whispered throughout the crowd. But the four happy fire quad members didn't notice the comments and took the news as nothing short of a Super Bowl victory. They slapped Tom on the back and kept telling him "What a lucky man he was" and "What a great girl Heather was."

Ben and the others paused to listen to Kushman get his just desserts.

"I would have paid to see this," Scott quipped.

"Yeah, and look at the jerk," Marcus added. "He's completely stuck. He doesn't dare disagree with those bruisers or tell them that it's not true."

"Not unless he wants to have his nuts for lunch," Ben commented. "And I would've paid to see that, too."

Kushman was now surrounded not only by the fire squad but quite a few of their fellow classmates who seemed to be enjoying the news that the TV lawyer was now going to be wedding the town slut. But the best part came a few minutes later, when one of the squad members informed Tom that he was having his brother-in-law put an item in the Kirklin paper announcing the good news. As soon as the guy said it, Kushman's face went white with fright and he bolted from the crowd, looking like he was about to be sick.

"Now that was damned entertaining!" John chortled. "You were right, Wendy. This was fun."

Ben and the others broke out laughing, as did quite a few of their classmates.

"Yep," Ben added, still chuckling. "I can't wait to get Monday's paper and read all about the engagement."

"And won't Heather be surprised?" Sue added, causing everyone to break out laughing again.

Scott stopped laughing long enough to tap Ben on the arm. "Hey. Here comes another floor show."

Ben looked over to where Scott was indicating and saw the last two firemen helping Ken Simmons cross the room. The firemen were holding up the drunken alumnus who was telling them about how his company "Shuplied the chiant beer mug" and how it was "All hish idea."

"Now there's a good advertisement," Marcus smirked. "Let me get Tom Kushman back here and see if he wants Simmons to do the decorations for his upcoming wedding."

The remark made everyone in the area laugh and Simmons quickly noticed the joke at his expense.

"Therrs the guy!" Simmons growled, pointing a shaky finger at Marcus. "He'sh the one whoosh responsible for thish!" He then jerked hard, breaking free from his two keepers and lunged at Marcus. Marcus's head was turned, talking to Vickie.

"Watch out, Magic!" Ben yelled.

But it wasn't quick enough. Just as Marcus began to turn, Simmons crashed hard into his back, shoving him directly at Vickie and sending them both sprawling to the floor. Ben started towards them when a white blur streaked past him, leaving a breeze in its wake. A second later someone jumped on top of Simmons, slamming him so hard against the floor that the thud could be heard across the room.

It was Wendy.

Everyone rushed forward to see the former "butch" turned beauty queen slam dunk the class bully. It was almost bizarre, watching the lovely legs and arms wrapped around the bloated bully, putting him in a full body lock. His face was scrunched up, locked inside Wendy's arm and elbow. He began pleading with her to let him go, his voice sounding shaky, as if his breathing was being hampered. It was then that Ben saw Wendy's left knee, bent and positioned against the man's larynx.

"Great move, Wendy!" Ben told her. "He never knew what hit him."

Wendy released her quarry a few seconds later and the man lay slumped upon the floor, like a dead cow carcass.

"How's that for an encore?" Wendy said, getting to her feet and brushing off the front of her dress, like she'd just stepped out of a car instead of putting down a two-hundred-plus-pound drunk.

The entire room broke into applause and people rushed up to her, congratulating her on the feat. *And why not?* Ben thought. It was the perfect ending to the reunion. The alumni of 1992 finally got to witness the class bully getting his comeuppance.

"Goddamn it!" Marcus grumbled.

Ben suddenly remembered his best friend and hurried over to Marcus and Vickie to make sure they were okay.

They were both back on their feet and Vickie was busy, wiping off some of the marshmallow mixture from the back of her dress. Ben asked her if she was all right.

"Oh, I'm fine," she replied. "Nothing that won't come out in the wash." She then glanced up at Marcus and smiled. "You okay?"

"Peachy," he replied but from the pronounced frown showing on his face, Ben knew he was anything but.

"Come on," Ben whispered to him. "Let's get you and Vickie out of here."

AND THE BULL SAVED ME

"What the hell for?" Marcus griped, his face red with anger. "What's running away gonna do? It's hopeless, Ben! What the hell was I thinking? I never should have done it!"

"Done what?" Vickie asked him.

"Never mind," he said. "It's not important. Come on. I'm taking you home." And before she could even answer, Marcus grabbed her arm and began hustling her towards the exit.

Ben took Sue's hand and they followed after them. Sue asked Ben what was wrong with Magic.

"I dunno. He's been acting kind of strange ever since he took Vickie on that tour. Where did they go, anyway?"

"Up and down the halls is all. Why? Did he mention something?"

"No. But I'm gonna find out," Ben said. "Do me a favor and walk Vickie out to Magic's car so I can talk to him alone."

Sue agreed and they managed to catch up to Vickie and Marcus just as they rounded the fire truck, still parked at the curb, next to the entrance. Ben took Marcus aside and told him he needed to talk.

"What is it?" Marcus grumbled, acting put out by the interruption.

"That's what I was gonna ask you," Ben replied. "What's wrong, Magic? Was it Simmons?"

"Not only him. He's always gonna be a prick. It was the others…"

Ben asked him what he was referring to and Marcus told him that someone had called Vickie a freak.

"Who?" Ben said, his anger flaring.

"A couple of guys I didn't recognize. They were standing by the shop class door when I gave Vickie the tour. I only took her walking to get away from everyone's comments about the mess in the gym and because we couldn't get out of here without bumping into twenty people telling me how this was my best *Magic moment* yet. I wanted to be the one to tell her, not some stranger. But then, when we passed those two guys, one of them called me the 'Town Freak' and then the other one called Vickie a freak, too."

"You know better than to pay any attention to what assholes like that think. Just ignore it."

"I can't, Ben! This time they weren't just saying it about me! They were making fun of her! They called her a freak, too! Just because she was with me!" He paused and frowned down at the ground. "Maybe you and Sue should find someone else to be the baby's godparents. I don't think Vickie and I are going to make it."

Ben could see where he was going and tried to talk him out of it. "Why? Because of what a few jerks said? So what? Who cares what they think? They're a bunch of closed-minded assholes! You shouldn't let them dictate your life!"

"It's not me I'm worried about! It's her! How can I ask her to put up with something like that? How can I ask her family to be associated with me? No person in their right mind would ask to be humiliated like that! And I care about her too much to put her through it…" He started to walk away but Ben stopped him.

"Don't you think you should ask her first? Isn't it her decision, too?"

"No," Marcus replied flatly. "She's too good a person. She'd stay with me even if it meant being humiliated." He sighed hard, like he had the whole weight of the world on his shoulders. "So I've got to make that decision for her." And before Ben could object any more, Marcus took off towards his car, his hands stuck down deep in his pants pocket and his shoulders hunched over, as though he was dreading what he was about to do.

"Shit!" Ben whispered, clenching his teeth in anger. It wasn't exactly the result that he and Sue had been planning for. Tricking Magic into bringing Vickie to the reunion was supposed to force him into telling her the truth, not break them apart. Ben saw Sue approaching from the other direction and walked the few yards over to join her at their car. There was a worried look on her face and he knew she'd have to know the truth.

"What's wrong with Magic?" she asked him. "He looks upset."

"Let's just say that our plan of getting him to admit to Vickie about his problem wasn't a big success."

"Why? What did he say? Is he still going to keep her in the dark? Even after everything that happened tonight?"

"It doesn't matter any more," Ben said, opening up the passenger side door for her. "Unless my guess is wrong, he's going to break up with her."

"What? But why?"

"Come on," he said, motioning her into the car. "Get in and I'll tell you all about it."

By the time Marcus pulled the car into Vickie's lot, a little while later, he'd already ran three or four scenarios through his head, trying to come up with an easy way to tell her. But none of them satisfied him. Lying to her or making up another story didn't seem right somehow. He'd lied enough to her already. His whole life had become a lie since he'd been going out with her. Now was the time to stand up and act like a man.

Even if it meant facing the rest of his life alone. Without her.

He pulled into one of the empty spots near the back entrance, got out and went over to her side of the car, to let her out.

"Aren't you going to park over behind the lawn shed? Same as usual?" she asked him as she stepped out onto the pavement.

"No need to," he told her, shutting the door and escorting her over to the back door of the building.

She put her arm through his and giggled. "You must have cooked up a new plan to get by Sanun. What is it this time?"

He held open the back door for her and followed her over to the bottom of the stairs. She stepped up onto the first step and turned around, slipping her arms around his neck. "Well? What is it? Can't you tell me?"

He swallowed hard and mentally braced himself for what he had to do. "I'm not staying," he told her.

"What do you mean?" she said.

He bent his head, avoiding her gaze.

"I'm not staying," he said again.

She hugged him tight and kissed him on the cheek. "It's okay," she said. "You don't have to hide the car. I'll make some excuse for Sanun. I'll tell him you found another wasp nest in my attic and that you had to guard me."

He lifted his head and gazed into her eyes. He loved her so much. How could he put her through a lifetime of what he knew would be one humiliation after the other? How could anyone do that to someone they loved so much? He bit his lip and mustered up all the courage he could.

If he really loved her, he couldn't do it to her.

"I think we should stop seeing each other for a while," he whispered.

Her eyes widened with fear. "What do you mean?"

He took in a breath and kept his voice devoid of any emotion. "I don't think we should see each other any more."

"But I don't understand," she whispered, acting stunned. "Why?"

He could no longer look her in the eyes. She'd know he was lying. "We're moving way too fast," he said, glancing down at the stairs. "I think we should give each other some time, so we can decide what's best for us." He stopped, not able to say anything else. The words were already trying to choke up in his throat and making him nauseous. "I have to go," he said.

"Please!" she said, her voice shaking, showing that she was close to tears. "What did I do?"

"Nothing," he said, his heart aching so hard that he was having a hard time breathing. "I just feel that we're not compatible, that's all." He pulled the car keys from his pocket, gripping them hard, wishing he could draw some measure of courage from the metal.

He had to let her go.

No matter how much it hurt.

It was for her own good.

"It's for the best," he said, turning his back to her and walking over to the back door, the words echoing in his head with waves of pain. "You'll see."

She didn't answer him. Instead, she burst into tears and ran up the steps.

The sound of her soft sobs could be heard as she ran down the hall. And with each sob, came a knife, plunging deep into his heart, killing it forever. She slammed the door to her apartment a moment later and as the sound reverberated throughout the building, the door to his heart slammed shut, too.

What other choice did he have?

How could he ask her to live such a life?

He couldn't.

He shoved open the back door and wished like hell he'd never been born.

CHAPTER FOURTEEN

It was a couple weeks later. Ben walked through the front door of The Point and waited for his eyes to adjust to the dimmer light inside the bar. It was Monday afternoon so the place wasn't busy. However, this was merely the calm before the storm. In a few hours, the place would be jumping with people coming in for dart ball league and the Monday Night Football Party. But right now there were only three people in the place. Two sitting on stools up at the bar and one familiar face in a booth near the back.

Jack.

Ben went over and took a seat across from him, more than anxious to discuss Magic's problem. He and Jack had been trying for days to talk some sense into their friend, but with no results. As soon as Ben took his seat, he noticed two full beers sitting on the table in front of him. *Interesting*, Ben thought, smiling down at the beer. Jack was setting him up for something.

"I take it one of these is for me?" Ben asked him.

"Yep," Jack replied. "And the other's for Magic. He should be here in about fifteen minutes. I wanted you here a little early so we could come up with a plan of attack."

The waitress came up to the table and set down a platter holding a cheeseburger and fries in front of Jack, along with a plastic squirt bottle of ketchup. "You want anything?" Jack asked Ben.

The aroma of the food caused Ben's stomach to growl and he suddenly remembered he hadn't eaten all day. "I'll take what Jack's having," he told the waitress. "And maybe you better bring a shot of JB, too."

The waitress took off with the order and Jack quizzed Ben about the JB. "Since when do you drink during working hours?"

"Since you lined them up for me," Ben said, pointing to the beers.

"I only ordered a beer for you so Magic would feel obliged to drink his," Jack explained. "It's bait. I'm hoping he'll listen to reason and figured…"

"That the alcohol would help in those persuasive efforts, right?"

Jack nodded his head yes and Ben laughed.

"What's so funny?" Jack said.

"Great minds think alike," Ben replied. "After you called me about this Alamo meeting, I got the same idea. The JB's for him, not me."

"Oh," Jack replied, getting back to his sandwich and fries. "You had me worried there for a minute."

"So what's the plan?" Ben snickered. "We gonna get him drunk, drag him over to Vickie's and make him take her back?"

"Nothing that drastic. But getting them back together is what I'm shooting for. It isn't gonna be easy. First we've got to talk some sense into him."

Ben rolled his eyes and sighed. "We've been trying that, for the last two weeks. It's not doing any good."

"But we've been talking to him separately," Jack reminded him. "I think we'd do better if we both work on him."

"Sort of like an ambush, huh? Jeez. This really is an Alamo meeting, *against* Magic."

Jack told him that an ambush was just what they needed under the circumstances. "He's absolutely miserable. He sits in his office all day sulking and won't even come out to talk to the kids during the dance game or the mother's league. I finally bullied him into coming out Saturday because we had the picnic for the kids' summer league in the parking lot and he had to help me run the grill."

"Well, that's something at least."

"Yeah, but he didn't have much fun with that, either. Even the kids noticed that he wasn't his old self. Now, every chance he gets, he runs back into his office or goes out walking with that portable CD player Vickie gave him. Mavis said she saw him last week, walking up and down Main Street, near the water department, acting as though he was out for a stroll with his headphones. She also saw him the next day, hanging around near that parking lot, next to the fire house, where Vickie parks her car. It's pitiful."

"Maybe he's thinking about running into her so he can talk to her."

"I doubt it," Jack replied. "Mavis said he was skulking around, at the side of the building like he was hiding. That's why she mentioned it, because it looked so silly. No. He's heartbroken and trying to sneak a peek at Vickie."

"Jesus," Ben said, enjoying the irony. "So now he really *is* stalking her. Sanun would love hearing that. Vickie's not exactly happy, either. She's been coming in for her piano lessons twice a week and keeps asking about him. And then, Friday…she started crying. And you know I don't deal well with crying females. I tried to explain to her why he broke up with her and she said she understood his reasons."

"Well, that at least softens the blow," Jack said as the waitress came up and placed the shot of JB in front of Ben.

"Not so you'd notice, by the way she was crying," Ben said, pushing the JB over beside Magic's beer. "I felt so sorry for her that I ended up promising her I'd talk to him."

Jack put his root beer down and smiled. "And did you?"

"That night. I called him but as soon as I mentioned Vickie's name, he hung up on me."

"That's the same response I keep getting from him," Jack said, pausing to squirt some more ketchup on his fries.

The waitress brought Ben's order a few minutes later and they suspended the *ambush* discussion for a few minutes while they ate their lunch. Jack pushed his empty plate aside and took out his tobacco pouch and pipe. Ben finished off the rest of his fries and asked Jack what the plan was.

"Pretty simple," Jack replied as he packed his pipe. "I figured we'd stick him in the corner here and make sure he hears what we have to say."

"This ought to be fun," Ben chuckled.

"Not for him. Especially once I start tellin' him a couple of whoppers I came up with and I don't mean fish stories."

Ben swallowed his mouth of fries. "Uh, these whoppers you're tellin' him…shouldn't I know what they are so I can keep a straight face when I hear them?"

"No time," Jack said, nodding in the direction of the front door. "Here he comes now."

"Okay," Ben said, "but I've got a few to tell myself so you'd better be prepared."

Jack told him he would and then motioned Marcus over to the table.

"This is no longer an Alamo meeting," Ben whispered. "It's a Liar's Club. We should be ashamed of ourselves."

"Not when it's for a good cause," Jack whispered back.

Marcus walked up to the booth and Ben got up and let him slide in.

Now we've got ya, Ben thought as he sat down next to him. "Here," Ben said, pushing the beer closer to Marcus. "We thought you might be thirsty. You want some lunch?" And he raised his hand to call the waitress back over when Marcus stopped him.

"I'm not hungry," Marcus said and then he pushed the beer back, across the table towards Jack. "And I'm not thirsty either." He paused and stared down at the shot glass full of JB.

"No problem," Ben said, reaching out for the JB. "I'll have the waitress take this away, too."

"That's okay," Marcus said, grabbing on to the shot glass and pulling it out of Ben's reach. "I'll keep this."

Ben felt Jack kick him lightly under the table and knew what he was thinking. As a rule Magic's preference was beer, only. If he was resorting to shots then he really was shaken. And that being the case, they'd have to tread lightly. One wrong word and their quarry would bolt, possibly trying to escape by crawling out under the table.

"Sure thing," Ben said, sticking his legs out, under the table, just in case. "And if you want a couple more of those, I'll be glad to drive you home afterwards."

Marcus let go of the still full shot glass and glared at them. "I know what you're doing. What you're both doing. But you can forget it. My mind's made up."

"We weren't doing anything," Ben said, bracing his legs, preparing himself for some sizable physical resistance. "But I might as well warn you. If you try getting out of that seat before you hear what Jack and I have to say, then you're gonna run into some trouble."

"You challenging me, Ben?" Marcus shot back at him.

"If I have to, yes."

"Now wait a minute, you two," Jack said. "Let's not get into some kind of half-assed duel here in the bar." He paused and directed his attention to Ben. "Let's calm down and leave the physical stuff out of it, right?"

"Okay by me," Ben replied, feeling like Jack was now pinning him into a corner, too.

"And as for you, Magic. Would you at least do us the courtesy of talking about it for a few minutes? That's all were asking for, is a few minutes of your time. That's not unreasonable, is it?"

"No," Marcus replied. "Okay. I'll talk about it. But I'm not changing my mind."

"I understand," Jack said. Then he told Marcus to drink his shot.

"Why?" Marcus said.

"Because you're gonna need it once I tell you what's been happening," Jack told him.

Ben bit his lip and tried hard not to smile. *Oh boy*, he thought. *Here come the whoppers.*

Marcus downed the shot and put the glass back down on the table. "Okay," he told Jack. "Go ahead and tell me. It's about Vickie, isn't it?"

"Nope," Jack said. "It's about Tim."

"Tim?" Marcus said. "I just left him at The Crystal a few minutes ago. What about him?"

"It's about him and Marty. Did you know they broke up?"

"No," Marcus whispered. "Tim didn't say anything about it. When did that happen?"

Jack told him it happened after Tim went to Sunday dinner at Marty's parents' place.

"Tim never mentioned anything to me…" Marcus protested.

"Me neither," Jack said. "Calvin told me about it yesterday, when we went fishing together."

"You went fishing with Calvin?" Marcus said. "Did he say how Vic…" But he broke off and stared down at the empty shot glass, not finishing the question.

Ben smiled over at Jack and mouthed the words "keep going, it's working" at him.

"I'm still showing Calvin the ins and outs of working the outboard on my old boat," Jack told Marcus. "He asked how you were."

"He did?" Marcus said, glancing up and acting surprised.

"Sure," Jack told him. "He still considers you a friend, even though you and Vickie aren't seeing each other any more."

"That's awful nice of him," Marcus replied. "What did you tell him?"

"I told him you were fine. I also told him about you going fishing with me this weekend on my new boat so I asked him to join us."

Here we go, Ben thought. *Pressure time.*

"Why would you do that?" Marcus asked Jack, his face going pale with worry.

"Why not?" Jack replied, puffing away on his pipe like it was no big deal. "You may have stopped seeing Vickie but that doesn't mean you and I have to stop associating with Calvin. I enjoy his company and he enjoys yours…"

"I can't go," Marcus complained.

"Sure you can," Jack said. "I already told him you were coming."

"I can't go," Marcus repeated. "You know I can't, Jack. He might start asking me questions about why I broke up with Vickie or worse yet, one of my *moments* could happen and then he'd know about me."

Jack asked him what difference it would make. "I mean you already broke up with Vickie anyway. Who'd even care?"

"I would," Marcus mumbled under his breath.

Ben decided to add his two cents. "Why does it bother you, Magic? Are you afraid that he'd tell Vickie?"

"Yeah."

Jack told Marcus it didn't matter. "Calvin already knows about you."

"What?" Marcus said, his eyes growing wide with surprise.

Ben tried hard not to smile as Jack explained it.

"He may not be from around here, but his clients are," Jack said. "He learned about you from them. But don't worry. Vickie still doesn't know about you. I told Calvin you didn't want her to find out and he promised not to tell her. But Calvin Garrett's not the kind of man who lies to his kids so I hope you appreciate the lengths the man is willing to go for you." Jack's expression turned solemn and he took the pipe out of his mouth and pointed it at Marcus. "I know you thought you were protecting Vickie but now the lie has gotten out of hand and it's affecting other people's lives."

"Whose lives?" Marcus asked, suddenly acting quite interested.

"Mine for one," Ben replied, deciding to add his own "tall tales" to the mix. "Because of all your lies, Sanun almost killed me."

Marcus asked him what he was talking about and Ben explained to him about Vickie buying one of the old Spinet's from him. "Remember? For her apartment?"

"Oh yeah," Marcus replied. "So she's really getting one, huh? I'm glad. It meant a lot to her."

Ben told him that he went to Vickie's on Thursday, to measure the doors on her apartment, to make sure they were wide enough for the Spinet. "But as soon as I drove into the lot and parked, Sanun came at me with his pipe wrench!"

"But why…" Marcus said, then he got a look of recognition on his face and whispered an "Oh shit! The license plates!"

"And the make of car," Ben added. "He spotted them both the minute I drove into the parking lot."

Jack told them he didn't get it.

"The lie I told to Sanun," Marcus said. "About John, Vickie's elderly friend, and how he was stalking her. I gave Sanun the make of car and plate numbers to watch out for, remember?"

Jack started huffing, laughing. "That's right! And they were Ben's! No wonder the guy went gunnin' for you, Ben."

Marcus asked Ben if Sanun hit him with the wrench.

"No. But I had to do some fast-talking to keep him from it. I told him about you lying to him so you could be with Vickie."

"You didn't!" Marcus exclaimed.

"Damned straight, I did! He was about to whack me in the skull with that thing." Then he paused and added slowly, to emphasize the point. "Besides, what difference does it make now if he knows the truth? It's not like you're gonna be spending any more nights at Vickie's place." He stared at his best friend, waiting for the words to sink in. A few seconds of silence followed after which Jack commented.

"See what I mean about it affecting other people? Ben ended up putting his life on the line because of the lies you told, to keep Vickie from finding out your secret. Isn't it about time to come clean?"

"But we're broke up, now," Marcus remarked.

Oh, brother, Ben thought. *Here we go again. Still in denial, even after the fact.* He decided to add another straw to the camel's back of tall tales. "My back's been killing me for four days now. I think I may have hurt it when I was trying to get away from Sanun. I'm gonna have to make a trip to the doctor to see if I pulled something."

Jack kicked him under the table and gave him a frown, as though saying "Don't pour it on so thick."

"Does it hurt bad?" Marcus asked Ben.

Ben glanced over at Jack and tried not to smile. "Not too bad. Another night on the heating pad should take care of it."

Jack changed the subject and asked Marcus how Tim was when he left him at The Crystal.

"Fine. He was oiling the lanes. Why do you ask?"

"Because of what happened to him last week," Jack said, tapping his pipe into the ashtray. "I think he's holding up well, considering."

Marcus asked him what he was talking about.

"When Tim went to dinner at Marty's parents place last Sunday, remember? Calvin and his wife wanted to meet him."

"Yeah?" Marcus said. "What about it?"

"Tim didn't say so," Jack said, "but I think he expected you to go along with him, for moral support."

Ben's ears perked up. This was the first time he'd heard about it.

"Tim didn't say anything to me about it," Marcus said, frowning down at the table.

"No, he wouldn't," Jack said. "He knows you and Vickie broke up so he didn't want to bring it up. Too bad. Maybe if he had, things wouldn't have turned out so bad for him."

"Why?" Marcus said. "What happened?"

"Well, no one ended up shooting at anyone," Jack said, "but Calvin said Tim was trying so hard to impress them that he came across as a jerk."

"Tim? A jerk?" Marcus said. "How could they think that?"

Jack told him Tim told a couple of jokes at the dinner table. "But Marty's Mom got offended by one of them and ordered Tim out of the house."

Ben bit his lip to keep from smiling as Magic asked Jack what the joke was.

"Something about conducting sex studies for Jacques Cousteau's son."

"The water park thing!" Ben chuckled, recalling the incident. He asked Jack if Calvin was also insulted by it.

"No. He thought it was really funny. But unfortunately, his wife didn't. She ordered Tim out of the house and forbid Marty to see him any more. Calvin said she was so mad, that he doubts she'll ever change her mind."

"Didn't Tim explain to her that it was only a joke?" Marcus asked.

Jack told him Calvin did his best to explain it to her. "But she wouldn't listen. I guess she's a bit puritanical or something."

"She didn't strike me as being that way," Marcus whispered; more to himself than to them. "She reminded me so much of Mom…" But he broke off at the last second and cleared his throat, like he'd said too much.

"Well, it doesn't matter now," Jack said. "The damage has been done. Calvin says Marty is so depressed that she stays in her room and won't come out. And Tim's not exactly his old smiling self any more, in case you haven't noticed."

"No, I didn't," Marcus whispered, acting remorseful.

"So you see?" Jack asked him. "Your decision affected more than just you and Vickie. A lot of people were depending on you and you let them down."

"I didn't mean to," Marcus whispered, seeming to get lost in his own thoughts.

Ben watched Jack give him a quick wink. The ploy had worked. Ben decided to help out the cause. "Uh…by the way, Magic," he told him. "Vickie's been coming in twice a week for her piano lessons but lately she's been having some trouble."

"Trouble?" Marcus asked. "What kind of trouble?"

"Trouble concentrating, I guess," Ben replied, shrugging like he wasn't sure. "She's too upset. She's always asking about you. Then yesterday she started crying."

"She was crying?" Marcus whispered.

Ben tried hard to make his face look stern, even though inside he was enjoying himself to no end. "Yeah? What the hell did you expect? You broke her heart and you won't even return her calls."

"I never meant to hurt her like that," Marcus whispered, reaching out for his beer and pulling it towards him. "I figured she'd get over it."

"Why?" Jack asked him. "Are *you* already over *her*?"

"Well, no."

Ben looked away, no longer able to keep from smiling. Jack was showing just what a master fisherman he was. Throw out the bait, wait for a proper response, the strike, and only then jerk it back and reel in.

"Vickie loves you," Jack told Marcus. "And I think you love her, too."

"That doesn't matter," Marcus said, fidgeting around a bit, like he wanted to leave.

Ben turned and glared at him. "Don't even think about it…" He was ready to give Magic a fight but it turned out, it wasn't necessary. Jack's powers of persuasion were about to pay off.

"You're a good person," Jack told Marcus. "I've never seen you intentionally hurt a single soul. It's not in your nature."

Marcus frowned at him, asking him what his point was.

"The point is that because you won't tell Vickie the truth about yourself, people are being hurt. People you care about and I don't just mean Vickie."

Marcus whispered that he didn't mean to hurt anyone.

"I know that," Jack said. "And I understand why you broke up with Vickie. But don't you think you owe something to the people who got hurt protecting you? Like, Tim, Marty and Calvin?"

"Yeah. I guess so."

"Don't you owe it to them to make it right? After all, Tim looks up to you and so does Marty. And as for Calvin, you owe him big time."

Marcus glanced up at Jack and asked him what he was talking about.

"Your *Magic moments,*" Jack replied. "At his place. You almost got the guy shot."

"Uh…Excuse me. I think I need another beer," Ben mumbled, getting up from the booth and hurrying towards the bar with his beer mug. If he listened any longer he'd end up laughing and the mirth wouldn't help Jack's cause any. Ben headed down to a stool at the end of the bar where Magic and Jack couldn't see him. He leaned down on the bar and covered his face with his arms, giving into the laughter. He kept it quiet so as not to make any noise but he couldn't keep from shaking. Terry came over and asked him if he was okay.

"I'm dandy," Ben replied, taking a deep breath from laughing "I just had to take a break from the greatest show on earth, that's all. You should hear what Jack is telling Magic. It's too funny."

"Don't tell me," Terry said. "It's about Magic's latest disaster, right? I already heard about it."

Ben stopped laughing and got up on the stool. "No kidding," Ben said. "Magic hasn't gotten around to telling me and Jack about it yet. Fill me in." He didn't want to tell Terry the truth, that since Magic had broken up with Vickie, he and Jack weren't getting regular updates, another good reason to get the lovebirds back together.

"It happened this morning at Mel's gas station," Terry told him. "Mel said Magic stopped in to put some air in his tires. But whoever last used the air hose got it wedged under one of the tires in that big display Mel set up."

"You mean the pyramid of new tires? The one with that giant blow up of the Michelin Guy on the top?"

"That's the one," Terry said. "So Magic goes to pull the air hose out from under the tire and the whole pyramid topples. Apparently, the tire Magic pulled out was one of the bottom supports. Suddenly the whole gas station and vicinity is full of tires, rolling every which way. Some ended up in the street and caused a traffic jam until Mel and his crew could get out there and pick 'em up. A couple more rolled over into the preschool yard and the kids were out on recess and started playing with them. I guess they thought it was part of the playground equipment. Mel said he had a time getting the tires back from them."

"No doubt," Ben said, pausing to finish the last of his beer. "It was standard issue playground equipment when I was a kid."

"Me too," Terry said, grabbing Ben's glass and going over to the tap to refill it. He came back a few seconds later and handed it to Ben. "And the best part was what happened at the station. After that tire pyramid collapsed that big Michelen blow up figure fell down, in front of the women's restroom, knocking the door open. Some woman was in there on the pot and once she saw that giant face leering at her she started screaming bloody murder. It took Mel twenty minutes to get her calmed down."

Ben started laughing. "That would be enough to scare the shit out of anyone."

Terry asked him if he'd also heard what happened on Friday.

Ben took a swig of his beer and tried not to act surprised. "Oh, yeah," he said, grabbing his wallet and handing Terry a ten for the beer and food. "But I didn't really catch all the details. What were they again?"

Terry went over and rang him out at the register and then returned with Ben's change. "Todd Maxwell was telling me about it the other day when he was in here."

Ben knew who Terry was talking about. Todd ran a small grocery and meat market on Main Street. Half the town did their meat shopping there because Todd had the best cuts in Northern Ohio.

"Magic stopped in to get ten pounds of those knocker wieners," Terry said. "The one's with the skins that are connected to each other."

Ben told him he knew what they were. "Magic gets them every year for the picnic he holds for the summer junior league bowlers. The kids love them because of the way they plump up so big when Jack puts them on the grill, out in The Crystal Parking lot."

"Someone else is partial to those wieners, too," Terry said. "Namely, the entire class at Miss Erskine's place."

"The kennel? Why? What happened?"

Terry explained that after exiting the meat market, Magic bumped into a couple of high school kids, coming from the karate class next door. "The kids were showing Magic a few of the new kicks they'd learned and accidentally knocked the package of wieners out of Magic's hands. So they helped him pick up the wieners, shove them back into the brown paper wrapper and Magic went on his way. But what he didn't know was that there was a hole in the wrapper, causing the wieners to spill out behind him."

"Didn't the kids tell him about it?"

Terry told him the kids never saw it because they headed off down the street in the opposite direction. "But a couple other people coming out of the karate class did. And so did someone else. Namely all the dogs in Miss Erskine's obedience class." He then told Ben that because of the seasonally warm weather, Miss Erskine left her front door open. "She's like my father: cheap, and doesn't want to run the air conditioner unless the thermostat hits a hundred. So the dogs are lined up with their owners, in that big front room, going through obedience training when they see Magic walk by, dragging a ten-foot train of those wieners behind him. All twenty-five dogs, plus a couple more that one of Miss Erskine's helpers were trimming, bolted from the shop and made a beeline for Magic. Todd heard all this crazy barking and looked out his front door. He said the dogs first scrambled after the wiener train and then knocked Magic down, trying to get at the rest of them. Todd said Magic must not have realized he was dragging the wieners because he didn't even seem to notice at first."

"How is that possible?" Ben said but as soon as he said it, he remembered something. "Did Todd say if Magic had on a set of headphones?"

Terry told him he did and Ben started laughing.

"So what do you know that I don't?" Terry said and Ben explained to him about Magic's CD player that Vickie got him.

"I guess that explains it," Terry said. "Todd said Magic never reacted until the dogs started fighting over the wieners and knocked him down, trying to get at the rest of them."

Ben thought of something. "So where was Miss Erskine and all the mutt's owners while this was going on?"

"Chasing after Magic and the parade of dogs!"

"Which ones?" Ben smirked. "The real ones or the ones from the meat market?"

"Both. Todd said it's the funniest thing he's seen in years." He then told Ben that the owners finally caught up with dogs in front of the courthouse. "And just then the mayor comes down the steps with the county DA and a couple of the court stenographers. The mayor starts laughing like crazy and yells, "The newspapers are right! The town really has gone to the dogs!"

"You talkin' about Magic and his wolf pack?" one of the guys sitting a few barstools away said. "A friend of mine serving jury duty saw it and said the courthouse personnel are still laughin' about it. He also said someone called the Kirklin radio station and suggested they do a daily *Magic moment* watch, like right before the news at six."

"You mean like a tornado or thunderstorm watch?" Terry asked the guy.

Hope to hell not, Ben thought, his heart quickening with worry.

"Hey, I never thought of that!" the guy said. "And you're right! That's what it would be. Some guy announcing Magic's latest escapade, just like that Paul Harvey guy doing those 'Rest of the Story' things. Maybe they could even sound off that tornado siren when one of them happens...that one out by the reservoir."

Terry waved the guy off, acting like he was talking nonsense. "They only use that thing for emergencies." Then he leaned down and whispered to Ben, "But a few of Magic's *moments* could be classified as 'emergencies' if you ask me."

"Don't I know it," Ben replied, glancing across the room to Jack and Magic's booth. Magic was gone and Jack was sitting by himself. Ben grabbed his beer and hurried back to the booth. He sat down across from Jack and asked him where Magic was. "Jesus! He didn't hear about the local radio station doing a daily show about his *moments*, did he?"

Jack stopped puffing on his pipe and stared wide-eyed at Ben. "No. He's using the phone to call Vickie! I finally talked some sense into him." Then he paused and started laughing. "A radio show? This, I've got to hear."

Ben told him about what the guy at the bar said. "And if it's true, then Magic's sure to find out and then he'll have to tell Vickie about himself."

"He's already told her."

Now it was Ben's turn to act surprised. "What? When?"

"Right now," Jack replied. "I convinced him to get it over with and tell her the truth."

"Over the phone? Kind of the coward's way to do it, isn't it?"

Jack told him that it seemed like the fastest and painless way to do it. "And do me a favor and don't mention the coward thing in front of him. He's already hurting bad enough. Let's not make it any harder."

"Okay," Ben said, turning around in the booth and making sure Magic wasn't coming back. "And now, I have a couple questions myself, if you don't mind…"

"About the lies I told him?" Jack asked.

"Yeah. For instance, Tim. Did Vickie's mom really order him out of the house?"

"No. As a matter of fact, that part of the tale was Tim's idea and I agreed it was a good one. Turns out that Calvin and his wife loved Tim's jokes so much that he now has a standing invitation to dinner every Sunday."

"Figures. I was havin' trouble buying that part about Marty's mom not liking Tim. I can't believe Magic fell for it."

Jack replied that people in love didn't think rationally. "That's why he also bought that BS you told him about Sanun, attacking you."

Ben smiled. "Well, that wasn't exactly a fabrication. Sanun did come after me, but not with a pipe wrench. It was a flowerpot."

"Flowerpot? That's more of a feminine weapon of choice."

"I know. That's why I had to elaborate on the lie some," Ben said. Then he told Jack that Sanun knew the truth about Magic, too.

"Everything?"

"He even knew about Magic's ruse with John not really stalking Vickie. He only went along with it because he knew Vickie was in love with Magic."

"So why did he come after you with the flower pot?"

Ben told him it was because Sanun thought he was a burglar. "He didn't attack me in the parking lot, like I told Magic. It happened in the hall, outside of Vickie's apartment. I was measuring the door, to make sure the piano would fit through and Sanun saw me and thought I was trying to break in. The part about me having to talk fast to save my ass was true enough, though. Otherwise I would have ended up with a flowerpot over my head."

Jack asked him how Sanun found out the truth about Magic.

"Vickie told him. She also told him everything else, like how she was trying to get Magic to trust her enough to tell her the truth." He paused and thought of something. "You know, I just realized something. That thing you told Magic about not being truthful to Vickie and how it's affected a lot of other people..."

"Yeah? What about it?"

"It's true, isn't it? I kept thinking how funny it was because he's been runnin' round like crazy, trying to make sure she doesn't find out every time one of his *moments* happens. But it's not just him; it's all of us. Everyone. You, me, Calvin, Sanun, Tim, Sue. It's become an epidemic!"

Jack agreed that it was getting out of hand. "But we can all stop worrying now. He's gonna tell her."

"And he's gonna get back together with her," Ben added but he'd no sooner said it than Jack shook his head no.

"I didn't say he was getting back with her. I said he was telling her the truth."

"Yeah, but..." Ben said, suddenly feeling like he was missing something. "If he tells her the truth, there's no reason for them not to get back together."

"Yes there is," Marcus said.

Ben glanced up and saw Magic, standing next to the booth. He wasn't smiling so Ben knew it must not have gone too smoothly.

"So?" Ben asked him. "You tell her?"

"No," Marcus said, sitting down next to him.

"Yep," Ben smirked. "I knew it. You chickened out."

Marcus scowled at him. "I did not chicken out. I couldn't tell her because as soon as she picked up the phone, she was already crying."

AND THE BULL SAVED ME

"Told you so," Ben replied, happy to make his point.

"She wasn't crying over me," Marcus said. "Her friend John died."

"That's too bad," Jack said. "What happened?"

"Heart attack," Marcus replied. "A couple days ago. Vickie just found about it today. John's sister called her. Vickie wants me to take her to the funeral tomorrow."

"And are you?" Ben quizzed him.

"Sure," Marcus replied, acting insulted at the question. "Why wouldn't I? Just because we're no longer involved, doesn't mean we still can't be friends."

"I stand corrected," Ben replied.

Marcus sighed and sat back, his body sagging against the booth. "Look. I know I've been a jerk lately but I've had a lot on my mind."

"Understandable," Jack said.

"And I didn't mean to hurt anyone with my decision, either," Marcus said. "Not Tim, not Calvin…and especially not the two of you. You're my best friends. You know how much you mean to me." He paused and sat forward, his expression turning stern. "So I know you'll respect that decision, whether you agree with it or not."

"We will," Jack agreed. "But we still think you're making a mistake. Vickie loves you. You love her. Don't be afraid to tell her that."

Marcus stared down at his hands and frowned. "I'm going to. Tomorrow. Right after the funeral. And I'm going to tell her about my problem, too. It was wrong not to be straight with her from the beginning. But maybe, if I tell her the truth, then we can still be friends. I'd really like that. To be involved in her life in at least some small way…" He broke off, unable to continue.

Ben felt sorry for him and patted him on the back. "It's okay, Magic. Whatever you decide, me and Jack are behind you."

"Absolutely," Jack added.

"Thanks," Marcus whispered. Then he got up from the booth and headed for the exit, without another word.

Ben waited until he was out the front door and then asked Jack what they were gonna do.

"What else?" Jack said, taking a large puff on his pipe. "We've gotta help matters along a bit."

"How?"

Jack puffed on his pipe, like he was thinking about it. "We need to set another trap," Jack said, smiling slyly.

Ben asked him what he had in mind.

"Magic's hurting," Jack said. "Vickie needs to know that. And she needs to know what he's planning to do."

Ben smirked. "You mean finally tell her what she's known all along?"

"Correct. If she knows what he's up to then she can prepare for it. Just in case he gets stuck…"

"And chickens out again," Ben said, finishing it for him.

Jack sucked the last of the smoke from his pipe and tapped the burned tobacco into the ashtray. "All right. Have it your way. If he…chickens out…she can jump in and give him a hand. Then she can tell him how much she loves him and if I know Magic, he isn't going to be able to walk away from her. Especially if she's crying and carrying on."

"But what if she doesn't cry and carry on?"

Jack stuck his hand in his pants pocket and pulled out a handful of change. "Here," he told Ben, handing him a couple quarters. "Call her up and make sure she does."

Ben stared down at the quarters and grinned. "Hell, I'll even buy her a big box of Kleenex." He got up and headed for the pay phone, thinking that if Magic knew how he'd just been played, Vickie wouldn't be the only one needing Kleenex. So would Mavis and Sue because Magic had killed their significant others.

Sometimes doing a good deed could get you in a whole shitload of trouble.

CHAPTER FIFTEEN

Marcus stared out the front windshield of his car and tried to think of something to say to Vickie. The drive from her apartment to the funeral home in Kirklin had been strained. They said very little to each other, merely exchanging pleasantries and discussing general topics like the weather. More than once he had to fight the urge to pull the car over and take her in his arms, but he knew that his decision had been the right one. She deserved someone better, someone who could give her the life she deserved. The best he could look forward to now was her friendship and he hoped she would give it. Having her somewhere in his life would be comforting, even if she *was* with someone else. At least that way he could watch over her…and maybe once in a while get invited into her world.

As they drove into town, she began talking about John and some of the stories he'd shared with her. He knew it was helping her to remember her friend and he was more than happy to be her soundboard. She began crying and he offered her some Kleenex from his glove box. He watched her smile slightly as she noticed how stuffed the compartment was of essentials, including Kleenex, Band-Aids, safety pins, burn cream and other safety items.

"You wouldn't by any chance have any aspirin in there, would you?" she said.

He reached over and pulled a large bottle from behind the Band-Aids and handed it to her. "You'll also find some bottled water in the cooler on the back floor," he told her.

She retrieved one of the bottles and took the aspirin. She was quiet for the next couple of minutes and he asked her if she was okay.

"I've just been thinking," she said, fiddling with the top of the water bottle. "I've never met anyone like you. Every day with you was a new adventure. I'm really going to miss that." Then her voice got softer, as if speaking to herself. "You'll never know how much." She began crying again and his heart went out to her. He drove into the funeral home parking lot and pulled into one of the spots nearer the back. He shut off the ignition and reached out to her. She went into his arms and for the next few minutes released all of her sorrow, which he knew included not only her friend John's death, but also him. He felt his own sorrow come forth as he held her tight, wishing he could keep her there in his arms forever.

But of course, he couldn't. It wasn't meant to be.

She finally let go of him and composed herself enough to face the funeral. He stayed by her side the whole time, alert and on constant duty in case she needed something, anything. There were only about a dozen people in the seats, no doubt because John had outlived most of his family and friends. A few minutes later the minister conducted the service and in spite of the few numbers in attendance, the emotion and tears were abundant. He held her hand the whole time as she joined the people mourning the loss of their loved one.

After the funeral, he accompanied her through the viewing line where John's sister and son were standing beside the coffin. As soon the elder woman spotted Vickie she began smiling. She looked about John's age and was wearing an elegant but aged blue satin dress. The dress had two pockets on the front, embroidered with lace and there were crumpled Kleenex sticking out of the top of both of them. She went up to Vickie and gave her a hug, introducing herself as Marion.

"You have to be Vickie," Marion said. "John told me so much about you."

Vickie told her she was and then introduced Marcus.

"Marcus Kerr?" Marion said, the smile growing larger. "Not Magic Marker?"

"Uh…" Marcus said, carefully watching Vickie's reaction. He didn't know how to answer the woman.

"I've heard a lot about you," Marion said, shaking his hand vigorously. "John loved hearing about all your adventures. He used to call you the Kirklin Hero and I had to agree with him. That was a lot better than what some people call you…The Kirklin Kl—"

"Uh…" Marcus said, grabbing the woman's arm and cutting her off.

"Vickie tells me John was quite a storyteller. I hear he had quite a few adventures himself over the years."

Marion's expression turned sad again. "Yes, he did. I'm going to miss him something awful. He was a lot like you, Marcus. People didn't understand him, either. But I did and everyone who loved him did..." She broke off and took Vickie's hand. "And he used to say that there was nothing more important in the world than friends. I want to thank you for being his friend, Vickie. It meant a lot to him."

Vickie hugged Marion and for the next few minutes, they both cried in each other's arms. Marion let go of Vickie and wiped her eyes with one of the Kleenexes. Vickie went over and stood next to Marcus, taking his hand and squeezing it tight.

"The flowers are beautiful," she told Marion.

"Yes they are," Marion said, gaining some of her composure and motioning to a large, white ceramic vase full of deep red roses, sitting in the middle of the other arrangements. "Especially the roses."

Marcus had to agree with her. The vase was stuffed full of spectacular rose blooms and seemed to make the other arrangements pale in comparison.

"The roses are from John's garden," Marion said. She told them that her son had arranged them. "And there's something else," Marion said. "It was one of John's last wishes that you get a big bouquet of his best roses. So those are for you."

Vickie clutched at her Kleenex and Marcus knew she was about to break down again. She went into his arms and as he held her tight, Marion whispered to him that the roses would be taken to the graveside and then Vickie could take them home. He thanked her and then led Vickie over to a corner where she could cry in private.

A few minutes later they were back in the car and following the funeral procession to the cemetery. The cemetery was one of two in town, this one dating back to the town's earliest history and containing the remains of its first leading citizens. John was being interred in the new section in the back and it took a few minutes to drive through the graveyard to the location. Vickie's tears had dried up some, aided by the car's AC, which he left on with the keys in the accessory position for a few minutes after parking the car. He then accompanied her to a brief graveside service where the other mourners had gathered.

After the service, the people began to disburse but Vickie remained at the grave, staring at the coffin. He didn't want to disturb her thoughts so he remained quietly at her side, waiting for her. The funeral workers busied themselves, picking up the vases and artificial green blanket draped around the casket. After a couple of minutes Vickie took his hand and told him she was ready to go. He knew she was still quite upset and asked her if she wanted to go somewhere for a cup of coffee, to talk.

"I'd like that very much," she said, walking with him to his car. "I know you don't want to see me any more but I still consider you my friend." She glanced back at John's coffin. "And you never know just how little time you might have with those friends, so it's very important not to take those friendships for granted." With that she broke down again and he opened up his jacket and put his arms around her, letting her lean against his shirt and cry it out.

She was so easy to love. She wasn't afraid to show her feelings, to her friends or anyone else for that matter. She was and always would be, his light, shining on him, the dark side of the moon. He laid his head next to hers. "You'll always be my friend too," he whispered. "And I'll always be there for you. No matter what."

She hugged him hard and he never wanted her to let go. She finally broke away from him and gave him a sad smile. "I can't afford to lose any more friends," she said.

He smiled at her. "Especially ones nice enough to give you roses."

As soon as he said it, he saw Vickie's expression turn to concern.

The roses.

They hurried back to the grave. The casket was still on the supports but the flower baskets were gone.

"The hearse!" he cried and they took off running towards the large, black car sitting about thirty yards away. It was closed up and two men were entering the car from the front, getting ready to leave. "The roses must be in the back!" he yelled at her. "I'll go grab the vase while you tell the driver what's going on!"

She sprinted to the front of the car and he ran up and tried the rear door handle. It was unlocked so he pulled it open and peered inside. The baskets and vases, including the one with the roses were sitting on the floor and held in place with a plastic twine with hooks on either end. The hooks were linked into U-shaped metal holders attached to either sides of the car interior. The rose vase was wedged between two others and as he leaned in to get it, he could hear Vickie yelling at the men in the front of the car.

Just as he clutched the vase, something pulled at his jacket. He glanced down and saw that one of the hooks on the plastic twine had come loose and worked its way into one of his jacket buttonholes. He reached down to free it when the hearse suddenly lurched forward. His feet went out from under him and he fell forward onto the car's floor, littered with leaves and flower petals. The other side of the twine was still attached to the car interior and before he knew what was happening, his body slid out the back door of the hearse.

He could hear Vickie scream as he landed on his butt in the stones. His jacket was still attached to the twine hook and he held on tight to it, dangling like a fish flopping helplessly as the hearse picked up speed and dragged him behind it. He tried to bend his knees to give him some maneuverability but the centrifugal force was too strong, causing his shoes to scrape across the stones and leave a dust trail in their wake. He wanted to let got of the twine, but kept imagining scenarios where the twine would jerk the jacket up over his head and choke him or else wrench his neck and break it. At least by hanging on to the twine, he was able to keep his body from flopping around too much.

The hearse hit a couple bumps in the road and some of the vases and pots clattered and fell over, releasing their contents onto the floor and consequently spilling over onto his head and upper body. He shook the water and vegetation from his face and tried to glance up. All he could see was the back end of the car and twine. The car took a turn to the left, onto the next path and his body swung wildly to the right, sliding across the gravel and up onto the grass. The grass and gravel scraped across the knees of his pants and he experienced a burning sensation on his skin. A couple seconds later the car sped up again and he was pulled back onto the gravel path, his body flopping from side to side, trying to right itself. He finally managed to get himself face down again and bent both of his knees, trying to "pedal" his feet in an attempt to jump up into the back of the car. But it was no use. Even as slow as the hearse was moving, there was no way he could build up enough momentum to propel himself forward. He suddenly felt like Fred Flintstone, scrambling not to start a car, but get away from one.

He tried to cry out but it only came out as a squeak and there was no way the men in the front would be able to hear it. A second later there was a ripping sound and he felt his jacket finally pull free as the buttonhole split apart. He could now let go of the twine and roll away into the stones. The worst that would happen is that he would end up with scratches and a few abrasions. He began to loosen his grip when he heard a car horn, blaring loudly behind him. He negotiated a couple more bumps, throwing him first left and then right, before he finally managed to look behind him.

It was Vickie, driving his car and honking the horn.

Instant panic caused him to clutch harder onto the twine. Now if he let go, he wouldn't simply end up rolling across the stones.

He'd end up under the wheels of his own car.

He wanted to laugh at the irony, but couldn't. More important things had to be attended to, for instance, the muscles in his arms, now aching from the strain. At least when the jacket was still hooked, it helped support his weight. Now all that stood between him and certain death was his brute strength.

He closed his eyes and held on for dear life.

His car horn started blaring again as Vickie veered the car to the right, off the path, trying to get around the hearse to force it over. But the gravestones were blocking the way on either side of the path, making it impossible to overtake the hearse. Just then the hearse took another right and Marcus became disoriented as his body turned over, going with the momentum of the twine. Once again he slid up into the grass and as he was being pulled back onto the path, his butt hit a small stone tombstone sticking up, close to the ground. His back and shoulders seared with pain as the rock monument collided with his body, causing it to flip around to the side from the impact. He grunted in pain and held on tight to the twine as he bumped haphazardly across the grass and back into the stones. The stones were almost a welcome relief as the ache shot through his back and legs. The hearse sped up, no doubt the driver didn't think anyone would mind if he broke the speed limit. Vickie was still laying on the horn but the hearse driver either had his window up or had the radio so loud that he didn't notice.

A couple of seconds later the gravestones were replaced with blacktop so he knew they were approaching the front entrance. Vickie took advantage of the situation and sped up, gunning the car towards the right side of the hearse. The hearse hit a bump in the road and his body lurched to the right, directly at his car. His shoes momentarily made contact with the driver's side door of his car and he could hear Vickie scream through the open window. She gunned the car forward and before he could even think to let go of the twine, the hearse swerved to the left, its tires spitting asphalt stones out like missiles as the huge car was forced over.

As both vehicles screeched to a halt, he finally let go of the twine. His body crumpled to the ground, the muscles in his arms on fire from the strain. He stayed face down on the road, catching his breath and simply happy he was still in one piece. People began yelling and he could make out Vickie's voice among the din as footsteps came towards him. Someone grabbed him, turning him over onto his back. It was Vickie.

"Marcus! Are you all right? Are you hurt?" she cried. "Can you move your arms and legs?"

He slowly tried to move all his limbs and croaked out a squeaky sounding "Yeah."

The two men from the hearse began apologizing and asking him if he was hurt. One was in his fifties, claimed to have some EMS experience and suggested Marcus be taken to the hospital.

"I don't think that's necessary," Marcus told him. "I just need to get my legs moving."

The other man, a tall, twentyish, nervous type that looked way too thin for the black suit he was wearing, kept babbling to Vickie about how he and the other man had the air conditioner and radio on full blast.

"That's why we didn't hear your horn," the first man said, motioning to the his partner to grab Marcus under his arms. They helped Marcus to his feet and as the blood rushed back into his limbs, the pain returned.

"Ow," Marcus moaned, carefully taking a couple steps. "That hurts."

"My poor baby," Vickie said, wrapping her arms around his waist, helping to support him.

"I think I can make it on my own," Marcus told the two men. "If I need any support, Vickie can help me." Then he smiled down at her. "After all, that's what friends are for, right?"

Her face scrunched up with emotion and she hugged him tight.

"You should still get checked out," the older man said. "Your body can experience trauma hours later."

"I'll watch him very carefully," Vickie assured the man. "If he shows any signs of that, I'll take him right to the emergency room."

"Make sure you do," the man said. "You can't be too careful."

Marcus thanked him for the concern.

The younger man then began babbling again, repeating how sorry he was. "It's my first week driving the hearse. But I never meant to hurt anyone…"

Marcus knew the kid was upset and told him not to worry. "It was an honest mistake. Could have happened to anyone. And don't worry. We'll just keep this among ourselves."

The kid started shaking Marcus's hand so hard that he had to bite his lip to keep from groaning. His arms were still feeling the pain from being dragged across the cemetery. The men retrieved Vickie's roses, which miraculously, had withstood the bumpy ride. After stowing them in the back seat of his car, Marcus and Vickie bid the two men adieu. The hearse pulled out of the front gate and this time the rear door was secured and no one was hanging out the back.

Vickie asked him if he was okay to drive.

"Sure," he told her. "I'm only a little sore." He glanced down at himself. The pants had holes in the knees and there were grass and scuffmarks from the stones peppered over the suit and pants. The sides of his shoes were now mesh with the shoe, rubbed off from the stones. His jacket was ripped and hanging in pieces where the buttonhole had been ripped out. He pushed up the sleeves of his pants and shirt and examined his skin. Apart from a couple small abrasions on his knees, everything seemed to be intact.

All in all, not bad for one of his *moments*.

"Are you really okay?" she asked.

"I'm fine," he said, giving her a smile. "Are *you* okay?"

She nodded yes hesitatingly, like she wasn't quite sure. "But it happened so fast! After the hearse drove away I remembered how you left your keys in the ignition and before I knew what I was doing, I was racing your car across the cemetery, trying to catch you. At first I wondered why you didn't just let go and then I realized you must have been caught on something. I had to save you, somehow. I kept blowing the car horn, trying to get those men's attention, but they didn't hear me." She paused and lowered her head. "No one seems to be able to hear me."

He asked her what she meant.

She gazed up at him. "You. Every time I tried to talk to you about certain things, you wouldn't listen."

"I heard you," he said, suddenly feeling remorseful. "I just didn't want to talk about it." He saw the words "talk about what" in her eyes and decided to be honest with her. He was tired. Tired of running from the truth, trying to keep her from finding out his secret and tired of running from his *moments*. What difference did it make, anyway? He'd already set her free and she'd already agreed to stay his friend. And good friends shared things. They didn't need to have secrets from each other.

"I have something to tell you," he said, feeling his resolve return.

She gave him a sad smile. "I'm listening."

Okay, he thought. *Here goes.* "You've probably been wondering about the things that've happened when you're with me." He paused and tried to think of an easy way to put it. "Uh, it's been happening to me for quite some time."

"Since your parents died," she said, finishing it for him.

He stared at her, not sure he heard right.

"It's been occurring for over ten years and no one can explain the phenomenon," she said, as if she was reciting it from a textbook. "Not even the psychiatrists can explain it. The time line of the incidents varies, sometimes a few days or even a couple weeks. Some people think it's spiritual, others think it's hormonal or emotional and still others have no idea."

He felt his mouth drop open as she continued.

"But you have a theory on why it's happening. You believe your parents' spirits are behind it, letting you know that they're still with you, that you're not alone—"

"I know that sounds kind of silly," he said, interrupting her.

She gave him a look of astonishment. "Why? Because other people don't believe it? Who's to say it isn't true? What if it is? You were closer to your parents than anyone else so who should know better than you? Besides, you have other special abilities, so it's not that incredible."

"What abilities?" he asked her, suddenly feeling completely overwhelmed.

"The ability to sense other people's deepest emotions, their sorrows and dreams. That's your 'gift,' not the strange things that happen to you. You did it with Marty, with me, with Dad."

"I didn't do anything."

"Yes, you did!" she said, taking his hand and squeezing it. "You just don't see it. You brought Marty out of her shell and helped Dad go after his dream. And look at George's family and how you helped them. And me? Helping me realize my own dream about taking lessons and getting my own piano. And you're forgetting The Crystal and all the people who love you. All the kids and everyone else's lives you've touched. You showed me and everyone how to relish life and not be afraid to try new things, experience life, because that's what *you* do. You don't let your *moments* stop you from enjoying life, you live your life the way all of us should, with hope and enthusiasm."

He smiled as he heard her say *moments*. "How did you find out?"

"John told me. He knew all about you. He also told me about how some of the people in town called you a 'jinx' and 'freak.' That made John mad. He said almost exactly what Jack told me…that what was happening to you was something to celebrate, not be frightened of."

"Jack? When did he tell you that?"

She told him about asking Jack and Ben meet with her. "They told me everything." Then she put her hand against his cheek. "But they didn't have to tell me what a wonderful person you are, I saw that for myself." And she gazed at him with that same disarming look. His heart melted. He bent down to kiss her when he remembered something.

"But…what about my *moments*? I can't ask you to live with something like that."

"Why not? It's my choice."

He sighed and felt his heart ache. How could he make her understand? He gently took her hand from his face. "Don't you see?" he whispered, so desperately wanting to hold on to her. "It would be like living with a bull in a china shop. I couldn't put you through something like that…I care about you too much…I love you too much to ask you to endure something like that."

"Don't you think I've thought about that? I *know* what I'm letting myself in for. Don't you understand? I love you. I'll do anything to be with you."

"Even if it means getting chased by elephants or…" he paused and swallowed hard, "lizards?"

She hugged him tight. "Even lizards. Besides, you're forgetting one very important thing."

He asked what thing she was referring to.

"That I was always there to rescue you."

"Rescue me?" he said, letting go of her and trying to figure out what she was talking about.

"You never saw it, did you?" she asked; acting amused. "Every time we were together, when one of your *moments* happened, I was always there to save you."

He thought about it, going over the *moments* in his head.

"Remember?" she said. "From the first date, the fire in the restaurant. The waiter threw the spaghetti on you but I'd already put out the fire with the pitcher of water."

"That's right, you did," he said. "Funny, but I never thought about it before."

"And at the zoo," she said. "I pulled you into that alcove, right before Benji ran us both over."

He thought back to the incident. He hadn't really thought about that one either. He'd been too focused on trying to keep her from finding out the truth about him. He suddenly remembered another one. "The wolfman mask," he told her. "When I ran into the woods and those kids thought it was the real thing. That girl was going to hit me with that Tazer gun until you explained what happened to her." He paused and thought of another one. "The water park. You saved me from those mothers when I was naked in the pool. And the emu at Old Man Pelling's place. You pulled me back right before the skunk let us have it!"

"I didn't think we going to escape from that one," she whispered. "But we did."

"And the giant beer mug, at the reunion!" he said, the excitement building inside him at each revelation. "You pulled me out of the way before it broke. And just now, with the car! You saved me again!"

She put her hands against her cheeks, like she was about to cry and nodded her head yes.

"It's true," he said, his heart bursting with love for her. He wrapped his arms around her and held her tight, a wonderful sense of happiness filling his soul. She was right. She'd always been there for him but he'd never seen it before. How could he have missed it? He suddenly thought of something and pulled away from her. "But what about the dinner with your folks? You didn't save me then. I ended up saving your dad."

"You're forgetting about something," she said. "Mom's glass room."

He thought back to the moment, the glass, and the panic attack. "That's right!" he exclaimed. "You held my hand and nothing got broken!" He paused and frowned. "And it should have! I was waiting for it to happen! But it didn't!" He gazed into her eyes, a sense of awe washing over him. "Because *you* were with me, protecting me."

Tears began to well up in her eyes. "I may have been protecting you, but you were also saving me."

"What do you mean?"

She smiled through the tears. "You've met my family. I love them dearly and Mom and Dad are sweet, but they're boring. It's like I've been waiting my whole life for something interesting to happen to me. And then I met you and we started having the most wonderful adventures. It was scary, but it was also so much fun! I was left laughing and breathless. It was incredible! And that's when I knew that I was destined to be with you. So who's to say your theory was wrong?" she whispered. "Maybe your parents *are* guiding your destiny. And they didn't just guide you anywhere. They guided you to…"

"You," he said, feeling every ounce of emotion come forth. He took her in his arms and kissed her, his own tears joining with hers.

It was so much like them.

She was so much like them.

And because of their love for him, they'd somehow reached out to another soul, sending her to him.

He loved.

He was loved.

And now, thanks to that *gift*, he'd never be alone again.

The dark side of the moon had finally found its light.

EPILOGUE

Marcus yawned and stretched as he waited for the bottle to heat. His muscles twitched sluggishly, coming to life and protesting the late hour. The beeper went off on the microwave and he pulled out the bottle and put on the top. He squeezed a couple drops onto his forearm and waited. Just right. He took off for the bedroom, his delivery momentarily interrupted as he stumbled over the car seat by the front door. He pushed it out of the way and heard something squeak under his foot. He bent down, picked it up and smiled. Adam's Winnie the Pooh squeeze toy, Sanun's present to him.

As he threw it into the car seat he heard his son bellow again, announcing to the world and everyone on the second floor that it was past time for his feeding. He hurried into the bedroom with the bottle. Vickie was propped up on a pillow and surrounded by her grandmother's yellow and blue comforter, gently rocking and humming to Adam. Marcus slipped under the covers and handed her the bottle. The wailing abruptly stopped as Adam directed his attention to his two AM meal. Vickie continued to hum to the baby.

"Isn't that the new piece Ben taught you?" Marcus asked her.

"It is. And Adam loves it, too. I put him in the bassinet the other day next to the piano and played it for him. He went right to sleep."

"Then he'll love his new bedroom," Marcus said, lying back on the pillow. "It's big enough for his bed and a piano. Not to mention the drums Ben's determined to get him."

She gave him a curious smile. "That's what you think. Sue told me Ben's changed his mind. He's getting Adam a guitar. Katie's getting the drums."

Marcus threw his head back and laughed, picturing Ben's face after a couple weeks of hearing his daughter *practice* in the den. "Ben's gonna be sorry! He thought he was going deaf listening to the kids wail on the Straitocasters. Wait 'til Katie lets loose with a couple of drumsticks. He'll change his mind."

She told him to lower his voice. "What's wrong with Ben teaching them music?" she whispered. "Adam's lucky to have his uncle so interested in his future."

"Uh-huh." Marcus nodded, enjoying teasing her. "And if Ben has his way, Adam will be the next Harry Chapin."

"So what if he is? You and I both love Harry's songs. You could use a little of Ben's enthusiasm." She picked up the baby and handed him to Marcus. He sat up on the bed and cradled his son in his arms.

"Your mom and dad would've wanted him to learn music," she said.

He adjusted Adam in his arms and gave him the bottle. "Knowing Mom and Dad, they would have bought him the drums and the guitar."

"I'll be happy if he does become interested in music," she said, reaching for her robe at the end of the bed. "Besides, it's better than growing up to be a race car driver, what you were having him do the second day he was born."

He leaned over and kissed her on the cheek. "It wasn't a race car," he reminded her. "It was only his crib."

She got out of bed and went across the hall to the bathroom. She came back a second later with a small towel and put it on Marcus's shoulder.

He took the hint and put Adam in place for a burp. "It wasn't a race," he told her, gently patting Adam on the back. "I was only trying to give him a ride. That's why they put wheels on those things. So you can roll them around."

She got back into bed beside him. "Rolling's one thing. Racing it past the nursery is another. I thought that grouchy old nurse was going to have a heart attack when she saw you pushing Adam and yelling 'ladies and gentlemen, start your engines!'"

Marcus told her that it didn't matter what the nurse thought. "Because Adam loved it. He smiled at me! And he did that even while that old hag was looking at us, so I know he loved it."

Their conversation was interrupted with the sound of a loud *Burrupp* coming from Marcus's shoulder. He laid Adam back in his arms and gave him the bottle again.

Vickie pulled the covers over Marcus and snuggled up against him. "But the really funny part was the next night, when all those other new fathers did the same thing," she said. "You should have heard the people in the waiting room laughing."

"I know. I was standing down by the nursery window when I saw them all coming at me. That redhead guy was right, though. That guy with the crew cut did cheat. His kid's crib was at least a foot ahead of the others. Obviously that kid's growing up under a bad influence."

Vickie giggled. "I don't think the hospital crew cared who won the race."

"Oh yeah? Well, the orderlies did. They were taking bets! I swear to God!"

"And how about that poor woman they were wheeling in from the emergency room?" she reminded him. "She was sure scared."

"Can you blame her? Her husband told me later that they'd just seen one of those news specials the week before about people stealing babies from the hospitals—right out of the maternity ward."

"Oh," Vickie said, snickering. "So that's why she started screaming."

"Yep. She took one look at those guys running down the hall with the cribs and assumed they were stealing all the babies."

"Probably why her water broke right after that."

Marcus made a face. "I know. Seeing it happen to you was bad enough. Watching it happen to someone else's wife was worse. Then that guy with the moustache kept complaining, saying his kid's crib was hampered by the mess that woman made. I bet that was the first race ever that was called because of placenta interference. Wonder what the Indy 500 would make of that?"

She leaned against his arm and sighed. "I wonder what they'd make of your *moments*. In case you haven't noticed, since we got married they've been happening more often."

Marcus shifted Adam in his arms, getting comfortable. "Well, at least I've been giving the Kirklin residents a break the last couple of years, since we've been living here."

She kissed his shoulder. "You've also developed quite a following with all the kids here in town. I can't take Adam anywhere without one of them wanting to look at the son of Magic Marker."

"Hey, that's better than what they used to call me—The Kirklin Klutz."

She reached up and gently stroked his hair. "It doesn't matter what they call you," she whispered. "As long as I can call you mine." She snuggled up against him and began humming the piano piece again. He finished giving Adam his bottle and watched him fall back asleep. Vickie took Adam in her arms again and snuggled against Marcus's chest. He pulled the covers up over them, closed his eyes and smiled, enjoying the sensation of being surrounded by his little family. It was a fulfilling and complete sense of happiness and one that not so long ago, he never thought would be his.

Strange how life could fool you. You never knew where fate was going to lead you. Sometimes in the most extraordinary ways. Sometimes it took elephants, wasps or emus…

"Or lizards," he whispered, chuckling softly.

"Lizards?" she said, yawning and nuzzling her face against chest. "What made you think of that?"

"Nothing," he said, giving her a kiss on the head and lying back down on the pillow.

She began giggling and he asked her what was so funny.

"Lizards," she whispered. "You might be seeing a few more of them in the future. You're forgetting that Adam's a boy. In a couple years we'll be seeing frogs, lizards, toads and bugs everywhere. He'll be giving your *moments* a run for their money."

Sure hope so, Marcus thought with a smile, drifting off to sleep.

THE END...ALMOST

Marcus slammed his car keys on the kitchen counter and clenched his teeth in anger. Vickie came over and hugged him. He didn't hug her back. He was too damn mad.

"I know you want to," she whispered, "but you can't spank him. His tenth birthday is only two weeks away and I won't have it marred with the memory of his father hitting him. Besides, we both agreed that no matter what, we'd never resort to corporal punishment. We have to stick to that."

He closed his eyes and fumed. "I don't understand why he'd do it! What's the reasoning? How could he do that to himself?"

"He must have had a good reason," she said, hugging him tighter.

"What? Was it a game or for kicks? How could he do that?" He stopped to take a breath and let it out but his anger didn't go with it. "When it first started happening almost two years ago, I thought to myself 'okay, so maybe it was hereditary.' I could deal with that! What I couldn't deal with was people calling him 'The freak's son' and 'Mini Magic.' I knew damned well what he was going through, having all the other kids follow him around and having people point at him and whisper behind his back. It killed me inside, knowing he was going through the same thing I did."

"But his *moments* weren't as bad as yours."

"Thank God for that! I kept praying that he wouldn't get hurt, or hurt someone else! I spent countless nights lying awake, trying to figure out why it would happen to him, too!" He sighed, feeling his frustration take over. "And now...to find out that he made the whole thing up..."

"He's a good boy," Vickie whispered. "He's never been anything but a source of pride to us. And his teachers are always saying how smart he is." She pulled away from him and looked him directly in the eyes. "And you know how much he loves us! But you can't lose your temper with him. He won't understand that. You can't just hit him and then expect him to talk to you. You have to reason with him."

"But why in the hell would he put himself through such humiliation? Put himself up for ridicule, in front of the whole town? And even after he was ridiculed, why would he keep it up? For TWO YEARS?"

She hugged him again, tight and he knew she was doing her best to try and calm him. But nothing could calm him. His son had suffered his same fate, being branded a jinx, an oddity, to be stared at and clucked over. But unlike him, Adam had staged it, faked the affliction and brought it all on himself. He felt his wrath begin to subside and finally hugged her back. "Okay," he whispered. "I'll talk to him. And I promise I won't spank him." He let go of her and headed for the staircase in the other room. "But if there was ever a kid who needed a spanking…" he mumbled to himself.

He went up the stairs to face his son.

Adam was sitting up in his bed, waiting for him. He was wearing his favorite pair of green shorts, Cleveland Indians T-shirt and the lace on his left Reebok was undone. There was an expression of fear on his face and his hands were folded, in his lap.

"Mom said you wanted to talk to me about…you know…" Adam croaked, "about what happened."

Marcus went over and sat down on the side of the bed. His son's expression was anxious and part of him wanted to make the boy suffer a little, to emphasize the seriousness of what he'd done. But he couldn't. It wasn't in him. "Your mother and I have talked it over and you're not getting a spanking."

A look of relief filled the boy's face and he sighed, like he'd been holding his breath.

"But you are getting a punishment," Marcus told him. "You're grounded for two weeks."

The boy rolled his eyes but made no additional comment. Marcus decided to get down to business. "I want to talk to you about this."

Adam grumbled and folded his arms in front of him. "Is that part of the punishment?"

Marcus pursed his lips, trying not to get perturbed. "No, that's not part of the punishment. I only wanted to understand your reasons, that's all."

Adam began muttering under his breath. "You'd never found out if Sarah hadn't blabbed. She should get a punishment for tattle-telling!"

"Your sister wasn't trying to get you in trouble. She's only six. She only thought she was protecting you from getting hurt."

Adam let out a "hmph" like he didn't believe it. "I wouldn't have gotten hurt. I told her I was okay. I've played with those groundhogs before. They was just little ones. I was only going to get them to follow me around at school. That's why I put them in that bag. So I could ride them on my bike."

Marcus tried not to smile. Wait until Ben heard about this. Adam had found a couple of "snipes" without even being forced into doing it. He then remembered what he was there for and cleared his throat. "But it's wrong for you to do that, Adam. You or someone else could have gotten hurt."

The boy sat up excitedly, like he was anxious to talk about it. "That's why I was putting them in the burlap bag. So I could hide them on the playground and bring them out at recess."

Marcus asked him why he'd want to do that.

"So they could follow me around the playground! Like I got those ducks to follow me into the drug store uptown and when those stuffed animals fell off that shelf at Kmart and all the other *moments* I fixed. And it worked!"

Marcus tried to think of a way to say it without hurting his feelings. "I know that sounds like fun, Adam, to cause those things to happen and make people laugh…"

"Oh, they don't always laugh," Adam protested. "Sometimes they get real mad, and even call me names. That lady at Kmart screamed at me and called me the devil's son when those stuffed animals fell on her. Katie and I thought that was weird."

"Katie?"

"Yeah. She's always helped me do my *moments*. She was the lookout when I put the string through the stuffed animals' tags. That's how we got 'em to fall down off the shelf."

Marcus couldn't help but smile and turned away. Apparently, Adam had a cohort in crime, none other than Ben and Sue's little princess. Ben was gonna shit when he found out. Ben had been bugging him for two years, wanting to know the details of all Adam's *mini moments*. Now he was about to find out that not only were they fake, Katie was in on it. *Uh-huh*, Marcus thought. *The look on Ben's face is gonna be one for the annals. I'm not gonna want to miss that.*

He wiped the smile from his face and tried to make Adam understand. "When that lady called you names, it didn't feel very good, did it?"

Adam shook his head no. "And I didn't understand what that man that was with her meant, when he called me an abobination."

"Abomination," Marcus corrected him and immediately felt like an idiot for saying it.

"Yeah," Adam said. "He really got mad after his wife got scared by those stuffed animals and crashed her shopping cart into that stack of paint cans, making 'em roll around the floor and knocking those people down. Katie and I didn't think anyone would fall. We just wanted the stuffed animals to fall down. That's why I used the string and stuck it on that duct tape, behind the shelf."

Duct tape? Marcus thought with amusement. He put the thought out of his head and tried to get back to the matter at hand. There would be time later to get all the gory details of two years worth of *mini moments.* Jack wasn't going to believe it, either.

"So you see, Adam," Marcus said, trying to keep his expression stern. "Calling you names isn't very nice, is it? It hurts, doesn't it?"

"Uh-huh."

He waited for the boy to see it, but knew he wasn't getting through. "People shouldn't call other people names, should they?"

"No," Adam replied. "But they call you names too, Dad."

"I know that."

"And it hurts you too, doesn't it, Dad?"

"That's right," Marcus replied, happy he was finally getting through to the boy. "And that's why I can't understand why you would make up those incidents."

"*Magic moments,*" Adam said, correcting him.

"Yes...*Magic moments.* Why would you do that, Adam? Why would you let people make fun of you like that?"

The boy started frowning like he didn't want to say.

"It's all right, Adam," Marcus said, gripping the boy's shoulder reassuringly. "You can tell me the truth. It's all right."

"I did it because they was hurting you."

Marcus blinked, not sure he heard right. "What? The *Magic moments?*"

"No," Adam said, looking down at his hands in his lap. "The people."

Marcus sighed and put his hand under the boy's chin, making him look up at him. "That's why I didn't want you hurt," he told the angelic face. "I didn't want you to have to put up with people pointing and staring at you. But because of you making up those inci...*Magic moments,* they did stare at you and make fun of you. You know that it hurt me when they did it to me and I prayed you'd never have to go through anything like that. Which is why I can't understand why you'd do something like that. Why, Adam? Why?"

Tears began to form in the boy's eyes. "I only did it because I wanted to be like you, Dad. I kept waiting for Grandma and Grandpa to come down from Heaven and make the *moments* happen to me, too. But they didn't. So I thought I'd do it for them until they could. I didn't want you to get mad at me. And I figgered if people started making fun of me, they'd leave you alone. I just wanted to be like you."

Marcus felt his heart break as the boy began crying. He wrapped his arms around his son and gently stroked his hair. "Don't cry, Adam. I understand. I'm so sorry." How could he have been so wrong?

He should have recognized what was going on. The way Adam kept his calm after every one of his so-called *moments*, almost like he was enjoying them. He hadn't said anything because he didn't want the boy to feel like an outcast, protecting him from some of the hurt.

And all along, Adam was protecting…him.

Adam pulled away and looked up at his father, wiping his eyes. "Is it okay if I still play with the little groundhogs? They wouldn't bite me. They're my friends."

"Okay. But we'll take them to a vet and get them checked out, just to make sure, first."

"And can I show them to Katie, too? She really likes the one with the funny stripes!"

Marcus smiled at him. "We'll have to check with your Uncle Ben and Aunt Sue first."

"Oh, boy!" Adam said as he quickly scooted across the bed. "I'm gonna call her right now. She was really worried I was going to get a spanking." He scampered towards the door and paused to look back at his father. "I guess that means we won't be doin' that *Magic moment* tomorrow at the school fair."

Marcus asked him what it was.

"Katie and I have been saving up bugs for about a month and were gonna let 'em loose in the gym."

Marcus chuckled and asked him what kind of bugs they had.

"Everything. Cockroaches, ants, spiders and we even found a couple of praying mantises in the woods."

Marcus felt a wave of alarm and glanced around the room. "And where are you and Katie keeping these bugs?"

"At her house. They're in shoeboxes and we've got 'em hid in her room. She's even got some of them hid in her drums." With that, Adam flew out the door and headed down the hall.

Marcus got up from the bed and followed him. He'd be making a call himself in a few minutes. Ben was going to be quite surprised to learn his little angel was a co-conspirator in a major fraud against the citizens of Kirklin. Not to mention that Ben also might be making a call to the Orkin man.

Marcus suddenly thought of his parents. They would have loved knowing their namesakes had been up to such mischief. It was just like one of their practical jokes.

He paused at the top of the stairs as it came to him.

It was not only *like* one of their practical jokes, it was *exactly* like one of their jokes.

He laughed and headed down the stairs, enjoying the revelation.

Yep. One of their jokes.

And knowing them, they were probably behind the whole thing.